Bad Be

by Martin Campbell

A story about poker and plumbing

Amazon Publishing.

Copyright © M Campbell 2016
A catalogue record for this book is available for this book from the British
Library.

ISBN 978-1-5262-0307-6

Bad Beat Hotel

CHAPTER 1

Shuffle up and deal

It started when the water stopped running. The tap coughed once, spat out half a cupful and the pipe under the sink gave a death rattle.

There were four cottages in the row, originally built for farm workers. Over a hundred years old, they had been re-roofed, re-wired, re-plumbed and rented out to anyone who could put up two months' cash as a security deposit, no references required. The farmer screened tenants, collected rent, and did any repairs to keep the cottage wind and water proof. The cottage walls were solid sandstone, as thick as the width of the doors. On the outside walls, the bottom two feet of the lime-based external render had disintegrated for want of a damp course in the walls. The cottages were south facing, but cold and damp most mornings. Between November and March when the sun got high enough over the hill opposite only to reach the chimneys, frost stayed on the windows for days. In the summer, the cottages acted like brick storage heaters and windows had to be left open at night to make the temperature inside bearable.

Bob Smeaton was the longest serving tenant. He was also the only tenant who still worked on the farm. When the water stopped he phoned the emergency number for the water company and then asked his wife to check on their neighbours. A white van with the water company livery, a four foot glass of clear water, arrived at 9.30. The two men from Scottish Water pulled away weeds and cleared lumps of clay soil to get at metal covers at the side of the road. They turned stopcocks off and on and checked the taps in Bob's cottage and the one next door, where the door was opened by a four year old in pyjamas. They told Bob that there was water running in the mains pipe at the road.

It was April; too late for frozen pipes. It looked like a burst somewhere on the stretch of pipe that ran 50 metres across the waste ground between the farm road and the cottages. It could take a day or longer to find the burst, shut off the supply further down the line and dig out an access hole. Then they would need to fit a collar on the pipe to seal it. If the metal pipe had rusted through it would take longer, digging it out and replacing the section. No traffic to worry about out here, but finding the burst somewhere in that waste patch could take a lot of man hours. The two men from Scottish Water left after twenty minutes with a promise to come back.

A bigger white van, with a six foot glass of clear water on the side, arrived an hour later. The van was pulling a trailer with a JCB 802 mini digger and multipurpose bucket, plus half a palette of bottled water. In the van were Jake, the JCB operator and foreman, and two diggers, Jamie and Alex. They were both modern apprentices, in training as Water Distribution and Sewerage Operatives. Jake had worked with water pipes straight from school, since before Scottish Regional Councils took over the industry in 1975. He still wore his original work boots, carefully nourished with dubbin every Sunday night. He gave the steel toe-capped boots that the company supplied every year to his brother, who worked as a builder.

Jake had two years to retirement. He believed that finding a leak was a special skill that no amount of modern apprenticeship training could teach. You could do it, or you couldn't. When Jake started as a tea maker and apprentice, there were no fancy training courses; you learned it all on the job, or you found another job. Back then, the Central Scotland Water Development Board employed a dowser, on a retainer. Mr. Callender was a crusty retired teacher, called out to tricky jobs, to plot the route of old pipes, laid before the days of water network drawings and asset plans. He was never James, and definitely not Jim; he was always Mr. Callender to everybody working on a site. Jake had never seen anyone so revered by diggers and supervisors alike. When he walked onto a job all other work would stop. It was like the class was about to start and everyone knew that you had to sit down, hands clasped, facing the front. He wore a battered tweed jacket over a checked shirt and woollen tie, with thick brown corduroys that looked like they could stop a bullet. Under his arm he carried a Belgian oak case containing *The Revealer*.

This was a pair of heavily chromed "L" rods about two feet long, with numbers on the rods and internally sprung-loaded handles. The rods were immaculate, polished to a high finish with Brasso and lint free clothes. When he took them out of the felt-lined case it seemed like they were generating light, rather than just reflecting it. People on site would watch him prepare like they were members of an audience at a concert and he was the conductor, raising his baton. He would listen attentively to what the site foreman had to say about what they were looking for, and what they knew, then he would walk a few circles, like he was limbering up. It was always the same routine. He grasped the leather covered handles close to his chest, the long divining rods swinging out in front, crossing and separating as he walked, like antennae. When he was satisfied that everything was working as it should, he would move to the stretch of ground that was being investigated, taking the audience with him.

If there was a start point for the pipe, above ground, the job was easier, but even on jobs with no such clues, Mr. Callender could plot the route of underground pipes in a ten minute walk across the site. The tips of his divining rods would cross, he would slow his pace and track the pipe in straight lines, making ninety degree turns without slowing and without error, every time. A workman walked behind him planting sticks. When Mr. Callender was over the leak he would stop dead, like an English pointer, nose up. He could even tell the men how much digging was going to be involved.

Even after all these years, Jake never understood how it worked, but he knew that it did.

Now there was no Mr. Callender and no divining rods. The kit was the *Schonstedt* portable pipe and cable locator and a mini-JCB. The job still needed three men, though, and a selection of the same curved edge spades and shovels to dig. High pressure jets to clear soil from pipes was a luxury of the teams working in the high streets; out here on the remote jobs, it was straight digging and clearing by hand after the JCB had taken the first few scoops. This distance from town, Jake knew that the pipe was probably buried more than the standard 900mm, to avoid frost and withstand the heavy tractor traffic. That meant more digging and more time.

Jake, Jamie and Alex climbed out of the van, stretching and sizing up the job. They were both keen lads, Jake knew, but sometimes their energy, or maybe just their youth, wore him down. It had been a mistake, he realised, to tell them about Mr. Callender on their first job together. Now they thought that all his stories about digging up pipes would be as interesting, as memorable, and they badgered him to come up with others. Were they keen to hear about Jake's adventures in the old days, or were they just taking the piss out of the old timer? Jake didn't know. Sometimes he felt like a grandfather trying to get two bairns to go to sleep at night without a book. When there was a lull in the conversation in the van, Jamie or Alex would pull a question from a seemingly endless list.

"Tell us about the most difficult burst you ever did Jake," *"What was it like when there were lead pipes in houses Jake?"*, *"Who was the worst boss you ever had Jake?"*

That morning it had been, *"When's the first time you ever worked with water Jake?"*, from Alex, the quieter of the two.

Jake had put him off with, *"Well, a long time ago boys, two hydrogen atoms met one oxygen atom…"* and they had both laughed, but he knew they'd be back for more.

From the mains cover on the farm road, the general direction of the pipe from the road to the cottages, across a barren patch of land, was clear. The flat stretch of grey earth was dead, and only the hardiest of weeds grew around what was now an old tractor attachment graveyard. For twenty years it had been the site of the farm's above-ground slurry store, a tank which could hold up to 600 cubic metres of straw-rich pig manure, silage and the occasional bucket of animal blood. The tank had been replaced by a slurry lagoon on a remote corner of the farm only when new Environment Agency legislation and the financial need to rent out the cottages forced the farmer's hand.

All three men did a slow walk and a quick visual, but found nothing that looked muddier than the rest of the dead ground. Jake took the listening rod from the van. He walked a line from the road to the cottages, poking the long metal shaft into the soft ground every few yards and cupping his hand around the angled rubber earpiece at the end. He was only going through the motions. Pressure in this pipe this far from the mains, he knew, was probably too low for him to hear any hissing or splashing or clinking of stones washed out of the soil. On poor land, with clay soil, a leak in a pipe could easily get channelled sideways for yards before it becomes audible on stones. He heard nothing.

Putting the rod back in the van, Jake gave Jamie and Alex a nod and they stubbed out their cigarettes and pulled on yellow waterproofs. Their first job was to drag a rusting two-furrow plough and a two wheel trailer to one side, off the track of the pipe. Alex and Jamie then walked a straight line between the road end and the cottages, like scene of crime officers, checking the ground for anything half buried that might snag the scoop on the JCB. Jake backed the excavator down the tailgate of the trailer and manoeuvred it into position, at the side of the road. It would be the same routine for the next four hours; get most of the soil off a section of pipe with the digger, then two men in the hole to get down to the pipe with spades, check it for the leak, then get out and back fill while the digger got started on the next section. They would take a break for lunch in the van.

The smell was on them from the first slurped scoop of the JCB bucket. The ground had a mustard coloured crust, but the soil underneath was a deep, wet brown with veins of black, permeated with years of fermented pig slurry that had leached out the tank. Even after years of being baked over summers and then frozen again, the stench leapt out of the hole, ripe and strong.

"*Now this is gonnae be fucking minging*", Alex said to Jamie, through the cuff of his shirt, pulled from his yellow jacket and pressed over his nose and mouth. It was different from cow dung, more sweet and sour, with an ammonia tang. It came in penetrating waves. First there was a pungent waft, sharp in the nostrils, when the JCB bucket broke the surface. Then, as soil from deeper down was scooped and dumped onto the surface, the stink was like a spray to the throat and eyes, so overpowering that Alex and James had to turn their faces away from the excavator.

As the trench got longer, and closer to where the centre of the slurry store had stood, the smell got sharper and the digging was tougher. Lumps of black earth, bound together by the slurry, were as dense as clay and kept their shape as they were dumped on the surface from the bucket. Alex and Jamie had to use feet on their spades to cut heavy slabs of the packed soil stuck around the pipe. They were spending twice as long in the hole as when they started the ditch at the road end.

Jake came out of the JCB to help. Although there was only room for two men in the hole, Jake went in for ten minutes for Alex, come out for ten and then went in again and gave Jamie a break. Jake was slower than the young boys with the spade, but they still made faster progress this way. It was hard going and all three of them were gagging with the stench in the hole, Jake dry-boaking the first time he went in. When it looked like they had cut more than half way across the waste ground, Jake called a break for lunch. Only Jamie could eat, the other two still smelling and tasting fermented pig shit when they tried to bite into cheese sandwiches.

There were clouds scudding across the sky on a strong breeze, but it was bright, and mild for April in Scotland. Three of the people who lived in the cottages were out, sheltering from the wind in the lee of the buildings, watching the trench get closer. Wrapped up in a waxed jacket, a man in his slippers was sitting on a garden chair smoking. He had a chunky scarf pulled up over his chin, met by a tea cosy hat coming the other way, and wisps of grey hair blowing about in between. A four year old boy with and mother were watching the show. The boy was delighted to see a real JCB in action. He was on his knees, with his yellow Tonka digger, scooping sandy soil onto a waiting tipper lorry, periodically shouting to his mother, "*Nup, still nothing there.*"

With ten metres to go across the waste land, Jake realised that they were going to have to dig up somebody's manicured back lawn. "*Bloody typical*", he thought. It was the only patch of flat, green grass for miles, and he was going to hack a trench straight through it. His hopes of finding the leak quickly and getting an early finish had long gone, but digging up somebody's grass meant even more time; filling in forms back at the depot, after the job was done, in anticipation of a compensation claim.

The smell coming off the slurry in the soil eased a bit as they got closer to the cottages as a breeze picked up. Jake went back into the JCB and they got a rhythm going, cutting another three stretches of trench without any problems, but also without any sign of water soaking the earth or spouting from holes in the pipe. Rust from the pipe was mixed in the lengthy mound of soil now on the surface, with some flakes as big as coins.

Using cast iron pipes became illegal in Scotland only in 1969 and the water companies were slowly, very slowly, replacing them. Jake had the set up for a saddle clamp in the van. It was a thick, adjustable doughnut with a soft inner layer. He had done repairs on cracks on old pipes, or smaller holes, where rust had eaten through the pipe. Sitting in the cab of the excavator, he was hoping that they still got the chance to use the clamp on the pipe before they got to the immaculate green lawn. Looking at the pitted state of the crusted pipe, he was wondering if there were leaks into it as well as out, and how long the people in the cottages might have had diluted rust and slurry coming out of their taps.

Three of the four cottages had fenced off patches of vegetables, fighting against weeds and rabbits, but the stretch of edged grass behind the centre right cottage was the result of many hours cutting, aerating, feeding and visits to garden centres. It was an achievement to grow anything on the edge of this contaminated patch. God knows what else the farmer had dumped into the dead soil after the slurry store was taken out.

The tenant with the lawn was out and nobody had a number for him. He had irregular hours and a car with a bust exhaust, according to the guy in the waxed jacket and scarf. Jake had to decide if the guy would rather have a water supply or a neat lawn when he got home. Permissions would take another day and the farmer who rented the cottages had already given the go ahead for whatever was necessary to get the water back on. Jake decided that he would just have to take the flak for digging up the bowling green. Then things got a bit strange

As the teeth on the digger bucket jerked and came down to take the first scoop out of the lawn, Alex shouted, "*Whoa Jake!*" and moved in front of the excavator, holding up a hand. Two squares of neatly cut turf were hanging on the teeth of the digger and another two, had been pushed to the side, revealing a bald patch of fine soil over a metre square.

"*Shit*", Jake thought as he peered out from the cab, "*this is just getting worse*". He was about to dig up the guy's newly laid lawn. That would explain why the green grass growing on this patch was so unlikely – it had come on a lorry from some turf suppliers.

When he got out the cab for a look and kicked around the grass, however, there were no other squares of loose turf. It was just that one patch with four straight-edged squares. Could be a weed killer spill, Jake thought, or maybe a lawn repair where the slurry made it most difficult to grow the grass. Or maybe, just maybe, best case scenario, it had been a waterlogged patch and they had found their leak. Now Jake was thinking that they should have started at this end, and saved a hell of a lot of time. Whatever the explanation, he was still going to have to dig.

Alex stacked the four square turfs neatly on the grass and Jake climbed back into the JCB and started it up. The soil was looser here, no lumps bound together, and it crumbled and ran back towards the hole as it was dumped at ground level from the bucket. After six scoops, Jake stopped and waved Alex and Jamie into the hole. With Alex's second shovelful there was the sound of metal on metal. He and Jamie dug out the loose soil, getting down either side off the pipe where it reached a junction. Alex climbed out to give Jamie more room to scratch away more loose soil by hand, using a trowel. Jamie worked quickly, on his knees, scooping the earth behind him onto the length of pipe they had just uncovered. He stopped mid-scoop and stood up, not raising his head. *"Jake, you better take a look at this."*

"Well, I will if you get out the road son, so I can see what you're staring at," Jake said from the edge of the trench.

They were looking at a pipe intersection. It was a master class in plumbing. The main cast iron pipe coming across the waste ground flared into four, more modern, copper pipe offshoots, one for each of the cottages, in a Christmas tree fitting. Three of these smaller pipes had been fitted with still-shiny brass stopcocks. Jake climbed into the ditch to inspect it more closely. He didn't know who had done this job – definitely not Scottish

Water – but he had to admire the finishing. The three pipes had been cut and the brass taps fitted neatly, jointed on either side, giving six joints in total. The threads on the joints had been wrapped with plumber's tape to seal the pipe threads against leaks. Only the pipe to the cottage with the lawn was untouched; the water supply to the other three cottages had been turned off at the brass taps.

The two Community Team cops who were called out puzzled over what to write in their notebooks. What were the charges? Vandalism? Malicious mischief? Damage to property definitely, but it was more than that, surely? The senior of the two cops was just hoping it wasn't some obscure denial of sanitation, human rights twaddle that would take hours to write up.

Around the hole the cop and his probationer stood with the three workmen and the old man from the cottage, who had joined them. The charges were going to be meaningless anyway, the senior cop was thinking; whoever did this was bound to be a nut job who wouldn't be appearing in any court. The Procurator Fiscal would never take this on. Cutting off somebody's water supply? It wasn't going to be in the public interest or worth the cost of the court to get somebody locked up in a cell for that, was it?

The probationer cop went by the book, taking statements and trying to piece it together. He spoke first to the woman from the end cottage, then the old man and finally to Bob Smeaton, who had come back from work in the fields, looking worried as he pulled up and saw the cops. The statements the probationer took were necessary but useless. Nobody had seen any digging. It was more difficult to take a statement from Jake. He wanted the probationer to write down what Jake was sure had happened, rather than what Jake had actually seen that day, and he couldn't understand why the probationer wouldn't do this. Alex and Jamie didn't have anything to add and were more interested in asking the probationer if cops had to deal with other crazy stuff like this.

When he had finished his statement, Jake walked over and stood beside the senior cop looking into the hole. He pointed at the taps. *"It's like I tried to tell your colleague here,"* he said, still frustrated at how little of what he had said the probationer had written in this note book,

"Somebody's dug a hole, probably at night, without making much noise. He's gone down 1.4 metres, fitted the three stopcocks there you can see and put back all the soil and the turf. Now could one man do that in a single night at this time of the year, with only eight hours darkness, before anybody in the cottages got up for breakfast and saw him? I'm telling you, it's hard to believe, but somebody's done it anyway"

"Well, sir, we will be making enquiries about all of that," said the senior cop, looking down the hole, rather than at Jake.

"That's good," said Jake, *"because what I really want to know – and you could ask him this when you find him - is how he knew where to dig in the first place and, how the fu…, how the hell did he know what size of pipe connections he was going to need for the stopcocks when he got down to the junction?"*

Alex came to join the others at the hole. *"The woman's asking if we can just switch the taps on the stopcocks back on boss, so she can get water, or if we're gonnae need to take them out?"*

Jake shook his head. *"Oh, that's a decision for the grown-ups Alex,"* he said, looking at the cop. *"I'll have to phone Head Office and try' n explain this mess, so we can get a job number, one way or the other about the stopcocks. And anyway, these boys might be needing the taps taken out for evidence, eh?"* Jake said, nodding again at the senior cop.

"Could be, could be," said the cop. He paused, scratching his chin. *"What you could do, I suppose, is just switch the taps back on but leave the hole open, until I find out what's happening".*

"Aye, we could do that, no problem," said Jake. *"At least that would let these folk get their water back on,"*

"OK", said the senior cop, *"I'll get you some gloves from the car, just on the off chance that we can get anything off the taps."* He knew there would be no prints as it had been exposed to moisture, but they might get fibres, if anybody wanted to get serious about this one, which he knew was unlikely. He paused again, still looking down the hole and shaking his head. *"I've been a cop for a while now, but I huvnae come across one like this before. We definitely need to talk to this guy."*

The curtains were drawn and there was no response to knocking at the cottage. The probationer cop was left on *locus protection*, one of the crappiest duties for newbies in the police. It meant standing about for hours, in any weather, doing nothing at the site of a crime. There was no drinking coffee, no pee breaks, and no mobile phoning.

The older cop radioed in to the station and then went to look for the farmer and a spare key for the cottage, and to find out what he could about the tenant who still had a water supply.

In the days that followed, The Dundee Courier went with *"Mr Plumb Crazy"* as an inside page headline, and a paragraph of the few facts that were known. In a follow up, a month later, the same reporter did a longer column, citing a plumbing expert, describing how Mr Plumb Crazy had dug down twice; once to check the pipe sizes and once to do the job, after dowsing the layout of the pipes.

CHAPTER 2

Texas Hold 'Em

Texas Hold 'Em is one form of poker in which each player is dealt two cards face down. These are known as "hole" cards or "cards in hand". Players must make the best five card poker hand from any combination of their two cards and the five "community" cards that are progressively dealt, face up, onto the table.
These community cards are dealt in three stages. The turning of the first three cards is called the "flop", the turning of the next card is called the "turn", and the final card turned is called the "river". There is a round of betting at the start when players have two cards, then after the flop, the turn and the river.
To stay in the game players must match the amount of chips bet by other players, or raise the bet to a higher amount, which other players then have to meet.
The player with the best five card poker hand, or the player who has bet in such a way that all other players have "folded" (got out of the hand, by mucking their cards — throwing them in) wins all the chips that are in the pot.

The main room was the shape of an indoor railway arch. It was the same damp cavern from September to May. Dried dance sweat and years of cigarette smoke permeated the vaulted stone ceiling. When the room was cold, it smelled like a meeting of long-term homeless people had just finished. It had been built as a passive wine cellar, resistant to outside temperature variations and maintaining 60% humidity. The thick sandstone walls, from 1912, had been patched where attempts by previous tenants to hang pictures with nails and screws had made crumbling holes. The landlords were responsible for roof, gutter and window repairs even though there were no windows. The internal works were the responsibility of tenants, with predictable quick fix, botched job results.

Overhead LED lights and the dual rotating disco balls were suspended on T-bars, which were fixed to steel plates in the tiny attic above the vaulted stone ceiling. Double chains hung through the ugly gaps, drilled through the sandstone with little skill. The holes could only be seen as the rotating disco fireballs went into fast spin cycle, and if you were looking up.

Over the previous twenty years the building had been a furniture store, a restaurant, a storage unit and a short-lived art gallery. Every business had used dehumidifiers, emptying pints of water out each day and eventually giving up, as the furniture, food and paper grew black or white mould. The last tenant, who'd rented the building as a day time café, claimed that fine silica particles from the unsealed sandstone could be seen floating down from the ceiling and landing on the sticky tray bakes.

Gossip 'n' Envy had been opened as a nightclub for twenty one months. The vaulted shape of the room was great for containing the sound, but it was a struggle to keep the high cavern warm and dry for drinkers on dance nights, from Thursday to Sunday. Thermostatic blowers were cranked up to maximum setting an hour before opening, then switched off. The DJ then made it his mission in the first hour to get punters from nightclub stage one; standing about looking anxious, and shivering, worrying that they had come too early, to stage four; a critical mass of sweating bodies, packed like penguins and moving vertically on the dance floor.

By nightclub stage three on the main floor of Gossip 'n' Envy, just before people could only move their arms, it was still possible to pick out the dancers who practised moves at home, using Wii *Just Dance*, editions 1-4. Most of the others did the same low-energy shuffle they had been doing since school.

Off a narrow corridor leading from the main vaulted room was The Melody Lounge, which had been set up as the bar and the designated chill-out room. The corridor continued to toilets and a fire escape, opening onto the car park at the back of the building. The Melody Lounge had been the wine cellar's old bottling room, and the temperature was more plunge pool than chill-out, regardless of the number of bodies dancing in the main room. People went into the Melody Lounge in two and threes, disclosed some

OMG gossip or bought drugs or did some beery fumbling, and got out again fast. Those who stayed longer were either too wasted to walk and had been parked there by mates, or had internal central heating fuelled by ecstasy. Both barmen in the lounge wore fingerless gloves, sleeveless body warmers and fuzzy beanie hats with ear flaps.

The car park at the front of the club was marked out with 45 degree angled spaces, used by insurance office workers from the adjacent building, Monday to Fridays and by shoppers on week-ends. Gossip 'n' Envy's rear car park, however, was exclusive. The gap between the side wall of the club and the five-storey insurance block opposite was wide enough for two cars as you turned off the road, but tapered to just two metres at the back corner of the club, as you entered the car park. The brickwork on the corner, and the wall opposite looked like a colour sampling kit, with rainbow streaks from the front wings, side mirrors and the car doors of drivers too stubborn to stop, reverse and find somewhere else to park.

There was enough room for a dozen cars in the space behind the club, but it was mostly taken up by motor bikes, and a few regular Fiat Unos and Ford Kas, slim and brave enough to get through. At the side of the fire exit there was a stack of empty aluminium beers kegs and broken chairs. The surface of the car park was pitted with some serious pot holes and an alarming dip in the centre where rain water, moss and mud would sit for weeks, shaded from the sun by the insurance building. A high rendered wall ran along the back of the car park. On the far left-hand side there were two white triangular signs which read, *Danger: Anti-Climb Paint,* either side of a drain pipe that had been used in the past to get to the skylight window of a newsagents for break-ins in search of fags and cash.

Vince had considered buying something narrow enough to park behind the club and guarantee himself a space. He liked the idea of a *Manager Only* rectangle, painted in bold, fuck-off yellow, on the tarmac. Yes, he liked that a lot, but as he told his last girlfriend, there might be "professional image issues" with being seen driving anything small enough to get through the gap into the car park.

Vince saw himself as a business man on the up in Perth. He bought his suits two at a time, had monthly haircuts at a place where you needed an appointment, and drove a car was a colour not found in nature, with an exhaust extension in bad-boy chrome that he'd had to order from China. He could suppress his Scottish accent when necessary, when he wanted to sound more sophisticated on the phone, although his ex- had told him it made him sound like he was from Cornwall. But that was only after the break up, he told himself.

He had taken the management job at Gossip 'n' Envy when the parent company Glossamer Holdings defaulted on loans, descended into administration, and closed all six clubs around the country. The whole financial house of cards collapse had come two months after a fire at one of the clubs and the newspaper pictures from a mobile phone, showing a car parked across fire doors. A short circuit in the club had left fourteen teenagers in hospital with smoke inhalation or crush injuries. Gossip 'n' Envy was the only club in the chain to re-open, under a continue-to-trade agreement, as the club most likely to. Vince knew that in the real world he was working to make money for administrators to pay off debts for Glossamer Holdings, but in his world the job was pure management glamorama.

He was the guy who had the big ideas to make it work where it had failed before. At interview, Vince had told them that about his plans for a nightclub management website, with a link to his YouTube clip. Yes, a lot of those around, he agreed, but them he hit them with his Mastermind Big Idea for directing major amounts of internet traffic to his pages. For Vince that was the key; getting as many as possible in the door, and back in the door the next week. You could work on what was inside the door later.

His plans for maximising sales and profits came from experience as a barman and knowing his town, sure, but his belief, his real belief that he could do the job came mostly from the $34.95 downloaded nightclub management training guide from *Nightclubpro*. The take home message from the course, repeated at the end of every page, was that by *"interacting effectively"* with the beverage, food and guests you could *"create the optimal environment for sustainable nightclub success"*. He was determined to make Gossip 'n' Envy the phoenix from the flames of debt and blocked fire doors.

Succeed and scale it up; that's how it was done. Sell the punters what they thought they wanted, then make them want more of it, then crank up the price. Vince knew Perth. He knew the nightclub marketplace of punters stumbling out of pubs at closing time, looking for more drink, looking for something to make the night longer, meaningful even. He knew how much people would pay for a drink at eight o'clock and how much more they would pay for a short measure of the same drink at midnight. He knew that most of his punters would be tanking up on cider and vodka before they hit the bars, pregaming at somebody's house for an hour, talking up the night ahead. Then taking half bottles in handbags to the pubs, keeping the costs down and the alcohol levels up. By chucking out time his punters were on the top of the wave, heedless of anything other than who knew where drink was still being served and who else was going to be there.

Vince had to fit all this knowledge into his nightclub strategy, getting them through the doors with the promise of more drink and more access to a fast draining pool of available women and men. If he could get his punters thinking Gossip 'n' Envy every time they left the bar the same way as others were thinking late night kebab, he had cracked it. Start local and grow national. Then the phone call from the manager of Lulu's or Shanghai in Edinburgh would come, he knew, asking him how much he would take to come in and work his magic there, take one of the big clubs to a new level. He was ready now.

In the first three weeks at Gossip 'n' Envy Vince had opened it up free, Thursday to Sunday nights, bar profits only. There was a cocktail hour, 8 until 9, then an hour of four-for-three on drinks. The DJ played requests and the bar staff were under instruction to serve anybody that could stand. Vince watched the numbers rocket. Then he employed two door-wide bouncers, with proper Door Supervisor licenses, drew up a list of all the violent head-the-balls that he had identified during those first three weeks and barred them all from the club. He knew most of them from the lists in other bars, or from the Court pages in the Dundee Courier. This was nightclub security genius, he thought; know your punters, start local and grow national.

Vince had introduced fancy dress theme nights, which were hit or miss at local pubs, with groups of guys turning up, not in disguise, just to gawk at the few women who could be arsed dressing up. He had looked at what the local students were doing for theme nights at parties and at the Student Union, but none of that was going to work with his punters; School Disco themes and James Bond nights were beyond their disguise capabilities, and none of them would have sheets clean enough or even know what a toga party was. So every other Thursday became Cowboys and Cowgirls Ho-Down at Gossip 'n' Envy, to bring in punters who preferred to be somebody else when they went out for a night. For the women it was the tightest jeans they could get into, avoiding having to sit down, balancing on heels that had them walking like praying mantes, wearing pink cowboy hats, bought for a hen night years ago. For the men it was the same going-out checked shirt as usual, but tucked in, with thumbs stuck in belt loops of worn work jeans, to make at least some effort at the look. Any workwear with a steel toecap guised as cowboy boots. The disc jockey wore a cream coloured Stetson, which he had claimed on his tax return.

There were special drinks at special prices, and signs on the bar encouraging punters to order either Cowboy beer (Coors, Bud, Miller) or a Cowboy cocktail; Cowgirl's Prayer (Tequila and cream soda), Texas Ranchero (Vodka, Tequila, Rum and Tesco cola), Midnight Cowboy (Tesco's Old Samuel Kentucky bourbon and dark rum), Cowboy Martini (Gin, lemon juice and sugar), Texas Tornado (Vodka, tomato juice and an olive). All the cocktails had a shot of cheap flavoured syrup to bolster the flavour and a mark-up of at least 400%. Vince also created the Cowboy Wobbly Stiffener (vodka jelly in shot glass) and started a successful rumour that it was laced with Viagra. With each cocktail, punters got a coloured paper napkin. Red meant you were taken (although it was unlikely that your partner was with you), green meant you were single and available, and yellow meant that you were taken but might be ready for some hometown Country and Western cheatin'.

On his first week in the job Vince had seen three generations of women from the same family on the dance floor at the same time, all trying to pull, to the sound of Brooks and Dunn's *Boot Scootin' Boogie* ("*I see outlaws, inlaws, crooks and straights all out makin' it shake, Doin' the boot scootin' boogie*"). The women were known locally as the Hanks, after the grandfather, father and son family line of Hank Williams, Hank Williams Jnr. and Hank Williams III. That, and the fact that Hank Williams Senior was an alcoholic and morphine addict.

"*Line dancing, tequila slamming, cowboy boot toting hoedown! Come on down!*" said the poster outside. In Country and Western tradition, there was a lot of tears before bedtime. The early promise of a loving he'in and a-she'in on the dance floor evaporated for most into drink-driven desperate endings and a dance floor littered with trampled napkins.

The night was a story of good loving gone bad, every week, but no-one remembered enough not to come back. First, there was an early hour when the club had just filled and happy, expectant line dancers stomped patterns across the floor. The blood alcohol levels brought everybody that could stand jostling for a space in one of the lines, moving like a synchronised dance troupe, from the viewpoint of anyone on the floor, at least. You didn't need a partner to dance in line and you couldn't go wrong with the steps. Billy Ray Cyrus was sounding unconcerned about his *Achy Breaky Heart* and Los Del Rio's *Macarena* was written just for the moment: *"When I dance they call me Macarena, and the boys they say que soy buena, they all want me, they can't have me, so they all come and dance beside me, move with me, chat with me"*. The stomping of feet beat out a hypnotic rhythm, and it was easy to stop caring where you were, or if you were here trying to pull. *Jolene* by Dolly Parton had everyone chasseing and cheerfully begging not to be cheated on, and then happily shooting the cheating Earl in the Dixie Chicks' song, as it turned out that he was a missing person that nobody missed at all. Any shouts heard above the music and singing were the happy kind; spontaneous whooping and wheeching as the lines of cowboys and cowgirls turned or names were shouted to get a stray dancer back into line. *"Back-together-forward and shuffle Charlene!"*

After about an hour, there was a definite tipping point in the night. It usually came about the time that the speed of *Cotton Eye Joe* by Rednex left most of the dancers just behind the beat, looking at feet, trying to adjust their stomping. The whole mood changed, like the beginning of a new song. It happened the same way each time, but despite the predictability everyone acted surprised. A just-too-loud, drunken comment shouted over the music, about somebody's brother or partner or hair or dress size or drinking took on special significance, with those close-by looking around to see who else had heard it.

The speed with which the drama heightened made *Cotton Eye Joe* look like a slow waltz by comparison. Within five minutes the news about the perceived slight had spread and anyone who was related, interested or emotionally incontinent had taken a side. The original incident was passed around the cliques of dancers again and again, embellished each time with half remembered past misdemeanours of the guilty party, cranking up the animosity. Troops of supporters rallied on both sides.

Ten minutes later there was at least two women crying, being comforted by at least six others, and a group of men either fighting in the car park, or holding two men back from doing each other some damage. Then the unhappy shouting started; *"Nobody says that about my…."*, *"That bastard needs to watch his mouth.."*, *"You need to control your brother, bud…."*, *"Your woman is totally out of order there…"* , *"You're needing a good kicking, pal…."*,

Everybody was caught up in the drama, and there was drunken competition for who had been insulted most. *"That bitch called me a slag, and that's her that's shagging her man's brother…"*, *"She said he was only going wi' me out of pity…"* *"He just called me a fat dyke…."*. The aggression was pervasive. Men stumbled out of the Melody Lounge, much too drunk to understand the reason for fighting but happy to jump in, punching and kicking anyone in their path.

The police were called, arriving quickly but getting out of their cars slowly, seeing the familiar faces outside the club and sighing as they put on their hats. Some weeks at Country and Western night it was a two song argument, some weeks it could last for three, but then it was over. Everyone piled back into the club, pledging allegiances or retribution. The DJ tried to pick it up, find tracks that would get dancers back to the happy shouting. *Honky Tonk Badonkadonk'*, encouraged women to be proud of what they were shaking. Last chance saloon for the DJ was Kenny Loggins' updated *Footloose,* which always brought a few thin lines to the floor, dancing on muscle memory. But the DJ was in downhill denial; the bubble was burst and the dancers who came back on the floor had already decided how the night would end for them, reminded by the fighting about where they were, and who they were.

The rest of the crowd stood around the damp walls drinking, faster than before, building up to one last despairing attempt to pull, be pulled or do something, anything that could be remembered and talked about the next day, the next week.

Regardless of the fights and other disappointments on the night, and to keep it simple, Vince used a tip from his *Nightclubpro* training and always had the DJ finish with *I've had the time of my life* by Bill Medley and Jennifer Warnes. Some ended the night drunk enough to believe that they had. Taxis arrived in a fleet, groups of women stumbled home in bare feet, and some stragglers wandered off on the rumour of a party.

Most came back through the doors the following week, with the same expectations.

CHAPTER 3

Heads Up

Heads Up poker is played between just two players. Any version of poker can be played Heads Up. The chances of having the best hand is much higher, statistically, than in a game with multiple players. Bluffs are more common in Heads Up, since you only need to bluff one player to win the pot, rather than bluff several players and risk getting caught when another player has a strong hand that won't be bluffed. A more aggressive betting strategy in Heads Up is effective.

Vince had once been a boxers' model. Just once, just one catalogue, when he was 19. Starface modelling agency had been auditioning at a hotel in Perth and Vince and a mate had gone along for a laugh. The agency didn't like Vince's pug nose or his mussed up hair, but he had been asked to model the boxer shorts. He had been absolutely chuffed to get a copy of the catalogue in post, four months later, with his arse in the boxers on page 236. He got to keep the boxers. *"Still my best feature"*, was his favourite line for the girls cadging a quick fag just inside the fire exit on dance nights at Gossip 'n' Envy.

He was the go-to guy in Perth. He had contacts if you needed 200 branded cigarettes that looked like the real thing, a bottle of Russian vodka with a few spelling mistakes on the label, or someone that could wire your meter so that the neighbour your never liked was paying for your electricity. If you wanted a box set of the latest American TV series, and didn't want the box, the DVDs or the cost, Vince had a mate that could put it all on a memory stick for you for a tenth of the price. He kept two phones; one for Gossip 'n' Envy calls and for filling in any forms that identified him, and another for his ducking and diving businesses. There was nowhere that Vince wouldn't take or make a phone call and he boasted that he worked taxi hours for business.

Many of his contacts in the town were, in fact, taxi drivers. These were guys who had been fabric mill or distillery or oil workers, engineers and managers who had been laid off, sacked or taken retirement packages. All drivers were required to be "fit and proper" to hold a licence, but driving taxis was not something they were proud of and very few said no when Vince offered a bit of extra cash in hand to deliver or do pick-ups around town. Boxes of Italian wine at half shop price and cheap bottles of vodka (with a bit of floating sediment) were favourites; Vince would take the orders by phone, wait until he had enough to make a run worthwhile then organise deliveries. Taxi drivers who had their own car worked best for Vince and for the drivers; they could do quick jobs before clocking on for a shift with the taxi company dispatch, or do drop offs on their way back to the rank. The taxis were also a good source of backseat conversations about who needed what, and for passing on Vince's ducking and diving phone number. Start local and grow national.

When Vince took the call from Gerry, what surprised him most was that it was on his official, Gossip 'n' Envy phone. Vince just assumed that Gerry didn't have his other number or he would have used it. Vince knew from the first minute on the phone that the proposition was dodgy; high risk, high return, a level up from what he was doing already.

Vince felt that glamorama tingle that he got only when a deal was going to be special. His body temperature dropped a couple of degrees and he quivered across his shoulders. It was a buzz from knowing that he, Vincent Quarrier, was still the go-to guy for a major set up like this, and the anticipation of making it happen like no-one else could, outshining any pretenders or any so-called qualified professionals asked to organise the same deal. What Gerry was looking for was use of the dance floor at Gossip 'n' Envy on Tuesday nights for a poker club.

Vince was brainstorming on an envelope on his desk even before that first call with Gerry was over, scribbling fast but having trouble getting his ideas to form an orderly queue. The space was quickly covered in Vince's *Nightclubpro* acronyms – OPE! (Opportunity Par Excellence!), IBFANG (interacting with the beverage, the food and the guests), MEMOR (minimise expenditure, maximise overhead recovery) – and miniature sketches of poker chips on a table, a three of hearts playing card and a front view of Gossip 'n' Envy, with the famous fountain of Las Vegas' Bellagio Hotel shooting skyward and arching across the car park. Vision, that was what put him ahead of the pack, Vince was thinking.

He pictured cars, conspicuous cars, drawing up outside the club, bringing out of town high-stakes rollers, somebodies not normally seen in Perth. These would be people with real clout, coming to Gossip 'n' Envy, all indebted to Vince for opening the club for poker. Thankful to Vince for facilitating the poker games, yes, but grateful mostly for his *discretion*, his professional handling of something this risky.

It would need to be done on the QT, definitely on the extreme down low, of course. Playing poker had all that James Bond, bow tie glitz, sure it did, but being seen in a casino was still a bit of a dirty secret for most; seedy gambling behind closed doors. This was not something these players would want to read about in the papers beside the article about all the splendid fund raising they were doing for the local community and Children in Need and the Rotary Club. Yes, the players would almost certainly be soft living, Rotarian class, at a minimum. The Tuesday night games might even attract some of the real money from outside town. The bright coloured corduroy brigade with their gravel drives and dinner parties, who owned nothing but land, but a lot of it. The top of the food chain who were the discreet gentry of Perth. But regardless of how much they had in the bank, none of them would want it to be known that they were spending chunks of it at poker. The moral weakness of gambling, or worse, the suggestion of common addiction had to be hidden at all costs. Yes, there would be many very good reasons for Vince's discretion. The main one being that the Gossip 'n' Envy owners and the administrators would sack him on the spot if they found out he was organising gambling in the club.

Vince prided himself on being a master of below-the-radar deals. They were quiet earners that ticked over, brought in a steady flow of cash and were illicit, but were not going to get him a criminal record. Planning, and knowing when enough was enough and it was time to walk away; that was the key. He always worked out what he could make on a sale or a re-sale without getting greedy, figured how long it would take him and who was likely to object if they found out what he was doing; the Police, the Council or other dealers.

He could do it, but the poker deal was going to take a lot more planning than wine and vodka delivered in the back of a taxi. If it came off as he expected, he would be the go-to guy for bigger deals and favours done, stepping up, moving in his new network. He would be dealing with guys who were not just poker players, but real *players* in and around Perth. He had to get it right, and first time. These would be people demanding high standards, used to good service whatever they were doing; posh, fussy bastards in other words.

There was much research to be done. Would he need to pay bouncers to keep the order, and bring in a waitress to circle the tables? What did poker players drink? Whisky? Rye whisky? Bourbon? Surely not Martinis? Food in casinos – what did they usually do in the casino in Dundee? He'd need to check that one out too. What about the lights; up or down? Would they want to use the Melody Room as a "losers' lounge" when they lost all their money? Vince was sure that he'd seen that somewhere. What about music? Did casinos play something in the background? Maybe just something funny when they first came in; *Poker Face* or *Ace of Spades*, or Kenny Rodgers'

Gambler? Yes, they would all like that. Something a bit more ambient, he thought when they were playing. He had some dark stuff in a box somewhere that might be OK, or about four volumes of ambient dub from the 1990s that could work. Maybe something a bit classier; some of that *Best of Opera* he had in the car just to impress people would create a bit of an atmosphere. But that was music for gangster movies, for slow motion machine-gun shooting, wasn't it? He scribbled it all down, but there was a lot to work out before he spoke to Gerry again. He was going to need a bigger envelope.

Vince had known Gerry, vaguely, at the High School, knew him as in somebody who stuck out in a herd of school uniforms. He had hair like a hedge. It was a cross between Elvis and a North Korean dictator. The sides were short and all the curls were on top, tightly knit and solid as a bird's nest. It wasn't the creation of a hairdresser. People at school who didn't know Gerry's name would refer to him as *"that guy with all the hair"*. That was when he was 15 and in the year above Vince. Gerry must have got a haircut about then, Vince figured, because he had no school memories of him after that.

He knew Gerry now only as a local worthy, a family man who did something with computers at the distillery, had done as long as Vince could remember. His face would appear in the paper every few months, smiling at some Rotary or Round Table (what was the difference?) charity gig, with a group of other, straight-down-the-line kilts, shirts and ties. Maybe not as straight down the line after all, Vince thought, if he was dabbling in gambling and organising poker games.

Vince knew a few others like Gerry, many in fact, who were family men by day, dark horses by night. These were the solid Perth citizens, with jobs that still had a pension scheme, living in houses with a trampoline and barbeque out the back, wild days long gone. Working hard at the office, but working even harder to keep their secret vices secret. Vince knew them by sight from pubs he had worked, but he knew their secrets mostly from being a man in the know, who heard what was going on in Perth. These were not the kind of secrets that drew these guys to each other to share. They were not like-minded fellows, joining the Masons or being part of some sad, Monday night metal detectors' club. No, the last thing these guys wanted to share was their secrets. There were lunchtime, half bottle drinkers, guys snorting coke in office toilets, guys who had to delete browsing history every time they used a computer because they liked looking at feet hair, or cartoon characters with nappies, getting their buzz from some off-the-wall, weird stuff. There were a lot of one offs. Mostly, though, there were guys who became somebody else when they took a drink, then regretted it.

In Vince's tagging system, the ones with brothers were the worst. Night outs, starting with the single brother being egged on in a string of pubs to try to pull any woman that had her own teeth and ending in any place that was still serving drink, with the married brother letching after anything that was still standing, eventually slobbering over a semiconscious teenager in a shop doorway, and being thrown into a taxi by his pissed-off brother. Weeks of lies and rehearsed alibis followed, and then the same thing was repeated. Another big family guy that Vince knew had cancelled his online Ladbrokes account when his wife looked at his phone and saw what he was laying out every week was enough to fill a supermarket trolley. So now he would stop at the pub then the bookies on the way home on Mondays and Tuesdays and lay out enough in an accumulator bet to make him physically sick later that night when Chelmsford or Leighton Orient failed to win the last game in a seven game parlay.

Then there were the sad bastards whose secrets had been laid bare in the courts or newspapers or Facebook; men who could never walk down Perth High Street again. Thomas McLean (51), Council planning officer, whose wife divorced him when she found the collection of vintage Hornby train engines that he had built up in the attic of their home, trading online with cash that she assumed was going towards the mortgage. James Randle (46), posing as 14 year old Jimmy in an online chat room, talking to 13 year old Stacey who was actually 28 year old Billy Bundock, a police officer involved in a clampdown to snare internet predators. Mark Cromar (35), solicitor, struck by a van in Tesco's car park and admitted to Accident and Emergency, wearing an all-in-one, velour hot pants suit beneath his a made-to-measure Armani.

Aye, Vince knew that all of this stuff went on, behind closed doors, off the public radar. He had his own secrets. Deals he did, that would have him nicked if he was outed by the law, sure. He moved stuff around, sold stuff, made himself a middle man, but unlike some of these other saddos, there was nothing, absolutely nada, that would have kids painting names on the door of his flat or, God forbid, his car, if his secrets were busted. So Gerry would have his secrets too, and Vince would be ready to use that.

It was a Friday night, early, as the DJ was setting up, rolling out wires, when Gerry came into the club to go over the arrangements. Vince had been rehearsing it, telling himself that he needed to play it cool, not sound too desperate for the business, make sure that Gerry understood that Vince was the man, was doing the major favour, putting his job - Christ, not just his job, but his *reputation* as a nightclub manager – on the line, taking a chance with allowing dodgy, probably illegal activities on his otherwise respectable premises. Vince would make a deal with Gerry, of course he would, but Gerry had to appreciate that Vince was the one taking the risks here, the one who could lose out, and big style, if it all went tits up. Yes, some appreciation was needed. What was in it for Vince? Could Gerry make it worth his while? These were the question Vince wanted Gerry to answer, but he didn't want to have to ask them. He hoped Gerry would know this, that there would be an understanding.

After the strained hellos and acknowledgement that they both remembered high school, but not much about it, Gerry sat down in Vince's office and got straight to it. He started by explaining the poker club membership, annual subs and registering as a Champions Poker League club, issuing membership cards, maximum pay out per player, maximum pay out per night. He told Vince how Christopher, another big family man that Vince remembered from school photos, was the club Treasurer. The whole time that Gerry was talking, Vince was trying not to look at what was left of Gerry's hair, wondering if it just stopped growing straight up like it used to. He was thinking about a price, nodding in the right places, keeping Gerry talking, planning his move.

There *must* be something dirty about it, Vince reminded himself. Christ, it was *poker,* seedy gambling, not some bunch of old biddies playing bridge or bingo. Gerry was still rambling on about club regulations that he had drawn up, the system of points awarded, trophies that could be won for each 13 week season, and the fact that although they couldn't advertise the poker they already had enough interested bodies to get started. When Gerry got on to his information about office bearers, and poker etiquette Vince had done with listening and cut in, *"Yeah, it sounds really good Gerry, well organised, like, but there's something I need to explain to you about Gossip n Envy. What most people don't appreciate Gerry, don't understand - and I know this from talking to the punters who come here - is that being the manager of a nightclub is about more than just being here to open the doors and make sure the bar is stocked. I've got responsibility for the image and the reputation of this place. It's me who has to market Gossip n Envy to the punters in Perth and make it attractive. It's me that has to make it a success."*

Gerry nodded, *"Yes, that is a responsibility Vince, I can see…."*

"There's a lot for me to think about here Gerry, a number of factors to take into consideration. My boss in Glossamer Holdings is on my case every month, phoning,

pressuring me to increase the takings, asking me for spreadsheets and customer marketing plans to bring in more foot traffic. So I'm planning the happy hours, the fancy dress nights, the Sexiest Shoes contests, the cocktails and all the other stuff, constantly trying to create a unique brand for Gossip n Envy, to make it a place that people flock to on the week-end. Then there's keeping the authorities happy. I've got to consider what the local Councillors and the police and the Perth and Kinross Licensing Board think. It only takes one complaint, by some moaning old git who doesn't like young people enjoying themselves, about the noise or bottles in the street or somebody peeing in the car park and there's letters in the paper, shouting for the nightclub to be shut down again. What I'm saying is I have to be careful, awful careful about protecting the reputation of the place, Gerry, and poker, well let's face it, it just doesnae have the best of reputations, does it?"

As Vince spoke, he made ticks with his pen down the side of the blank pad on his desk, looking up at Gerry after each one. He was working through what he had rehearsed. He finished with a knowing nod to Gerry and an arching of his eyebrows, and took a swig from an open can of Coke.

Gerry paused and put his papers on the corner of Vince's desk.

"Well, I don't know Vince. Poker like this in a club open to the public has to be all above board, as I was explaining — there's no dodgy stuff allowed, nothing illicit like there used be. The Gambling Commission has cleaned it all up. It's a bit like your Licensing Board for the drinking at the club; everybody has to stick to the rules."

Gerry looked across at Vince, who was now rocking in his high backed leather seat, hands clasped on his lap.

Now Vince's looked directly at Gerry, not speaking, holding eye contact until Gerry looked away.

"Ye see, Gossip 'n Envy is a business first, Gerry. That's the main point I'm making here. Don't get me wrong, I would love to see the building used more by the local community during the week. That's all good for the image, makes it look like we're making the effort, sharing the love. Carpet bowls or some women jumping about doing Pilates or whatever - that would be dead safe. But for me to be associated with organising poker? Now that's a

big risk," Vince said, *"not knowing what locals and the neighbours would make of it."*

Gerry picked up his papers again while Vince spoke and looked through them, but found nothing that he hadn't said already. He shrugged, looking across the desk, trying to decide whether to push it again or just thank Vince for his time. He'd had a plan to get the poker club into Gossip 'n Envy, but he'd said his piece. Now he didn't know where he was with it. Which is exactly where Vince wanted him to be.

Vince sat forward in his chair and spoke more slowly, doodling whorls on his pad. *"Aye it's risky right enough, but I think we could help you out getting it started here at Gossip 'n Envy",* he said, nodding. He paused until Gerry looked up.

"In fact, I think we could be helping each other out, if you know what I mean Gerry, making these poker nights a real success for everybody."

Gerry spoke quickly. *"Well, yes, that would be great, I'm sure all of the members of the poker club will really appreciate that Vince. We've been looking forward...,"* he started.

"Well, it wasn't so much the members that I was thinking about Gerry, actually.... it was more about what the success of the poker club could mean for you and me."

Vince was in deal making mode now, in his comfort zone, trying to draw the first move from Gerry, which he knew would put him in an even stronger bargaining position. But Gerry just looked at him, blank, and the silence stretched out too long for Vince. He pushed on.

"Well, look Gerry, we're the two guys making this happen, right? It doesn't fly without us. You're the man bringing the punters in here, right? That's what you're good at. They're going to be drinking, they're going to be laying out money on the poker and they're all going to be having a good time. Me, I'm the go-to guy for this, the man facilitating this, making sure they have everything they need, making them comfortable, making them want to come back, all that hospitality stuff – that's what I'm really good at. Now because me and you are doing most of the work here, I'm thinking that you and me should be getting some return, some of the benefits from this enterprise, right?"

"What kind of benefits Vince?" Gerry said, puzzled.

Oh, he's a cagey bastard, Vince thought; trying to get me to come up with some figures that he can then negotiate on. But he's trying to kid a kidder here. Vince smiled, confident that he could cut the deal that would suit him, but realising now that it might take a bit longer. He had to give Gerry credit though, for playing it deadpan, stringing it out, waiting for Vince to make the first move. He was smarter than he looked.

But to Vince this was bread and butter; this is what he did for the day job, and he always got the price he wanted. Vince wondered if maybe this faking ignorance act was something Gerry had learned playing with all his soft poker buddies, getting people to make a move and do something stupid in a poker game, so he move in and skin them. But this wasn't some kid-on card game, this was Vince's world of business deals.

Vince smiled. *"Well, I'd be guided by you on that one Gerry – you know the punters, and how much they're likely to be spending, eh?"* he said, putting his elbows on the arms of his chair and leaning back again. This time Vince decided to go for the old keep-quiet-and-let-the-other-person-speak-first trick. After ten seconds Gerry was still scratching his ear and looking at Vince, puzzled.

He spoke, hesitating between words, *"I'm sorry Vince, I'm, eh, still not clear here on this. Are you talking about a…, talking about the poker club paying a charge for the room in Gossip 'n Envy, or were you thinking about a commission…., or something else?"*

Vince smiled again, sensing progress at last. *"I'm talking about both Gerry, but not just a cut for me. You're doing some of the work here too, and I think it would only be fair that we should both benefit from the profits on the night."*
He paused, again raising his eyebrows and nodding at Gerry's papers.

"Look, what if you give me an idea of how much you think the poker club will be taking in profits and we can make a deal about splitting that right down the middle? Fifty-fifty would be the simplest way, eh? Would that be somewhere to start?"

Vince knew that Gerry would want to go for a lower figure on Vince's cut but if he could just get him to agree on the 50/50 split now, he could take it from there on the first night, when the poker money was on his office table, being counted. He could renegotiate the split, taking into account his "unforeseen overheads", when Gerry was there being dazzled by the sight of hard cash.

Vince looked across the desk and he could see from his expression that Gerry wasn't happy about taking a hit on his profit margin. His pudgy face was like a big bairn that had been caught with a bag of sweeties and told to share them out. Well, Gerry had to learn that it was tough all over. Vince was a business man, not some charity worker, and it was bloody obvious that Gerry and his poker club were a low overhead, big profit business, like some working-from-home type scam. The punters were going to be paying some whack of fees to Gerry, and then bringing in extra money on the night, possibly big money, to the poker tables, while Gerry, straight down the line family man Gerry, was spending next to nothing on operating expenses. How much could a pack of cards, some folding tables and some plastic chips cost? Buttons, that's how much. And when they were bought, they were bought, right? You didn't have to keep forking out for them every week. So apart from some prize money, that came from the punters in the first place and could be kept down to amounts that sounded like a lot, more so after a drink, all that was coming out of Gerry's cut, in hard currency, was what he would be paying out to Gossip 'n' Envy, and to Vince, obviously.

Vince was on a high, celebrating his deal making skill in his head and missed Gerry's reply.

"*Sorry Gerry, what did you say?*"

I said, "*Any extra we make goes back into the poker club, Vince,*" and then, after another pause, "*You, see the Gambling Act doesn't allow poker club office bearers to take any part of the winnings.*"

Vince's fixed grin did not change as he dug his nails into the arms of his chair. Fuck! Gerry was making this a lot more difficult than it should be, getting arsy now about what was legal and what was not in playing poker, which was almost certainly not.

"Right, right Gerry, I get that bit about all the rules and regulations and membership fees and Licensing Board and stuff. I agree with you, one hundred per cent. We have to make it look like it's all on the up and up and keep it straight for the punters, so they think they're getting a good deal from us. But, come on, I mean, inside the club here, on a wet Tuesday night in a back street in Perth, in November – are any Gambling Act inspectors likely to wander in to check what's happening. Really?"

Gerry looked away, off to one side of the desk, *"I'm sorry Vince, but I have to put the membership money and the prize money through the books, record everything on Excel and produce accounts at the end of the year. It's Christopher who does the books, and he's even more of a stickler for this stuff than me…."*

Gerry stopped mid-sentence when he saw Vince sigh and shake his head, pushing himself back in his chair.

Gerry put both hands flat on Vince's desk and spoke more quietly, *"But the extra punters in here midweek are bound to boost the bar takings for Gossip 'n' Envy, I guess, Vince, right? Would that be something that you get a cut of?"*

Vince was fuming, feeling a vein in his temple pulsing. Gerry, the crooked bastard, coming out with all this Mr Honest John, play-it-with-a-straight-bat shite had him fighting to keep calm. Oh, this was really rich, two-faced crap, especially coming from Gerry. The same Gerry, who worked with computers of all things, and who would have definitely downloaded whole TV box sets onto memory sticks for Christmas presents, nicked hours and hours of music and lifted hundreds of movies without paying a penny, was telling him that he couldn't possibly be involved in anything illegal. And to top it all, he was now suggesting what Vince might want to do in his own fucking club! Was that really Gerry's best offer; that Vince would skim off his own bar takings?

Vince called on his *Nightclubpro* training – always there when he needed it- to stay focussed, to prevent himself telling Gerry to fuck off. SEE TAFT (Stay Energised, Eyes on the Target, And Follow Through), that was what was needed. He crossed his arms and spoke slowly, separating the words, as if he was being recorded.

"Bar takings wasn't what I had in mind Gerry. Bar takings need to pay the barman that I'd have to bring in special, just for the night, just for you and your poker pals." A spray of saliva hit the desk as Vince spat out the word "pals".

"I need to take that money on the night over the bar, just to pay the barman and break even." He stopped to take a breath and then continued. *"Ye see, this is a business here Gerry, as I was trying to explain to you, it's no a community hall or a church club. I was hoping that you would realise that and you and me could come to some arrangement here, but that's just not happening, is it? I want to help you out here with getting your poker club started. Absolutely. But not if it's gonnae cost me to do it."*

Gerry interrupted Vince, lifting a finger in the air, *"Ah but you might get some new weekend punters out of this Vince,"* he said, *"that would bring in a bit of extra cash, surely? If the poker players who've never been here like what they see in Gossip 'n' Envy they might come back for one of your theme nights for dancing and drinking and bring a few mates, eh?"*

Vince blew out a long breath and slumped in his chair, looking at the ceiling.

"To be honest Gerry, that's a bit of a long shot," he said.

He was trying to stay energised, but feeling and sounding flat and bored now that he had made his best play and the negotiations were going in circles. It was like trying to explain something to a child who wasn't old enough to understand.

"The punters who are in here, pissed out of their skulls, dressed up like cowboys, see I don't think they are from the same tribe as your poker playing Cool Hand Lukes, and your Johnny Aces..."

"*Well, I don't know Vince*" Gerry said, smiling, "*you might be surprised at the different type of people who play poker. We get all types, and I know for a fact that some of them have been in here before on nights out, before the place went bust after that business with the fire door down south. You might want to see how it works out. You never know with this stuff.*"

The remnants of the polite smile that Vince had managed to keep throughout the negotiations disappeared. He spoke in a monotone.

"*Well, you see, that's the problem right there, Gerry. After doing this job for years, I do know about this stuff. I do know what works in pubs and clubs, and I know it even before it works. I have to. Because it's a really thin line between success and failure in the nightclub business and I have to walk it.*"

"*With this one Gerry, I just don't get a good feeling and I'm not convinced that it's a goer. Sorry.*"

Vince said, shrugging and putting his hands on the arms of his chair ready to stand up.

Gerry spoke even more quickly, one last stab, "*What about selling them snacks from the bar Vince – you're bound to have a big mark up on nuts and crisps and stuff?*" Vince stood up without replying.

"*How do you bump up the profits on your other nights when people are in here dancing? D'you sell them glow sticks to wave about, or have drinks promotions, or raffle a bottle of something or…*"

Vince stood behind his seat and pushed it under the desk, not looking at Gerry.

"*It's like I said Gerry, your punters and my punters are basically different animals. Your poker buddies are not going to be too interested in jagerbomb drinks promotions or first-pair-of-knickers-in-the-air competition or a chocolate fountain at the side of the dance floor, I don't think.*"

The idea hit Vince at precisely the wrong time, as he moved towards the office door. He stopped and looked at Gerry, slump-shoulder deflated, packing the demo membership papers and cards into his canvas bag as he got to his feet. There was a way to salvage this, but he had to move fast. It would have been better to have followed through with it while they were sitting, make it seem planned, like it was one option in the negotiations. He would have to improvise.

"*Well look Gerry*" he said, rubbing his chin and pulling his lips tight, "*I can see that this is something that you've put a lot of work into and I don't want to be a complete wowser here, stop you organising your wee poker game and having a laugh with your mates.*"

"*I'd feel bad about that. God knows, there's next to fuck all to have a laugh about for most folk in Perth these days. Maybe, just maybe, there's a way forward here.*"

Gerry put his bag of his papers on his seat and turned his palms up.

"*Now I'm totally confused Vince. Are you saying yes or no here? I thought we were finished?*" he said.

"*Well there might be something to try,*" Vince continued, "*but you've got to see this from where I'm standing. I would be taking a big gamble here, which is pretty rich, considering we're talking about poker, eh?*" Vince snorted.

"*You have to appreciate that there's not much in this for me. I'm a business man, Gerry, and I've got to think about the bottom line, which is, you think it would work; I still don't,*" Vince paused, looking at Gerry for a reaction, but getting none.

"*But I'm not a totally heartless bastard, Gerry, despite what some other heartless bastards in Perth might tell you,*" Vince laughed.

Gerry stood holding his bag. "*So, what are we talking about now, Vince?*"

Vince moved back toward his desk, to put some space between them.

"*OK, let me be straight. What about we try it one night a week for a month and see what happens? I'd hate to pass on any wee opperchancities for Gossip 'n' Envy, even if it's a long shot. You know what I mean Gerry? We'll look at the numbers and any bad publicity for the club and if it doesn't work out after the month, I'll have to pull the plug and you'll be looking for somewhere else, but at least you'll get to play four games here at least. What do you think?"*

Gerry had prepared himself for a quick hand shake and out the door, an hour wasted, and now…well, now he wondered what had changed in the last two minutes. Was Vince still looking to spring some last minute, profit sharing deal on him, and hook him in after he agreed to a month's trial?

"That's, well that's….. very….reasonable of you Vince, very civil – I appreciate it. I can see you're trying to make it work here in the club as a business, and…and maybe this will bring in more punters, one way or another."

Gerry paused, not sure if he should say more, or quit before Vince changed his mind again. He waited a beat for Vince to come back with some conditions on his offer, then kept going.

"I'll let the boys know that it's just a trial, and I'll make sure that they spend at the bar when we're here Vince. I can absolutely guarantee that. I know everybody'll really appreciate it Vince, you allowing us in, and if there's anything….."

"Aye, nae bother Gerry, let's just try it and see how it works out, eh?"

Vince moved towards the office door and held it open.

"Great Vince; I'll be here about half an hour early on Tuesday to get things set up, and I can speak to you then. I'll just need to push the tables together, put the poker tables on top, and you've plenty of chairs and…".

"Aye, OK, OK Gerry, I'm sure it will be fine".

As Vince walked him out along the dark corridor, Gerry stopped to look at the club posters, framed on the wall, noticing for the first time the damp patches along the top of the wall. He stopped at the country and western poster.

"Did you know that pair of Kings in poker are called cowboys Vince?", he said, pointing.

"What?" Vince said, half turning.

"A pair of Kings, Vince, in your hand, in poker, see, we call them cowboys," Gerry continued, *"like the guy in your poster there for one of your dressing up nights. Aces are*

called bullets, and if you have Queens we call them…..."

Vince cut in, talking over his shoulder as he continued walked down the corridor, *"We call them theme nights, actually, not dressing up nights, and they're very successful. I'm thinking about extending the number of nights we open. If your poker is half as successful, you'll be doing alright Gerry."*

Gerry walked quickly to catch up with Vince at the entrance to Gossip 'n' Envy.

"Oh, right, I see what you mean Vince. I think the poker here could be a real winner."

There was an awkward pause, then a handshake, offered by Gerry and ended quickly by Vince.

"Like I said Gerry, we'll see how it works."

Vince locked the main door and walked to the bar, where he drew a whisky from the optic and took it to the office. He punched his phone onto calculator mode, put in some numbers, tried it again with ten percent more, re-calculated and sat back. Vince was the go-to guy; it might work.

"We get all types", Gerry had said, *"Some have been here before"*, *"They might bring a few mates."*

Vince really hoped they would.

CHAPTER 4

Crazy Pineapple

Crazy pineapple is a poker variation. There are two differences from Texas Hold'em. Each player gets four cards instead of two to start, and must discard two cards after the flop, when the three community cards are put on the table. It is also a game with "wild" cards. These are cards that can count as any suit, any number. There are five possible wild cards in Crazy Pineapple and the dealer decides how many will be active: both of the one-eyed jacks, (J♠ and J♥), both black twos (2♠ and 2♣) and the "suicide" King (K♥), so called because he is holding a sword to his head.

The Mental Health (Care and Treatment) (Scotland) Act 2003 provides for "*Advance Statements*" for people who have mental health problems that are episodic. These statements are witnessed and signed documents in which a person specifies how he or she wishes to be treated for a mental disorder.

The person writes the statement when he or she is "well", in anticipation of times when they are too "unwell" to make their own decisions. In an Advance Statement a person may express a preference for individual therapy over group therapy, or a preference for certain types of medication, for example those that do not cause them to put on weight, or make them drowsy. The Advance Statement might also make it clear that the person is vegetarian or has other dietary preferences. The wishes that a person expresses in an Advance Statement can be overridden by a health professional however, if a clinical judgement is made that refusal of a particular treatment would not be in the patient's best interests.

When a person needs treatment for a mental health problem the status of an Advance Statement is judged by considering the age of the statement, how relevant it is to a patient's current healthcare needs, and the medical progress that the patient has made since the time the Statement was witnessed and signed. What is written in an Advance Statement cannot oblige a medical practitioner to do anything that is illegal or unethical; it is simply a statement of *preferences* in the context of how the patient is treated.

Francis Robert McMurdo's Advance Statement was dictated to a medical secretary and witnessed by his local GP at Francis' Health Centre. After reading the Statement to Francis, the secretary had suggested some changes to grammar and vocabulary to make the Statement clear and unequivocal. Francis agreed to these changes and signed the Statement.

"In the event of my incarceration (again) in the Glenalmond Unit or any other hospital place with locked doors I wish the following to be taken into consideration in how I am treated:

- *My preferred form of address is Mr McMurdo, Rab or Robert . I do not wish to be known as, and will not respond to the name Francis.*
- *I have strong religious beliefs and I reserve the right to express these in what I say and do, or sing.*
- *In line with my religious beliefs, I will choose what I wear and when. If some people are offended by the way I dress, that is their problem, not mine.*
- *In my room I request no green curtains, carpet, bedding, towels, paintwork or lampshades, i.e. none. No green medication tablets either.*
- *My Advanced Statement preference is to receive no medical treatment whatsoever from anyone wearing a crucifix, no matter what size (the crucifix, not the person).*
- *No fiddle, accordion or so-called traditional dancing music to be played in my presence.*
- *My condition is worsened by the showing of any football on the television (that should be obvious by now to all so-called medical staff that know me). I reserve the right to have the television channel changed or the television switched off, no matter who wants to watch it.*
- *My religious beliefs prevent me from consorting or fraternising with*

members of certain other religions. This should be respected at meal times and in any group meetings that I am obliged to attend. My Advanced Statement preference is to know the religious affiliation of all other patients and staff in advance of fraternising with them in any way.

☐ *Under no circumstances am I to be disturbed in the morning when I am sleeping – I will get up when I am ready and not before.*

☐ *No visits from my wife, that is, none."*

Rab had been taken out of the Criminal Justice system and referred to the health care system during preliminary court proceedings, when it became clear to the Sheriff and to Rab's defence solicitor that he was unable to understand the charges against him (breach of the peace, threatening behaviour likely to incite public disorder, religiously aggravated breach of the peace) because of his mental disorder. The solicitor made a case for compulsory treatment measures under the Mental Health Act, and the Sheriff agreed, even although he was not convinced that Rab understood these any more than he understood the criminal charges against him.

In the two-fold information leaflet given to relatives, the Glenalmond Inpatient Unit was described as "*a safe environment for assessment, treatment and therapeutic work for a full spectrum of mental health conditions, based on a planned and integrated whole system approach to care which is delivered in conjunction with the community services and is designed to promote recovery.*" The sliding glass doors at the main entrance to the one storey, L-shaped building and the internal doors at the entrance to the accommodation for the sixteen patients were both security code operated, with the code changed weekly. This was for the safety and security of patients, explained the same leaflet.

In reality, the security code on the doors was to stop people running away. This had been a major problem during the first year of opening when the unit operated a therapeutically admirable, but completely unworkable open-door policy. Police and ambulance services had lodged a formal complaint with the hospital management about the number of call outs to return patients, mostly from the local Shots Bar or from a muddy bottomed fishing loch half a mile from the hospital.

The male and female corridors of the Unit met at the corner of the L-shaped building in a communal dining and recreation room, although both corridors also had their own, smaller TV rooms and even smaller smoking rooms. Smoking in the men's room was how Arthur first met Rab.

Designated rooms in psychiatric hospitals and psychiatric units were exempt from the Smoking, Health and Social Care (2005) legislation by virtue of the Prohibition of Smoking in Certain Premises (Scotland) Regulations 2006. Nurses had argued that a ban on smoking would make patients aggressive and more difficult to manage, and would also take away lifestyle choices from a vulnerable population. Nurses, a health profession with a 30% smoking prevalence were not exempt from the smoking ban of course, but the smokers' room in the Glenalmond Unit was well used, by the day, back and night shift staff, only at times when it was free of patients, of course. There were no distractions from the main business of smoking in the small room. Eight mismatched chairs sat around a low table, bolted to the floor by metal brackets on each leg. On the table, two battered ash trays were fixed by half inch bolts through two inch washers, secured by steel nuts under the table. The wiry, brown carpet tiles were moved around regularly to put the worst of the cigarette burns under chairs, where they were less visible. The walls and the ceiling of the room had been gloss painted and had an eggshell finish of nicotine, sticky to the touch. There was one small window with an aluminium surround that had been painted so many times that the window no longer opened. The tempered glass was dull with streaks of yellow from the cigarette smoke. The window looked out to a small sitting area and an adult size trampoline, for patient recreation. This was the result of a fund raiser by the Hospital Friends charity. A laminated sign on the nearby picnic bench read, "*Strictly no smoking on the trampoline*".

Arthur Salter's Advance Statement was short, and had been made only after encouragement by his doctor.

"*In the event of my incarceration I wish the following to be taken into consideration:*

- ☐ *My preferred form of address is Arthur or Mr Salter*
- ☐ *My Advanced Statement preference is to have any medical treatment that I am to receive discussed with me beforehand*
- ☐ *I have no known allergies or food intolerances*
- ☐ *I have a preference for tap water, rather than bottled water*
- ☐ *I would like to have a range of reading material available during any inpatient treatment and my preference is for books (fiction) rather than magazines*
- ☐ *I have a preference to get outside to walk at least once a day, accompanied or unaccompanied*
- ☐ *I would prefer not to share a bedroom other patients*"

When Rab came into the smoking room, Tyler Dupree, the main character in Arthur's current book, was struggling with the fact that all the stars in the universe had suddenly disappeared. Arthur looked up from his book and nodded. Rab blanked him and went for the chair that was furthest away from Arthur, although that was still only two leg lengths. Rab lit up as soon as he sat down, took a double drag on the cigarette, and stared out the discoloured window. He sat forward with his elbows on his knees, rocking slightly. Arthur didn't smoke, but the smoking room was the best place to read.

Arthur realised that a mysterious shield had surrounded the Earth, blocking Tyler's view of the stars, and he was keen to find out more, but he couldn't concentrate on the implications of this event with someone else in the room. He put the book on his knee, using his finger as a bookmark.

He looked across at Rab and nodded again, but Rab continued to squint out the window through the smoke. Arthur had learned, after many missed opportunities and what-ifs in his formative years, that the best way to start a conversation was to say something, not think about it until it was too late. He waited a beat and then dived in.

"My wife was here, you know. They said it was for depression, but I know what she was really doing was checking the place out for me. She liked to check stuff before I try it, you know, make sure that it's OK".

He put his book on the table, spreading it face down to keep his place.

"That's a good woman for you."

He sat perfectly still, looking at Rab.

Rab took a long drag on his cigarette, blew out the smoke and said, *"My wife's a lyin' hoor, who fucked up my life."*

Arthur reached for his book, stopped, then stuck out his hand instead, moving it into Rab's line of sight.

"My name's Arthur, by the way".

Without moving, Rab said, *"People call me Rab."*

Arthur kept his hand dangling between them for another five seconds and Rab was embarrassed into shaking it, a quick grasp, before dropping it. Arthur noticed the knuckle tattoos.

"So, been in this place before, Rab?"

Rab looked up, not at Arthur, but at the door, then at his half-finished cigarette, doing a quick calculation on leaving.

"Nope – first time. It was this or the jail, bud, and I wouldn't give those fuckers the satisfaction of locking me up for speaking my mind."

He sat back in the chair, clenching one hand around his wrist, still holding the cigarette.

"Some tight arsed neighbours objected to me playing my music and singing too loud and now I'm stuck in this shithole. What happened to the principles of free speech in this

fucking society, eh? What happened to my human rights and my right to tell people what I think? What happened to my freedom to celebrate my heritage?" he said, his voice rising.

He took a double drag of his fag again, trying to calm himself. *"Bastards!"* he spat out, and sat back in the chair, crossing one leg over the other and rocking against the back of the chair.

Arthur waited until Rab's breathing slowed, then leaned forward, *"Ach, it's no too bad in here – you'll be OK. I'm one of the regulars, so I know the score. There's no bills to pay, three meals a day, even if they are mostly sludge, and you get to meet some right interesting characters. There's some good guys, like us, but some of the punters when they come in at first are totally doolally tap, you know, living on Planet Zanussi. It calms down though, and you get a laugh sometimes."*

Arthur stopped and smiled at Rab, waiting for a response. Rab continued rocking and ignored him, lighting a second cigarette from the glowing stub of the first.

Arthur had learned that is was important to keep a conversation going, especially if you were the one who had started it.

"Deolali was an army camp in India, Rab - don't know if you knew that? The boredom there used to send the troops mad. They were all hanging about in the heat doing nothing for weeks, a bit like in here, and they went doolally. That's how the name came about. Of course, we're all mad in here already, according to them, so maybe the boredom is supposed to calm us down."

Arthur gave a short laugh at his own joke. Rab glanced at him out of the corner of his eye and then went back to looking out the window.

"Something else that you might not know if it's your first time is that even when you get out of here, and you need after sales service, they do home delivery. Aye, some young laddie who's a Community Psychiatric Nurse comes to my house and speaks to me. I think he enjoys it, but it's difficult to know, because he never looks that happy. Probably thinks he has more problems than me, at his age, I reckon. He's still better than some of the staff in

here though – I can never work out if they get promoted and come here, or get promoted and get out of here."

The mention of staff seemed to trigger a reaction in Rab, who uncrossed his legs and turned towards Arthur. Arthur kept going.

"Just watch that psychiatrist in here when you see him Rab. He's as tricky as a bag of snakes with his questions and he doesn't like it when you......see, he's got me stabilised on those Tic Tac tablets, but he's got some tablets that you definitely don't want to be taking because....."

Rab leaned forward, towards Arthur and cut in.

"With a name like Arthur, I'm guessing you're no a fenian, are ye?"

Arthur stopped, confused, trying to remember what he was explaining and how Rab's question related to this.

"Sorry Rab, a what?"

Rab took another draw on his cigarette and made eye contact with Arthur for the first time since he'd been into the room.

"You know, a fenian, a pape, a taig."

Rab's eye contact was unblinking.

Arthur hesitated before replying, looking away as Rab kept the eye contact.

"Ah, right, I see what you mean Rab - am I Catholic? No, no, I don't believe in any kind of God, haven't for a long time, not since..."

"Ah'm no talking about God, bud", Rab said in a quieter voice, putting one hand on the edge of the table and pointing a finger at Arthur with the other.

"I'm asking about your religion bud, your faith, your cause."

Spots of saliva sprayed out and hit the table as Rab spoke.

"My religion? You know, I honestly can't even remember what I was before I wasn't anything Rab."

He laughed nervously.

"Those Tic Tac tablets make you forget stuff from a long time ago and sometimes even

from yesterday. I think I might have been Baptist or some kind of Presbyterian, or maybe Episcopalian? I think it was one of the ones that was difficult to spell, I remember that, definitely, from Sunday school, when you had to write it down. But it's been a long time since I was anywhere near a church Rab, expect for weddings and stuff, and…..."

"Well at least it was a church, bud, as least it was a church," Rab said, falling back into the chair again and drawing the last life out of his cigarette. He reached for another in the pocket of grey tracksuit bottoms that looked like they had been washed out without ever being washed. He was wearing a baggy T-shirt, frayed at the collar, and a pair of grey trainers without socks. As Rab lifted his feet onto the low table, Arthur caught a waft of stale body odour that cut through the permanent smell of tobacco fug in the small room.

Arthur ran his finger around with the cover of his book on the table looked again at Rab, wondering what might be safe ground to keep the conversation going. He lifted the book, then put it back down. He just could not be in a room this size with someone and not talk.

"If you're worried about not getting to church Rab, they have a guy in a dog collar who comes in on a Sunday afternoon to speak to anybody who's religious, because we don't get out much from here when they're short on staff."

Arthur saw Rab tense his body in the chair and the look on his face made Arthur realise that talking about the church was definitely not safe ground.

"I don't need any fucking church for my faith, bud, and I definitely don't need some Holy Joe spouting shite about the baby Jesus. I keep my faith all in order in here," he said, tapping his temple so hard it must have hurt, with an index finger that showed a smudged capital "F" just below the knuckle. He put his feet back on the ground, one of the Velcro fasteners on his training shoes ripping loose as he did so.

"It's my faith that keeps me going, see, and even though I've been persecuted for it, I've never given up the cause, and I never will," Rab continued, his voice rising to a near shout, directed at the closed door of the room.

"*That's good Rab,*" said Arthur, trying to calm it down by speaking more slowly, "*I wish I had something I believed in as strongly as that, but I never found any…*"

But Rab wasn't finished.

"*See, there's only believers and non-believers, bud. They bastards in power have tried to grind us down for years, stopped us meeting, stopped us writing the truth, tried to change our history, but we just keep coming back each time. We have to keep fighting to express our identity. They just keep knocking us down and we just keep coming right back at them. We don't do walking away.*"

He thumped on the table with a clenched fist, causing cigarette butts to jump in the ashtray.

Rab was breathing fast, his neck reddening and the colour creeping up his blotchy complexion. He was flexing his shoulders, sitting straight in the chair and looking like he was ready to say more, much more.

Arthur composed himself, ready to get out; he'd seen a few of the men in Glenalmond kick off, for stuff that seemed trivial to everyone else. It was usually a quick flare up, then everybody settled down again. What surprised him was just how fast Rab had changed. He had gone from slumped in the chair to rage mode in fifteen seconds. His face was now the same colour as his neck and Arthur could see beads of sweat along his hairline. Rab grabbed his T shirt in a clump and pulled it away from middle of his chest, then repeated the action at one shoulder. Arthur caught the same acrid body odour each time.

As Rab swapped his cigarette to his left hand, he was distracted from his rant. The cigarette had burned out while he was speaking. He flicked the dowt onto the floor and slapped the pockets of this tracksuit bottoms, now empty. Making a sound like someone constipated, he stood up marched to the door.

"*Anyway, it was good to have a chat with you Rab,*" Arthur said.

With eyes fixed on the floor, Rab walked out.

'It's good to find somebody else in this place who isn't totally Tonto, if you know what I mean,"* Arthur finished, sitting alone as the door to the smoking room closed.

He sat back in his chair and tucked his chin into his neck, "*Louis, I think this is the start of a beautiful friendship*" he said, in his best Bogart-in-Casablanca accent.

"Engaging the patient in therapeutic programming that is available seven days a week", was one of the stated aims of Glenalmond. In reality, there was a lot of down time. Meals, TV time and a morning group meeting – to talk about meals mostly – were every day. There was a music activity group on Thursday mornings. *"This is not music therapy and I am not a music therapist"*, the harassed music facilitator said at the beginning of every session, trying to find an instrument, mostly percussion, for everyone who turned up. He was a believer in the power of mindfulness; meditation to improve musical abilities- and he tried each week to incorporate rhythms and silences into his sessions. It was hard work. Few patients had played any instrument since school days and the attempts at contemplative silences were regularly interrupted by patients asking what everybody was waiting for.

There were two groups that some patients, including Rab, were obliged to attend by the conditions of their stay in Glenalmond. The anger management group was run by the hospital psychologist and a string of different assistants on Tuesday afternoons. The communication group on Wednesday afternoons was run by two nurse therapists, who would introduce the theme for the day before splitting the main group into two Circles of Trust, based on the charge nurse recommendations about which patients to keep apart that week. In the past, all groups in Glenalmond had been psychologist-led, as part of the therapeutic ethos, but when budget cuts started taking effect, ethos was replaced by expediency; training and paying nurse therapists was cheaper than psychologists, took less time and still ticked the box for

"Engaging the patient in therapeutic programming", for those who would otherwise go without.

Participation in both groups was part of Rab's therapeutic care plan, one condition of the legal agreement that kept him out of prison. He was required to both attend and contribute. At the beginning of the communication group one of the nurse therapist would restate the aims of the group and the rules for participation, for new patients and for those that needed a reminder.

"Improving your communication skills will ensure that your journey of excellence in Glenalmond continues. We will facilitate honest, direct and respectful communications. You will be safe in this group to talk about your experiences and your feelings. Everyone in the group will support and encourage you to speak freely. In this group we will recognise the strengths in each other and we will view any difficulties that anyone has as opportunities for them to grow and learn."

They would then break into the two subgroups and each nurse therapist would remind those in the Circle of Trust about ground rules, appropriate and inappropriate behaviour in the group, the need to respect opinions of others and to let them have their say. Finally, the rule that was most often broken; the need to respect confidentiality.

"Anything personal that anyone says here today must stay within this group – it is very important that no-one talks to others outside the group about what we discussed, or says anything hurtful to anyone in this group after the group meeting has closed. Are we all clear on that?"

Everyone would nod their agreement, in the same let's-get-on-with-it way they would tick a box at the end of three pages of small print agreement on a computer screen.

Jane, the nurse therapist for the group that Rab and Arthur had been assigned to had been doing the job for two years. When she finished her nurse training she had worked in low secure units, NHS and private residential services, and then gone on to do a Cognitive Behaviour Training course. More recently she had started an evening class in the use of massage. Jane was delighted to be a nurse therapist, or more accurately she was delighted not to be a nurse. Two months into her training she had realised that caring for people who couldn't care for themselves wasn't for her. Saying and doing the right things she could manage, but keeping people clean, fed and alive just bored her very quickly. It was the repetition of cleaning, taking bloods, taking temperatures and saying the same thing over and over that did her head in. That, and her irritation with uncooperative, ungrateful patients who crapped the bed. Before she had finished her basic training, she was already applying for other qualifications that would get her out of wards with people stuck in beds, and off the crazy shift patterns that screwed up her holidays.

The Cognitive Behaviour Training course gave her an edge. It allowed her to leapfrog the nurses with whom she qualified; most of them were grinding out years on the wards, trying to climb the ladder to assistant unit managers, at best, if they kept their head down and didn't complain too much.

She was now a nurse therapist; no night shifts, no wiping arses, and in demand. The approach she took to running groups was one that she had learned in an afternoon and polished up in less than six months. She found that it was best to learn enough techniques and tricks to convince other staff that you knew what you were doing, but not so many that you had to use notes or books to remember them. Because using notes might give the impression to other nurses that anybody with the notes and books could do what she was doing, and that would not be good. Other nurses in Glenalmond didn't treat Jane as a senior, but they didn't treat her as just another nurse either. There was some resentment from staff who had known her before she was a nurse therapist, of course, but most nursing staff were just grateful that she came to Glenalmond regularly and took some patients out of circulation for an hour to give the real nurses a break.

The approach Jane used in groups was one of facilitating communication. The aim was to allow patients to overcome the barriers that prevented them from accepting the changes they needed to make, either in the way they thought or in the way they behaved, or both. It was easy enough to explain what she was doing in patient reviews, and to make it sound convincing. In the low secure units where she had worked she had seen this approach used effectively, when the level of motivation of the patient was matched by that of the staff. She had also seen it fail miserably. For fellow nurse therapists, a patient with the label of "resistant to treatment" was the ultimate challenge, a real test of whether you could succeed where other therapists had failed, end the search for some unique form of communication that would save the patient from years of incarceration and misery. Jane was less optimistic about patients who were resistant to treatment ("tough nuts to crack" was her old ward manager's worn out joke). She drew the line at putting any of her effort into patients who needed to change not just their ways of thinking or behaviour, but their *predisposing personality style*. These were conniving, long-term patients who had long ago forgotten when they were telling the truth and when they were lying. They would invent stories about themselves and about others, including Jane, and then just as easily deny that they had said any of it at the next meeting. Spending any time with them made Jane feel utterly exhausted, the same sort of fatigue that came from giving blood.

So when she finished her CBT training, Jane made the move out of low secure units in search of easier nuts to crack, and found them in general mental health services. They were easier to crack, she thought, but they were still nuts. Staff were also less well trained, and less likely to question what she was doing.

The theme for the group she was running today was "Just for Starters", and for the patients the first exercise was about making small talk. For Jane, it was an exercise from one of her manuals about building relationships and working through levels of self-disclosure, starting with small talk and working up to discussing emotions and experiences. It was an easy one to remember and it could be repeated every few months as patients were discharged and new ones arrived.

Jane kicked it off.

"So let's start this by talking about how you get into conversation with someone that you have never met before. So.. we'll imagine that I don't know you and you don't know me, and we are sitting on a bus together, or in a café, or..... we're walking our dogs in a park, for example."

She looked around the six faces in the Circle of Trust, deciding where to start. She could see that Arthur, more smartly dressed than was necessary for an inpatient in polo shirt and shoes that had been polished. He was leaning forward, ready to go, as always, but God knows where he would take them, Jane was thinking, as she moved her gaze around the group.

"Now Tom, I know that you can be a bit anxious when waiting to talk in the group – do you want to go first, get it over now, or would you prefer to wait?"

"Don't mind," Tom mumbled, looking down.

Anytime of the day, Tom looked like he had been dragged from his bed where he had fallen asleep, fully clothed. He had heavy eyelids and his cheeks sagged around a mouth that seemed too small for this face.

"OK, in that case I will come back to you, when you've heard what the others have to say. Is that OK?"

"Don't mind," Tom said again, not raising his head.

She had another quick look around the other faces, considered Raymond, and then gave in to the inevitable.

"Anyone else want to start us off then? Arthur?"

Arthur was off and running before she had finished saying his name.

"Well you could say something about the person's dog, if they had a dog – how old is he, what's his name, does he chase cars – that sort of thing, or you could ask the person if they had any other pets, or you could show them the tricks that your dog could do – sitting, fetching things– or …"

"Yes, what Arthur suggests is good," Jane said, *"it might be OK to start the conversation about dogs, because that's what we would call a "neutral" subject, like talking about the weather, or commenting on something happening in the park. My only suggestion would be not to ask too many questions about the dog right away, until the person has responded to your first question and you knew the person a bit more."*

Jane looked around the faces for nods, or some signs of understanding from the others. Nothing.

"OK, that's a good starter, Arthur. Thank you. Now, what about if you were on the bus?" Jane said, looking around the faces again.

"Does the person have the dog on the bus?", said Arthur, quickly.

"No, forget the dog just for now Arthur. Let's try it without the dog this time", Jane said, keeping calm, smiling, thinking ahead about how to bring someone else in. *"How do we get the conversation started on the bus."*

No heads came up, except Arthur's. She waited it out. One of the tricks that she could remember without notes was just waiting, giving it twenty seconds longer than what felt comfortable.

"Is it moving?"

It was the first time that Jane had heard Rab speak in the group without being asked a direct question. When he spoke it was in quick bursts, without spaces between words and without any compromise on his accent, which was more Dundee than Perth, and more announcement than inquiry. It made everything sound like a challenge, like you had just insulted him, or as if some argument had run its course and he was inviting you to settle matters outside.

"Is what moving Rab?" Jane said.

"Bus".

"Well it could be moving, yes, or you might still be sitting at the bus stop or in the bus station waiting to leave." Jane was puzzled. *"Would it make a difference, do you think",* she said, making a basic error of asking Rab a question to which she did not already know the answer.

"Well it's gonnae look just a bit fucking weird if you start talking to some complete stranger when it's moving, eh? I mean, fair enough if you're stuck in the bus station and you forgot to get a paper to read and you're both just sitting there twiddling yer thumbs, with nothing happening, you might say something like, "Fucking buses, eh? Always late." But if the bus is already bumping along the road, and you start talking to somebody it looks like you're trying to chat them up. Either that, or they're gonnae think that you've just walked out of this place," said Rab.

"Well…..", Jane said, trying to pick her words carefully, without making it sound like she was reading them. She wanted to find something positive to say to Rab and keep him involved, without giving him any encouragement that might make her legally liable in any way for Rab terrifying some stranger on a bus in the future.

"OK - that's a good start, Rab, everyone, but let's move on. I think we're getting the hang of this now."

Jane knew that progress was zero, but the book called for positive feedback after each contribution.

"Let's try the coffee shop scenario now. That might be a better place to start a conversation, when people are relaxing."

She glanced at Rab and said, *"And try not to swear in the group Rab – remember what we said about being respectful."*

She said it as fast as she could, addressing the group and avoiding Rab's dead eyed stare.

"Let's think about what you might say, to someone if the café was busy and you had to sit at a table that had someone sitting there already. What if you wanted to engage them in conversation?"

Rab was still staring at her and he was on it before she had finished speaking.

"Man or woman?"

"Well let's try a man first, shall we Rab?" Jane said, still not looking at him.

"How old?"

"Eh, OK, this is good, getting the details... let's say that the person was about the same age as Rab."

Jane was now looking at others in the group, one at a time, trying to catch someone's eye, nod them into the discussion.

"What would be a good way to start a conversation in those circumstances?"

Everyone else in the group had been intimidated by the thought of speaking and now the heads went down even lower as Rab began to get worked up. Arthur was still ready to chip in, but even he knew that it was easier to step back when Rab got started.

"Is he white or black, has he got hair, is he ginger, and what's he wearing? See, I like to size people up before I talk to them. I don't just talk to anybody and I definitely don't ..."

Jane turned to him, trying hard to keep her voice in calm, group facilitating tone and failing.

"OK, Rab, OK, for the purposes of this exercise let's just imagine he looks a bit like you; same age, same looks, wearing the same sort of clothes. Does that help?"

She smiled, wishing that Rab would just do his usual strong-and-silent-type act more often in her group sessions.

"Well, number one, see, I wouldnae be seen deed in wan of thae places, drinking coffee, folk sitting about kidding on they've got nothing better to dae, and number two, if this was real I'd just sit down, say nothing, let him deal with it. The tables are for everybody. But, but, if I had to speak to him, I'd keep it short," said Rab, *" 'cause you don't want every c...., everybody knowing your business. I'd probably just say, "Hello bud, I'm Rab and I'm a plumber". Because that's all he needs to know."*

Rab jerked back into his chair, arms folded.

"Well, that might be fine as a starter, Rab," said Jane. *"Thanks for that and thank you for speaking up and sharing that with the group, and for getting this conversation started."*

She recognised the signs in Rab and she knew that it was important to take action now, before the whole session became an audience with Rab.

"Now, how about someone else comes in here, yes? Someone to give Rab a rest for a minute? Raymond?"

She spun on Raymond like a teacher with a question for someone who had not been paying attention.

Raymond worked at the tax office. He was thirty two, small and wiry, but with a slump of the shoulders usually seen in much bigger men. He had a thick, dark fringe that almost covered his eyes and a hairstyle like a German WWII helmet. Whenever he spoke in the group, he pulled on the end of a charity moustache that he had grown originally for Movember, six years previously. He started to pull on his moustache now, but Arthur was in first, leaning forward to look at Rab on the other side of Jane, *"I didn't know you were a plumber, Rab...."*

Jane raised an open palm to Arthur, her voice just louder than his, *"Arthur, could we let Raymond speak in the group please, and you could maybe continue your conversation with Rab later?"* she said. Arthur raised his own palm in apology and sat back.

Raymond spoke slowly, *"Well, if it was a woman in the cafe I might say something about the weather, or I might comment on how nice the scones were ..."* He paused.

Arthur cut in again, leaning back in his chair this time, behind Jane, to address Rab, *"Plumber Rab, eh? I've done a bit of plumbing in my time. It's satisfying when you do a good job, isn't it? It's not an easy job either, mind..."*

"Arthur!" said Jane, in a voice that was calm, but loud enough to stop conversation in the second Circle of Support, at the other end of the room.

"Raymond is talking to the group. Please!" This time her hand was raised as if to stop traffic.

"Oh, right, apologies Raymond. On you go," Arthur said, raising two hands this time in apology.

The nursing staff on the Unit became most interested in the group activities when they were cancelled. The nursing view was that therapy was done by "outsiders" and nurses did the real work on the Unit. Therapy was tolerated because it occupied patients, if only for an hour. But it was an hour's less work for nurses, and that was OK.

All inpatients in Glenalmond had detailed individual care plans – a summary on the office noticeboard, an easy read copy given to the patient and an electronic copy of the full plan and notes from periodic reviews on the password protected hospital database. These plans were based on National Institute for Health and Clinical Excellence Quality Standards and included the recommendation that each person should have *"access to meaningful and culturally appropriate activities"* seven days a week. The care plans were written with the help of a Mental Health Promotion Specialist (MHPS) and the staff on the Unit. Each person had a designated nurse, responsible for ensuring that the care plan was delivered. The activities on the care plans included helping to prepare snacks on the Unit, one-to-one teaching sessions on Aids to Daily Living and visits to "community facilities". In times of budget cuts, this meant anything that was free; local museums, galleries, garden centres, shops and participation in further education classes. In truth, more hours were spent writing and updating the plans than were spent on the activities in them.

Any reasons for a patient not participating in certain activities had to be recorded in the care plans, but there was always a reason not to do something: *"Patient was not on good form today.", "Said that he just didn't feel like it.", "Decided to have a long lie in today.", "Didn't want to go out today because there was a murder in one of the TV soaps and he didn't want to miss it.", "Had an argument with another patient this morning and was still upset about it this afternoon.", "It was raining and he didn't really fancy it."* Reading the care plans, it was sometimes difficult to tell whether the reasons were those of the patient or those of the designated nurse.

Glenalmond had a games cupboard. It had dominoes (two full sets), draughts, a Solitaire board with pegs, Monopoly (top hat missing), Trivial Pursuit (Young Players Edition), Bingo (staff needed to call numbers) and Osh Vegas, a crime-solving board game that nobody could understand. There were also two decks of playing cards, dog-eared from years of Whist, Gin Rummy and Pig. One was a good quality deck by The Bicycle Company, waterproofed against spills, and the other deck was a freebie from a whisky maker, with some cards missing corners.

Playing cards in hospitals divided opinion. The British Medical Association had issued a 2011 report strongly encouraging the playing of games in hospitals, *"To help battle boredom, improve psychological wellbeing and better treatment outcomes. A greater focus is needed on addressing the psychological and social needs of patients, improving the patient experience, speeding recovery and thereby saving hospitals money."*

Playing cards was one kind of game but playing games and gambling were, of course, different.

Any form of gambling on NHS premises, and especially in settings with "vulnerable" patients, was viewed in the same way as people bringing in alcohol or recreational drugs. The act of doing it was bad enough, but the dangers of exploitation and abuse associated with it made it a no-brainer, especially in a system set up specifically to safeguard patients' welfare. With long waiting lists for in-patient NHS places on addiction and substance abuse programmes, sanctioning addictive substances or activities on the premises was like throwing petrol on a fire.

As well as the dangers of fuelling addictions, many things brought in a hospital could become hard currency. Older nurses at Glenalmond told stories of patients' medication, cigarettes and tea bags being exchanged for sex in the old hospitals, where patients with enough mental illness to be incarcerated, but not enough to be in a locked ward, wandered the wards and the grounds without much surveillance, or much staff interest in what they were doing outside of meal and bed times.

Fruit Ninjas in cowboy hats was how poker started in Glenalmond. How to slice a banana or a cucumber by throwing a playing card at it from six feet. It all began one night when six patients too anxious or too depressed to sleep were sitting up watching graveyard TV with two bored night staff.

There was the European Poker Tour, Late Night Poker Ace, Poker Stars, and the poker dream of dreams, the World Series of Poker (WSOP). The Glenalmond insomnia group started to watch any late night poker show, understanding when something big happened in a game, but only knowing why it was big, not understanding why there was applause or laughter or replays. Then, gradually, over many nights, they picked up why players were victorious or gutted in defeat, why they were raising or calling or folding as the cards came out, and why the crowds around the tables were oohing and ahhing. As the number of players around a table dropped they got more interested, as blinds went up, players pushed in all of their chips, or stood up from the poker table in preparation for a showdown.

In each hour of late night TV programming there were twenty minutes of highlights, actual poker play. Seen through the hole cams buried in the table, TV viewers were privy to the two cards that each player held and opponents were trying to guess. The rest of the hour was taken up with poker star profiles, ex-poker star analysis, commercial breaks, and monotonous summaries of what had happened before the commercial break, which seemed to be aimed at viewers with no short term memory. Buried in there, among all the table action and the commercial padding that surrounded it, was two minutes of distraction that first drew in the patients and staff of Glenalmond to poker. It was the grip and wrist action needed to make the 4♣ as deadly as a Ninja throwing star.

Arthur had seen it first on Full Tilt Poker. Embedding a playing card in the flesh of half a water melon from a distance of four feet was entry level, fruit Ninja. Drawing-a-small-crowd level was slicing a banana, or a soft cucumber, and Masters level was making a performance living out of chucking cards into apples, cutting pencils in two and slicing through a tower that held up an egg, letting it splash into a glass of water below.

It was explained how seasoned pros went with holding the card parallel to the ground and gripping it between index and middle finger, or even middle and ring finger (the Ferguson Grip), but for accuracy and short term success, beginners were advised to start with holding the card between thumb and middle finger, with the index finger running to the corner (the Hermann grip).

Arthur remembered what his old driving instructor had told him about establishing good habits. He favoured another variation of grip, the Ricky Jay, with his index finger on a card corner, thumb on top of the card and three fingers along the long side of the card. It felt awkward at first, but more comfortable as he practised, twenty minutes at a time. He had seen Ricky Jay, a magician turned professional card thrower, embed a card in the rind of an uncut water melon from a distance of ten feet. To Arthur that was bordering on magic.

Arthur threw cards –"scaling" it was called- at tired looking pears in Glenalmond's fruit bowl, but the cards were so dog eared that they couldn't be directed and went flying off at random angles. Ricky Jay used laminated casino-quality cards, fresh out of the box. But Arthur persisted.

"*It's all in the wrist action,*" he kept repeating, as 52 cards flew over and under the table, "*like throwing a handful of rice in a paddy field, but with a killer flick.*" He tried the other deck, which still had a few edges left, managing to land seven cards in the bowl, and inflicted a paper cut on the ear of Greg, another patient, sitting too close to the table.

Greg didn't react at all to the cut, and only noticed it when Arthur started to apologise. At first, it seemed to have blown over, but later in the evening Greg was given his PRN medication when he became agitated, asking if he should tell his brother about his ear when he phoned.

"Will my brother think I did it tae myself? He'd be mad about that, see, 'cause I scratched my arms with a key before, and he shouted at me for ages for doing that."

Arthur kept up the twenty minute practises for another two weeks, finally accepting that his scaling skill had plateaued, at least with the cards and the fruit that he had to work with.

In the twenty minutes of real, poker play there was a lot happening. Arthur started to watch. The poker plays couldn't hold a candle to scaling, but at least he could imitate them without a set of brand new, laminated cards and someone holding up a thin cucumber.

He started by taking quick notes whilst watching and then laying out the same cards from big money hands on one of the oval wooden tables. He then played the hands out, blow-by-blow, moving around the table as he did, putting on a different voice at each seat, hamming it up for himself and anyone watching.

"I think you've got nothing Cisco, nothing," said Arthur, pushing, a pile of coasters into the middle of the table, and talking out one side of his mouth, *"you've been card dead for an hour, and now I'm burying you."*

Flipping over 8♥ and then 7♣ to make a straight with the 9, 10, Jack showing on the board. Moving to the next seat, turning over a pair of sixes and burying his head in his hands.

He would then gather the cards and re-deal, laying out the hands for another memorable showdown on WSOP.

"*Check these bad boys and weep, sucker*", turning over two Kings to match the final, river card turned over on the table. "*A set of Cowboys just ain't what you want to see, is it, even if they took their own sweet time getting here.*"

Then standing up, at the next chair, throwing down an Ace and a Queen, to make two pair, "*That was a terrible call, really lousy. I had you right up to the river. You were fishing for cards,*" in an irate New York accent, "*that's not poker, that's gambling.*"

Moving back to the previous chair, "*Yes, that is gambling, my friend. That's what I do*", in a Southern drawl, sitting down, tipping an imaginary hat.

When Arthur was on a hypomania roll, it was difficult for anyone except Arthur to keep up. His rambling would jump around connections that only he knew, with bits of songs, lines from movies and whole conversations, real and imagined. He would talk faster and faster, moving around the room, punctuating what he was saying first with hand gestures, then with whole body theatre. It all speeded up to the point where he would slump in a chair, exhausted, or have to be walked to a chair and asked to calm down. When he was focused on just one topic that outsiders could understand, which was rare, like the scaling or playing out the big hands, he was more entertainment than the TV. And that's how the first games got going.

The learning was by osmosis; sitting night after night as hundreds of games and thousands of hands were played and re-played on TV, and learning by watching the Arthur show, in which the best showdowns and mega bluffs were repeated, sometimes card by card and word for word, sometimes just in highlight form. The two night staff and five of the regular late night patients, including Arthur, would sit around the table, playing slow-dealt hands of Texas Hold 'Em, with blow by blow commentary as each hand came out.

Everybody learned, but not all at the same time. None of the patients was too proud to ask, in the middle of a hand being played, if a flush was better than a straight, or a full house, or if two pair beat three of a kind, but the nurses started to get pissed off when the result in a hand had to be explained again and again.

One of the night staff forked out on a new pack of cards, with two jokers and a card showing the ranking of poker hands; what-beat-what. Then there were arguments over where this card was kept, and if it was OK to ask to see it during a game. But they stumbled on. The shuffling and the dealing got a bit faster and the instructional commentary was needed less.

They had all picked up the basics except Tom, an overmedicated former chef. He learned the hand rankings after a few weeks, but he needed constant coaching on the rules; when to post the blinds, when to check or bet, when to turn over his cards, and when not to. It slowed the game down and players got irritated with the repetition, but they needed Tom to keep the numbers up, and Tom won enough of the Solitaire plastic pegs that they used as chips to keep him interested.

Mad Hotel, they called their late night game, after Arthur informed them in one of his more accessible stream of consciousness, manic rambles that Texas Hold 'Em was, in fact, an anagram of Mad Hotel Sex. They decided to drop the sex bit, because that made it sound a bit seedy, but having a clandestine name for their games was something all the players liked, a lot, as soon as Arthur suggested it.

It was an in-joke for inpatients; a secret reference that made them feel part of something in which other patients and especially other staff were not included. It was also a good ploy to avoid interest or suspicion among the day staff, who had more professional scruples than the permanent night staff. It was nothing new for patients, and the locals, to refer to Glenalmond as the crazy hoos or the bat house or the nut factory or the fruit farm, so making references to the Mad Hotel fitted right in. It was the beginning of the Glenalmond poker players' argot, a secret language that only ever had a few words, but which gave those who used it the buzz of being exclusive, and part of something special that they had created.

Raymond and Tom, two patients who would otherwise speak only if cornered by a nurse or a therapist, would sit together at lunch and signal each other that a game was on, like two prisoners in adjoining cells, tapping on pipes.

"Ye going to the Mad Hotel tonight Tom?"

"Aye, I thought I might make a reservation."

"This place is like a Mad Hotel sometimes, eh?"

"It's a full hoos in here today, but you can always get a seat later when it's quiet..."

Daryl would listen, content to know that Mad Hotel was real.

If Daryl had been a patient in the same hospital 150 years ago, the cause of his mental illness might have been written up as, *"disappointed in love"*, a recognised trigger event then for periods of both mania and depression, second in popularity only to *"religious excitement"*. The apparent cause of Daryl's current illness was, in fact, disappointed *with* love. His case notes told how he had spent five years happily married to Jenny, his childhood sweetheart, until one day she found him sitting in the garden, in pyjamas, explaining to next door's dog that he had realised while watching a day time chat show that neither God nor love existed. He had spent the next three years bouncing between Glenalmond and home, going back home slowly each time, in-well planned stages, and coming back to Glenalmond fast, in a Friday night emergency admission. There was never a need for police support; no struggle, no bundling him into the back seat of a car. He always came quietly. Too quietly in fact, because by the time Jenny had admitted that she couldn't cope, Daryl would have stopped eating or taking medication for at least three days and be in his bed or a corner of the house, comatose.

The hospital's consultant psychiatrist liked to test junior doctors, working on rotation at the hospital, by sending them to Glenalmond to meet Daryl, when he was in a talking phase. A patient who didn't believe that God or love existed and had given up on getting up in the morning as a consequence? A patient who was articulate and could explain in detail why he was depressed? For the junior doctors it was a text book puzzle where you got to look up the answer at the back of the book later. They all went at it with a clinical vigour.

"Look at it this way Daryl," they would say. *"When it comes to things that we can't see, like God or love, absence of evidence is not necessarily evidence of absence."*

The doctors would win the argument every time, and leave with a smile and a recommendation to the consultant for more cognitive therapy, medication or both. Daryl would stay in Glenalmond, unconvinced that anything had changed. What was real was still real, and the rest was in people's heads and nowhere else.

For Daryl, Mad Hotel was real and, unlike God or love, it existed for just a select few. Absence of evidence during early and back shifts was not evidence of absence when the night shift came on.

Most of the night nurses were counting down to retirement. They had started before 1995 and had doubled up on their NHS pension each year after twenty years' service because they had Mental Health Officer. Working in direct care of mental health patients was considered so stressful and wearing that staff needed special pension consideration. This was a government acknowledgement, backed by policy and funds, and sympathetic public agreement, until the pension pot started to run dry and Mental Health Officer status was scrapped

There were eight permanent night shift nurses on Glenalmond male wing, plus an occasional bank nurse to cover holidays and sickness. Six of the eight, including all of the men, had chosen to work the night shift early in their career and live their lives on four nights on, three off. They moved around wards when needed, avoiding whenever possible staff meetings, paperwork and staff training. They were time-served nurses, who saw themselves as professional tradesmen, willing to do a job, but only on their terms. It was difficult for the hospital management to find staff willing to work permanent night shift and this gave the night staff protection from pressure from above to implement new practices. On the few occasions when changes to working practices were forced on the night shift, they had a secret sickness rota that kicked in, with the six nurses taking it in turn to phone in, on a pre-arranged schedule, giving the ward manager just enough time to get someone from the nurse bank, at crippling cost to the hospital budget. Hospital managers didn't like to upset the night shift.

Mad Hotel became part of ward routine. After the nine o'clock handover, after the bedtime medications, after everybody who was going to bed was settled, the cards and solitaire pegs came out. The two nurses would join the game only after a few rounds had been played, after they had checked that the corridors were quiet.

Cards, ace to six or ace to seven, were spread face down on the table and everyone picked one to determine seating positions. Ace was the starting dealer, but a player could have the dealer button in front of him without having to actually deal the cards, because not everyone could deal. The standard and the speed of shuffling and dealing got better, over a period of weeks, with fewer cards flying off the table or being flipped face up during the deal.

Despite late night TV and daytime practice, Arthur never mastered the riffle shuffle, favoured by the casino dealers, or the Faro shuffle, favoured by guys who just liked to show off. It was hard enough to shuffle the dog eared cards the old fashioned way, battering one half of the pack against the other until they interweaved, without causing more damage, split edges and creases. During play in Mad Hotel, Arthur was able to spot the 8♥ in another player's hand by a single diagonal crease that marked it out, although this advantage had yet to lead to him winning a pot of chips. Most nights, one of the two staff would end up with all the pegs in front of him and players would congratulate or curse him and start again. First one o'clock, then two became the absolute, final, we-have-to-stop-now time.

They experimented with substitutes for the real poker chips they didn't have. The solitaire pegs were OK, but they rolled around a lot and fell off the table. They tried the Trivial Pursuit plastic pieces of pie, then draughts pieces, dominoes (not enough of them), Jelly Beans (good, but the different colours confused players and Tom starting eating them between hands) dried kidney beans (promising, but too small) and paper clips (OK, but difficult to count). The red and black game pieces from the all the draughts sets worked best, because they were the right shape and could be stacked like poker chips. When one of the night shift brought in an extra set from home, this gave them 72 pieces in total, which was just enough. The black pieces became high value, one hundred dollar chips, the reds were twenty dollars and the solitaire pegs they kept as tens. The blinds were always ten and twenty in late night Mad Hotel.

Arthur kept up a stream of commentary as the cards were dealt and players checked, made bets or folded. He was told to shut up at least once a night when his chat became one too many balls to juggle for someone trying to work out what he had in his hand, what was on the board, and how many chips he had left.

He knew when to shut up, without prompting, in hands when hundreds of dollars in red and black chips started going into the pot, or when one of the players had a bad beat, with strong cards losing to a weak hand that had hit some highly unlikely combination of cards on the table.

When he was playing, Arthur distributed pearls of poker wisdom for the other players, collected from late night TV pundits, gambling songs and combinations of both.

"Play in the opposite style to the rest of the table; if they're tight, play loose, if they're loose, tighten up." *"If you know how a man plays poker, you will know the man."*

"*You've got to be in it to win it.*" "*Good poker is hard work guys, but great poker is courage.*" "*You've got to know when to hold'em, know when to fold'em.*"

His favourite, repeated at least three times a night was, "*Every chip you waste on bad calls in the early games won't be in front of you to double you up when you get a big hand*".

When the game started, however, Arthur's optimism in what cards would appear on the table often outran the probability of specific cards being dealt and he ended up chasing lost causes in the first twenty minutes of most games, before losing all his chips and becoming dealer and commentator for the rest of the hands.

Cutting deep into the pack before dealing, he would mumble, "*Run silent, run deep – have you seen it? One of the great submarine movies, that is. Clark Gable and Burt Lancaster – who wouldn't like to play poker with those guys, eh? Bungo Pete, he was the Japanese captain in the movie, sunk all these American ships, eh? Sometimes I feel like that, you know, like I've been torpedoed and I'm sinking, but I swim back up to the surface. Shipwrecked, fourteen days in an open-necked shirt, a bit like being in here really…*"

Arthur wasn't looking for a reply from others at the table and he didn't get one. They were all happy not to have to deal, and if the only price was having to listen to Arthur ramble, that was OK.

Without the need to concentrate on his cards *and* give poker advice, Arthur's table talk moved from a cricket commentator ball-by-ball speed, to a horse racing canter. It also became less about poker and more about him.

"*You've got to play the cards that you're dealt, even when you know you've got the worst hand at the table.*" "*Aye, poker and life are like a journey, really, but I missed the bus.*" "*Full house and empty arms – that's me.*"

On his first deal of the night Arthur would open the game with the maxim he had created for Mad Hotel, adapted from the communication group, and spoken as a mock prayer.

"Improving your poker skills will ensure that your journey of excellence in Glenalmond continues. We will facilitate honest, direct and respectful communications. You will be safe in this group to talk about your experiences and your feelings. Everyone in the group will support and encourage you to speak freely."

For players at the table, it was like going into a pre-match football huddle; even though they were playing against each other, and there would be winners and losers, they were all proud members of the exclusive Mad Hotel club. The players at the table, Arthur, Daryl, Raymond, Tom and Greg all knew why they were in Glenalmond; they knew, even if they didn't understand, the reasons that they didn't get a bus to work in the morning and go back to a home life of some kind at night. But they also knew that for a couple of hours at least, they could forget where they were and the fact that you needed a pin number to get out the building. They could hold it together, keep focussed, sitting at a real poker game, just enjoying it.

There was learning how to play cards, and then there was table etiquette. They watched how it was done at World Series, and if it was good enough for the World Series in was good enough for the Mad Hotel. So when Daryl was scooping up a pile of black chips, won from a luckless Tom, there was no gloating over the victory, no triumphant, in-your-face dissing of the loser. Cards had to be kept visible to all players at all times and here was no throwing cards across the table when you lost, no stomping off in a huff, no name calling other players, even if you had done it earlier that day. There might be commiseration from other players or a quick comment about a good hand, but the chips were gathered quickly and the next hand was dealt. You could stand up, behind your chair, if all your chips were pushed into the middle and this could be your last hand, because that's what they did in World Series of Poker. You then had to sit back down again when you got beat however, rather than shake hands and walk off as the World Series players did, because you had no losers lounge or cocktail bar or hotel-supplied room to go to.

Swearing by losers was tolerated, but only just, and on the understanding that the swearing was directed at the cards, rather than at the winner. You waited your turn to check, bet or fold, and you were allowed a minute, if you needed it, to make your decision before the dealer called you on the clock. You protected your cards at all times, which meant keeping them hidden and close to you. You didn't show your cards while a hand was still going on, and you definitely, most definitely did not tell another player how to play a hand, even when you saw what he was holding. If you showed one player your cards at the end of a hand, you had to show it to everybody. Arthur kept players right on the rules and on the etiquette.

Some of the Mad Hotel players got stressed when they tried to bluff to win a hand, showing tell-tale shaking hands, but could hold and play unbeatable cards without looking the least excited. Others would shake with anticipation when they thought they had a winning hand, but could bluff without giving off any signs. Tom and Daryl were the poorest poker players. Tom would over bet on small pairs, under bet when he had the best hand at the table and ask questions during a hand that gave away too much information to his opponents about what he was holding. When Daryl had a good hand he held his cards in his hand, close to his body, looking back and forth between the cards on the table and his two cards. It might have been a poker "tell" too subtle for most of the players to notice, if Daryl didn't combine holding cards in his hand with loud breathing through his nose, so strong that the cards in his hand quivered in the blast of air from his nostrils. When he had a poor hand, he left his two cards face down in front of him. But Tom and Daryl were Arthur's lieutenants on the enforcement of table etiquette. They enjoyed the security of good manners protocol at the table as much as the playing of cards. They had both struggled in different ways with knowing what to do, when and how outside of Glenalmond, and even within

Glenalmond, but at the refuge of the Mad Hotel they had the confidence not only to do the right thing but to keep others right.

The etiquette in the Mad Hotel games took a bit of a kicking and struggled to survive after Rab joined. All the time they had played, he'd been awake and around. Arthur had invited him into the game a few times but Rab was, "*too busy to play fucking stupid card games*". He was a walker, pacing around the table first, then the circumference of the room, then the length of the corridor, then back to the table, walking on the same stretches of carpet again and again, rolling his head as he made his turns, like a stressed animal at the zoo. He would circle the table more slowly when there was a big hand in play, a big pile of plastic in the centre, delaying the next stage of his routine, waiting until the hand was played out before heading off to the corner of the room on his usual route.

One night he just sat down and asked to be dealt in; well, didn't ask, just pulled up a seat when everyone else had gone to bed and the cards came out. Whether he'd picked up the game from watching TV like the rest of them or from watching the Mad Hotel games or both, he didn't say, and nobody asked.

At the late night TV poker tables, the recognised styles of play were tight-aggressive, loose-aggressive, tight-passive and loose-passive, with good players knowing each and able to switch between styles, depending on the size of their chip stack, their position on the table and what other opponents were in a hand. Rab's style at the Mad Hotel table could be described as radge; threatening in all that he did. It went well beyond the frequency with which he would raise or re-raise other players or go all-in, pushing all his chips into the middle. With Rab, it was aggressive dealing, firing cards at players so they had to stop them flying off the table, loud slapping of plastic onto the table when he was betting, and tight lipped staring at anyone who dared to raise a pot to which he had already committed chips. He muttered aggressively during hands, like Dick Dastardly's cartoon Muttley. Not words that could be made out, but clear enough for everybody to know that he was pissed off. The late night poker commentators might have said that he tried to "control the table" with his tactics. To Daryl, Raymond, Tom and Greg he was trying to bully them into folding good hands, or not playing any hands that Rab was in. They would have been much more intimidated if they had not seen their late night poker heroes do pretty much the same thing, staring down opponents, getting them to fold, giving other players the silent treatment, behind sunglasses, hats, hoods and headphones. They didn't like the abuse of the table etiquette, but they saw Rab's play as an exciting, addition to Mad Hotel; the new boy trying to get an edge on other, more established players. Rab would take it to the limit in every hand he played, trying to push players off hands with wild over raises, muttering that Daryl or Raymond were donkeys or eejits when they lost a hand to him, his complexion going a deeper red as he spat-swore under his breath when Greg raised him. But he was always able to reign it in, just. His aggression was at a level that would get him thrown out of any casino, but just below the level where Arthur would politely remind him about etiquette, or one of the nurses at the table would say, "*Enough Rab*".

His table name in Mad Hotel became "No-Fold-Rab". If someone raised and Rab had already put any chips in the pot, even just the minimum, he would call or more often re-raise, regardless of what the bet was, regardless of what he held, ignoring the pot odds. "*No fucker pushes me off the pot,*" was one of the longest intelligible sentences heard from Rab when he was playing poker.

At the table, Arthur liked to mix up his game. He would tell himself that he was playing tight aggressive for a few hands, then loose-aggressive, then wild bluffing, just to keep it interesting. If any of the other players noticed his different styles, they never said. He liked to mix it up with his personas too, bringing a different one to the table each night and trying it out, to see how if he liked it, to see if it was worth keeping. He didn't need the laughs – he got enough just playing the characters, whether or not anybody recognised where they came from. Sometimes even he didn't know who they were. He would start off as Arthur-does-Clive-Owen as the Croupier *"Welcome back Jack, to the house of addiction,"*, he would say, working that role for a while, then jumping to being Ace Rothstein in Casino, *"The longer they play, the more they lose, and in the end, we get it all, Daryl"*. Without noticing, he'd move to quotes and other voices that he didn't recognise, didn't know if it was some movie character he couldn't remember, or somebody else, some Arthur-does-Arthur-doing-Arthur who only came out when he ran dry on movies. Keeping it going was as much a challenge to him as playing the cards; more sometimes, when he had had a dark day.

For the others, too, it felt good being somebody else for a few hours. Being the pretend, late-night poker player, instead of the all too real day-time patient. Making the moves with the best hand and scooping the chips, or bluffing with the worst hand and not being caught. Being a badass, even if you knew it was in a Mickey Mouse game. Just for a while, even for just one hand a night, forgetting the reasons you happened to be there playing poker in the first place. Being somebody different.

Late night Rab, however, was the same as daytime Rab. He didn't like losing, he didn't like being beat by some reject, nut factory patient, or by some overpaid, lazy bastard night nurse. For Rab, to lose face at anything, even a fanny game of cards, was Just Not Acceptable. When he got beat, he would go down fighting in every hand, pushing in all his chips if that's what it took, because showing that he wouldn't be pushed about was better than folding his cards like a fucking woos. When other players pushed all of their plastic into the middle of the table they said, *"All in."* When Rab did it, he said, *"No surrender"*. If he could have stood at the table the whole time he played, he would have, just to show them that he could.

When he won a big hand he punched the air, too close to the face of whoever he had just beaten and said, "*Yes!*" through clenched teeth. When he lost, he muttered and threw cards into the middle, and when he lost the last of his chips, he got up, avoided the proffered handshakes and did his caged animal walk up and down the corridor, on full volume muttering until he was calm enough to sit back down.

Rab never finished higher than fourth in any of the late night games. When his luck held, and the way that he played it was mostly chance, he might double up his chips, fluking the right cards when he went heads-up against somebody who had dared to take him on. But he only had one style of play and he would haemorrhage any chips that he did win in the next few hands, burning out quickly.

Nobody was going to go homeless or lose a job if the Mad Hotel games came to the notice of the day staff or the hospital managers. There would be disciplinary action against the night staff, a verbal or a written warning at worse, but it wasn't gross misconduct. Two night nurses had been sacked after two warnings the previous year; one for swearing at patients, telling one woman she wished she would die, and the other for downloading porn on hospital computers. This definitely wasn't in that league, and what was the difference between a game of Whist or Bridge and a game of poker anyway? Mad Hotel had been going for nearly five weeks with no damage.

The night shift nurse manager was supposed to do a tour of the wards, just to show face and make sure there were no problems. Both of the night managers had been promoted from night shift posts, and both knew that you phoned ahead to the ward before you popped in, if you wanted to keep the night shift sweet and to avoid seeing anything that would require you to fill in forms. Some nights, a shift manager ended up working a ward shift to cover late call offs, but never on Glenalmond, where they took care of their own and called in somebody that was on days off. The probability of a nurse manager turning up uninvited to a game of Mad Hotel was very low. But Rab took a different view on these odds.

One week after he started playing, he moved his original place at the table to a seat that had a better view of the main door to Glenalmond. A week later, he started to get up from the table when he wasn't in a hand or when the cards were being dealt, stretching his legs he said. He would walk to the door, cup his hand on the glass, and peer down the path to the main hospital building. The leg stretching got more and more frequent, then one night during the seventh week, as the cards and draughts and solitaire pieces were being brought out, Rab sat down at the table and blurted it out.

"This is serious stuff, here, you know. A fucking poker school in here? If we're caught at it, we're all so fucking busted. Nobody will walk away from this clean."

He pointed at the nurses first.

"You two can say goodbye to yer pension," and then moved his finger like a gun around the table, *"and the rest of us can say cheerio to getting out of this shithole anytime soon."*

The nurses exchanged a look that agreed it was just Rab, having another rant, and went back to final checks on the corridors.

It was Daryl who spoke first, as he counted out the blacks and the reds for the game. He spoke in a monotone.

"Well Rab, to be honest, I wasn't planning on going anywhere for a while anyway."

Rab turned on him, lowering his voice, and looking over his shoulder first, checking how far the two nurses had walked off.

"Aye you might say that, but we're only in the mad bastards ward now, but if they found out about this we'd be moved to the mad, bad bastards ward, I'm telling you. The place with the heavy duty nurses, wearing Doc Martens, forcing you to swallow the horse tablets."

He spoke loud enough to make sure everybody at the table heard. When he had finished, he stood up and started pacing up and down, pointing at the table.

"*We shouldnae be playing out here in the open either. That's so bloody obvious. We should move the game to that wee smoking room, out of sight.*"

"*The smoking room's too wee Rab, and it's OK, nobody's gonnae walk in on us, unannounced at two in the morning,*" Arthur said, pulling out a chair and pointing at it, encouraging Rab to sit, knowing that if he could get Rab shuffling cards, it would calm him down.

Rab ignored the chair and Arthur. He did one circuit of the table, then stopped mid-stride, pointing again, but only at the carpet this time.

"*Mad Hotel might even have to go dark, until things settle down,*" he said, turning to look at everyone individually, to make sure that each of them appreciated how serious a measure that would be.

They didn't.

"*What you mean play cards wi' the lights oot?*" said Tom. "*See, that's no gonnae work for me Rab, my eyesight's no the best as it is.*"

Rab stared at Tom, exasperated, and did another circuit of the table, stopping opposite him. He spoke in a whisper, staring at Tom.

"*You're clearly one of the uninitiated, bud. In the Sons of Light we sometimes have to go dark, stop operating for a while, until it's safe to start again. This game might need to go dark, there might need to be a sworn pact, and....*"

Bruce, the older of the two night nurses, had walked quietly across the carpet and appeared behind Rab.

"*Look Rab, if you're on about all that secret handshake, trouser leg masonic gibberish again, you need to calm down. This is just a friendly game of poker, and nobody is gonnae be coming through the skylight from a helicopter with guns to break it up, even if you think they will.*"

The other nurse, Dave, walking back into earshot, laughed. He pulled out a chair and started to shuffle the cards.

Rab walked back around the table to his seat, but stood behind it, still determined to make sure everybody understood the gravity of the situation, even if it meant talking now when the two nurses were there.

"We could learn a lot from how the Lodge operates, you know. Calling this game Mad Hotel – now that is smart. It might keep it under cover for another few weeks, but you need to think about other secret language to keep it safe, throw them off the scent. I think if we call it something else for next week, and then change the name again after that we'd be one step ahead of the goons."

He looked around the table for agreement.

"The Compass – now that would be a good secret name for next week, and then…."

Dave tapped the edge of the pack against the table.

"Look Rab, you're the one most likely to get this game broken up because you talk about it too much. Now stop talking shite and sit on yer arse if you want to be dealt in."

Rab remained standing.

"Aye, well, I'm telling you we need to keep all this Mad Hotel strictly sub rosa, if you know what I mean, and I just hope you all remember that it was me who said it, me who warned you, when they start taking us into a room, one at a time, for questioning."

Rab pointed at each player around the table as he finally sat down.

"I know things that only I know, see. When I was an aspirant for the Lodge I was in the darkness for a long time before I stepped into of the full light of the knowledge."

Arthur looked across at Rab, puzzled, trying to work out if this was a line from a movie he hadn't seen, or if it was some secret plumber's code, to prevent the skills of working with water falling into the wrong hands.

The game started and Dave dealt in silence. Everyone folded to the big blind on the first hand. Apart from players declaring a raise or calling, there was no talk at the table for the first four hands.

"*Rab's right you know,*" Arthur broke the tension finally, speaking in his best Humphrey-Bogart-meets-Sean-Connery accent.

"*Mad Hotel is a dangerous game, but that's why we play it.*"

He nodded his head, slowly.

"You play a hand and you regret it; maybe not today, maybe not tomorrow, shweetheart, but soon and for the rest of your life. Once you hook up with Lady Luck, it's only gonnae end one way - either you win or you lose."

Tom had put his cards down to listen. He couldn't concentrate when Arthur got going. Arthur pointed at the deck of cards.

"The question you have to ask yourself is this: how far are you gonnae chase that red Queen down the rabbit hole, in the hope that she's got a sister to make your pair or a brother to give you a straight? Can you make the commitment to stick with her, through good times and bad, knowing that it might all end in tears? You might think about baling out, but then you've already invested all those chips on the Lady. You might think about staying with her, but the costs are rising higher and higher. Maybe she broke your heart last time, maybe it'll be different this time, maybe she's sorry for what she did..."

Arthur's voice rose and he spoke faster, more urgently.

"Arthur," then louder, *"Arthur!"* Bruce interrupted. *"The action's on you to play. I think you should focus on the game here, so that you can stay in for a while instead of going one of your rambles and losing all your chips before your arse has even warmed up your seat as usual."*

Arthur paused, then fixed his gaze on Bruce.

"The only point in making money is so you can tell some big shot where to go," he said, more slowly, but still in character, leaning back in his chair, *"so deal the cards big shot."*

Bruce shook his head, suppressing a smile, and dealt the next hand.

CHAPTER 5

Cincinnati

Cincinnati is a poker variation. Each player is dealt five cards, (instead of two, as in Texas Hold 'Em) and there is then a round of betting. Three community cards are then dealt on the table, followed by a second round of betting, a turn card followed by a round of betting, and finally a river card and a final round of betting. Each player makes the best five card poker hand he/she can make from the five cards in hand and the five community cards, in any combination. The game produces very high poker hands because of each player has ten cards to make a best hand. Full houses, quads (four of a kind) and straight flushes occur much more frequently than in Hold 'Em or other forms of poker. Players have high expectations of having killer hands.

Gossip 'n' Envy, the nightclub was called. Gerry hated the name, especially the 'n' in the middle. But he hated gossip even more, hated it with a vengeance and got irritated with himself for hating it so much. Gossip was for people who were empty, void of anything else to talk about. It was all that he-said-she-said-so-I just-turned-around-and-said shite. Garbage Of Stupid Silly Ignorant People, he called it. Gossip was what vacant nobodies wasted hours on, when they didn't have a hobby, like poker, or a real social life, like being in a poker club. Gossip had them screeching, "Oh my *God!*" in the High Street, loud enough for people on a passing bus to hear, ranting about some sad bastard that had shagged some other sad bastard, or had tried to, or might have tried to, or didn't. Gossip didn't have to be true, no, that wasn't necessary, it just had to be detailed enough. You didn't need to know any of the people that you were talking about either, and the only rule was that none of them was present when you were dishing the dirt.

Some of it was envy, plain, simple and so bloody obvious.

"To be honest, I wouldn't want her job, travelling about the country in hotels and stuff, if that's what makes her face look like that all the time. I heard that she's really miserable, despite what she says".

Some of it was bitter, starting off somewhere else and ending up as revenge gossip.

"She totally blanked me in the street, so I started that rumour about her and that weird guy at Asda with the club foot and put it on Facebook; let's see how many people Friend Request her now!"

Gossip escalated. If someone told her drinking buddy, in that do-NOT-tell-ANYBODY- about-this whisper, that for a *fact* some neighbour was seen sneaking out of some other neighbour's flat, the drinking buddy was obliged, just had to, trump this with some half remembered gossip about how that same neighbour had been seen at the pub, once, by her brother's mate, who was hung like a horse by the way, and he was only drinking shorts, because the doctor had told him that his wife wasn't getting pregnant because he was drinking too many pints, but the real reason that she wasn't getting pregnant was because she was still taking the pill, because she didn't want to have a baby with him, as she already knew he was shagging around. And so it went.

Now *scoom*, scoom was different from gossip. First off, scoom had to be true and second, the person that it was about had to be there to confirm it. So it was honest. Scoom wasn't whispered, it was spoken loud enough so that it didn't have to be repeated. It was restricted to one person, one incident, and it was said because it had to be said, not because you hated somebody's guts and wanted to make up reasons to justify it. True, the person who was the subject of the scoom would rather it was kept secret. But what was a secret anyway? It was just some extra juicy scoom that everybody didn't know about, yet.

That was one of the things that Gerry liked about poker games. Any elephants in the room were shot on sight. No mercy was shown. If you turned up, you should expect to talk about it, whatever it was, regardless of how raw it was. You could give it out to those who had had a hard week, but you had to suck it up too, when the scoom had your name on it. Denying it wasn't an option, because scoom was true and the evidence had you. You could keep your head down, laugh it off, but it was better to fess up with basic details at least. Because the alternative was worse; somebody would spin the evidence into a story worse than the truth, or think up crap jokes that you would be peppered with all night. Concentrating on your poker game would be impossible.

Some information was so well known that it hardly qualified as scoom, but it had to be brought out and aired anyway.

"We huvnae seen you at the poker for a while Russell - been working?"

"Aye, working up at the Big Hoos for a couple of months, trying to keep oot the road of some boys in there that I still owe money. Managed to get put in a different block from most of them, but everybody's got mates who've got other mates they owe a favour, so y've got to watch yer back the whole time, know what I mean?"

"What were you in for this time?"

"Ach, just the usual – being stupit. I got caught holding a stash for a boy and I couldnae very well say it was his, could ah, then they found my stash as well, so I was done for dealing it. It'll be the last time I hold a stash for anybody, I'll tell you that right now. Two months wisnae hard time. You've got all your meals, nae bills to pay, fitba on the telly most nights, and naebody nipping ma ear about money."

Then there were players who had habits and nights and weekends they wished they hadn't, but there was no festering gossip to make it worse, just straight questions and insults. You could laugh it off or bounce it back, if you were fast enough.

"I heard you shagged that wee dwarf after you left us on Saturday night, Welsh."

"Aye, well she was no Snow White, but I was happy, that's for sure."

"Saw your name in the Telegraph again, Donny. You're gonnae need a new suit for the Court."

"Naw – it'll never go to Court. I'll plead insane at the time of the crime. I was oot of ma heid on vodka and Red Bull when I was lifted."

On that first Tuesday night they played beneath the fireball, suspended from the ceiling of the nightclub Gossip 'n' Envy. The previous Saturday had been advertised as a *"Mustang Stampede - Boot Scootin' Dances with DJ Sandy aka LazArus"*. Tonight it was Texas Hold 'Em Freeze Out with TD Gerry, aka Gerry.

Gerry spent his days maintaining Whisky Workbench, a software system to manage production, quality and stock control and the all-important traceability of the whiskies produced by his employers. Gerry liked systems. You knew where you were. He was good at making them work and fixing them when they didn't. It was one of the very few things in his life that he was good at, and enjoyed. Usually it was one or the other, but with systems it was both. He enjoyed poker and he liked to think that he was good at it, or at least getting better.

On the rare occasions when Gerry played poker at the casino he called the dealers' percentage cut of each hand "the angels' share". It was a term used in the distillery business for the whisky that was lost to evaporation during aging. It was only about three percent, but across the distillery and across the years it was thousands of litres of whisky in fumes that simply floated away, like the thousands of pounds that the casino took from punters, on the five per cent rake in each poker hand. This subtlety was lost on Barry, who thought that angels share was some reference to Gerry's God-like status as Tournament Director at the home poker games they played in.

Late night TV was where Gerry and Barry had first seen poker played. Just sitting there one night, suffering drama withdrawal, having finished off yet another police-and-thieves, bad asses defeated by badder assess, American box set, desperate to find something that was even half as good on live TV, flicking through the channels. They watched the poker and they watched again the following weekend and then they spoke about inviting a few mates to Gerry's house for a game. It took a few weeks to organise, to persuade enough people that it was worthwhile, driving out to Gerry's and not be able to drink. That first poker home game, Gerry and Barry agreed, was just to see if it would work.

Gerry wondered at the time if it was any different from his daughter watching *Britain's Got Talent* on TV, and then stomping about in her room, with her mates, trying to do the dance steps. Probably not, he thought. She wanted to do the dance steps and he wanted the home games to work. She just did the steps again and again and again until she and her mates had absolutely nailed the dance, in her head at least, and Gerry and Barry read up every online how-to guide that they could find on home games.

On the night, it was fine. The five players that came to that first home game were so many pages behind that Gerry and Barry felt like experts. They took it slow; two pound buy in for each Texas Hold 'Em freeze out game, winner takes all. They went from there to working out how to organise a game with more than one table in Gerry's small kitchen. It had all started from that late night TV poker and the success of the home games.

As Gerry looked across the dance floor of Gossip 'n' Envy, he saw that late night TV had a lot more to answer for. Like Sunday morning footballers, amateur poker players had perfected the mannerisms but not the skills of their heroes. They were aping the look, wearing the gear and the pose of the TV stars. For "poker nervosa" players it was an actor's disguise. Players who would otherwise be a twitching collection of poker tells sat down at the table as calm as winners. No trembling hands or slumped shoulders (weak hand), no wide eyes, sitting ramrod straight (a strong hand or the absolute, unbeatable nuts), no choked, higher voice, trying to declare a raise, no double checking cards.

Phil "Unabomber" Laak, a professional player with a trademark dark-grey hoodie was aped by Jake "Eyetie" Bolatelli, who was never seen without a black, woollen tammy, pulled down to his neck, covering what some believed was a full head of hair. The former "Tiger Woods of poker", Phil Ivey, inspired Mitchell Marshall, a security guard at the local ASDA supermarket, to wear an oversized LA Lakers jersey, over his green work shirt. The look, Mitchell said, made him feel rested at the table.

Style woke up to reality however, when players tried to go beyond the baseball caps and Vegas bracelets and lucky chips of their chosen heroes and imitate the professional players' moves on the table. Bluffing on unlikely hands against players who believed any pair was a winning hand, or trying sophisticated check-raises to represent some fantasy power hand on a table of eight callers resulted in bleeding chips very quickly. On that first night in Gossip 'n' Envy and for the next few weeks it was fast learning and mostly fast losing for those who turned up.

In poker terms, the problem was that the dazzlingly complex plays were only dazzlingly complex to the player making them; either nobody else at the table had a clue what the move was supposed to represent, and just kept betting, or other players were too busy making their own dazzlingly complex bluffs, semi-bluffs and power plays to notice what anybody else was doing.

Memory was also a problem. To make the show-stopping moves, you had to remember who had made the first raise, who had called or re-raised and when, and who had checked their hand and when. Hands ended with a winning player being complemented on something he hadn't done knowingly, but more often it was a clumsy stumbling towards the final, river card and the player who was too stubborn or too naïve to fold winning the chips.

Players would stay in role right to the end, aping how their heroes might take defeat in a major hand. This could be morose and silent, or incredulous and loud, depending on the poker hero. It was also considered good form on professional poker on TV to shake the hand of the player who took the last of your chips and knocked you out of the tournament. It was just a bit of poker etiquette, simple enough to do, but of all the acting done by the pretenders, the sporting hand shake was one of the most challenging performances.

First off, shaking the hand of a player who had just condemned you to the walk of shame from the table, sent you to spend the rest of the night sitting on the side-lines while the game continued, didn't come easy. The hand shaking had to include some words, and that made it even harder. *"Well done"*, or *"good game"*, or *"well played"* were as far away in sentiment as it was possible to be from what losing players were feeling when they had to shake the winner's hand. Finally, the act of touching flesh, shaking hands, with a stranger was a rarity for most of the guys who turned up to play at Gossip 'n' Envy, and it made them feel uncomfortable; self-conscious about being self-conscious. You touched flesh with those you knew, that was the usual rule in Perth, unless you were trying to sell something.

It was easy for players to swear, to be somebody else, to do stuff they only did at poker when the noise level was constantly at shouting pitch. Jake "Eyetie" Bolatelli and Mitchell "Phil Ivey" Marshall would come out of character, briefly, to yell some abusive welcome to somebody arriving late, and players would compete to shout over one another.

A stream of distracting comments flew across the table and between tables. In the big hands, when a mountain of chips was the prize, speech play was part of the game. There were wind ups - *"I don't think you've got much"*, when calling a bet, to goad the other player into throwing in more chips against a stronger hand. There was feigning weakness, *"I'm behind here, but I'm going to call to keep you honest…"*, *"I'm chasing cards here…"* , *"I'm fishing for a miracle card here…"*. The word play was lifted straight from *YouTube* clips of hands played in TV tournaments. But not all of the dialogue at the tables was scripted.

"Who's the action on?" said Welsh, looking up and switching concentration back to the game after checking the Liverpool score on his phone.

"*If you've got to ask....*" sighed Ewan, nodding at Christopher, who was sucking on the broom of hair below his bottom lip and staring hard at the three cards turned over on the flop.

"*Allright, allright*", Christopher muttered, nodding, "*I'm still thinking here...*".

He rubbed at the sides of his mouth a bit more and then re-raised the bet to three times the big blind, on the strength of his top pair. The three remaining players folded and he scooped up the chips, putting them in neat stacks. Two hands later, Welsh made a simple mistake at the table that revealed much more than the two cards he was holding.

Ewan had just started on his round of dealing, and there were four of the eight players still left in the hand. Ewan raised on the turn card and two players had called him. The action was on Welsh, who had laid his two cards in front of him, half over the white betting line on the poker table. He leant back in his chair. Mistaking the position of the cards as a fold, Ewan swept them into the pile of discarded burn cards, as part of his dealer tidy up of dead cards.

"*What the fuck are you doing?*" screamed Welsh, making a grab for the cards, just too late, "*I'm still in the game, ya fucking bawbag!*".

"*Well ye shouldnae put yer cards over the line, then – I thought ye had folded them*", said Ewan, trying hard not to sound defensive.

"*Ye cannae get them back now – they're mixed in the pile*".

Welsh was on his feet.

"*I'm naw taking that fae you, ya idiot - get the TD over here to sort this out!*".

The Tournament Director was Gerry, who was already on his way over from one of the other two tables, in response to the shouting.

Gerry wasn't big, he wasn't a funny guy and he wasn't hard; none of things that would get some stranger respect in a mob as rowdy as this. He would be the fifty-something, lumpy around the waist, pie-eating football fan in photographs from any Scottish game over the last fifty years. Now that his thatch of hair had been replaced by wispy remnants that didn't need combing, his main stand-out physical feature was his walk. Whether as a result of being on his feet too soon as a baby or having a growth spurt at the wrong time, his feet were at sixty degrees to each other. He rocked from side to side as he walked. From the front it looked as if he was about to turn a corner, left or right, any minute. It ruled him out for any sport that involved running, but he played a mid-handicapped round of golf. His dress code for golf, for work, for home or for poker was a checked shirt, jeans that were smart enough not be called jeans and soft leather boots.

No, Gerry wasn't the TD because he could shout louder than anyone else, and he would never tell anybody to shut the fuck up, but he did know more about poker than anyone in the room and even the wild men knew that somebody had to keep the order if any poker was to be played.

He made his way to Welsh's table, squeezing between players too focused on cards to notice anything different in the shouting. He targeted one person randomly at the table, asked him to explain what had happened, after waving down the four different versions of events that he was being given as he arrived. Then he took Welsh aside, asked him quietly what his cards were, calmly sorted through the small pile of discarded cards, before sliding two cards in front of Welsh and telling Ewan to get on with the game. There was some protest from Ewan, about mucked cards being dead cards, but he knew the TD decision was final. Problem solved, apparently.

The hand played out and Welsh turned over a pair of Jacks to make a set with the one on the board and took the pot. He threw his cards across the table at Ewan, with enough force for one of them to flip up and hit him on the chest. Ewan stopped gathering up the other cards and stared at Welsh.

"*What is your fucking problem Welsh? Not getting enough?*".

Welsh looked at him for a few seconds and then said, "*Is that what you said to my sister on Friday night Ewan, was it? I mean, for fuck's sake, she's only 18, and you're letching after her like she was a widow".*

"Letching? That's what she said, was it, or is that you talking?"

The table was silent for a moment, then Welsh muttered, *"Just deal the fucking cards Ewan, OK?"*

On that first night in Gossip 'n' Envy the players' reviews, if they had ever been published, would have been described as mixed. Gossip 'n' Envy's rating under *Things to Do* or *Attractions in Perth* would have been off the scale that stopped at terrible. There was poker and there was a bar, and that was it. Did the place have atmosphere? Yes, there was definitely something; the vaulted ceiling and slowly rotating disco fireball guaranteed that nobody present had ever played poker in such a room. Were the punters friendly? Everybody was welcomed by Gerry, as he took names and Christopher took the buy-in cash. Names, or at least grunts, were exchanged at the tables, after players had been randomly allocated table and seat numbers. Were refreshments available? Prices at the bar were steep for a midweek, before-closing-time venue, but there was no crush to get a drink and the young boy at the bar, twenty at most, was efficient enough. The main cause of the mixed reviews would be the medieval temperature in the room.

Collars were turned up and chins were tucked in as players came into the room. Even when they sat down in groups and got started, the only difference was that hands emerged from sleeves, as combined body heat around the table raised the temperature in that part of the room at least. Players sat holding ears or noses or tucking exposed fingers under oxters for warmth between hands being dealt. Gerry wasn't expecting any gushing thanks from players for getting the venue for their first night as a proper poker club, for organising a bar, real tables, new sets of chips, but he wasn't expecting what he got.

"*Fuck sake Gerry, it's Baltic in here – is the heating bust?*" Ewan shouted across the room.

Players who had arrived with artic quality headgear and sleeveless gloves on that October night kept them on, and fleeces, body warmers and anything with a zip collar was a plus. Only for reasons of cool and being noticed did Stevie and Russell sling their jackets on chairs, to play in the same sleeveless, wife-beater T-shirts that they both wore, regardless of the season. Goose bumps pushed through tattoos. Stevie and Russell did regular trips to London to buy supplies, and cheap flights to Majorca, Turkey and the Greek Isles to sell on site. Ecky and Vicodin mostly, for the clubs, but meow too, because you could get it by post and save the cost of the London trip. Gerry had offered an extra ten, on top of the twenty that went straight into the Vince's pocket, but Vince knew how much it cost to heat the place, and he made a business decision not to switch the heating on until he saw who turned up. He also guessed that gambling addicts would play without the heating. He knew they would still spend money at the bar, and he knew that he would clear enough on bar takings to pay the junior barman cash-in-hand for four hours work. Gerry had complained about the heating, but Vince had reminded him that heating wasn't part of their deal. On that first poker night the heating was off.

The Gambling Act stated that for organised poker games, "*no charge can be made for taking part, nor any levy considered to be a charge imposed on the stakes or winnings.*" The get-out clause for Gerry was a "*£10 maximum per person per night stake*".

Between them, Gerry and Christopher, the self-appointed club treasurer, had calculated how to take enough out of the winnings to pay off Vince without the slush money appearing in the books of the poker club. Christopher took some convincing; he was a stickler for keeping it all legit. On the dance floor by poker club week one, stage three, just before the blinds went from fifteen to ten minute intervals, there were three kinds of people left in the main Texas Hold 'Em freeze out game; players, lucky non-players and unpredictable drunks. In the books and on TV you could learn about another player's "tells" – twitches, smiles or just looks or that gave away the strength of his hand. Everybody had tells, suppressed them if they were aware of how they showed, or used them as double bluffs to mislead other players The pokerclack; tutting when the cards came out to mislead others into thinking you were disappointed, or shrugging or sighing before betting were all tells with a purpose. Players who drank too much lost their tells, together with other poker inhibitions, and sometimes facial expression of any kind. Drunks at a game like this were difficult to read, randomly aggressive, pushing in chips, making calls when the odds said don't. It was hit or miss if you went heads up for a big pot of chips up against someone who was drunk.

Players who were knocked out early in the main game would get a cash game going; a tenner to start, with unlimited rebuys. A "side game" as Christopher had asked for it to be called for legal purposes, or a "sad losers' game" as it was referred to by those playing it. Players in the cash game took cigarette breaks outside the club in ones and twos, or asked to be dealt out when they went for another drink or to the toilet. On that first night, Vince drifted about the bar, weighing up the players as they walked about. He was also looking for tells; something that would let him spot the players with something to hide.

It was not what he expected. Vince was constantly looking past the next person through the door, for the one behind, scanning the crowd for the high-stakes rollers, somebody who looked the part, somebody who had travelled to the game sitting in the back seat of a car, chatting to his driver, somebody who would be wearing a coat that just demanded a cloakroom and a hanger. Somebody who would justify putting the heating on.

Instead it was *deju vu*, or it would have been, except there was nothing mysterious about the feelings Vince had that night. The players that he recognised were the flotsam of the Gossip 'n' Envy dance nights; reliable public nuisances who were the jacket holders for the main players of the in-house brawls and car park wrestling at the club at weekends. There were half a dozen new faces, dressed like they were made up for a 30-year High School reunion; clean hair, for those who had it, jeans that had been ironed and shirts with a brand label that said "how much?" The rest Vince knew by sight, and most by name and reputation.

They were the B team in the weekly Country and Western dramas, just off the main stage, shouting encouragement to the action of others, comforting the same people when that action led to a slap in the face. On weekends they were the worst kind of personal adviser anybody could have. There was always something else that could be said or done, something to make it all better, that made it all worse.

Russell and Stevie Mahon were there, body-abuse thin brothers who had done jail time at Perth Prison for joint assault outside Gossip 'n' Envy, after a string of similar fights. Some hapless drunk called Stevie "ferret boy" and required dental surgery as a result. Vince couldn't afford to ban them from Gossip 'n' Envy because of what they spent, and he had given up trying to understand why they came. They rarely spoke to anybody in the club, never danced and spent their time standing near the bar, slugging pints at a rate that made it look like a magician's trick. Russell had the complexion of an acned teenager, belying his age, a consequence of his take out diet and a take-out lifestyle. His brother had darker, leathery skin and hair so black it looked like a pensioner's dye-job. They only became animated in the club when entertaining each other with crude impersonations of dancers on the floor. For Vince and his quest for *Nightclubpro* inspired success, the brothers were definitely not in that "unserviced demographic" of club goers that he sought to attract.

Vince recognised Kodiak Stone and his side kick Melvin Binns, aka The Sleeve, as they came up to the bar. They were loud, walking, talking ads for

their business. Eyebrows, lips, septums, cheeks, nipples and scrotums; all
hygienically pierced and studded at a fair price, and all guaranteed to attract
more looks and comments than humdrum ear piercings. They had a shop,
open between 2pm and 10pm four days a week. *Well, nobody wants a piercing on*
a Tuesday, or before noon, now do they?"

Kodiak was over six feet, heavy and bald and wore Doc Marten boots
with eyelets to shin height.   He created a space, even on a packed dance
floor, when he was in Gossip 'n' Envy at the weekend. He had told Vince
once that his dance style was based on a rapper sword dance, first devised by
coal miners. To Vince, it just looked like he was stomping in circles to
anything with a beat, and a dance partner was optional.

"It's difficult to recreate the dance exactly Vince, since the Doc Martens don't let you
point and flex properly, see?"

From wrist to shoulder, Melvin had one arm completely covered in tattoo
ink. It was not a detailed design gone wrong and smudged, just a deep violet
sleeve that looked like he had dipped his arm in potassium permanganate.
Celtic shaped whorls crept out of his standard black t-shirt, and his initials,
ink needled in some gothic Frankenstein font, could be seen above his left ear
when his number one haircut allowed. A black "Hello Young Lovers" Frank
Sinatra trilby completed the look. Melvin didn't dance.

Kodiak and The Sleeve came to Gossip 'n' Envy to have a good time, of
course they did. Vince knew that it was also a great shop window for their
business, 666.ink. He had seen the increase in the number of club goers with
new tattoos and he had imagined the below-the-waist piercings. Vince
admired their knack of advertising and the hours he knew they put in; late
night opening, attracting bevvied customers and giving them permanent
reminders of temporary feelings. He just wished Kodiak wouldn't take up so
much space on the dance floor.

Mitchell and Shirleyanne were also there for the poker on that first night.

It was the sight of them coming through the door that finally burst the bubble on Vince's hope of the out of town high-stakes rollers visiting the club. He decided then to save on the heating. They were a forty five year old couple with no secrets, who had once posted an "instructional video on love making" on *YouTube*. It was recorded on a mobile phone, propped up at an angle where most of the screen, but not enough in Vince's view, showed feet. They were happy to talk about the YouTube clip to anyone, or to invite strangers from the pub back to their flat for a demonstration. The video created little interest in the town, but confirmed the reputation of Mitchell and Shirleyanne as skanks, some of the large group of punters that Vince didn't want at Gossip 'n' Envy, but failed to discourage.

It was a low point for Vince. The club full of the town's debris had him doubting. But he was Vince, the go-to guy who was ready to move up and he didn't do self-doubt. It made him feel like shaking his head hard to get rid of it. With every face that came through the door, the reality grew and the despair got worse. There would be no customised cars outside, no unknown high rollers eyeing up the opposition across the tables and there would definitely be no need for a waitress to circle the tables. But he was the man who made the right decisions, saw the openings, brought together the pieces that made things happen. But that night he was also the man responsible for this train crash of a crowd.

He was trying to think fast, running over all the possibilities, working out the best move to stop things getting any worse. His online course taught him about night club problem analysis. It was 1-2-3 easy stuff to remember; identify the problem, identify all the relevant alternatives, select the best possible alternative. But this was no simple, *"your neighbours have complained about the noise from the club"* scenario, no easily-fixed, *"anticipated footfall is 10% short of target for the month."* This was different, this was real. It was a scenario that said, *"You really are just a seedy night club manager, now managing an even seedier night club. Welcome to reality Vince".*

Vince knew that you could have ideas, which were temporary, or you could have a vision. He had chosen vision. It could be used when times were tough, to push aside obstacles on that long path to Vincent Quarrier, nightclub owner. Thinking about the next step up the ladder, the move to the big city, the phone call that would come; that kept him going. The vision was further away than it had ever been on that first night. The more he tried to focus on what needed to be done, now, tonight, the more the intrusive thoughts came. This was it for him, stuck in Gossip 'n' Envy with a room full of Scottish trailer trash and skanks until the club finally went bust or he was sacked.

Just when he thought the crowd couldn't get any further from what he had imagined, what he hoped for when he had closed the door as Gerry left their meeting, Vince saw Frank the Penguin walk into the club, wearing a worn out *Megadeath* T-shirt and drinking from a can of supermarket lager, the other five cans tucked under his arm. Frank the fucking Penguin - what sort of circus had Gerry brought to the club? Vince went to his office to write down what needed to be done, before he did what he felt like doing, which was smashing a fire alarm and locking all the doors when everybody in the club tonight was back out on the street, where they belonged and where he didn't have to look at them.

CHAPTER 6

Anaconda/ Pass the Trash

Anaconda is a poker variation takes its name from the "snaking" of cards around the table. Each player is dealt seven cards and a round of betting takes place. Each player then chooses and passes three cards, face down, to the player on his left and another round of betting takes place. Then each player passes two cards to the left and another round of betting takes place. Finally, each player passes one card to the left and there is another round of betting. Players who are still in the game at this stage place their best five cards on the table face-down in a stack. Players turn over their top card and a round of betting takes place. (The player with the highest card bets first). One by one, all the cards are turned over and after each card a round of betting takes place until all the cards are shown and the winner is the person with the five car hand, or the player who has shown his cards and bet in such a way that all other players have folded. Anaconda involves more rounds of betting than any other poker variation.

Steph had missed the first and third week of poker because of an airport run. Two American golfers who were, they told him, *"back in the old country"*, although they had never been to Scotland before. As the first point of contact, he was used to being asked about Scottish history. They fired questions about genealogy; theirs, never his, and the real Scotland. Steph never disappointed in pursuit of a bigger tip and the bits he didn't know, he just made up, convincingly.

Steph Longhouse was a long term taxi driver, whose only other job in life had been as a RAF maintenance engineer. Into the RAF as an apprentice, straight from school, worked his way up, did 21 years, travelled a bit, east and west, straight out the other end with a lump sum but no job. Owner of two houses, his ex-wife's and his dead father's, Steph was now a man with something to prove but nobody to prove it to. His conversation starters were variations on the same theme; his successes, great and small.

"I got five packets of bacon in the supermarket this morning, only one day past the sell by date – stuck them in the freezer – result!", "So I picked up an airport fare who wanted

to see a bit of the scenery. I drove him the long way to his hotel and he tipped me £25 on top of the £110 on the meter – back of the net!", "We had a lock in at the Two Keys last week – I know the barman and he just locked the doors at eleven and we all drank black sambucas and pints until three in the morning – excellent!"

He was a one man show. Owner of his cab, a spotless diesel Hyundai with 133,000 miles on the clock, and a mini television on the dash board to kill time at the Perth rail station, where he spent most of his waiting time. He made money that he no longer needed on airport runs to Edinburgh and Glasgow and occasional, one-off school runs.

Driving was driving and drinking was drinking, was Steph's view, so he always kept off the drink for eight hours before driving, but when he drank, he drank. Two cans and a vodka chaser at home before the game of poker with some mates at the Two Keys, with four pints an hour during the game. The drinking changed his poker strategy from tight-aggressive to random betting over the evening. Despite having played poker off and on in the RAF for twelve years, he still kept and used a credit-card size "ranking of poker hands" guide in this top pocket – flush beats a straight beats three of a kind etc. He never could remember how the hierarchy of poker hands went. He knew little about how to play poker, and he didn't pretend that he did. Some nights he would hit a lucky card and scoop a big pot, but more often he would end the night out of the game, watching other players and re-telling RAF stories that the table had heard, many times.

Steph stopped smoking regularly.

"Jacked in the cancer sticks – feel a lot better for it," he would say.

He would then have a mad affair with his road bike, cycling for hours during his time off.

"Not as fit as I was in the RAF, but I've still got it!", before taking the offer of a fag from another taxi driver while waiting on the stand, and reverting to fifteen a day.

"Hisnae killed me yet!"

He was twitchy when he was off the fags; shrugging his shoulders, rubbing his neck, running his hand through his self-cut grey hair and stroking a non-existent moustache.

Steph knew Gerry from his airport runs. He had taken him to catch a plane for some computer courses in Manchester or London. All that hi-tech fannying about left Steph cold. Taxi drivers with GPS who couldn't do their job without it were not real taxi drivers, he thought, they were just blokes who could turn left and right when a computer told them to – no great knowledge needed for that. It really hacked him off when somebody got in the back of his cab and immediately started footering aboot with a mobile phone, bleeping and clicking, totally ignoring him after mumbling an address. Steph had a mobile phone, of course he did, couldn't do the job without one these days. But it was a real phone. It was older than his Hyundai and it still worked fine. You could speak on it and you could send a text, and it even had a timer, to tell you when you were safe to drive.

Steph kept an old sign in his cab from Hackney Carriage regulations, stuck on the dashboard under the television.

"The maximum hours of working for any horse shall be six (6) hours per day and all horses shall be rested after three (3) hours for at least half an hour, during which time harnesses, shackles, bridles and other such items must be removed from the horse except for a head collar."

He tried to stick to those rules for himself.

His phone was a Nokia 3310. *"Bulletproof, in battleship grey"*, Steph liked to say. Unsuspecting punters who laughed at his ancient phone in the Two Keys were issued the Steph phone challenge.

"A fiver says this phone can do something that your iPhone/smartphone/computer-in-your-hand can't do".

Only strangers who drank as much as Steph would take up the challenge.

After maximising an audience, most of whom knew what was coming, Steph would walk them outside the pub, toss his solid phone three feet in the air and let it bounce on the road, before picking it up, wiping it off and dropping it in his pocket, smug in the knowledge that he had won the challenge, once again.

In poker, Steph's favourite two cards, on which he would bet irrationally and in the face of any odds, was the "Negreanu" hand (middle rank suited connectors, made famous by Daniel Negreanu, a Canadian-Romanian professional). This was one hand, in fact the only hand, he could remember from all the poker magazines he had read. On the few occasions that he won, Steph would tell the table why it was such a good starting hand. He came to the poker for an audience, even one that wasn't listening. He had started off at home games at Gerry's – six or seven people – but that didn't suit his hours. He moved up to alternating Tuesday and Thursday poker games at the Two Keys, but that was getting tired, with the same four or five guys every week. He had been to Gossip 'n' Envy before his wife left him, but didn't remember much about the place.

He used to have a few cans at home before they came out, to save on the prices at the bars and night clubs they visited. Julia would always drive. Unreasonable behaviour it said on the paperwork, but he liked to say irreconcilable differences to anybody who asked, even if the behaviour was grounds for the divorce, not the differences. Julia liked to say unrecognisable differences – she told him that when he was drunk she didn't know who the fuck she was married to.

He looked around the club as he came in and saw a familiar cloud of breath rising over each of the tables. It felt colder inside the vaulted room than it did outside. Steph counted at least thirty bodies, most of whom had been in his cab at one time. He patted the poker hands guide in his shirt pocket and took out cash for his first paid-for drink of the night.

Gerry had his laptop set up on the bar and he took names and typed them onto the PokerMax screen as players came into the club passed the bar. When all the names were in, the poker software allocated players to seats at the four tables, and calculated prize money for the first four or five players, depending on numbers. The prize money maximums and minimums could be set. Everybody who turned up got two league points for being there, two points were given for knocking a player out and the ten players who were left at the end scored from one to ten points for the winner. It was possible to win the tournament on the night by knocking out no one except the player who finished second, but that would be a passive strategy, and a dumb one to try. You could see your chip stack shrink quickly, unless you hit an unfeasibly long run of good cards. If you played to win, you were aggressive, you targeted players low on chips, separated them from the herd, pushed them with your bigger stack, and knocked them out to build up your stack, and your points. Raisers usually won, callers usually lost.

Steph found himself at a table with some familiar faces, including club secretary Christopher, who was getting ready to deal. Steph knew him from his taxi runs; he was some kind of teacher with extra duties at the High School, where he would direct taxis in the morning. Bit of a dry baws – absolutely no sense of humour. He didn't make jokes and didn't laugh at them from what Steph remembered.

"Small and big blinds please", Christopher said, tapping the felt in front of the two players to his left. *"The blinds will go up every twenty minutes before the break."*

He dealt the cards without further comment, and players slumped a bit lower in seats, using one hand as cover while the other hand bent back the cards to the reveal eight different combinations around the table. Most players just looked at the two cards, but some players teased themselves, preferring to reveal one card at a time, deciding after looking at the first what they would do if the second made a pair or was suited, or was a connector.

Melvin the Sleeve, who was on the big blind, placed his chips on top of his cards without looking at them. He was looking instead at everyone inspecting what they had been dealt, looking for signs of delight – sitting up straighter and looking around the table, eyes widening, raised eyebrows, putting the cards back down quickly, or disappointment- a sigh, putting the two cards together ready to chuck them in, a distracted look around at other tables. He didn't expect to see anyone leap up from their chair and punch the air, but any information he could get was useful. Some players had tells. Kodiak, his mate, his main man, who was at the next table, had an unusual one. When he was on a good hand Kodiak would bounce in his chair. Not like a child on a trampoline, just a small up-and-down rhythm that was difficult to see, but could sometimes be heard from creaking in the chair. Kodiak was bigger than most people and the joints in chairs were tested when he sat on them.

"No drinks on the table please, and it's you to act", Christopher announced, without looking up from his cards.

One of the newbie players, Kyle, who was used to having a glass or a cup by his computer when playing poker, lifted his pint from the wooden veneer that ran around the table and put it on the floor, between his feet.

"Aye, sorry about that," he said.

Sitting next to The Sleeve, he picked his cards up again for a second look. He started counting chips onto the table, one after another.

"Ah'll raise two hundred", he said.

"Whoah….. let me stop you there!" Christopher said, loud enough to make the player sitting next to him knock over his chip stack.

He held up both palms in front of Kyle, the internet player.

"That's a string bet. You have to declare the size of the bet before you put chips in the pot, and it's also a bet, rather than a raise, because there is no current bet."

The new player looked at the chips he'd put out already and moved to take them back, then stopped, confused.

"Aye, OK, Christopher, OK, I think we all knew what he meant," said The Sleeve, *"the boy's new to the game, so let's make him feel welcome at the table, eh?"*

Turning to Kyle, The Sleeve said, *"Just put all of your chips in at the same time, son, or say how much you're betting before you put in any chips, OK?"*

"Just keeping him right," Melvin, *"so that he'll know for next time"*, Christopher continued, taking the new player's two hundred bet and stacking the chips in front of him, over the betting line.

"The bet is two hundred to you", Christopher continued, pointing with a flat hand to the next player.

Christopher's table was always the quietest. The shouting, the mock insults, hoots of laughter and chairs scraping back as players went all in or got knocked out – shouts of *"man down, man down"* - came from the other three tables as the game progressed. Christopher's strict adherence to the rules of poker and his frequent reminders at the table were like a wet blanket, smothering any banter. No drinks on the table, no phones on at the table, clearly stated bets, raises or calls, verbal intentions are binding, no coaching other players, or speculating on what cards another player has, no showing cards to any other player, whether they are in or out of the hand, no folding out of turn; Christopher knew them all.)

Knowing the rules of the game suited him. For Christopher it also meant no mates at the table, but that was a price he was willing to pay. It saved a lot of bother, in his view. Patience, experience and persistence he repeated to himself as he dealt; PEP. It was a mantra that had served him well. He knew that other players at home games and in Gossip 'n' Envy too, had little or any of these. They were there for the quick win, the five minutes of bragging rights for knocking out someone they knew, or just to get routinely drunk on the cheapest alcohol they could find and try to remember enough detail the next day to bore someone with the terrible injustice of bad beats suffered on hands they should have won. Christopher was there for the long haul, waiting for the opportunities, calculating the pot odds – how much was in the pot, and the inferred odds - how much was likely to be in the pot, and making his raises and calls, systematically. No emotion was involved or necessary. That was where he got his buzz. A poker player could not and should not let emotion affect his game, or long term strategy, which was to win more money than everyone else in the game. That was why he came, that was why he had agreed to do the organisation, handle the cash, keep the books auditable and help Gerry out in setting up the games.

Greed was not good, greed was evil. It was accumulating wealth just for the sake of it, and taking pleasure in the suffering of others in doing it. Taking it from the weakest in a silent feeding frenzy. He saw them at the tables, sharks, picking out the fish, gutting them before they knew what had happened. Sharks, even betting against each other for the right to fleece the new guy, to take all his chips in as few hands as possible, just for the bragging rights later. They would chat, welcome him to the game, gather information and strike. Job and finish. Next.

Christopher refused to play that game. No one in the home games, or now in Gossip n' Envy was losing more money than they could afford, but there was a line to be drawn, a moral line. His own standards were important, even if it felt like he was playing in a cesspit of people devoid of morals, people with no notion whatsoever about the concept of consequences of behaviour. The idea of taking money off others and being deceptive, the very basis of poker, bothered his Christian principles a bit to begin with, when he and Gerry talked first about organising games. The idea that someone had to lose for him to win was hard to reconcile with having a good attitude and concern for his fellow man, something he heard most Sundays. But it was not enough to stop him playing. In his head he had rationalised it, separated playing poker and gambling.

Gambling and poker were different. Gambling was evil. Soldiers at the foot of the cross gambled to see who would win Jesus' blood-stained gown, taking pleasure in the ultimate suffering. Gambling was seductive and addictive and caused misery. Families lost all they had. Men and women stole from employers, from partners, from family, just to gamble. Poker, on the other hand, was a game, like other games that other Christians played, and had played since the time of Jesus. Four-sided sheep's knucklebones were used as dice in primitive board games. Games where players moved and captured pieces had been played by Christians, by families, for centuries. And what was poker, if not a move-and-capture variation of those games?

Christopher celebrated his God-given skills to pit his wits against others at the table, some Christians, some not. The pleasure was in doing this well, not in causing distress and misery to others. That would be wrong too. When he didn't play he missed it, and this still bothered him. But not enough to stop. The rules of poker gave Christopher focus on what needed to be done, his desired direction of travel and destination. Like his mantra, PEP, the rules allowed him to filter out the many distractions at the table. Some around the table lived in the moment, seeing nothing beyond it, seeking a quick fix. They experienced joy or despair and expressed it loudly only on the turn of the next card. The sharks at the table lived for their next victim, seeing a few hands ahead, positioning themselves for the next kill.

For Christopher, the pleasure was in the strategy and the manipulation of the game, the planning and the execution of his moves. For this, he needed focus. He didn't want to hear talk at the table about who had shagged somebody's sister or who had been arrested at the weekend for pissing in public or breaking somebody's nose. That was talk for the pub, for the street, not for a poker game. It broke his concentration, and as the irrelevant talk at the table grew, so did the sloppiness of the play, the lack of adherence to the rules and to the etiquette of poker, in his experience. There would be players folding cards out of turn, throwing chips in without declaring a raise, saying "raise" instead of "bet", and his pet hate, players with a pile of unsorted chips in front of them that were impossible for other players to count. It was about playing properly, nothing more than that. He could take the flak from Melvin at the table and the crude impersonations from Russell and the badmouthing behind his back from the others. In his day job he had learned doing the thing right did not make him popular, but it did make him right, always.

The flop on the table showed 8♣, K♦, 4♦ with just Steph and Melvin still in the hand. Melvin had raised to four times the big blind pre-flop and everyone except Steph, now on his fourth paid-for pint, had called. Melvin checked and Steph bet half the pot. Melvin flat called instantly and the turn card was 2♠. Both players checked, each after some thinking or bluffing time, and the final, river card was 8♦.

Melvin said, "*All in*" instantly and pushed his remaining chip stack forward.

Steph first rubbed his neck, then lifted his cards and sat back in his chair, checking this cards and running his hand through his hair.

"*Keep your cards on the table at all times please*", Christopher said, tapping the green felt in front of Steph.

"*Well I've got a bit of thinker here*", Steph said, ignoring Christopher and looking at Melvin with eyes that had the dark bags from three days of early morning and late night airport runs. He was bending alternate knees up and down, tapping his heels on the wooden dance floor.

"*Take your time*", said Melvin, sitting back, looking relaxed with his fingers steepled in his lap.

He started and then quickly stopped himself from a Kodiak bounce in his chair.

To buy some more time, Steph asked, "*How much is there?*", nodding at Melvin's final push of chips.

"*The total would put you all in, all of your chips*", Christopher said quickly without looking at either player.

Steph paused for another ten seconds, then said, "*You know what, I'm going to call because I've got everything I own in that pot of chips*", pushing his remaining chips forward.

Melvin turned his cards before Steph had finished speaking, "*I have the nut flush*", he said, looking directly at Steph with no expression on his face as he turned over the A♦ and Q♦, giving him the highest possible five card diamond flush.

Steph looked down at the two diamonds, then up at Melvin and then said, "*Mmm, I have an eight*", turning over his first card and placing it in the centre.

He looked around the faces at the table, and then said, "*and another one*", flicking his final card face up in front of him, smiling.

He had quad eights, four of a kind. Higher than a flush, higher even than a full house.

Melvin's chair scraped across the wooden floor as he got to his feet, holding fists by his side.

"*You fucking slow rolling bastard,*" he said, slowly through clenched teeth.

"*There's nae need for that sort of stuff.*"

He stood still, staring at Steph.

"*Ah, come on Sleeve*", Steph stood and reached his hand across the table for the usual commiseration handshake to a player knocked out.

"*I didn't mean anything by it – just a wee bit of entertainment for the rest of the table, eh?*"

Melvin continued to stare at him, tight lipped, ignoring the hand.

"*Totally uncalled for in a friendly game*", he said, shaking his head.

"*Slow rolling is a fucking insult Steph.*"

He pushed his chair further back, turned and walked, stiff legged, out of the room.

Steph sat back down and looked around the table for a pair of eyes to talk to.

"*For fuck's sake, boys, it's me. I wouldn't know how to slow roll anybody,*" he said, "*you know me, I'm not that good a poker player*", laughing.

The other players found mobile phones to look at or looked over to the hands being played out on adjoining tables. Nobody around the table looked at him, or moved to push the piles of chips that were now his toward him. He was forced to stand up again, stretch across the table to gather together the chip stacks and slide them to his end of the table.

"*Ach, I'll see Sleeve through the week and straighten this out, buy him a pint – result!*", he said, now talking without looking at anyone.

Christopher dealt the next hand in silence. There was a raise from the big blind and everyone folded. He gathered up the cards and started to shuffle again. As he did so, he said, "*You may not have meant to slow roll him, Steph, but that's what it looked like. Just for future reference, it's considered bad poker etiquette.*"

Steph looked at Christopher, then around the faces at the table, to check if he was being serious. But he knew that Christopher was always serious.

"*Look, Christopher, I really wouldn't slow roll anybody – I was just turning those cards over slowly to get a laugh at the table. I was lucky to hit the quads on the river and Sleeve was lucky to hit his flush. That's just poker, eh?*"

"*Big and small blinds please,*" Christopher said, ignoring him and tapping the felt in front of two players as he dealt.

After two more hands played in silence, players at the table were back to chatting in twos, but they were blanking Steph, treating him like some of his airport fares did, he thought. He folded his next two hands, and decided that he needed a break.

It was still ages until the halfway break so he stood up and asked for his cards to be folded while he went outside for a cigarette. Christopher nodded and acknowledgement and kept dealing. Steph got up and walked across the floor, catching the quick looks from other tables, where news of his move had spread. Christ! It was only a game, he was thinking, almost saying out loud, as some players looked at him as if he had killed Sleeve in a hit and run accident. It was only when he reached the door that he remembered that he was off the fags that week. Bugger.

As he stepped outside, the cold air made him think about going back for his jacket, but the idea of walking back across the room put him off. Steph was trying to decide if he would prefer to see Sleeve still hanging about in the car park, square it up with him then, or if it would be easier to see him later in the week, by which time he might have calmed down. Either way would be fine. It was no big deal; just a misunderstanding that could be sorted out. Some of his ploys worked, some didn't, and God knows it wasn't the first time that he had offended somebody. You had to at least try to be funny and if some people didn't laugh, so what? It was better to give it a shot, rather than mope about like a misery guts, moaning about everything, as life flew past.

Life was short. If he had learned anything from living with Julia, it was that. She always wanted to try something different, go different places, even when they were already in a different place.

He was well up for the travelling about when he first met her. He'd already done a stint on the RAF bases in Cyprus and Gibraltar, bouncing about the Greek islands and Spanish bars in his time off; some great mates and memories. They all got married off before he did, dropping off the radar for the weekends away, drinking or doing a bit of fishing. They all turned up for his stag night though, for one last blast, ragging him all night about him being the last chicken in Sainsbury's, the last pork sausage left on the shelf. He was 37- hardly a crumbly- and he thought that he and Julia were getting married at the right time for both of them. The first two years were great, for him and most of the time for Julia, he thought. She didn't like married quarters routine and the pack drill of the RAF. All the standard box RAF flats, RAF social clubs and especially the RAF wives, all cut from the same, bland stand-by-you-man cloth. So they agreed that he would take the package that he had earned for his years' service and he bailed out with a decent pension. His old man helped him out in buying the house and doing it up; result! Back in Scotland and all to play for.

His father helped him again when he paid Julia off for her half of the house. She didn't want her half of his pension. She didn't want any contact of any kind even in writing. When she left she made that very clear, to him and to anyone else who would listen, or could hear her shouting.

As he stepped out the front door of Gossip 'n' Envy he hunched up his shoulders and pulled together the neck of his shirt against the cold breeze. So now he was out here without any cigarettes, but he couldn't go back in. That would look stupid. He looked around for a spot more sheltered, in the lee of the wind, and it was then that he saw movement at the corner of the building, near the back. It was dark and Steph could see only the red glow of a cigarette, glowing red as it was smoked quickly. Was it Sleeve? He hadn't noticed any other players knocked out of the tournament. Better to get it over with, he thought, rather than let if fester until later in the week, when it might be harder to say something.

"*Sleeve, 's that you? You alright there?*"

Steph raised one hand in a half wave.

At this, the figure looked up. It wasn't Sleeve. Steph recognised the night club manager. Vinny? Vince? Vincent? – he couldn't remember the name. He'd never had him in his taxi, but Steph had seen Finny, or whatever his name was, on the road in that hellish colour of car he had. What would you call it – mustard? ochre? A curry-jobbie colour, that's how Steph would describe it.

"*Aye, aye – ye just taking a break from all the action then?*"

Vince said, keeping his cigarette sheltered from the wind in the palm of his hand as he walked towards Steph. Steph took a step back, nearer the door.

"Aye, that's right – just giving the other boys a chance to win a few hands and catch up with me, y'know."

Steph laughed, feeling awkward without a cigarette.

Steph didn't much like the way this sharp boy in a suit was looking him over in the light of entrance to the Gossip 'n' Envy, his scummy club, making him feel like he'd been caught doing something he shouldn't.

"Cigarette?" Vince offered, after a pause, flicking opening the pack of Kingsize with his thumb.

"Always good on a cold night, and you look like you could use one."

"Nah, no thanks, I'm off them just noo", said Steph, as his hand came out of his pocket instinctively and he pushed it back in.

A fag would be good, he was thinking, after his play with the quad 8s and Sleeve; it would take the edge off a bit. He wouldn't take a fag from this slick with the hair gel though, even if he was the manager of the place. The longer he stood there, the more he felt he was being inspected. Who did this boy think he was, and what was he doing out there anyway, lurking about in the shadows?

"It's hard to quit," Vince was saying, still looking at him, *"I've done it hundreds of times"*.

Steph was thinking it was a line so old that even he wouldn't have used it.

"Last time I did it, my girlfriend bought me a packet and told me to start again. She said that I was moping about like a bear with a sair heid."

Vince chuckled to himself, and put his back against the wall, next to Steph.

"Aye, it's no easy to chuck the fags, that's true."

He took another drag of his cigarette and blew out the smoke, letting it drift across Steph.

"If you did go back on the fags, just let me know – I could get you cartons of two

hundred, cost price. These are top quality, branded, mind - no rubbish."

Vince glanced at Steph, who was staring out across the car park. Vince couldn't tell yet if he was interested, but he pushed on.

"Maybe you need something else to help you to get over the hump, straighten you out in the meantime?"
Vince said, stepping closer.

When Steph said nothing, he continued, *"I could put you in touch with somebody, if you like."*

Steph was only half listening, looking at the makes of cars line up, and thinking up a farewell line that wouldn't come across as offensive, before heading back inside. He could smell the hair gel now, and he caught just the end of Vince's last sentence.

"What did you say?"

Vince came closer still, glancing back over his shoulder.

I said, *"You're looking a bit tense there, bud, like you could use something to help you feel a bit more mellow."*

He looked at Steph and nodded, smiling.

"I could fix you up if you're looking for something."

No crazy prices and guaranteed to …"

Steph had heard him right the first time. Now he swung around to face Vince, moving fast, and stuck a finger in his chest, pushing him back against the wall. He was shaking with the sudden rush of anger, adrenaline still pumping after the incident with Sleeve. His voice was higher than his usual cigarette-induced growl.

"Listen pal, if I want to feel mellow I'll drink a few more of your overpriced pints in there and then maybe go home and have a good wank and go to sleep. I don't need tablets or sticking stuff up my fucking nose like a fiend to feel better, so just fuck off back to hole you crawled out of," his voice louder as he spat out the last words.

Vince held up his hands, sliding away, along the wall, out of fist range.

"OK, OK, no offence intended, bud. Just a friendly offer I thought you might appreciate. No damage done here. No need to take it sore."

Steph stomped past him, back into the club, feeling worse than he did when he came out.

Vince gave it five minutes, then went back inside and straight to the bar.

"Give me a lime and soda with ice, Graham," he said without looking at the young barman. That was a bad judgement call; not like him. Steph's bed-head hairstyle and the bags under the eyes looked like a tell, but they weren't. It turned out that Vince had got it wrong this time. He was a jumpy bastard, right enough, twitching like a user, wringing his hands. It could have been because he really was off the fags. Vince didn't want to chew it over too much, beat himself up about one mistake. He knew from experience that it was vital to bounce back, absolutely crucial to move on quickly to the next success. You had to play the percentage shots in a long game, not go into a tail spin just because you got one or two wrong. It was more difficult to spot the tells in those who still had a choice and Vince had misread Steph.

There would be other punters at the poker who would be interested in being put in touch. He had the contacts and the phone numbers that they would pay for. It was still a question of choice for those who came to the club. If they still had money to spend on drinks or gambling or taxis then they still had choice. They still had jobs, or redundancy payments, or partners stupid enough to bankroll them. Vince had seen what happened when the choice was gone, and going out at the weekend or going out at night was replaced with just going out, 24/7, to find a hit. He called them the Martini fiends, after an old TV advert for the drink: *"Martini – anytime, anyplace, anywhere, there's a wonderful world you can share, it's the right one, it's the bright one....it's Martini"*. Vince's Martini fiends were more anywhere, anyhow, any more for the desperation of acts they would do for a hit. They were drained of life and the only energy left was used to think of how to get the next score. The choice was gone.

The poker club crowd still had choice, but some of them would become Martini fiends. Vince had seen it. Somebody would make good money off them before heroin became the reason to live, so why not him, why not Vincent Quarrier? He worked for his money and he deserved it. Some of these freeloading bastards had never worked a day; just leeched off the state or other people who did work.

He looked over the tables for likely marks, scanning for likely tells. The shades to hide the baggy eyes and the prisoner wannabe look to disguise the weight loss were usually good signs, but not here. There were too many posers in the club wearing dark glasses and jeans hanging off their arse, crying out for a belt. A few were more peely-wally white than the average Scotsman, but that could be as a consequence of too many hours of Grand Theft Auto and internet porn, rather than substance abuse. Vince could spot shaky hands at tables and some players holding chips, rubbing them together or turning them over and over in sweaty fingers. All possible tells, except every second player was doing it.

Drugs delivery anywhere in the city within the hour and Vince took his percentage cut on every satisfied customer referred. That was the quality guarantee. Vince avoided using his phone for any of the deals. He supplied the numbers, the customer phoned the dealer, and the package was delivered to Vince for distribution. Group discounts were available and this was where he made the big money hits. Hen nights at the Gossip 'n' Envy were usually up for a few Disco biccies, to make everyone feel that they really were best mates. Ecstasy was for groups, and he could take a few hundred quid with return customers on the same night. With heroin, the best he could do was ones and twos. Nobody on skag cared enough to give a flying fuck whether somebody else was scoring and feeling relaxed. But with heroin he was guaranteed repeat custom for months, at least until the choices ran out.

Vince scanned the crowd again and picked out two potential customers who might be interested in his contact numbers. Crucifixes were another good tell; not anything dainty and discrete, but wooden or cast metal black things, to top off a just-over it, Goth look. The two guys he spotted had the unhealthy, worn-out-from-partying look that Vince had heard described as heroin-chic, but on them it just looked like hadn't-washed-in-while slob. He would watch and pick his time.

CHAPTER 7

Bad luck, bad beats and bawbags

To lose a hand, to lose a game, to lose all your chips on the turn of one card was hard. It hurt. But if you had played your best game, bet when you should, folded when you knew you were beat, stole a few pots and based your play on the pot odds, then you could walk away from the table with no regrets, knowing that if you played like that each time, you would win more than you would lose. It hurt, but it was no big deal; you forgot that particular game and moved on. Simple.
But you never forgot the games when you had played your best and gone out to a bad beat from some bawbag. You had a hand that was an odds on, 96.4% favourite to win and some bawbag called your raise with some donkey hand and hit a miracle flop. That hurt a lot.

Rory came to the game to relax and to play loose poker. He left school at 16, kicked about doing supermarket and garden centre work and at 18 picked up a job paying out winnings to smiling punters at one of the four bookies on Perth High Street. Over four years he worked his way up to trainee manager, organising shifts but still taking bets and paying out money. He learned how to calculate odds along the way.

Staying with tolerant parents, he was drunk on the week-ends, eating curries, out chasing women at clubs with the school mates that were still around, all joking about sex but all desperate; (Q: "*How do you get a fat bird into bed?*"; A: "*Easy -piece of cake*" etc.). That all changed when a man with a hood and bad teeth- all the detail that Rory could remember- walked into the bookies on a Tuesday afternoon and held the point of a bread knife under Rory's chin. He took £455 from the day's takings, and made Rory redundant. He was off work for three days, talking to police and taking the time that his multinational employer, William Hill, considered enough to "sort himself out". Apart from constantly hearing the blood rushing in his ears, and feeling too hot, he was OK when he came back to work. It lasted for a whole week. He was serving customers and smiling, right up to the point when one of the bookie regulars who had read the local paper pulled a banana out of his pocket and stuck it under Rory's chin.

He didn't understand half the words his doctor used, and he couldn't see the connection between himself and some guy who had seem his mate blown into small pieces in Afghanistan, but he did understand that his job at the bookies was over. Being in the house all day with his mother was the motivation for doing anything but that. He did the job centre, he did the job clubs, he did the taster sessions (unpaid) with the call centre and even the vegetable processing plant, where nobody spoke English. In the few interviews that he got to he could hear them thinking as soon as he walked in the room – "*Too fat; next!*"

With no rent to pay, no food bills, and nobody to spend his money on, he had built up some cash in the bank. Years of meeting punters in the bookies had taught him how long money lasted however, without a job to keep you out the pub. To avoid his mother in the house he would play online in his room; $3 and $6 games, where he would scoop regularly, playing against poker starters. He staked himself in a few twenty five, then fifty dollar online tournaments, and cashed in those too. He was careful, systematic, knowing that when his stake was gone, there would be no more to spend; no more online and stuck in the house with his mother.

His online playing became his nine to five. He had a set strategy, calculating pot odds, adjusting his stakes, and checking his balance daily and weekly. He disciplined his playing, made it into a job, taking tea breaks, even keeping a poker face online, and keeping emotions out of it. It was solo but it was soulless. He switched off the onscreen chat, focussing on cards and how players onscreen played them. He kept written reminders by the computer and took notes about regulars, screen names who spent as much time as he did watching the coloured chips flying across the screen and the cartoon-pretty croupier deal the cards at double speed. He knew from his reading that one of the less publicised aspects of playing good poker was that it was slightly boring. You followed a script; reading the cards, then folding, checking or raising accordingly. You played the same way every time, adjusting only for position. Sometimes you played like you should and lost, and sometimes you made a mistake and won, but over the piece you knew that you had to tick the right boxes and play a steady game.

He made enough over the week to live on, grinding it out, playing the occasional tournament when his balance was high enough, but making his bread and butter winnings from cash games with fixed blinds. He would sit in, make enough and get out. As he got faster, he would play in up to four games at the same time, multiple screens on his computer. He would pick some regular speed, some fast and some turbo, glancing around the tables planning his next moves.

He made enough to put petrol in his car and go out on the weekends. When he went to the poker club at Gossip n' Envy on Tuesdays it was for respite, for the chat, definitely not for the poker. It was a break from work. He took his buy-in money for the main tournament, a tenner for a cash game and enough for a couple of drinks. He left at home his poker face and his systematic strategy for grinding out meagre winnings over hundreds of games. That's what he told himself, but he still got sucked in, playing to win, when the cards hit the table.

Reading books about football didn't make you a better player, unless you could already control a ball with your first touch and drop a shoulder to go past a defender, but reading about how to be like the greats of poker, could that work? God knows, and Rory knew, there were enough books. Monthlies and strategy online pages, with professional players competing to be the first to tell you how to think like them, play like them and win like them, and how to spot the schmuck, the fish at your table, so you could take all that they had. To Rory, it was one of the great mysteries of poker. If these guys had spent thousands of hours and pounds discovering the secret of how to go home with their pockets bulging, rather than their head buzzing with memories of wrong moves and bad beats, why would they broadcast it? Why would they share the secrets, in print and on websites specially created for the purpose? The stars who did were all men, except for Isabelle "No Mercy" Mercier, Jennifer No-nick-name Harman and an occasional journalist bloggers who invited you to come closer, listen carefully, so they could disclose the magician's true secret, to you and thousands of others. Why didn't they just shut up and continue to scoop the pots, bank their winnings, until they had enough to lie in a glass bottomed boat in the Maldives sipping cocktails? Why? Because there was a piece of the puzzle missing.

Rory could follow Doyle Brunson's super system in power poker, always playing tight-aggressive, adapting only for your table position, the size of your chip stack, what you knew about the other players, card knowledge, the stage in the game, whether you were in a major tournament or a smaller sit-and-go game or a cash game, the pot odds, the implied odds and, of course, the relative strength of your hand. You could mix it up, avoiding the predictability of being a tight-aggressive (TAG) fish , playing any two cards super aggressive on one hand, then slow playing your pair of kings on the next, controlling the table. You could play the long game, letting more aggressive players thin the herd before you made your crucial moves on big pots. You could practise hard at working out what range of cards your opponent might have in his hand and the range they might have you on, and work at trying to get your opponents to put you on a different range. All of these strategies worked, but none of them worked every time. And this was where the magician's trick stated to come unstuck.

The same killer move that you made with the same cards and with the same players on any two consecutive night could have you either commiserating losers or trying to find someone at the bar patient enough to listen to your blow-by-blow bad beat story. You had played it perfect, using Doyle Brunson's super system or some other never fail system, but it had gone wrong.

Despite making it his job, playing dry as he called it, Rory still got suckered occasionally; knocked out of his regular, steady orbit by some unlikely-bordering-on-impossible combination of cards that wiped up all his sophisticated set up play. The catharsis of telling somebody, anybody, about these bad beats meant that he would have to re-live it one less time in his head over the next hour, or sometimes over the next month. Tuesday nights were good for dumping his bad beat stories on others, trying to draw a reaction that would make him feel better.

When he was deciding if he could make a go of it as a full time job, Rory read. It was mostly free. He read everything he could find about online gaming strategy, protecting your stack, playing limit and no-limit games, learning from your mistakes, bluffs and semi-bluffs. He read more. He figured he had the time and if he could learn more than anyone else sitting at the three dollar and six dollar tables, he could blow them away, every time. Then, one afternoon, in the middle of reading a very wordy, online article, full of spelling mistakes, about whether it was ever justifiable to play suited connectors after a re-raise, a thought came to him, suddenly and powerfully. He dismissed it at first as ridiculous and because of what it meant for him and his game. But it came back, a few minutes later, more convincing and more demanding of his attention. He stopped reading about how to play poker that afternoon and never read about it again; it was that decisive.

It seemed so obvious, but the fact that he'd taken so long to realise it made him feel so dumb, which was another reason for denying it. He realised that the real reason why the top magicians of poker were happy to share their tricks was that they only knew part of the trick. They could sell the strategies and jaw-dropping plays that they had used along the way to their first million or their first sponsorship deal in books and online betting sites. They could disclose wonders of how to play Negreanu's connectors and get paid off, how Doyle "Texas Dolly" Brunson won both his World Series of Poker tournaments by playing the trashy 10-2 hand, and a top hundred other moves that were all calculated to make you think the same thing: it could be you! Publishers and sponsors paid well for these stories, and amateurs and no-clue players would be drawn in. The bottom line however was that it had been profitable for 40 years to reveal so called secrets that other players knew already. In that, there was no secret.

No, the real mystery of poker, the holy grail, was whether there was a system, a formula, some comprehensible algorithm for how to play in any tournament, any cash game, any heads up, amateur or professional, and go home with more money than you came with, every time. Not more than half the time, not on average over a thousand hands or a thousand years of games, but every single time you sat down at any poker table. A second, more important, question was whether anyone had already found this system. Rory knew from his experience that the bookies had winning tied up in horseracing. You might have a system to reduce the haemorrhaging of your cash across the bookies' counter, you might have a computer that could devise a system that would produce winnings (or produce profits for people selling the systems) but there was no horse racing system that allowed you to beat the bookies more than half the times that you bet.

Free advice on Z Pattern running line betting, surface switch angle betting, Dutch betting and even horse-and-tail horse body language was freely available, to everyone. The 1111222334 sequence horse number betting scheme had you going back to the first number in the sequence after a win. Like poker, there were online wizards of odds, just queuing up to help you win more and lose less. There were big money betters changing allegiance regularly, worshiping then discarding system after system, in search of the

Golden Fleece, the great unfindable.

Despite the proliferation of systems, the majority of horse betting punters were still walking in off the street and betting on a whim or a gut feeling or because they remembered that a horse called Ballysomething once won a race. The vast majority of money bet in a bookies was placed by punters whose only system was blind optimism, and whose cash was only ever going to go in one direction across the bookies' counter.

But there were no bookies at the poker table. In non-casino poker you were playing against other schmucks, not against William Hill or Ladbrokes or Coral. There was a finite number of starting hands, a finite number of flops, turn and river cards that could appear on the table. Rory know all of the dry facts by heart. You could have 1326 possible combinations of starting cards in your hand, but that could be boiled down to 169 *types* of hands, grouped as 13 possible pairs, 78 suited and 78 unsuited hands. All good news so far for devising a simple system for calculating the odds of your first *two* cards being higher than those of any other single player. Two card, two player poker however was not a known game.

The complicating factor was that there could be up to nine other players at the table, and when the flop, turn and river were dealt on the table the number of combinations of hands if all ten players stayed in was more than 21 octillion; not million or billion, but octillion. A number that big could give you the same sort of headache you got trying to think about the universe being infinite - yes, but what was *beyond* the bit of the edge of the universe that was still expanding, etc. The 21 octillion number of possibilities could also have you believing that statistically, by the law of averages, by calculated odds, over thousands of hands, your 2♠-3♥ off suit starting hand had to sweep the board sometime in the next hundred years, so why not now? Did a winning system exist that was going to make sense of such numbers? Rory had realised on that cold afternoon in his bedroom that if such a system did exist, he was not going to find it on the pages of PokerStrategy.com or playwinningpoker.com.

Gerry thought there might be a system. Rory remembered listening to him one night as they sat in the sad seats; both knocked out of the main tournament early and waiting for enough losers to be able to start a cash game. Gerry understood computers. He said the elusive poker system was just like the search for factoring big numbers. In maths theory and in software development labs around the world, the quest for how to factor very large numbers had heated up. Every message sent by smart phone, email and text between two mates or two countries could be encrypted to prevent unwanted eyes. Computer encryption codes had become massive money makers.

At the level of Facebook and gossip, encryption was handy, to avoid getting a slap; at the level of commercial espionage and national security it could save millions of pounds or save lives. A system called RSA encryption was devised in 1978 by Ron Rivest, Adi Shamir and Leonard Adleman, a small group of cryptographers; a job that was still associated in Rory's head with cracking cunning codes in Biggles and TinTin stories. RSA involved the electronic choice of and communication of two numbers. One was a "public" number, widely available, for encrypting the information; the other private, like a personal PIN code, for decrypting or decoding the incoming message. The security of RSA ultimately depended on the fact that one of the big numbers in this transaction was a multiple of two unknown and unknowable prime numbers. This would be easy to figure out if the numbers were seven and eleven, for example, and the big number was 77, but modern encryption was using increasingly large numbers, where "large" meant a number that would cover pages when written out in full. Bearded mathematicians and cryptographers, fashion-free men with jumpers tucked inside their trousers, were working day and night on quantum computers, searching for that eureka moment; a fast way to factor, or "disentangle" any two prime number that had been multiplied together.

If there was a eureka formula for poker it was still out there waiting to be found.

There were nights when poker players who believed in the winning system, the magic formula, thought they had stumbled onto it. They could look at a hand and know. Know that it would win, know what other players were holding and know just how much to bet to build the pot, before striking and winning. Instinctive calculations without numbers, made in a split second, they had found the true path, the Tao of poker.

Rory knew too. He'd once had a fortnight of invincibility, cashing in every game in which he played. He called the sound system that was now installed in his clapped out car "the zone", in memory of the money he had used to buy it, all of it won in those heady two weeks. But being in the zone was like being on a night out, having mates laugh at everything you said, hitting the funny bone every time you spoke; you couldn't keep it up. You tried telling the same jokes again and they didn't work second time around, and you were soon back to hit and miss.

Rory had read the pages of the players who had found the route to the zone. If you could get there, you could feel the game, pick up on players' tells, get your big hands paid off, bluff on your rubbish hands, avoid bullets, build momentum and control the table. When you were there, other players backed off. It was like you exuded danger, playing in a rhythm as your chip stack grew like a Lego construction. Being in the zone was like a drug you couldn't buy. You wanted it for every game, and you wanted it even more after you had been there, to the zone, but you couldn't find it, and you certainly couldn't fake it. Frustratingly, for a place you could seldom find, you knew exactly where it was. The zone was waiting in that half-way house somewhere between being so immersed in a game that your neck muscles ached and you almost laughed out loud whenever you had a strong hand, and that state of being so who-gives-a-fuck detached from the hands that you only looked at your cards when you were reminded that it was you to play. You didn't sit there waiting for a good hand, you just waited to pick your spots. You knew, with one hundred per cent certainty when they happened. It was the right combinations of cards in your hands, cards on the board, hesitation by other players, relative sizes of chips stacks and probability of the next card. Then you struck, building the pot, or feigning weakness; whatever it took to draw in as many chips as possible to the centre of the table and then, invariably, from there to your growing chip stack.

You were alive in the zone, invincible, with nothing more to prove. All the pointlessness of having too much work, of not having enough money, of sweating about trivia was gone. You could hear others talk, distracting you, trying to put you off your game, or congratulating you for nailing hand after hand, but all the noise was outside the zone, just bouncing off your invisible shield.

Coming down was hard. The details, the memories that you brought back from the zone were random and unreliable as a morning after. It was like finding a handful of the runic letters that Arne Saknussemm had scribbled as clues to his impossible *Journey to the Centre of the Earth*. You knew it was possible to go there because you had been, but you couldn't remember how. You had had a great idea and you had forgotten to write it down. You had typed up everything that you would ever have to remember for the rest of your life, edited it, formatted it and then you had pressed delete by mistake. You could spend hours searching for it, believing that it was there somewhere, but you knew, after the first few minutes that it was going to be time wasted. It was gone.

Players worked on breathing. The shared knowledge was that anybody who had been to the zone remembered something important about breathing through your nose. It was nothing specific, just being conscious of something that you did normally without thinking. Finding the zone was a misnomer, because the more you searched, the more you read and the more you perfected your Zen breathing the further it floated away.

Rory believed in the logic of systems and the existence but elusiveness of the zone, but sometimes his faith was tested. After a particularly bad run his belief that the more he practised the luckier he got would weaken. Could the whole up/down, I am a poker God/I am the fish at the table, be all down to luck and the randomness of who was shuffling and dealing? No, that couldn't be true. Rory's livelihood depended on that reality being ridiculous.
If you played ten thousand hands against the same guys ever week for a year, would you all end up with the same bank roll, more or less, all things being equal? Probably not, because all things were not equal. Sitting at your table could be any combination of top feeders, grinders, loose cannons and poker flotsam.

At the Gossip 'n' Envy on Tuesdays there were top feeders, scooping the easy prey from the surface of the pond. Players like Welsh who fed on those who just came along to see what it was like to play against real people, instead of an electronic dealer and online players from the Russian Federation or Latvia called Johnny Diablo or Pigrider47 or Swingingdick53.

Welsh was in fact, Scottish. He had acquired the name in his early school years, because of his resemblance to a scandalised politician with protruding ears. He made his money in cash games, after he had been knocked out of the main tournament. He had a knack of making new players feel like they were having a good time, as they dipped into their pockets for another ten pound top-up and Welsh's chip stack grew by the same amount. His poker strategy was classic loose-aggressive, more commonly described as *"playing like a fucking maniac"* by others at the table. The level of aggression in his play was closely correlated with the number of beers drunk.

Each week, he was condemned to repeat the same Groundhog Day tournament game many times; sensible, odds determined play, deteriorating to random all-in bets in later rounds and elimination, never victory. He held the record of being the player with the most tournament points to end on negative cash equity at the end of a 6-month season of poker.

Body language at the table could give a poker tell to those observant and sober enough to notice. The information from Welsh's standard slouch in his seat gave away little. In the intervals between exchanging a stream of friendly insults with players on other tables, and giving football score updates from his phone, he would throw some chips into a pot after a casual glance at the cards dealt. He scooped up winnings from the pot and shrugged off any big-hit losses with equal indifference, and kept a steady stream of non-poker chat going whether he was in a hand or without cards. If playing poker was gripping, thrilling and all-absorbing, someone had forgotten to tell Welsh. Then there were the grinders. These were the players who made it to the final table more weeks than not, made it to the money places more than half the time they got to the last eight players, and didn't make a big deal about it. Jake "Eyetie" Balatelli, played in three live games a week, plus four, ten dollar screens at once online on weekends, having staked himself originally with four hundred dollars. His stash had crept up to $1800 over six months. He was a steady-eddie player, betting or folding according to the odds on most hands, taking an occasional chance on a big pot, but keeping track all the while of his chip stack on the night, his cash stack for that week, that month and that year. Seldom spectacular in his plays, rarely cracking a smile, Jake was just someone who was there or thereabouts when the prize money was being paid out at the end of the night.

If you could avoid the top feeders and the grinders, you still had to get past Boyd, and wild players like him, for whom dropping a hundred or even two hundred pounds in a single night of poker didn't mean nearly as much to him as it did to you. He was most often out of the main tournament and onto the cash games in the first fifteen minutes of the night, earning him the nickname of "Man Down", which was the shout given to alert the Tournament Director that someone had been knocked out of the main game. In Mississippi steamboat days he would have been a grifter, an itinerant gambler with a good looking hat, searching for a game and a hapless traveller that he could fleece; in modern day Scotland he worked for an agricultural accountancy firm, helping farmers to prepare annual accounts and tax returns. He set aside 15% of his salary each month and gambled it, on cards, live and more often online, football accumulator bets, horses and puggies. His favourite £50 bet at the bookies was Liverpool to score before the 27th minute in any game.

If you decided to take on Boyd in the main tournament you were going to either double your chip stack early, or go out of the tournament; there was no middle ground. If you played against him in the cash games, he would come and come again, pulling an endless stash of twenty pound notes from his pocket, to buy back into the game and betting higher until he won back his money and yours, or wore you down to the point where you got out with what little you had left.   Given the option, Boyd would be spending his money on nights out with women. He was a single man with no overheads, and no contacts outside work and poker, trying hard to convince himself that he had made a choice.

Rory knew the basic odds of winning, but he also knew avoiding players was down to luck, or rather down to the random seating allocation of the PokerMax Poker League Software. You could get one or two big players on one table, raising on every hand. If you kept your head down, avoided wild bets, you could win chips and progress in the tournament, by picking up scraps. Lesser players could be reduced to a handful of chips and you were a scavenger, feeding on the dead insects stuck to the front of the train when it stopped in the station. Or the big players at your table could get into some macho face off, betting against each other, or picking on some newbie. Like some old "Lost World" movie, with two dinosaurs fighting over the prey, you could escape with some chips while they were distracted.

Welsh played the same, laid back, who-gives-a-fuck game each week, except when he was on a table with Boyd. A darker, uglier side came out when he was goaded by his long term poker buddy. Since school they had a relationship like a stale marriage. Their weekly "last-longest" side bet, on which of them would go out of the tournament first, quickly escalated from banter about lack of poker skills to insults about hairlines, waistlines, and cock size. They would bet against bookies' odds on football games, horses and dog races and bet against each other on dominos, darts and Chinese poker, a variant played in any gaps before tournaments.

When they sat down at the same table in the main tournament, it was over fast. The winning hand was not who had the best cards at the table; it was who had the better hand between Welsh and Boyd. They would raise and re-raise quickly, way beyond what was in the pot, frightening off the rest of the table, and then slow it down when just the two of them remained. It was kamikaze poker, with each of them ready to go out of the tournament, rather than back down.

So Rory had learned that there were top feeders, grinders, players to be avoided and, dodging through this random obstacle course, there were players who had been playing since before it was possible to play online, before the age of computers. Tam, aka Armadillo Slim, was the oldest player at the club. Tam was a basic systems player, finishing in the top ten of the league each season simply by turning up every week (two points) and playing his game to a strict set of rules that he had devised over the years. He would raise any flop with a Jack or a 10 in it, raise five times the big blind if a pair appeared on the flop, and go all in if nothing higher than an 8 was on the board. With a few minor exceptions for position and other re-raises, that was it; that was Tam's system for winning at poker. Tam was old school. He dressed for poker, and specifically for Western Texas Hold'Em, wearing a selection of braided leather bolo ties, ending in silver aiguillettes, always with a white shirt. Rory's epiphany, back on that wet afternoon in his bedroom, was that players who wrote about poker only told part of the truth, but sold it as the whole truth. Playing a system, searching for the hidden formulae or gambling on luck, it all came down to you. *"Working on mysteries without any clues. Workin' on our night moves"*, said Bob Seger. He was singing about how to do sex, properly, but doing poker properly? Most players Rory knew were still fumbling in the dark, trying to get to first base with some pride still intact. It was basic winning or losing quietly. To win was to lie and take other people's money. It was much harder to be a good winner than to be a good loser. When you lost a game, or you were knocked out of the tournament, you smiled, you shook hands and walked away, or walked as far as the table where the cash game had started. You just bottled it up and said nothing when you lost, whether it was a bad beat, or you had just totally misplayed your hand, or it was some bastard who had just sucked you in with a few small bets and then taken all of your chips with his monster hand. You could talk about it, in detail, later, if anybody asked and if you really wanted to see what someone who was really bored looked like. Bad beat stories were like listening to jokes you had heard too many times; you knew the ending and you were just hoping that you could feign interest for long enough for it to be over. To win well was to lie well and take all of the chips at the table, without making the losers feel any worse than they already did. You didn't laud it over a player that you knocked out, even online, you didn't shout when you won and you didn't belittle players, even if that same player had knocked you out the week before and called you a fucking donkey.

It was more than bog standard table etiquette. If you were good at winning, really good, you could tell the noble lies; say things that made people feel less empty and devastated as they got up to leave the table. This was a trick that few could master and it came off most times as just patronising or sarcastic – *"Unlucky pal"*, *"That was rough"* or *"Tough break"*. Those who were good at it spoke to the player, not to the table. They offered a few quiet words about how they would have played the hand just the same as the loser did.

At the end of each league season, for the Gossip 'n' Envy games, there was polite but not ecstatic applause when the league winner went up to pick up the trophy. Every player was sitting there thinking about games that they had lost to the winner. Poker was important at the time. When you were driving home after the game, it was easy to rationalise how you had played. Your wins could all go down to your dead-on analyses of the players and their cards, your system, combined with your Vegas-like audacious moves at just the right times. Your losses and glaring cock-ups? Well obviously they were because of bad luck, bad beats and complete bawbags like Boyd and Welsh.

CHAPTER 8

Chase the Queen

Each player is dealt two cards down and one card face up, initially. A total of four cards are dealt face up eventually and then a final card face down to all players. In this poker variation the card that is dealt immediately after any Queen is dealt becomes wild. For example if a player is dealt a Queen face up and the next player is dealt a 6, then all 6s showing on the table and all 6s in players' hands become wild.
There are rounds of betting after the initial deal, then after each card is dealt. Each time a Queen is dealt face-up any cards that were previously wild are nullified and the card following the Queen becomes the new wild card. If a Queen is the very last card dealt face up, then there are no wild cards. The outcome of this game is extremely unpredictable. What was poker gold one minute can be worthless the next, and what was dross can suddenly become the hand everyone wishes they had.

Midnight to one o'clock on Friday and Saturday nights in Perth Infirmary Accident and Emergency (A&E) was rush hour. It was the most people making the most noise. Ninety per cent of the footfall into A&E was drink related accidents, or just drink related drunkenness. There were underage cider drinkers with alcohol poisoning, drug and drink cocktail collapses, police bringing in people too drunk to charge or take to the cells, mates bringing in mates who had been lying in pools of spew and piss, bloodied, topless males, knickerless females; all of them too drunk to remember if they were victims or assailants. All of these emergencies were accompanied by other drunk people, all trying to shout loudest to be attended to first, or punching and kicking doors, doctors and nurses before during and after they were taken into a cubicle and treated.

The non-informative statistics showed that most who attended the A&E Department on weekends had minor, non-life-threatening (NLT), non- limb-threatening (NLiT) injuries and illnesses. In A&E, abbreviations and acronyms were used to speed communications between medical and administrative staff. The drunken non-life-threatening, non-limb-threatening injuries were referred to collectively by staff as FDGB (Fall Down Go Boom), an acronym that had started to appear on patient records until two ambulance crew were disciplined.

In contrast to the weekend rush, midnight to one o'clock on a Thursday in A&E was quiet. There were usually a few ambulance runs with road traffic accident (RTA) injuries, breathing problems or chest pains brought in from home, self-referrals for late night falls or early evening sports injuries that got worse. Most were walk-ins.

Four drug ODs in one hour on a Thursday night was call-for-reinforcements time. The waiting time clock on the wall jumped from twenty to fifty five minutes. One women was brought by ambulance from the city centre McDonalds, a man had been carried down four flights of stairs from a party and bundled in the boot of a hatchback and police had been called to a couple lying semi-conscious on the back seat of a taxi. All four passed from A & E to Critical Care and the doctor who admitted them suspected a bad heroin batch. None of the patients was an injector, but the symptoms were consistent with other cases of adulterated heroin that the consultant had seen the previous year, when a combination of war and a fungus infection on the Afghan poppy harvest had resulted in an increase in use of paracetamol and talcum powder as bulking agents in street heroin. All four patients were given naloxone by IV push and hooked up to a saline drip. A&E contacted Public Health and Police to get alerts out quickly, and the Police started an investigation that night, looking at the movements of the four.

They had been found within half a mile of each other, all semiconscious and with high temperatures and rapid heart rate. From witness statements, the woman from McDonalds and the man from the party had had what sounded like febrile seizures around the same time, and the couple in the taxi had fallen ill a bit earlier. The man from the party was known to Police for minor drug busts, but none of the others had anything on file. The couple had been picked up from a bar and were on their way home, according to the taxi driver.

The two detectives assigned to the case got some helpful information about the time that each person had collapsed and their behaviour immediately before. In addition, the hospital reported finding two pink tablets in the pocket of the man brought in from the party. The most useful clue, however, was the fact that all four patients had been admitted to A&E wearing cowboy boots.

Questioning of reluctant witnesses at the party led the police to Gossip 'n' Envy. Vince was keen to be of assistance to the two CID officers, making them comfortable in his office and including in his answers to their questions detailed descriptions of the two men who were most likely, from his observations, to have sold the tablets at the club that night. The account that Vince provided included the hair and eye colour of the two dealers, and their movements in the club. It was comprehensive. It was only when one of the officers asked him to go over the details again, so that it could be written as a statement, that Vince realised how difficult it was to make up the same story twice.

Seven months later, when the court case was finally called, *The Perth Gazette* reported:

"A 33 year old nightclub manager has begun a nine-month sentence behind bars for selling Ecstasy tablets at Perth's Gossip 'n' Envy nightclub.

Vincent Quarrier was found guilty of being concerned in the supply Ecstasy after a three-day trial. Police discovered a bag containing 56 Ecstasy tablets and £900 in cash in the office of the nightclub on the night of 20th September. Their investigations had led them there after four people who had visited the club that night had been admitted to hospital, suffering serious health problems. The trial heard that Mr Quarrier had sold ecstasy to the four late-night revellers through an intermediary. The pink Ecstasy tablets, all bearing a skull and crossbones decal, the court heard, had been adulterated with unknown substances. Sheriff Lennox Paterson told Quarrier: "The taking of drugs in this town and the consequences of that drug taking has figured in these courts over a number of years and I have had to hand down custodial sentences in an effort to try to discourage more people from doing precisely what you did."

Quarrier, of Milton Road, had pled not guilty to supplying the class A drug and possession with intent to supply at the nightclub, but the jury delivered their guilty verdict after just an hour of deliberation at the end of the trial.

During the trial Quarrier had claimed that he was not a supplier and that the Ecstasy was for his own use. He contended that he bought the tablets in bulk to save money. Quarrier, who had no previous convictions, was described by his solicitor Mark Bell as a hardworking and upstanding member of the local business community.

Quarrier denied describing the four victims of the adulterated ecstasy tablets as, "some E-tarded burn-outs who'd be better off dead" when questioned by PC Hammond of Tayside Police on the night of the incident.

In appealing for a non-custodial sentence for his client, Mr Bell told the court that Mr Quarrier had been drawn to drugs in a difficult period of his life, following the death of his mother, three years previously.

Judge Paterson said that a custodial sentence was necessary to emphasise to others the dangers of drug that could kill, and the consequences of dealing in these drugs, especially from a club open to the public, "We must ensure that all pubs and clubs are safe for the people of this town and stay within the law and the terms of their licence. This court will continue to take action against any premises which fails to do so."

Following Quarrier's arrest in September Gossip 'n' Envy was closed. Perthshire Licensing Board were due to make a decision next week on the licence of the club, but the parent company, Glossamer Holdings, who were operating the club under a continue-to-trade agreement, has already indicated that the they will not be applying for renewal of the licence and club is unlikely to re-open in the near future."

The main doors and the fire exits were chained up by Perth & Kinross

Council, who owned the building. Within a week the vaulted stone ceiling had returned the main room inside the building to its original 60% humidity, ideal for wine storage. A half-hearted Facebook petition to Save Gossip 'n' Envy attracted 23 cut-and-pasted messages to accompany the signatures. None of the signatures came from poker club members.

Gerry was pissed off with Vince's stupidity and greed and pissed off that the closure had happened after he had kept Vince sweet and put in the effort to sign up enough players to make the Poker Club work, but now he was getting really pissed off with players texting him, asking him what *he* was doing about organising games, like he was responsible for Vince selling drugs out of his club and getting caught. Christ! He was doing all this for nothing; no pay, no glory and certainly no word of thanks from these ungrateful poker junky bastards.

Without him there would have been no Poker Club. He was responsible for making it happen. Everybody, especially the snidey bastards constantly texting him – " *U getN somit sortD Gerry? When's d nu leag sTRtN? ny nws?'* - seemed to be missing that fact. But they were fast enough to decide that he was responsible when it stopped happening. They had had a taste and now they wanted more and they were giving him a hard time about it.

He was pissed off with Vince, pissed off with all the idiots texting him and just plain gutted that the whole thing had gone bust. All the work he had put it, he was thinking, repeating the rules, marshalling the tables week after week until these street savages could sit on a seat and play poker and behave like civilised, socialised human beings, at least for a few hours. It was all wasted. He was left with boxes of chips, decks of cards, dealer buttons and some redundant PokerMax Poker League Software on his computer, but no venue and no poker club. Each time a new *what-the-fuck's-happening-Gerry?* text pinged on his phone he came closer to closing it all down, sending out a brief group text of his own, telling them all to fuck right off.

The Civil Service Sports Association, also known as the Civil Service Sports Association Club and as CSSC Sports & Leisure, was based in a narrow building by the Perth Railway Station. The land was owned by Network Rail and the building had once been an engine shed with a capacity for two diesel locomotives. It had been subdivided, insulated, mostly with coats of paint, decorated, and run as the "Civvy" since 1979. The flat, tarred roof had been laid with neat lines of spiral barbed wire at one foot intervals giving it a corkscrew hairstyle, after two break-ins through the skylight in the first month the club was open.

The Civvy sold subsidised drinks to current and retired members of staff from "Government Agencies and Non-Departmental Public Bodies"; mostly former railwaymen and Royal Mail employees. Former Miners Club members had been included in the eligibility criteria as a gesture of solidarity, and a measure of sympathy for the collapse of the mining industry in Scotland. The main bar, which was just longer than one railway engine, had darts, a pool table and 58", difficult to ignore, wall mounted TV. The bar was the main focus of activity and income.

The Civvy bar also served meals that looked like meals – meat, veg, potatoes separated on the plate- to appreciative members, and to signed-in guests. The other room in the Civvy was the Function Suite, used each week for the local dominos league, and hired out at reasonable rates for meetings and celebrations. The regulars in the function suite were the photography club (Tuesday), a Real Pilates instructor (Thursday) and a small but enthusiastic War Games group, (De Bellis Multitudinis Rules for Ancient and Medieval Battle 3000 BC to 1500 AD) on Sunday afternoons. The accordion and fiddle club, who met to rehearse on the last Monday of each month played two, 30 minute sets in the bar on the last Friday of each month in exchange for use of the room.

The Civvy paid a nominal rent to Network Rail for the converted buildings. The Committee Members who ran the club were unpaid, and the only salaries were for the bar and catering staff, and a part time caretaker/handyman. The biggest bill by far was for heating. In a building designed originally as a garage for trains, there had been little thought to energy conservation. Any smoker from the Civvy who stepped outside on a cold night could lean against the wall of the bar and feel the heat on his back. Arched, metal-framed windows ran the full length of the building, with just a single width of brick between each window. The windows, designed to maximise light in the original engine shed, were now covered in black out curtains as thick as carpets. But the heat still seeped out. Portable gas heaters were wheeled around the coldest spots of the building. A hard winter the previous year had the radiators doing 24 hour shifts, just to prevent pipes from freezing, and drinkers and diners had to wear scarves and hats inside. Another hike in heating oil prices was the catalyst for the September Committee meeting to include part-time closure of the club on the agenda. The motion to close on Tuesday, Wednesday and Thursday nights was defeated by 4 to 3, but the monthly update on the accounts which followed made it clear that the club would not survive beyond the end of the financial year without extra income. The roof needed to be re-timbered and the moss-covered roof felt replaced, the rust on the windows was eating its way both in and out and the mud patch that was the delivery area needed surfaced.

An Extraordinary General Meeting of the Civvy members was called and the Committee was given permission to apply for funding to save the building and to look for new premises for the club in the meantime. The Civvy Committee members met with Perth & Kinross Property Sub-Committee and negotiated a one year lease of the Gossip 'n' Envy building. Although the council had told the Civvy Committee that they had a "portfolio of premises" available, Gossip 'n' Envy was, in reality, all that was on offer.

A Press release from the Council said:

"The Council are extremely keen for this building, which has a chequered history, to be put back into use as a community facility. We can confirm also that the Civil Service Club is currently preparing an application to the Big Lottery Fund for refurbishment of their original premises at Station Road and the Council will assist the organisation in this process in any way we can."

Gerry got the news before it went out in the Perth Gazette and realised that he had to move fast. He made the phone call from work, something he only did in emergencies. He needed to get in there quick, and make his proposition attractive enough before the Civvy had other, more sensible offers to consider.

It was logical for him to take Christopher to the meeting. He was the safe choice. Respectability and responsibility? Christopher had them spades, and in all other suits. Christopher was the Poker Club treasurer and he could explain how the club operated, and everything the Civvy needed to know about membership, annual subs and registering. In meeting Christopher, the Civvy Committee could be convinced on how trustworthy and, well, ordinary the typical Poker Club members might be. Given the opportunity, Christopher could talk like a politician about poker club governance, campaigning for wider public understanding on the importance of knowing the differences between rules and regulations, gaming and gambling, fees and charges. Gerry knew that in a tight spot Christopher would be able to respond to Committee questions even when he didn't know the answer, just to avoid the embarrassment of not knowing. Christopher could be a deal breaker if the Committee were swithering on a decision. Yes, Christopher was the obvious choice. But Gerry took Tam instead.

Tam took his table name, Armadillo Slim, after one of the first celebrity poker stars, Amarillo Slim. The variation was a reference to Tam's pock marked face and wrinkles. Gerry guessed that Tam was the only player at the club who had been playing poker longer than him. He wore his trademark bolo ties, except at work, where his job as a prison guard manager required a plain clip-on black tie to prevent being choked. He arranged his own shifts to make it to the poker on three weeks out of four. But it had been no weeks out of four since Gossip 'n' Envy had been chained up, and Tam was missing being Armadillo Slim.

Gerry took him to the meeting with the Committee when he realised that Tam, as a Government Agency employee, was the only person he knew who was eligible to be a *bone fide* member of the Civvy. Christopher would have respectability, but Tam would have a different kind of credibility, Gerry thought, with the blazers who were likely to make up the Civvy committee. Having Tam renew his long dead Civvy membership and ten signing in thirty plus guests to play poker seemed unlikely, but it would be a starting point for negotiating with people that Gerry had never met.

Gerry arranged to meet Tam at Costas on Saturday morning at ten to go over the game plan for their meeting, which was set for 10.50. Not 11.00, the Civvy secretary had repeated on the phone, just to make sure Gerry knew when he and Tam would be expected. Tam spent his time in the short queue in the coffee shop complaining about the prices, and the customers, or coffee shop mugs, as he called them, breaking off only to thank Gerry for paying for the drinks. His stream of observations was just loud enough for Gerry to hear.

"Somebody's having a laugh here Gerry. Three quid for a cup of fucking shaving foam? How can people no see through that, eh?"

As they sat down, he took a sip of his tea; milk, three sugars.

"And you have to stand in a queue for twenty minutes with a bunch of other mugs for the privilege of giving them your money— I bet these guys in the coffee shop's boardroom were absolutely pissing themselves when they thought that one up. Charging the price of enough milk to keep a family going for a week for a few coffee beans, some hot water and a squirt of crazy foam? You could not make that up, because nobody would believe you."

Gerry glanced around the busy tables. "

Yeah, you're right Tam, it is quite pricey. But if people are willing to pay that, then that's business, eh?"

Tam continued to shake his head.

"If a lot of people want to drink coffee, it's supply and demand. Think about your work Tam- if there was no crime around, you'd be out of a job, know what I mean?"

Gerry put his elbows on the table and leaned towards Tam, lowering his voice, keen to get to the script.

"Now, this meeting at the Civvy, I thought we might…"

But Tam was like a dog worrying a stick. He just couldn't put it down.

"I mean, look at all these mugs sitting by themselves with their computers and their fancy Star Trek phones. Do they all come here 'cause they've forgot how to speak to people face to face, or because they're all Johnny-no-mates? The place is like a home for saddos, all paying through the nose to be crammed into this sweaty hole."

Gerry sighed and sat back.

"Tam, we've only got half an hour…"

But Tam was looking over Gerry's shoulder, reading the board behind the baristas.

"Flat white? Marocchino? That's a coffee is it? Who makes this shite up? And since when was a cup of coffee a fucking "beverage"?"

Gerry tuned out and looked around the tables, but there was too much noise for anyone else to hear Tam. He waited for Tam to talk himself out. When his ranting reduced to mumbling and head shaking, Gerry tried again.

"Right Tam, I'll cut to the chase here, 'cause we're short on time. You're the only guy I know who could legitimately be a member of the Civvy, so I'm hoping that'll make a difference with these blazer and brass button Committee guys when we meet them."

Gerry knew that it would be a one-shot deal. If the Committee didn't like what they heard, the Poker Club would not be going back to the cavern at Gossip 'n' Envy next week or any week. There had been only home games since Vince was busted, and Gerry was still getting flack – complaints about not being invited to his place for a home game and a string of phone messages about the home games in other people's houses.

Tam confirmed that he had been to the old Civvy engine shed, once. It was a prison guard's retirement do years ago and all that he could remember was that the place smelled like someone was cleaning an oven. He told Gerry that they had presented the guy with an old bell from a steam engine. (*I mean, what would a retired guy do with a brass bell Gerry? Pretty stupid gift if you ask me…"*) By the time he had told the whole story it was after 10.30 and they had to move.

As Gerry and Tam opened the familiar doors into Gossip 'n' Envy, now reborn as the Civvy, the PA was blasting out *Rhythm is a Dancer* by Snap!. Eurotechno crap, Gerry was thinking, wondering why the staid Civvy would be playing it.

The parent company had done a deal with the Civvy on the equipment left in the building when the doors were chained up. The Civvy got to keep some of the bar furniture that hadn't started to grow white mould, and the Gossip 'n' Envy PA system, which was years better than the one left in the bar at the engine shed. It was a combined mixer and amplifier and four full range speakers. Nobody on the Civvy staff knew much about subwoofers, but the sound quality was impressive, whatever was played. The accordion and fiddle club opted not to use the PA set up when they played in the bar, but the Civvy had plans for money making, live music nights, when it could be useful to attract local tribute acts, who always went down well with members. Before re-opening the Gossip 'n' Envy building again, the Civvy Committee had arranged for the bar to be re-decorated (peach white) and had the mirror ball and rotating lights in the ceiling taken out of the main room.

"*I'm as serious as cancer when I say rhythm is a dancer – now who would sit down and write something like that Gerry, I ask you?*" said Tam as they walked along the corridor.

"*It's a good tune for dancing, granted, but the lyrics put you right off. Now if you want a really good lyric for a song, you can't go far wrong with Hank Williams. There was a man who….*"

Gerry stopped dead and Tam almost walked into his back. Gerry spoke to Tam without turning to face him.

"*Tam. This is not going to work if you're gonnae girn, and rabbit on about the music, or about whatever else gets up your humpf when we're in there*", he said through clenched teeth, pointing to the door to the bar.

"*It'll be like a job interview in there, right?*" he said, "*We've got to make the right impression if we're gonnae get the poker club going again. This is last chance saloon for us Tam- if they don't like what we're saying, we're busted, no more poker for you, for me or for any of those other punters. So no bitching and moaning in there, agreed?*"

Tam drew back a step.

"*Nah, I mean, aye, aye Gerry, right, I got the message, I was just commenting on the song, like,*" Tam replied, looking down, then to either side.

They stood for a moment, saying nothing, one behind the other, facing the door.

"*So I see the bar's in the back,*" Tam said, breaking the silence.

"*And…?*" Gerry said, wondering where this was going.

"*Well it's like that old joke about American bars and women, Gerry, you know, poke her in the front, lick her in the back. You know, like poker in the front, liquor in the back, or is the other way around? It probably is, when you think about it, eh? I can never remember jokes, see…*"

"*Tam!*"

"*Right, Gerry, right. I'm focussed, totally focussed. Let's do this interview thing.*"

Gerry's first thought when they opened the door into the main room was Communist Russia. The Politburo Committee of five had pushed three tables together and sat behind them in a row, in the centre of the room, with two bare, mismatched chairs for Gerry and Tam laid out in front. The only splash of colour in the Committee was one member's red striped tie, that looked like it had been colourised onto a black and white photograph. There were four men and one woman.

The Chair of the Committee, a ruddy faced man with a tweed jacket straining to contain him, stood up and waved them in.

"*Now I know one of you is Gerry,*" he said, in introduction, looking at Tam.

Gerry recognised the voice on the phone and stepped past the two chairs, to shake hands with him. He was then unsure whether he should shake hands with everyone else, but decided against it, and went back to the chairs, where Tam was already sitting, looking around the room. Gerry looked directly at him opening his eyes wider as a warning, as he sat down.

"*This is my colleague, Tom Winters*", said Gerry.

"*People also call me Armadil...*" Tam started, twiddling his boot lace tie.

"*...and Tom has actually been a member of the Civvy in the past*", Gerry cut in quickly, "*although he's lapsed a bit, not been to the club for a long time, because of his shifts, working up at the prison.*"

Get that in quickly, Gerry thought, get them thinking that there would be other members of the poker club who were reputable, Civvy clubbable members, or at least older guys, with respectable jobs.

"*The Committee would like to thank you both for coming here today to discuss your request to use the main room*", the Chair began, speaking as if the room was full.

He introduced the Committee members by their function first, name second: treasurer, secretary, events' organiser, and vice chair.

"*Here at the Civvy, our main concern is, of course, the interests and enjoyment of our members, although we pride ourselves on involving non-members of the local community in the activities of the club. We have raised money for many deserving charities locally, and our members have pulled together on a number of occasions to fund worthy causes outside of the local area. As you may know, Gerry, we also serve the community by allowing our rooms to be used for meetings and functions and by other groups. These have to all be carefully vetted by the Committee, as I'm sure you'll appreciate, and they must comply fully with our club policy on room usage."*

Gerry nodded and smiled understandingly and glanced down at the table in front of the Chairman. A black folder lay there, closed. Gerry was sure that he must be reading from a script, but he wasn't. Out of the corner of his eye, Gerry saw Tam to his left, with his head thrown back, looking straight up, at the holes left in the stonework where the mirror ball had been taken out.

The Chairman continued, *"Now I have to be honest at this point Gerry, and say that in a preliminary, pre-meeting discussion our committee expressed surprise at receiving a request from a gambling club."*

He paused for effect, looking at his fellow committee members on the other two tables and smiling, priming his joke.

"Gambling is the sort of thing that we might normally associate with smoky saloons on riverboats, or even with other vices, if you know what I mean."

He raised his eyebrows and nodded at Gerry, who opened his mouth to defend the poker club, but then stopped.

"However, having said all that, the Committee are willing to listen to your proposal with an open mind, and to consider it on its own merits, taking into consideration what benefits it might bring to our members, and perhaps to yours."

The Civvy treasurer, sitting to the right of the Chair made an approving murmur.

As Gerry got ready to reply, he saw Tam lean forward, and he knew, just knew, that he was going to ask the Committee about the hole in the ceiling. Gerry moved further forward in his own seat, nudging Tam as he did so, and replied before Tam could get started. He fell into the same committee-speak of the Chairman.

"Thank you, members of the committee for inviting us both here today, and for taking time out of your weekends, and for considering our proposal..."

It was a long fifteen minutes, and by the end of it Gerry was aware that he was repeating himself. He gave the Committee the same spiel he had given Vince, way back when, about poker club membership, annual subs, accounts and membership cards, throwing in a bit more about the Gambling Act 2005, to make the poker club sound more legitimate and less, well, riverboat. He tried to make eye contact with all five of the Committee as he spoke, but two of them kept their heads down the whole time, scribbling notes.

Gerry finished by thanking the Civvy Committee again for their consideration, and then repeated the reassurance that the poker games were more of a community club than a serious competition for any financial gain. He closed by reminding them that the club had run successfully for some months without any problems in the same venue previously. This was a risk, because any of the Committee members who knew what went on at Gossip 'n' Envy in the past would now have combined the image of riverboat gamblers with an image of Perth degenerates who drank, danced and took drugs.

The Committee had some questions, about the number of players and rules on behaviour at the poker table (*No fist fights and no derringers permitted at the tables, I assume Gerry?* quipped the Chairman). What a wag he was, Gerry was thinking, what a complete wag. They also asked about the noise levels and any extra nights that would be needed for the Poker Committee and annual general meetings. These were all questions that Gerry was able to field easily, mostly by making it up and sounding confident.

The Secretary, who started all of her questions with "so.." ,was curious about the length of Tam's Civvy Club affiliation. After clarifying what she meant, the Secretary then had to wait while Tam went through summary of his years in the prison service, thankfully brief, in order to arrive at the correct dates of his Civvy membership. The rest of the time, Gerry managed to prevent Tam from rambling off topic, by diving in when Tam cleared his throat to speak and by leaving no gaps in the exchanges between questions and answers. When the half hour was up, the Chairman tapped the table twice and asked his Committee for any other questions. Gerry and Tam were asked to leave the room while the Committee *"made their deliberations"*, and when they were brought back in, ten minutes later, it was for a conditional yes.

The Chairman read through sections of the Civvy Club policy on room usage, sounding like a priest delivering last rites, and pausing for Gerry's agreement to each requirement. Although Gerry acceded readily to each one, he knew there would be problems.

Firstly, evidence of the *"status and standing"* of the poker club would be required. That one was not a problem, in fact Christopher would relish putting together columns of numbers and detailed but dull poker club regulations.

Secondly, *"Bookings for functions by any Civil Service club member will take precedence over bookings by non-members"*. The poker club would just have to wear that one and see how many conflicting bookings there were over the next few months, Gerry figured.

"All non-members purchasing alcohol in the Civil Service Club must be signed into the club by a member".

Now that was going to be a major headache, Gerry knew. It would not work unless he could find some Civvy members to join the poker club - unlikely- or get Tam to spend twenty minutes signing in everyone as a guest at the start of every week – equally unlikely.

Finally, *"A full guest list of Non-Members entering the building would be required at least 48 hours prior to the event"*.

Gerry could supply a list of poker club members two days before, sure, but could he say who on the list would turn up on the night or who would turn up who wasn't on the list? He was going to have to bluff his way through that one and just give them a list of every name he knew each week. How would they know anyway, unless they did a school role call?

The Civvy had agreed to let them use the main room for a trial period at no charge and for Gerry that was enough; the poker club had a foot in the door and he could work with that. He could negotiate on all the other conditions of use, especially when the Civvy Committee took a look at the increase in bar takings after a few weeks of poker club drinking, and saw the real "merits" of filling the place on a midweek night, when it would otherwise be what he would call dead and what Civvy members would call quiet. The photography club had Tuesdays so that meant Gerry was offered Wednesdays. Not ideal, because that meant the poker would be competing with TV football, and live, wet and windy St Johnstone games some Wednesdays through the winter. But it was take it or leave it, and that's how he would put it to the poker club punters. They could come to the Civvy and play poker, or they could sit in a pub or in front of a TV – their choice. Some of them would be able to do all three, if they got knocked out of the tournament early enough and went through to the Civvy bar and its 58 inch TV.

He kept the text to the poker group list short. *"Poker bak on NXT wk @ gossip & NV. Wed. nyt NXT wk. 7pm registration, 7.30 shufL ^ & deal. Txt bak f u cn mAk it.'"*

The first week they got 24, some griping about playing poker at an "old men's club", but by week three word got out and they were back up to four tables of nine and ten.

By special arrangement, and only after another narrow Civvy Committee vote, all poker players on a Wednesday were made guests, who could be signed in by Tam, as a member of the Scottish Prison Service and the Civvy, having renewed his membership. For the weeks that Tam wasn't there another Civvy member, usually the barman, was given a five pound bung by Gerry to pre-sign the sheet. A full list of names, the same one each week, printed and with signatures had to be checked by a Civvy Committee member before poker could begin.

For the first weeks of the new arrangements, a few regular Civvy members from the bar came in and walked around the poker tables, attracted like curious children to a new activity. They were drawn to particular tables in the main room by the level of shouting or laughter, and moved around the room, sipping from their pints, watching. The poker players treated them as invisible. It was like a zoo enclosure but without the Plexiglas. The older Civvy member were able to observe at close hand, but not understand, the animals' behaviour. The novelty soon wore off and the two camps on a Wednesday were established, with poker in the main room and Civvy members and TV in the bar. The poker players spent only enough time in the bar to buy drinks, or to plug a few quid in the puggie.

As Gerry predicted, the extra takings over the bar outweighed the Civvy Committee's reservations about having gambling in the club. There was a hard core of Civvy regulars however who begrudged having a horde of loud, foul mouthed non-members in the building, treating the place like they were members. These long standing members were clumps of drinkers who were in four nights a week and sat in the same seats in the bar. The chairs that they sat in had been brought from the old engine shed bar. It had been traumatic for the older Civvy worthies to give up the peace and familiarity of the old shed and move to "a bloody disco". They had taken lawn bowls plaques, horse brasses and old train photos from the walls of the shed and put them up in the new place. Even Dallas, the Civvy cat had been brought to Gossip 'n' Envy, although he left after just one day, in disgust, and moved back to living under the old railway shed.   In the move to Gossip 'n' Envy, the puggie came too. It was a B4 category, fixed-odds betting terminal called The Wild West, and it lit up a dark corner of the bar, flashing Shoot Outs, Quick Draw, Posse Prize and Bonanza! across four reels, three rows and 24 possible paylines. The Civvy members had the volume reduced to the lowest setting. The main room in the Gossip 'n' Envy building was the same damp cavern, with pitted walls that absorbed heat and reflected back none of the weak light there was in the room. Like the Civvy members, the damp walls seemed impervious to the changes. The Civvy had gone for a working-men's-club look about the place, but coming into the building the feeling was of an empty night club in day light hours.

The hard core members enjoyed a moan. It gave them common ground and an easy conversation opener. Without work to complain about, anything else was fair game. They were good at what they did. One member would pick on something from the TV news or the front page of the tabloids as a starter and within a few minutes they could collectively work it up into something that was a national scandal, which would never have happened back in the day. Something Perth and Kinross council had or hadn't done, footballers' wages, drinking on the street, the indulgences of politicians, state of the railways – these were all the easy ones to get fired up about. There was a familiar, warm feeling in sitting with mates in the Civvy, agreeing that the world outside had gone to hell in a handcart. To an outsider it might have been a depressing and destructive marathon, sitting there every night, wearing away at the joy of living, picking off targets one by one, but to the Civvy hard-core it *was* the joy of living. Knowing that you could sit in your designated seat with a pint in hand, with guys you'd known for years, and gripe about anything that came up your humpf, without fear of disagreement or criticism; that was happiness.

They took badly to what happened outside the Civvy, and they took worse to what happened inside. Now they were barely settled in the new place, trying to make it like it was, and it was being overrun by louts, drinking beer, subsidised from Civvy members' fees by the way, and shouting so much when they were playing cards in the main hall that members couldn't hear the TV in the bar.

There was resentment from the Civvy staff too. One barman made a point each week of serving every Civvy club member at the bar before turning to any poker player for orders. Gerry made the effort to keep relations workable, getting there early every Wednesday to listen to complaints that Civvy members had relayed to the Civvy Committee, and trying to say what they wanted to hear about putting things right. He could do tact and patience and being pleasant, and the smiling and saying that he would make sure noise was kept down and no drink was spilled on the floor and toilets were flushed after use and no cash games would be played by those knocked out of the main game, and…and… but he found it all so exhausting. He took it because he hoped it would settle down after a few months, and because knew that there was no alternative.

Gerry did poker announcements at the start of the game each week: who had won last week; who was top of the league; time and place of one-off tournaments being organised locally and anybody raising charity money looking for cash. He slipped in the Civvy complaints as announcements, trying to keep it light, trying to avoid saying "complaints", trying to make it sound like the requests were coming from him, rather than from the Civvy club members, although most players knew he was relaying what had been said, after first translating it into plain-speak for the poker club members. He was hammering away every week in those first few months, feeling that he was making some headway, even with the drunkest, loudest poker players with the worst toilet habits. Even the worst of the drongos at the poker tables understood the bottom line. Being kicked out of the Civvy would be the end of the poker club and the end of their own Wednesday fix of Texas

Hold 'Em.

After ten weeks, the number of complaints was down to two or three a week, and for the first time Gerry had enough time to enjoy playing his poker again, not having to strain his neck like a meerkat all night, looking for trouble brewing on other tables. The number of players stabilised at enough for four tables, and poker players and Civvy members were co-existing, tribal routines established. There were still minor gripes, but no new ones. Then there was the Donny and the puggie incident and Gerry was back to the beginning, or worse.

Before the random seating plan for the main game was up on the screen each Wednesday, and during the fifteen minute break at nine o'clock, a few poker players would play the Wild West. Fifty pence bought you one spin on the electronic puggie, two pounds got you five, including various holds, nudges and combination plays. The nudges feature made players feel that they had an element of control over the outcome of the spins, but the chances of winning on the machines, with or without nudges was, in the hard reality of fixed odds betting terminals, exactly the same. Poker players would huddle around the machine in threes and fours, waiting for the crush at the bar to die down, as the arsy barman served Civvy members first.

It was a loud shout from the bar, loud enough to be heard throughout the building, that put Gerry back into meerkat mode.

"That wee shite should be slapped!"

Donny was born to be a competitor, but just not at poker. He spent a method actor's amount of hours working on his moves, rather than his game. Late night TV hours watching his idol, Phil "The Brat" Hellmuth; recording it, playing it in slo-mo. With a bad boy reputation and an online clothing company (Power Brat Apparel) built on holding eleven World Series of Poker (WSP) bracelets, Hellmuth played the spoilt rich kid of professional poker convincingly. His trademark leaping up from the table in a tantrum was a poker sponsor's delight, in a televised sport that that usually involved even less movement than fat-boy-darts. The sponsors loved it and Donny did too, playing it back again and again each time, just to watch individual player's reactions and the bull fighter adulation of the crowd behind the rails. Donny had perfected his own trademark move, more suited to the Wednesday poker club than WSP. It was an overturned chair, pushed back as he stood up from the table, with a follow-through swearing rant, that could he could sustain for five minutes. Any hand in which he lost more than half his chip stack was the trigger for his move. The inept or random poker plays that preceded his rants seldom had any connection to the content of the rants. Donny rehearsed and adapted his rants from some bigger games in bigger places:

"God I set him to bluff all of his money and he did and I didn't call – un-fucking-believable", or "This guy slow rolls me. I mean I know he didn't mean to slow roll me – he doesn't know what he's doing here, but it is the rudest fucking thing in poker", or "Queen-10? You raised me with Queen-10 and then hit a straight? You're an eejit! That's not poker you're playing, that's bingo – you won't last another twenty minutes here!"

Donny saw himself being recorded while he was ranting, visualised it on the largest flatscreen, with the best camera angles and close ups. When his chair hitting the wooden floor didn't get enough reaction, he would raise his voice until he was sure that every player in the room had at least looked his way.

He talked a good game, and he could recount, in detail, great plays made by other players and what you could learn from these plays and from the poker greats. He could tell you sit-down strategies for tournaments and for cash games to maximise your take. He could tell you how to play and win against top players in the club. He knew some killer moves for each table position and for each blind level in tournaments. As soon as he sat down to play, however, the rational analysis ended and Donny's game disintegrated. He just couldn't play the knowledgeable poker player and "The Brat" at the same time, even in his head.

Some weeks when it was busy, Donny didn't have enough room to overturn his chair, because of the tight seating positions. Denied the space, he would channel more energy into the rants, and they could get out of hand. He would become an actor having difficulty coming out of role, pacing, pointing and swearing, looking panicked, not so much unwilling as unable to wind his neck back in.

When he started playing on Wednesdays, Donny and his audience shared the joke when he kicked over the chair and threw a wobbler. Here was young Donny, playing to the gallery. What a laugh he was, eh? It was added entertainment. Look what he's doing now! Listen to what he said this week! But over the weeks, players started to concentrate more on their game and Donny's repeated antics became distraction, rather than entertainment. He started to lose mates, or what passed for mates, at the table. Guys who would take the time to chat with him would blank him the following week, after being subject to a rant that he pushed too far. He escalated the rants, trying to win back his audience, but in doing so he became the one thing he was trying hardest to avoid; ignored.

Donny could not get the balance right. If he started off losing a few big hands he could go into ranting mode almost from the off; if he got a run of good cards and won a few pots he would gloat about it at the table and then play super aggressive and loose, trying to intimidate players with his run of luck. Then he would over bet on nearly every hand and slam his chips down, loud enough for the room to hear, or smack the table with an open palm when he was checking, confusing aggressive poker play with physical force. His frustration was made worse by knowing that if he was advising someone in his position he would know exactly what to say to build his chip stack. He did not stay chip leader for long, disintegrating and ending the night telling the same bad beat stories to anyone who would listen for long enough.

"I raised with my Ace Queen suited and this wanker calls me with a pair of fours and then pushes all in on the turn, with nothing else on the board. So obviously I called him, because I know he's got nothing, but un-fucking-believably his shitty pair hold up against my Ace Queen!"

Before he was barred from the Civvy, Donny had been the only player in the club ever to have been yellow carded by Gerry, as Tournament Director. Donny had pushed it too far, coming back to the table one week to kick the chair that he had already knocked over and then call the winning player a *"fucking empty bawbag"*, twice. This was out of order even by Perth Poker Club standards. Gerry walked him outside, talked him down for 15 minutes, and sent him home.

The chaos of Donny's poker play was like the rest of his life. He didn't think beyond the next hand when he played poker and outside of poker he didn't think beyond the next day.

Back in the Civvy bar, Donny was doing celebration laps, waving the Super Bonanza voucher that the Wild West puggie had coughed out on his first spin: four sheriff badges straight across the middle row. He jigged in front of the Civvy hard-core members who had contributed almost all of the 50p's that made up Donny's £250 prize money. To a rising volume of threats and men getting to their feet, Donny wove his way around tables, waving the voucher and milking the moment, playing to the handful of poker players who had come in and were standing at the back of the bar, shaking their heads.

By the time Gerry and Barry got to the bar Donny was outside, grabbed before his third lap of the bar, a shoulder each, by two ex-miners, who were walking him straight out the main door. He was smiling through bloodied teeth, being held against a wall, when Barry got to him.

"*OK boys, c'mon, no need for this, he's just a daft laddie,*" he said, holding up both palms and trying to get between Donny and the two Civvy members.

There was a pause before the ex-miner holding Donny at arm's length bounced him off the wall once, and then turned, muttering, "*Fucking eejit*", as both Civvy members walked back to the front door. They stomped in as Gerry came out. He looked over at Donny, assessing the damage to his mouth, and to the poker club's chances of continuing at the Civvy. Donny rubbed at his mouth, the back of his hand showing three small squares of duct tape. He read online that it was the most effective, and cheapest treatment for the warts that he was constantly battling with. At the tables, some players suspected it was a con, to get out of dealing, but nobody wanted to take the chance of catching Donny's warts.

"*Ah, for fucks sake Bagman, I was only winding up the old ones, gi'en them a bit of excitement in there*", Donny said, spitting blood and smiling as Barry took his turn to pin him against the wall. (Barry was The Bagman; a joke that was funny only to new players. The reference, to his day job as a debt recovery officer for Scottish Power, was now out of date since he had moved to sales, but the joke persisted because it was a lazy joke whenever he won a major pot and scooped up his chips-"*The Bagman collects his dues etc.*".)

Barry eased his grip and Donny stood back, pulling his shirt back into place. Barry knew that it was pointless, a total waste of his energy to talk to Donny about what he had done. Many better men and women than him had tried over the years, first at school and then later in every one of Donny's short term jobs, and short term relationships that he had blown.

Gerry kept it short. He told Donny to go home and not to come back next week. To shut him up and soften the blow, he took Donny's voucher back into the bar and collected his £250, thrown in a pile of loose notes on the bar in silence.

Two emergency Civil Service Club Committee meetings followed that week. A vote to stop non Civvy members playing the Wild West and a vote on ending poker nights completely were both narrowly defeated, but a vote to bar Donny from the building was unanimously passed. Gerry was asked to tell Donny that he was being suspended for a period of six months for, *"conduct that in the opinion of the Committee rendered him unfit for membership, or attendance as a guest of a member"*, which was section 11(a) of the Civil Service Club Byelaws. Gerry phoned Donny the same day and told him that he was barred for six months from the Wednesday poker for behaving like an arse in the Civvy. Gerry hung up before Donny could respond.

Two weeks before he was barred, there had been an error on the bar code scanning at Tesco's Superstore in Perth on a Wednesday night. Three crates of six-pack Budweiser were selling for nine pounds, instead of twenty seven. One text from a poker player's brother in Tesco's sparked ten others and word got round the poker tables in less than two minutes. In the middle of the game, phone calls were made to wives, brothers, mothers and stay-at-home friends. Soon the poker club looked like a plane full of passengers about to crash, speed dialling contact lists. All orders and pleadings were over in six minutes, apart from Donny's.

He phoned his skint and disabled father first, as the only home-based link in a complicated, but coordinated plan. Torn from an evening of English soaps on TV, his father was despatched to the nearby Tesco's to rendezvous with Colin, Donny's cousin (transport) and Donny's girlfriend, Natalie (cash). Nine crates of Bud and forty minutes later Donny's father was back home. For Donny, an otherwise slick operation was spoiled only by the drunken fight between him and his cousin the following night, after they'd had some of the Budweiser. They argued and then took a few swings at each other over what had, or had not happened between Colin and Natalie in the back of Colin's Vauxhall Combo van after they had dropped off the beer, Donny's father and his wheelchair.

In all of the time that Gerry had run the poker club, only two players apart from Donny had been asked to leave. For the other two is was permanent. They were caught colluding while playing on the same table, and then later of dipping chips at the break. At the table, they worked by sending signals to each other about the strength of their hands, to maximise their collective chip stack before the nine o'clock break, then added to their stacks by dipping a few high denomination chips from the chip boxes. One would distract Gerry with some questions about the computer or the scoring, while the other took a handful of chips from the box. Eagle-eyed Christopher was the first one to get suspicious, after the two players, between them, knocked out a string of players. With more eyes watching them the following week, their system was quickly busted. Gerry had a quiet word and asked them not to come back. Word got out quickly. Cheating at poker in a professional game was seen as something vaguely daring; being a poker outlaw and outwitting the casino, busting the bank in an ingenious scam and making off with millions. It was Monte Carlo glamorama. In an amateur game, where everybody just turned up and took their chances, cheating, and taking money from players who had worked for it made cheaters the worst kind of scum. It was stealing money from your own people while pretending to be friendly. It was the lowest forms of deception. It was worse than housebreaking in the same area where you lived, worse than dipping purses from people you knew and on a par with mugging drunks. The two barred players were local building site workers. They were blanked in the street by other poker players and everyone else who heard what they had done.

On the night of his return to the Civvy after his six month ban, Donny did a tour around the poker tables, high-fiving seated players and telling them how much they had missed him. Later he had to be pinned against a wall, by Gerry this time, to stop him going into the main bar, and to stop him shouting, loud enough to be heard, about the great weekend that he had in

Glasgow spending his £250 puggie winnings.

CHAPTER 9

Crazy Tahoe

Crazy Tahoe is a variation of Texas Hold'em with two differences. Both the black twos (2♠ and 2♣) are wild cards, and each player gets three cards instead of two to start. Players must discard one card, face down, after the flop, when the three community cards have been put on the table. The wild twos can represent any card that a player chooses, whether they are in a player's hand or face up, as any of the five community cards on the table. In this variation, the two lowest value cards in the pack become the highest. If a player is holding two black twos in his hand, he cannot be beaten.

When the names for the tables went up on the big screen at the start of the night there were some that most players looked for. Stevie and Russell, or Welsh and Boyd at the same table meant that everyone would have to wait twenty minutes for one to knock the other out before everyone else got a chance to play. As part of his game, Russell also did poor impersonations of any the player who knocked him out of the tournament. They were so poor in that if you were not sitting at the table and had not seen who had knocked him out, you would have difficulty naming the person that he was impersonating. He'd combine these antics with a swearing rage at the player for stupid or lucky play as he left the table. If Kodiak or Sleeve was at the table it was good to have something to listen to on earphones, because it was going to be loud, very loud. Having any of the top five players in the league at the table slowed the game down, with everyone taking all the thinking time available before making any moves. Thinking how to clock up points by taking players out, and how to avoid taking on big stacks at the table and going out themselves.

Finally, players looked up at the screen to see who had the serious bad luck of having Rab on the table. Baseball caps and dark glasses were useless. Earphones, no matter how high the volume, no matter how good the noise cancelling, were not going to stop Rab affecting your game.   Any carefully thought out tight-play and check-raise strategies were going to need maximum concentration.

Rab was also Frank the Penguin, but not when he was in earshot. The T-shirts that he wore at the tables would be retro in five years' time, but until then they were just-missed-the-boat, charity shop jaded. They showed lists of tour dates on the back and the faded screen print logos of bands that had broken up or were now playing pubs instead of stadiums on the front. Rab didn't care about music, didn't own a music player of any kind or a collection of songs in some cloud. He went for the name. Something solid was good. He wore T-shirts from *Hard Stuff, Steeler, 44 Magnum,* or names that got him a second look, like minor bands that had gone bust - *Nuns on the Dole* or *Rubbing My Nipple for Luck.*

His favourite, least washed T-shirt, and the only one he had ever bought new, showed the smiling face of Diamond Dan, The Orange Man. This was a square jawed, Buzz Lightyear lookalike, created by the Orange Order of Scotland as the face of a publicity campaign to educate the public about the rich heritage of the Order and its place in history. The name of the Protestant superhero had been chosen by Northern Ireland schoolchildren. "Diamond Dan, The Orange Man" had narrowly beaten "Sash Gordon" in a close competition.

Rab was a seasonal plumber. In the winter months he charged pathologically high rates for emergency 24 hour call outs, and survived the rest of the year on the profits and subcontracted jobs from his few remaining contacts in the building trade.

He had an online ad in the local Business Directory. This assured customers that McMurdo Plumbing and Heating was both CIPHE and SNIPEF licensed, which had been the case at one point, three years previously. The two colour ad showed a chunky, smiling workman with clean overalls and spanner in hand, urging customers to *"Remember the name!"* Rab did own a set of tools, and a call out to your home was indeed memorable. Polite customers who had work done by Rab, nearly always in emergencies, put the lingering, fetid smell down to something that had been in the blockage, or had built up in a leak in the drains. At the poker table however there was no such alternative explanation; Rab didn't wash much and he stank. He smelled like ear wax, a lot of ear wax that had been collected and kept somewhere warm for a while. Players caught a waft when he moved the air around, when he was dealing or as he moved to take chips out of the pot. Any comments from players too new or too drunk got the standard response from Rab.

"Fuck off – that's hard work you're smelling...".

Sitting at the table, Rab always looked as if he was just about to stand up, or launch across and head-butt the player opposite. His upper body remained tense for the entire game, leaning forward. This spooked many new players, distracted by Rab's pose, thinking that there was some major history of aggression between Rab and someone else at the table. A combination of the waves of stale sweat and the air of menace caused old and new players alike at Rab's table to fold hands that they would normally play, or go outside for a break with the smokers even when they didn't smoke.

Finally divorced, in a case that redefined acrimony, Rab had moved back in with his mother. He had a daughter he never saw, but wanted to, living with an ex-wife he never wanted to see, ever. His mother had gained local hero status ten years previously when the national media covered her campaign against paedophiles, released from prison, being accommodated in a local housing scheme. Spurred on by the promise of more tabloid coverage, she had organised protest marches which quickly went awry. The photos on the inside page of the redtops showed the graphical challenges of using bedsheets as banners and also the variety of spellings for "paedophiles". The campaign ended in farce two months later when one of the protesters spray-painted a paediatrician's house.

Based on an instant and permanent assessment, Rab categorised other players at the table as good guys or complete wanks. He spoke little at the table, other than to grunt, or to add to one of his partisan rants from the week before. Talking to no-one in particular at the table, he would introduce some new, *"pure factual"* information to back up his claims, which other players may or may not have heard the week before, depending on where they were sitting. They were conspiracy theories – although they were very much more than theories to Rab - about the police, the courts, the Scottish education system, football referees and the Scottish Football Association. There were gems of information that Rab *"just knew"* and would resort to when anyone drunk enough challenged him and it looked like his theories might collapse in the face of information that was even more *"factual"* than his own.

"You can argue with opinions, bud, but you can't argue with pure facts," he would say, and the argument was closed, in Rab's mind at least. He had special, insider detail that was so irrefutable but equally so confidential that the details and the source of the facts could not be disclosed to anyone not committed to the Cause.

"Did you know that the bastarding Council – that's the Council that we're paying for, by the way", said Rab, looking up at the big screen as if he was reading it there, *"have just limited the number of marches going through the town on weekends?"*

Players at the table who still had cards checked them again, and players who had folded looked toward the muck pile of cards in the middle of the table, longingly, wishing they still had cards in their hand to look at.

"See, that's an affront to my human rights, right there, restricting my freedom to celebrate my heritage in a traditional Protestant way", Rab continued.

"Yeah, walking past a chapel, banging a drum at a Catholic funeral-that's very

traditional," muttered Russell, just loud enough for Stevie to hear.

On Rab's left hand the letters U, V and F covered three consecutive knuckles. The Ulster Volunteer Force had officially ended its armed campaign in Northern Ireland in May 2007 after 41 years, and the name was only shouted now by groups of hooded-up 14 year olds throwing stones and bottles at police cars or at any group of 14 year olds who would throw stones back. The UVF nickname of Blacknecks was derived from their original uniform, which included black polo neck jumpers. Rab didn't go so far as to wear the uniform, although the tide mark of unwashed dirt around Rab's neck suggested that he was carrying on the tradition.

Rab's right hand knuckles read F, T and P, with a botched letter covered up on his third finger, between the T and the P, where Rab's lack of left hand dexterity with a bottle of India ink and a needle stuck in a propelling pencil had let him down. Fuck The Pope was a slogan that had lost most of its shock value over the fifty years that it had been daubed on toilet and lock up garage walls, and now on Facebook, mostly by those who were, according to Rab, "*denied the opportunity to protest their repression*".

New anti-sectarianism legislation had made illegal any songs and gestures that could be regarded as offensive acts. This included "threatening communications" or signs. These further attempts by the papist cabal to outlaw the promotion of the Cause did not worry Rab, in fact he welcomed the recognition that these moves brought. The fact that parliament, the Big Brother of clampdown, was seeking to appease the masses and deny basic civil liberties to law abiding citizens, was an admission that the Cause was again on the rise. Like all good armies, the Cause was one step ahead, always prepared for what their opponents might do.

Those committed to the Cause had a *strategy*, a get-out-of-jail card, passed around only by word of mouth at meetings, for those who needed to know. It was a long term plan that required Rab to campaign every day against the tyranny of being persecuted in this own country, by his own government and its lackeys. He was ready to stand for the Cause, to stand for freedom of expression and fight the new repression. When the police caught up with Rab and his tattoos – "*Only a matter of time, in't it, before the biggest gang in the world come for me again?*", he would give up, "*nobody and nothing in the interrogation - nobody and no amount of torture would bust me*". His knuckle tattoos, the meetings he attended at a selection of upstairs' rooms in local pubs, and the collections taken at those meetings were all for the same Cause. He would tell that to those police scum and the scheming, lawyer bastards. He was looking forward to seeing those fenian lawyers' faces in court at the trial when he sprung it on them. When he told them that the collections, the money and the tattoos were all for FTP, Frank The Penguin, and the UVF, Union of Volunteers for Frank, who had chosen to sponsor the eponymous penguin at Edinburgh Zoo. He would be pissing himself, watching them trying to build a criminal case against him on that.

Why Rab bothered to turn up and play poker was a mystery to everybody at the tables, except Arthur, who remembered from their days in the Mad Hotel. Like all good players, Rab mixed up his play, keeping it varied. But the variations that he used were not to be found in any book of poker strategy. The bets he made were unrelated to pot odds, implied odds and the rank value of the cards in his hand. He had a durable and unwavering belief that the miracle cards he needed would appear on the next turn.

He bet on hands that just "*seemed good to him*". This unsettled many players, who were used to having respect shown when they raised with a pot sized bet or went all-in with a lot of chips to steal a pot. The result of having Rab, his rank body odour and his wild betting at the table was the unpredictable movement of piles of chips, with top players being knocked out because the three consecutive diamonds or the two fives and a nine needed for a full house occasionally turned up for Rab at the right time.

Only Arthur knew that Rab put a lot of faith in diamonds. It was Rab's belief that the secret to winning at the The Mad Hotel games was to trust your diamonds, always, and they would repay your faith. Any pocket pair that included a diamond, any face card that was a diamond, any two diamonds in his hand and Rab was going to bet against anybody, through the flop, through the turn card and all the way to the river, regardless of any odds, regardless of what was showing on the table. It was his unquestioning loyalty in Diamond Dan, The Orange Man, Rab's Superhero. To the River and Beyond…

Poker was the only time in Rab's week or in his adult life when he would knowingly sit down at a table with papes. He could usually spot them, as part of his instant assessments. Like a Homeland Security list of terrorist characteristics, Rab had a list of definite and probably signs. Black hair combined with dark eyelashes and blue eyes– probable; red hair and green eyes – probable; skin colour darker without tanning – probable; Irish accent from anywhere but East Belfast – definite; wearing anything green above the waist – definite. Normally, he would avoid talking to them, listening to them or even looking at them. They would be blanked as if they didn't take up any space in Rab's field of vision.

But that night he was struggling. His normally infallible sensors were sending mixed signals. He couldn't work out if the two Latvians sitting at his table were papes, foreign prods or communists. His confusion was made worse by not knowing if communists could be papes at the same time as being communists. For once, he wasn't sure enough of his facts.

One of them - Benedictus, Rab thought he was called - had just re-raised Rab's initial pre-flop bet. With half his stack now in the middle, Rab had a decision to make. He could go all in with the rest of his chips and see if Bendy–fucking-dickus had the balls to call him, or he could fold, back down and be a complete woose. Not much of a decision, really. He looked at his cards a final time and then thumped the rest of his chips into the middle, in a multi-coloured column. "*All in*", he said, leaning further across the table and staring at the Latvian.

Bendictus asked for a count and Rory, who was dealing, had to reach across to re-stack Rab's jumble of chips into piles to see how much he had. "*Another 1400 to you, Bendiks*", Rory said. Rab moved back in his chair, arms folded, still staring. The Latvian separated 1400 chips, put them to one side, then counted what would be left in his stack if he lost.

"*I will call*," he said, annunciating each word, and putting the chips into a single column and standing it beside the chips in the middle.

Rab turned over 6♦ 8♦ and stood up behind his chair. This was the standard all-in, ready-to-leave-the-table pose, although Rab didn't take his jacket off the back of his chair. He believed. Diamond Dan would come through, ride to the rescue once again. Even when the Latvian turned over his pair of tens, Rab noted that neither them were diamonds, which increased his own chances of a flush. In Rab's world of miracle card predictions, he had a lot of outs.

Three more diamonds to hit the board would give him his flush. He even had straight flush possibilities, and a straight chance. A pair of sixes or eights on the board would give him trips. Believing was what was needed. The flop came 3♦ J♣ and K♠. Rab still believed. His straight possibilities had gone, but two more diamonds would do it, or runner-runner sixes or eights. The turn card was 3♣, but Rab still didn't lift his jacket. Only when Rory turned over the river 10♦ did Rab move, turning away from the table and dragging his jacket off the back of the chair in a single movement as he went. Rab decided not to shake hands with Benedictus, just in case he was a pape. The ten foot square of blue light dominating the room showed just seven players left from thirty nine starters. The data projector was linked to the PokerMax Poker League Software on Gerry's laptop. The tournament information was displayed on a tombstone-shaped panel of light, curling up the brickwork on the vaulted wall. As well as the player count, it showed the number of players left, current blind level, next blind level, time remaining on current blind level, total time played, time to next break, average chip stack and prize money to be paid to first five players.

When the game came down to the final table that night there were two baseball caps, two pairs of Blue Shark sunglasses, one collar up, one nail biter and Arthur. Simon had paused long enough to get hurry-up sighs from three players, then bet four times the big blind. Two players folded and the betting was on Stevie.

"You only relax when you've got a big stack, did you know that?", said Russell from across the table, goading him.

"Aye, well that's where you're wrong again, poker smartarse – I only relax when I've got a bigger stack than you," Stevie fired back, without looking up, tugging on his baseball cap for emphasis, *"and don't talk to me when you're not in the hand, dickwad."*

Stevie looked at Simon for any sign of weakness, saw none, and flicked his two cards into the mucked pile in the centre of the table, muttering, *"I'll let you have this one Simon. Fold".*

Russell continued his chat now that Stevie was out of the hand.

"Well you were looking well relaxed on Saturday night when I saw you with yer brother."

At this, Stevie sat up, pushing his cap back on his head.

"Aye, we'd been to his hoos for a bit of wacky backy vaping before we came out. Did ye know that if ye keep the heat low enough in the bowl and don't go daft on the inhaling, ye get the buzz, but ye don't take in aw they toxins and stuff? It's practically a health food!" said Stevie, laughing to himself.

"Aw well, that'll wipe out the damage of those forty fags a day that you're smoking then, eh?" said Russell, getting a laugh from a few at the table.

"I found a really good way to relax myself", said Simon looking between Stevie

and Russell as he scooped up the chips from the pot.

"My wife's hairdresser passed it on, actually".

Everyone at the table slunk a bit lower in their chairs, looking at the big screen or across to the cash tables, avoiding eye contact with Simon.

He went on, oblivious to the signs.

"You breathe in for a count of twenty, slowly, right?" Simon said, looking around the players for a nod of interest.

"Then you hold it for a count of just five, before breathing out for a count of fifteen. The trick is that you do it all through your nose, and you can either have your eyes open or closed. It's pretty cool actually, and the effect lasts for a while – you should try it!"

Simon finished, raising his voice, looking around the whole table for any sign of interest.

Stevie couldn't decide if this guy was taking the piss about his vaping with his brother, or if Simon was just being his usual posh, wanky self. He decided to leave it, and ignore him, hoping that Simon would just shut up. Why did he have to keep chipping in with his stupid fucking stories, every week, trying to be "one of the lads" when he was never, *ever* going to be that? Fuck knows how old he was – it was impossible to tell with rich folk like him who were like a car that had been kept in the garage; no mileage on the clock. He wore those stupid long shorts in some tweedy material that looked itchy as fuck, and shoes that you could hear coming. And what was it with the turned up Elvis collar- it was poker they were here for, not fucking karaoke. Somebody should have a quiet word and tell him that it just wisnae cool to talk at that volume *all the time*, like everything he had to say was something everybody just *had* to hear.

Simon brought a different card protector to the table each week, and every one had a story. There was always some newbie naïve enough to ask and then have to sit and look interested as Simon bored him senseless. For the other players it was like watching someone walking towards an open manhole cover.

Mini paper weights in the form of animals were his favourite. He could and would tell you where he bought each one, how he got it back to Perth, whether flights to Scotland had been delayed and what the weather was like. Other card protectors had stories that lasted for four hands and more. The wooden mouse with clogs on, that some girlfriend had given him for his birthday, was the first part of a sequence of gifts that ended with an airline ticket to Amsterdam.

Tonight it was a mini Eiffel tower with King Kong hanging on it, and he had already waved it about, trying to get a response. Stevie knew that if nobody asked about his Eifel tower Simon would change his look-at-me strategy and move up to something more desperate. He would start muttering under his breath, then escalate it until somebody said *"What?"*. Or he would look at his phone, and say, *"Oh my God"*, or *"I don't believe this!"*. It only took one person, anybody, just one, to look at him inquiringly and he was off on some rambling story that nobody wanted to hear. What. A. Fanny.

Chat amongst the players had stopped.

Stevie had raised to 300, Russell re-raised to 1200 and the betting was on Arthur. He looked up at the table over his bifocals, flat called the 1200 raise and returned to his book.

It was never less than 500 pages, always science fiction and always second hand, from the same cancer charity shop. Arthur was reading it, but other eyes were on it, despite the need to ignore it and focus on the game. Arthur rubbed his earlobe between finger and thumb, then silently turned a page. Stevie turned his Las Vegas betting chip (from eBay rather than Nevada) over and over in his hand, considering the 900 re-raise as other players folded around the rest of the table, calculating how much he had to put in in relation to how much he could win, then thinking whether he felt good about his cards. He rocked imperceptibly on his seat, one hand on his two cards on the table, trying to sense any vibe, any good or bad karma, coming from the cards. It was difficult to sense anything. Kodiak, sitting next to him, had only his right earpiece in, forcing the rest of the table to listen to the music blasting out of his left earpiece, dangling on his chest. It sounded like someone wearing a suit of armour was falling down a very long flight of stairs.

Arthur took a book each week. The way he thought about it was like a thoroughbred with blinkers. He just needed to see what was in front. The swearing across the room, the aggressively slapped bets and raises, and the speech plays were all just scenes at the side of the track he was on. He could follow the plot in the book and on the table equally well, and never be out of the book long enough for emotions to interfere with his game. He experienced a strange merging of worlds. He became the avenging sci-fi hero of the poker table, with special powers to conquer adversity. In his books, he favoured quiet heroes over guys with muscles. Who needed pecs when you were good at what you did? You could get the job done and not make a big deal about it. Sweep all aside, then move on, quietly.

Players folded around the table to Stevie, who muttered "*bluffing bastard*" under his breath and called Russell's raise, pushing his black 500 and four white 100 chips into the middle.

The flop showed J♥, 4♥, 10♥, and Stevie said, "*Raise*", immediately, pushing 2000 chips forward before the three cards were even straightened on the table.

"*Have you hit your flush with that flop, ya bastard, or do you just want rid of me?*"

Russell said, holding his two cards an inch above the table for a few seconds, and looking at Stevie, before throwing his cards into the muck pile. Stevie said nothing and pulled his cap lower on his face, squinting at Arthur under the peak.

Arthur, looked up from his book at the flop and Stevie's raise, put a finger in the book to keep his place, stacked all of his chips into two neat columns with his other hand and slid them onto the green felt.

"*All in*", he said, "*for 7600*".

Everyone went quiet, expect Kodiak.

"*Ha. You got caught with your hand in the cookie jar, there Stevie boy, trying to steal that one?*" he blurted out, too loud and with too much glee.

"*Shut up if you're not in the hand*," Stevie shot back from under the cap.

Stevie was trying to play mean and aggressive, representing Hearts or representing a high pair, but his promising A♦ 10♦ starting hand was now just a pair of tens with a decent kicker and, he suspected, was now worthless. Arthur's style was to go all in with a pile that high only when he had something strong. He didn't do much bluffing. Stevie was in for two thirds of his stack. If he folded the blinds for the next hand would leave him with a chip and a chair.

Could Arthur have a King-Queen and be chasing the straight? Unlikely, going on past form. Was he sitting with a pair of Jacks or a pair of tens? Less likely. But he wouldn't have stayed in for the initial 1200 raise with nothing. Did he have an Ace in his hand or already have two Hearts and a made flush? Much more likely, going on past form. Whatever Arthur had in his hand, Stevie's knew that his own hand was now weak, with all the other possibilities out there. He might hit another ten, giving him trips, or some miracle pair of Aces, but that was about it. He was left without a choice.

"*I've just got a thousand at the back Arthur, but I'm going to call, although I think you're well ahead.*"

Stevie pushed in the remainder of this chips in and turned over his A♦ 10♦. Arthur took back 5600 chips and turned over his suited A♥ Q♥; the nut flush. Only two aces or two tens, one after the other - odds off the scale - would save Stevie now and he knew realistically that he was drawing dead. The turn card was a meaningless 2♦ and there was another Heart on the river. Stevie was already on his feet before the river card was dealt. He shook

Arthur's hand quickly, punched Russell's shoulder and then Kodiak's, just too hard, and stormed off to the bar.

"*If I had stayed in,*" said Simon, "*I would have had...*"

He was drowned out by a chorus of "*Could have, would have, should have - but you didnae stay in!*"

Arthur pulled the chips that he had just won towards him and started to stack them in columns of a thousand each.

Russell looked round the piles of chips in front of each player left on the table, without looking at the players, and realised that he now had the shortest stack. With only six players left, they were now on the bubble for the money; the next player out got none and everybody else was cashing. For Russell, to go out on the bubble was even worse than being the first player out in the tournament, early in the evening. To be bubbled meant that you had spent two hours playing, concentrating, making your moves, just to be the nearly man. He had to double up his stack quickly or he was the next man on his feet.

Russell knew that Kodiak wasn't going to hear anything he said, and Simon would launch into some more of his fanny prattling if he spoke to him. The two with the Blue Shark sunglasses were Latvians, who didn't speak much Scottish. So that left Arthur for him to try to noise up, to give himself some kind of chance, some edge to take out a player and end up in the top five money.

"*You don't play poker for the money Arthur, do you?*" Russell said, pushing his cap to the back of his head and shuffling for the next deal. Russell knew that bending the cards up into the bridge in the riffle shuffle reduced the lifetime of the cards, but he also knew that the move got him respect at the table, and sometimes an edge, especially with new players, who mistook fancy shuffling for poker skill. It took Arthur a moment to look up, hearing his name. He put his index finger on the line on the page that he was reading and turned to

Russell.

"*I play poker for succour Russell,*" he said.

"*Aye, and there's nae shortage of suckers come here, that's for sure,*" Kodiak shouted over the volume of his earpiece, shaking in his chair, laughing at his own joke and not caring if anybody else did. Russell ignored him and continued to look at Arthur.

"*So it doesn't matter if you don't win this game then, eh? Is that what you're saying Arthur? The money doesn't matter - you just come along for the craich, for the ruthless banter?*"

Arthur slipped his bookmark, a bus ticket, into a page and put the book under his seat.

"*Well it was a choice between poker on a Wednesday or Bums and Tums Fitness on a Thursday, and I didn't fancy that,*" Arthur continued, now looking directly at Russell.

"*So that's why I'm here tonight at the final table.*"

"*Oh, so you aim to be at the final table? So that means that you do play for the money after all Arthur?*" Russell continued.

Arthur paused, glanced up at the blue screen on the wall, and switching to a clipped American accent, and talking out one side of his mouth.

"*See, Fast Eddie Felson can play big-money poker for forty straight hours on nothing but talent kid, and if you're coming with him you better be ready to go all the way.*"

Kodiak stopped chewing his gum, his mouth open, and looked over at Arthur and Russell, as did the two Latvians, who had been chatting. Russell had seen Arthur come out with this off-the-wall, weird stuff at the tables before, speaking in that same voice, saying things that meant nothing to anybody at the table, or nothing that he could understand anyway. Was it supposed to be funny, or was Arthur trying for a Simon look-at-me moment? Russell didn't think so. He didn't know if it was Arthur's attempt to get an edge, to spook other players. If fact he didn't know what the fuck Arthur was talking about and with everyone now looking at him for a reply, he was wishing he had tried to wind up Kodiak or one of the Latvians instead.

In the awkward silence, Russell re-shuffled the pack again, bending the cards nearly in half, looking up at the screen, to see if there was something there that had set Arthur off.

"*Aye, right Arthur,*" he said, just for something to fill the gap.

Arthur picked up his book and went back to reading.

Arthur liked playing poker. All were welcome at the Church of Lies. Worshipping at the Church of Lies; that's what Gerry called it. "*This is the Church of Lies*", he'd say at the start the night, "*now shut the fuck up and deal.*" This was the club in-joke. One week, just after he started, a newbie had misheard, "*Shuffle up and deal*", and the joke had stuck.

It was honest lies, Arthur thought, straight lying and deception by players trying to take his chips, with no pretence that it was anything else. There was nobody there being paid to lie to him, to tell him what he wanted or needed to hear, or even worse, what they *thought* he needed to hear. No support services, just the ruthless banter, as Russell had said.

Some players might sugar coat it, sure. Welsh would tell him how well he had played a hand, or a game, or nod admiringly at Arthur's chip stack, sticking out his bottom lip and raising his eyebrows. Others would draw him in, talking about what was going on in the town, on the TV, on the cash tables. Some were obvious, like Russell, and some were smarter, like Boyd, who would distract the table with wild tales you couldn't ignore and throw in equally wild bets to control the table.

But Arthur knew it was all part of the game and everybody in the room knew it too. They all shared in the same joke, the same deception. It was all about finding ways of moving chips in your direction, willing them to be pushed into the middle by other players and then back out to add to your stack. He had learned from playing at the Mad Hotel and now on

Wednesdays when to push, when to call and when to fold, by judging probabilities. He looked at the cards in his hands, the cards on the table, how many chips he had, how many chips the person pushing chips had and, lastly, who was raising. He did a quick calculation and then made his move. It was nothing fancy. He was pleased when he won a hand or placed in the top five for money, but he wasn't devastated on the weeks that he didn't. There was still the ruthless banter to enjoy and he would sometimes tune in, between games, like searching for a radio station that was broadcasting something that would hold his interest for a few minutes at least.

Everybody sitting at the tables wanted to be there. Nobody was being detained. Even Donny, borderline arrestable any night of the week, except Wednesday. He kicked over his chair most weeks, but he always came back and sat on it. Even Rab, taking dogs' abuse for how he smelled, how he looked and what he said, came back for more straight lying. Even Rab and his world of protestant cowboys and catholic Indians and papal conspiracies. Frank the Penguin, Rabid Rab, Diamond Dan; there was a seat in the Church of Lies even for him.

There was an order of service at the Church of Lies; dealer, small blind, big blind, play or fold in turn around the table. If you could follow the order and play by those basic rules, you were welcome to join and stay, no other requirements, all previous sins forgiven. All worshipped at the Church of Lies, every week, spending time and money and trying to convince themselves and others that what they believed in was real; that it was not just a sham, a faith in the false hope of winning.

On the next hand Russell smiled as the Latvian with the unpronounceable name went head to head with his fellow countryman and took him out with pocket Queens against pocket Jacks.

"*Cha-ching!*" Russell said, "*we're all in the money now boys*," as Bendiks stood and left for a cash table. Russell lifted a chair out and the five remaining players spaced out their chairs to give themselves more elbow room at the table. Arthur put his book on the floor again to take his turn at dealing. Two hands later, Kodiak chased his flush all the way to the river and a fifth Heart didn't appear, letting Russell double up on a pair of eights. Kodiak then went on tilt and bet the remainder of his chips blind on the next hand, losing out to Simon's Ace high. Kodiak made as little contact as possible with Simon's hand as he left the table.

Then there were four: Russell, Arthur, Simon and Meinekinus. Kodiak picked up his fifth place money from the table where the computer sat, and used the mouse to record that he had been taken out by Simon with two clicks on the list of names. The blue screen showed the blind levels, and the timer counting down to the next doubling of the blinds.

Arthur dealt again, bet four times the big blind when the action came around to him and Simon and Meinekinus folded to the bet.

"You got the small pocket pair and don't want to see any more cards on the board, Arthur, eh?" Russell said, fishing for any information in Arthur's reaction, but getting only a half-smile and no eye contact.

He prodded again, *"Will you show your cards if I fold?"* he said, looking at Arthur, who was now without his book to retreat to.

"I'll show you my cards if you call, Simon." Arthur said, politely, getting a laugh, despite the fact that the same question and answer was heard most weeks at the tables.

Russell did a calculation on his chips and folded, not willing to make his final stand on the hill on what he had in his hand – small suited connectors. He decided that he could hang on and finish third at least.

No mates at the table; just players eyeing up your stack of chips and working out the best bet to make it theirs at the right time. When Russell said, *"You'll be bullying us all with that stack you've won,"* Arthur understood, everybody at the table understood that it wasn't a compliment on Arthur's play. It was clumsy but it was honest lying, to try to relax Arthur and give Russell more of a chance of chipping away at his stack.

There was not a pretend mate in sight, Arthur knew. There was no one telling you that your welfare was his number one concern, nodding in the right places, encouraging you to dig up feelings, work through the stages, while he shifted the cuff of his white shirt, surreptitiously checking his watch to see how long before he could stop pretending, make his excuses and move on to the next schmuck.   When Simon or Russell or Kodiak spoke to him at the table it was for information about his hand, or to check his reaction to a move they made; plain and simple. It was honest lying that everyone understood.

Meinekinus looked down at the A♥Q♣ in his hand and pushed all in.

Russell, who was again short stack at the table, called immediately and turned over A♦Q♥.

"*Split pot boys, not worth fighting about,* " Simon said quickly, burning the top card and dealing out the first three, 5♦, 9♦ a 10♠. He burned the next card and dealt the turn card, 3♦.

"*Three diamonds - ah, now, that makes it a bit more interesting,*" he said, putting the deck down on the table and sitting back, pausing for effect.

"*Just deal the last card Simon, and stop fucking about*", Russell said, through tight lips, conscious that the blinds were about to go up again, but more irritated that Simon was trying to milk the moment.

Simon burned the final card before turning over the river card with what he hoped was a poker croupier's flourish. It was 8♦, giving Russell the unlikely Ace flush in diamonds.

Meinekinus picked up his A♥Q♣ and threw them on the table, "*Sudi!*" he said.

"*Hey, sorry about that one bud,*" said Russell, shrugging and looking anything but.

"*That was a bad beat,*" he said, looking not at Meinekinus but across the table at his few remaining chips.

With the blinds increasing every ten minutes, Meinekinus lasted just two more hands before being blinded out. Then there were three.

The chat died down again and chips moved around the table for the next three hands, with Simon, Russell and Arthur defending their big blinds, but nobody making any significant moves.
Simon had the lowest tolerance for silence.

"*We're all playing pretty tight and cagey here guys, eh? Not like earlier, eh, with all the jokes and plenty of chips swishing around the table? I guess it's time to concentrate on the big money, eh?*"

Arthur slipped his bus ticket into *The Hyperion Cantos* again and put the book under his chair to take his deal. "*The animals looked at each other differently when the water hole dried up,*" he said quietly.

Russell looked up immediately at the blue screen, then down at Arthur's book. He really wanted to know, but he didn't want to show his ignorance by asking where it came from, or what it meant. It was easier just to ignore it, he decided, to treat it like Kodiak's loose earpiece, squawking out maximum volume metal, or like Rab's rants about his life on planet protestant. It was best to just tune it out.

But Russell did want to know, and every time Arthur did it, he wanted to know even more. He might settle for knowing if Arthur was talking to the rest of the table, or just to himself. That would probably be enough. But he wanted to ask more, even knowing that he wouldn't understand if Arthur explained, or knowing that the answer would be something that he could have well done without, thank you very much Arthur.

The last time Russell had been at a final table with Arthur, Kodiak had been ribbing him about being so quiet, trying to push him off his even keel.

"*Softly, softly, catchee monkey – is that how you play it Arthur? You're like a wee*

Buddha sitting with the book there, watching it all happen, then making your move, eh? The quiet man of poker, trying to spook us all off our game Arthur. "

Arthur took it with smiles and nods, but Kodiak was relentless, wouldn't leave it, kept pecking away, trying to distract Arthur from his book and his game, asking if all Arthur's plays were coming out of his book, asking if it Arthur preferred reading a kid's book to talking to adults. At the time Russell thought that Kodiak had gone past the point where he was trying to unsettle Arthur and was getting irritated because Arthur wasn't reacting.

"You look as if you're enjoying playing the quiet man of poker Arthur, having fun without laughing, dancing on the inside, eh? You making us all wonder if.."

It was then that Arthur had looked up from his book, across at Kodiak and said with a smile, *"That's the problem with having bipolar disorder Kodiak – it's only fun half the time."*

It got uncomfortable laughs and made Kodiak the quietest man at the table, at least for the next two hands.

So Russell decided not to ask Arthur about the animals and the water hole.

As the blinds rose to near maximum level, Simon finally pushed all in, on a pocket pair of eights. A good shout, he thought, when they were only three handed. He was called by Arthur, who was on A♠ 9♣. The flop came 4♣ 9♥ 5♠ and turn and the river were both meaningless face cards. Arthur's pair of nines took the pot and Simon finished third.

"Ah, well boys, that's me for another week," Simon said, getting up.

"You've got to know when to hold them and know when to fold them, like Kenny Rogers says, eh? It's been a pleasure to sit at a poker table with you as always."

He reached across and shook Arthur's hand, then turned and fist bumped Russell.

"Let's all get together like this again next week," he finished, raising his pint and toasting Arthur and Russell. Russell had already started dealing.

Heads up with Arthur, who had at least twice the chips, was going to be a short game, Russell was thinking. He had enough chips for five big blinds left and playing heads up he was going to have to push and double up quickly, or be blinded out.

Arthur moved his chair, so that he was sitting opposite Russell and kicked his book under his seat. With heads up, the order of dealing changed, with the dealer being the small blind and acting first, before the flop, then acting last after the flop had been dealt. Christopher, who got very excited about explaining that rule to players, had come over to update Simon's elimination on the computer, and to give Simon his third place prize money. He offered to deal for Arthur and Russell, to speed up play, reminding them that the game had to finish in the next 15 minutes because that's when the building would be locked up.

"*Yeah, yeah, I know that Christopher,*" Russell said, irritated about being reminded of the same thing every fucking week. He held the two cards that he had been dealt against the table and bent back the top half of the cards to check them.

As he did so, Arthur said, "*I'm happy to split the cash and just play for the league points, if you like.*" Arthur put his hand over the two cards he had just been dealt, to let Russell know that he hadn't looked at them.

Russell looked up from his cards, first at Arthur's stack of chips then at Arthur. His first thought was that he had miscounted what Arthur had just won from Simon, but Arthur's neat piles confirmed that he had almost three times as many chips as he did. Russell could feel his heart rate increase, knowing that Arthur, and Christopher were waiting for his answer.

His next thought was that this was a new one from Arthur's bumper bag of tricks, to make Russell think about the money and not about the cards. Or maybe Arthur didn't fancy his chances against Russell in a heads up? Unlikely, Russell thought.

"*It would work out at eighty three pounds each, if that's what you were wondering,*" said Christopher, when Russell continued to hold his chin, looking at the chip stacks.

Russell ignored him and started talking to Arthur, just to give himself more time.

"So you would just chop the cash, now, like that, even though you're well ahead on chips?" Russell asked. *"You sure about that?"*

"I don't play for the money, Russell…"

"Yeah, yeah, I know Arthur, you play for the suckers, whatever that means." Russell said, getting more anxious about making a decision. *"You told us that before…."* he tailed off into silence again.

Christopher stopped shuffling and put the deck of cards down in the centre of the table.

"Well it would be a bit irregular, of course", he said, *"because the player who wins the tournament wins the first prize, and that prize would be the points and the money. What the winner does with his cash winnings would be up to him, of course…"*

"Yeah, thanks for that Christopher," Russell said, holding up one hand to stop Christopher distracting him.

Russell knew that he was in a good spot, but he started chewing the inside of his cheek because of the decision he had to make. He didn't have a problem with splitting the prize money; a guaranteed £83 in his pocket now, before any more cards were dealt, would be welcomed, and given the size of Arthur's chip stack it was logical to take up the offer. It was a no brainer. Plus he knew from experience that in a heads-up Arthur was hard to beat. He could just grind it out, play safe, and make his superior chip stack work for him. Russell had seen him do it week after week. Russell also knew that after the next few hands, the blinds would go up again and then he would be forced to push all his chips in on any two cards. The odds shouted take half the cash, now.

Deals were done in bigger games than this. Russell had seen in the World

Series Circuit. The last three players would look at the blinds, check their stack and decide to chop it three ways, rather than loose fifty thousand on the turn of a card.

All of that was straightforward. His dilemma was what to tell Kodiak and Stevie, and The Sleeve, if he asked. No pals at the table, no favours, dog eat dog – that was the rule. No matter who you played, you played to win, no exceptions, whether it was in the casino, here on the tables at the Civvy, or even in some vicious-friendly home game with your mates. You gave away nothing and you took nothing. You didn't hold back just because someone was a mate and was low stacked when you had the nuts – you gutted him and left him with nothing, skint and beaten. Even if you knew he was on his last tenner, you took it. Even if you knew he would have to sit and watch everybody else have a good time playing for two hours because he needed a lift home, you took all his chips anyway. No second thoughts about it. There were no exceptions because you knew that's what anybody else would do to you if he got the chance. Anybody except Arthur, that is.

Stevie had taken fifty quid off Russell once in a home game, inside the first half an hour. When Russell bought in again with his last fifteen quid, Stevie had made a point of going all-in every hand against him, until he put him out, then left him to scrounge taxi money off Gerry, just to get home. Stevie was a good mate, but when he played poker he treated his mates worse than fuckers that he hated. No pals at the table then. That was the rule.

Russell was holding his two cards, trying to think, trying to stop his heart beat racing, as Christopher and Arthur waited. How could dress this one up? How could he tell anybody who asked that Arthur had offered him half the cash and he had gone for it, like some poncey gentlemen's agreement?

He could tell Kodiak and Stevie that Arthur and him had been going back and forward with the chips, run out of time, ended up even, split the cash. But that wouldn't work because there were still fifteen minutes left. He could say that Arthur was a mug, say that he had shafted him for the cash, got him to chop the prize money when Russell was well behind. That might work, as long as somebody from the cash table didn't get busted in the next few minutes and stroll over to watch the final heads up, and see what was really happening. But none of it would work, he realised, because Mr Dudley-Do-Right Christopher was dealing and would he was bound to blab about how they had chopped the winnings, and how the rules allowed for it, even it was a bit irregular.

Stevie and Kodiak would rip the piss right out of him if they found out.

"*You and your pal Arthur split the cash did you, Russell*", he could hear them say.

"*A wee friendly game was it? When you two moving in together, going oot shopping to pick oot curtains for your wee house? Is he gonnae lend you some of his books to read at the table next week?*"

They would keep it up for weeks, months, every time there was a split pot on a hand, every time Arthur was at his table, every time Russell won any cash on the tables.

"*Not sharing that pot with yer wee pal Arthur tonight Russell? Maybe you should give him a call before you take it all for yourself, eh?*"

Fuck it. He couldn't do it.

He kept his eyes down on the table and said quietly, "*That's good of you, Arthur, but I'll just play it out to the end, I think.*"

"*That's OK, Russell. I just thought I'd offer,*" Arthur replied, looking at his cards for the first time.

Christopher dealt for them and the game was over eight minutes later. Russell raised on a K♣ Q♥, Arthur flat called, the flop came Q♦, 6♦, 8♥ and Russell pushed all in. Arthur had called the initial bet with a pair of eights and took all of Russell's chips with his set of eights. They shook hands quickly and Christopher got to his feet and went to the laptop to record the final result.

As Christopher opened the money box, to give out the cash to the two players, Russell could hear Stevie shout over from the cash table, "*Ah Russell, you didnae spunk away all those chips I gave you earlier and let wee Arthur beat ye in the heads-up, did ye? What a fucking woose, you are!*"

Arthur took the hundred pounds first prize and Russell had sixty-six. The cash game finished up and a few of the regulars stayed behind to pack up the chips and put folding poker tables back into bags.

Gerry gave Arthur a lift to the game on Wednesdays, on the understanding that he found his own way home, by lifts or by taxi, because neither of them knew when Arthur would be out of the main tournament and he didn't hang around to play on the cash tables. The numbers went from the high thirties, down to eight for a final table, then to last man standing. Gerry was always the real last man standing on a Wednesday, packing away the laptop and loading the aluminium cases of chips into the back of his car. Tonight Arthur was still around, with his winnings, helping with the tables, so Gerry offered to drop him off on his way home.

The lift to the poker was on the understanding that Arthur talked, but Gerry was not expected to answer. That was the deal. This was no unspoken agreement; Gerry had told Arthur after the first journey together that he had to concentrate on the driving and Arthur had asked if Gerry minded him talking as they drove. Gerry didn't mind; Arthur's chat was little different from having the radio on.

When he was playing, Arthur was in his book between hands. He would speak to say his hellos to those he knew, or to bounce back some attempt to get information about his cards. Sometimes he spoke as Arthur, and sometime as one of this poker personas, but some weeks he said next to nothing for the whole game.

He was a different Arthur in Gerry's car on the way to Perth. He talked from the time he clicked in his seatbelt until Gerry put on the hand brake in the car park at the Civvy. That night, as they left, turning onto the side road, out of the car park, Gerry checked his watch, thinking about how many hours sleep he might get before work. Arthur saw him look at his wrist and picked up his stream where he had left off on their arrival, almost four hours earlier.

"Who knows where the time goes, eh? Sandy Denny sang that. Don't know if you remember her Gerry? I don't think she knew the answer either. She had the voice of an angel did Sandy Denny, even on the scratchiest of vinyl you could still hear that. She had such a pure tone when she sang. Fell down a flight of stairs and banged her head – did you know that? It killed her about a month later. She just tripped. At least it wasn't *one of those heroin overdoses, or hanging on a doorknob glamourous deaths, eh? Her voice was like a musical instrument it was."*

Gerry waited for a gap in the traffic and turned right, onto the main road, picking up speed.

"Some people who say they're sane claim to have seen angels, Gerry, did you know that? Coloured mists and lights hanging about, three paces behind, following us around. But then some people say they've seen God as well, eh? I don't think so. Angels are not souls of people who have died, floating about, waiting for something to happen. That's crazy talk. No, I think some real people are angels."

"Like Melisa. She was an angel Gerry. You could tell when you saw her. Just meeting her, you knew, just knew there was something different. She looked like one, even when she was sleeping. She slept on her back, like something in a fairy tale. She hardly seemed to breathe. Gave me a fright a few times – I had to give her a shake just to check that she was still breathing. I thought you only did that with babies, you know, anxious parents reading too much about cot death. We had a laugh about that one. Aye, she was an angel. I know that sounds like crazy talk, but that's what I see when I look at all the photos. I've kept some old ones that I dig out sometimes. To be honest, it's fifty-fifty whether I end up sighing or crying after I've looked at them, but I just couldn't chuck them out."

Gerry was half listening, practised in tuning in and out, as they got up to cruising speed and the late night traffic thinned.

"We didn't get to go on honeymoon until a year after we were married. I don't know if I ever told you that Gerry?"

Gerry tuned in. This was new territory for the car journeys and he didn't know what was coming next. But then, with Arthur, Gerry would have a lost a lot of money if he had been forced to bet on where Arthur's rambles were going to take them. Gerry usually tuned out, listening only when Arthur had an unusual turn of phrase or was talking with too much enthusiasm to be ignored.

"Well, it was a full year before we had enough spare cash between us to go away anyway. We picked the Lake District because the car we had was a real banger, an old Fiesta, and it was conking out on longer drives. It was the distributor I think. But we reckoned it could make it that far, one way at least."

Arthur paused, looking out the passenger window.

"I never saw her look better than when we were there."

"Breakfasts, she just loved the breakfasts at that place. She would have had them three times a day if she could. She would swan about the terrace at the hotel with a plateful of eggs and fancy breads, and a glass of champagne to kick off the day. Champagne, Gerry, real Champagne, for breakfast on the terrace! It was like we were in the movies."

Arthur tipped his hand to his mouth, pinkie finger straight up.

Gerry nodded and raised his eyebrows, unseen in the dim light, to share Arthur's wonder at the thought of champagne for breakfast.

"We did a lot of walking in the hills during the day, pottered about the shops in Kendal, then back for steak dinners and hunkering down at the hotel bar for the night. She loved it. I liked it too, and I loved seeing her like that. It was like she was drinking the air when we were out and getting high. I'd never seen her that colour in her face – glowing, she was, even with full make up on."

Arthur held his hands up, either side of his face, fingers wide, to emphasise how much Melisa had glowed.

"The water there tasted different. She said it was more bubbly and sweet, but I knew it was because it came from the hills, high up. It had more ions, you see. It picked them up on the way down the hills. Any water coming from that height had to be good for you. It was supercharged with ions by the time it came out the tap. I could taste it. It was like double espresso, but without the palpitations and the jitters. It made me feel like I could do anything! I tried to explain it to her, but she just laughed. She said that I was always trying to explain stuff, instead of just enjoying it."

They were about half way to Arthur's place and slowing behind a line of traffic, as two lanes merged to one for some late night road works Gerry had seen signs for earlier.

"She would speak to total strangers, sitting in the hotel or when we passed them out walking. Easy as you like, cracking on about what a great place it was, how we were here on honeymoon, what a beautiful day it was. I'd never seen her do that before, never. It was always me who did the talking, doing the necessary if we had to ask for directions or booking up stuff, taking things back to the shop, or when the phone rang. You get it, she'd say, or That'll be for you Arthur, I'm not expecting any calls. But not when we were at that hotel. She'd be picking up the phone, ordering sandwiches and drinks on room service, picnic lunches like she did it every day, like she lived there."

Arthur hands moved as he spoke, always ahead of what he was about to say; mimicking carrying the breakfast plates, arms swinging, walking on the hills, or hands spreading out or pointing in advance of what was to come. Gerry had seen interviews with football managers with hands like Arthur; down the channels, in around the back, over the top, keeping it tight, hands mirroring each other, or taking turns on the stage, but rarely meeting in the middle, rarely touching.

Gerry had been thinking about a difficult programme at work the next day and whether to do this in the morning and get it over with, or risk having enough time to do it in the afternoon. They had just got through the single line traffic and were almost at Arthur's turn off on the road when Gerry became aware that Arthur must have stopped talking for long enough for him to have worked out a detailed work timetable for the next day. Gerry indicated left to go up the slip road and glanced at Arthur to check if he had nodded off after his long night at the tables. He knew that it could be exhausting, having to concentrate for that length of time, when you made it all the way through to the final table.

Arthur turned and looked back at Gerry. His voice was quieter, the enthusiasm of the Lake District hotel gone.

"She must have used the phone to book it while she was ill. I worked that out from the timings. The same room, the exact same room we'd been in. She must have phoned up and described it, booked it, put the phone down and waited for two weeks. She liked to plan stuff, know what was around the corner, get it on the calendar. She was meticulous like that. The deal with us was if it was written on the calendar it was happening. If something came up at work and there was something on the calendar for that night, I had to change the work thing, get somebody else to do it, no questions, no exceptions.
Of course, she didn't write that on the calendar."

Gerry was listening now.

"But she had put a dot on the date. It was in blue ink and it looked like it could have been a stray drop from the painting of the Venice canals above, for April, except that the pen had been pressed hard enough to make indents in May and June."

He paused again, as Gerry turned the tight left into the unlit road and pulled up.

Arthur didn't reach for the door handle immediately and they sat with the engine running. Gerry felt edgy without the distraction of driving, knowing that not listening was now not an option. Arthur might tell him more than he wanted to hear and he was worried about the knowing, and out of his depth about how he to reply. As Arthur shifted his position in his seat, Gerry dived in, closing it down in an embarrassed panic, before Arthur could say anymore.

"Well, that's us here, Arthur. Well done on winning it tonight. You've still got it, eh? You must be doing something right with those cards and those books of yours. Some more points on the board as well – that'll move you up the league a bit, and a bit of extra cash never goes wrong, eh?"

Arthur smiled in the dark, glanced at Gerry, then towards the door, searching for the door handle.

"Yeah, it's good to win now and then. Thanks again for the lift, Gerry, much appreciated."

He got out and tapped the roof of the car twice before walking towards the row of farm cottages.

CHAPTER 10

Omaha Bingo

Omaha Bingo is a poker variation, although it is one not played in casinos.
It is normal Omaha with a noughts and crosses twist. Each player gets four cards in their
hand and nine community cards are dealt in a grid of three rows of three, face down, at the
start of the game.
For the flop, the four corner cards of the grid are turned over; for the turn the four remaining
outside cards are turned; and for the river, the remaining card in the centre is turned. As in
regular Omaha, players must use two of the cards in their hand, plus a straight line of three
cards on the board, across, down or diagonally. The best five card hand wins. The game is
called Bingo because of the grid of cards on the table and the need to use straight line
combinations, as on a Bingo card.

Injuries in poker were rare, during the game at least. Boyd's party piece story
was telling strangers how he broke his neck playing Omaha Bingo. He'd been
out drinking and six of them had gone back to Boyd's for a home game.
Dealer's choice, which for Boyd was Omaha Bingo, every time, because of
the number of possible permutations when cards were turned. For at least
seventy per cent of hands played, he would raise the hell out of the pot,
frighten off most players, then take it down with some weak pair or some
miracle combination of cards. No Limit Texas Hold 'Em was described by
Doyle Brunson as the "Cadillac of poker", but Omaha Bingo was Boyd's
choice of second hand car; a comfortable old banger that nobody except him
liked to drive, which suited him fine. He was fast, very fast, at working out the
number of possible outs – possible made hands - he had when the first four
cards were turned, and faster at calculating the size of bet that would thin the
field and leave him with just a single player to beat.

He also knew how to control the table from the start, using his stop/go
system on cards. He would split his four cards randomly and designate two of
them as his "stop" cards, which he would then look at. The other two cards

he kept face down and only used if any other player put in a significant size bet or raise. If no one bet against him, he would keep his "go" cards face down until the end of the hand. This stupid and irrational system, done with a running commentary, paid out for Boyd, more times than any calculated odds. One reason was that none of the players, including Boyd, knew how his go cards would match what was on the table and this led to ultra-cautious play by others. The main reason, however, was because poker memory was selective. The players that Boyd knew well remembered his system winning massive pots against strong hands many more times than he actually had. He had just been getting into his stop/go-ing on the night of the accident, enjoying other players groaning and swearing at his crazy betting as cards were turned. He was in his favourite chair, playing poker in his narrow, pokey kitchen, with a bellyful of beer and his choice of Omaha Bingo. It was as relaxed as he got. He rocked back in his chair, taking it all in. When the back legs of the chair made an angle just beyond ninety degrees with the tiled floor in the kitchen, Boyd's weight did the rest. The chair slid from under him. His knees slammed against the table, demolishing players' towers of neatly stacked chips and lifting the pot of chips in the middle half an inch in the air. Above the clatter of the chair hitting the floor there was a louder crack as Boyd's head connected with the solid wood worktop behind him on his way down.

Around the table, the other five players almost joined Boyd on the floor, doubled up with the kind of uncontrollable laughing that can strain a muscle. He was drunk enough to laugh too, despite the pain, lying on this back with his legs splayed around the chair. It wasn't until Welsh tried to help him up that he realised something was seriously, terrifyingly wrong. He sobered up in seconds, screaming loud enough to cut off the laughter, telling Welsh not to touch him, scaring him enough to back off. It was an Ambulance job; he had cracked vertebrate in his neck and was immobilised for four weeks.

Boyd told the story again for the benefit of the two people who had not heard it, as they waited for players to turn up for one of Gerry's rare weekend home games. Welsh had heard it too many times, but still laughed, regardless, because that's what you did when one of your mates told his favourite story. By eight o'clock everyone was there and settled with a drink, balanced on window sills, small tables and shelves. Bowls of snacks had been passed around then put away, to prevent finger marks on the cards.

"*Try it with two – go on, just try it*", Welsh said.

"*It'll blow my heid aff!*", said Barry, getting two out of the packet as he spoke.

"*Naw, you'll be fine. I've done it before wi' three and it was a bit hot, but it was awright*", said Welsh, willing Barry on.

Barry slipped both wasabi peanuts under his tongue and closed his mouth. The other six players around the table glanced over, but continued with the hand. The ruddy complexion on Barry's nose, cheeks and forehead, a combination of rosacea and too many beers, went darker, then turned the colour of his tongue. He looked at Welsh as his vision blurred from watering eyes. After twenty seconds of pretending, trying to show that it was no big deal, he grabbed for his bottle of Becks and gulped.

"*Bloody hell Welsh, that stuff is toxic!*", he spat out, in a rasping whisper, "*Ma throat's paralysed and I cannae feel ma cheeks.*"

Welsh laughed, looking around, encouraging others into the joke.

"*I've never put two under my tongue, ya numptie. Them nuts are extra spicy!*"

Everyone else at the table except Simon gave a polite chuckle or a smile, just to bring the joke to an end and get back to the game.

The home games at Gerry's house brought a combination of those he liked to invite to his home, and those who could make it. He had to invite enough for a game – five was a minimum- but not so many that he ran out of seats in his kitchen. It was a balancing act; putting out texts the day before to see who could make it, starting with favourites, waiting for replies, then working down the list on the day of the game.

Tonight it was Christopher (same village, and generating too many awkward questions to not invite), Barry (local, and usually at a loose end on a Saturday night), a package deal in which Welsh had brought Lee and Boyd (no transport), Steph (on a rare night off from the taxis), and Simon, who had phoned Gerry after hearing about the game from Pat, a home game player who had been invited but couldn't make it.

"Thanks a lot, Pat," Gerry was thinking, as he looked across at Simon pouring another two fingers of Lagavulin single malt from the bottle he had brought with him.

"See, we don't sell this stuff, Christopher, but if we did I would be keeping it all for myself", Simon said, before throwing it back in one gulp.

After telling Christopher for the third time that the he had first discovered whisky from Islay when he was a student in Glasgow, Simon stumbled on the fact that he and Christopher had both been at Glasgow University at the same time.

Simon rattled off a list of "absolute characters" called Binky or Gussie or Spody, who Christopher simply *must* have known, but didn't. He then ran through his memory of all of the "totally memorable" social events that he and Christopher might have been at, again with no success. After a few more false starts on bars and restaurants, Simon gave up trying to put them both in the same place. A combination of the Lagavulin and his inability to find a shared history annoyed Simon, who didn't like failure.

"We were there at the same time Christopher but, Jesus Christ, you just look so old," he said, exasperated.

Without a pause in the deal, Welsh muttered loud enough to be heard, *"You're right, he does look old, but I've got some bad news for you Simon – your face looks like it's made of elbow skin too."*

Simon claimed to be from Glasgow, but had an accent that said it was a part of Glasgow that didn't have bus stops, but probably did have at least one delicatessen. He worked as a wine merchant in his family's business. He didn't actually take wine orders or organise deliveries or handle cash; that was done by what he described as the "hard working drones". He saw himself as the public-facing executive arm of the business. Most of his work time was hosting wine tastings at select venues, giving and taking business cards, and passing interested buyers onto the "girls" who manned the wine stands, in hotel function suites, art galleries and marquees in the summer months. Skilled interacting and commercial networking was how he described it. Swanning about drinking and getting paid for it by his father was how those at Gerry's poker table saw it. He was invited to the home games when Gerry got down to the least-worse names on his list. He could be relied on to turn up and to continue to re-buy chips all night, or until he was too drunk to play, as happened that night.

By half past ten the bottle of Lagavulin was empty, most of it in Simon, minus a few nips eked out to others. He had knocked over two glasses, one of them his own, and was tipping his cards to show them before the end of hands. No one at the table had any qualms about taking his money, as he continued to over bet on nothing hands and call every raise. No pals at the table, dog eat dog; that was the rule. It got embarrassing when players realised that they were no longer playing against each other, but competing to take Simon's chips, which he was no longer sober enough to count. Tolerating Simon at the table, even as a calling station on each hand, became too much for Boyd when a third glass was knocked over, and he snapped.

"Look Simon, you're completely moroculous there and you're playing like a blind jakey – time to pack it in, eh?" Boyd said.

Simon took a few seconds to react to his name and a few more to locate who had spoken to him. He got up, unsteadily, supporting himself on the back of his chair. He wiped the back of his hand across his mouth before he spoke.

"*Well firstly Boyd, Mr self-appointed Tournament Director, I will leave the table when I'm ready to leave, not when you decide, and secondly,*" he said, turning over his two cards and waving them at Boyd, "*you are wasting your time and effort using your quaint Scottish colloquialisms on me, because I have no idea about what you're talking, as I speak only the Queen's English.*"

Queen's English came out as "Squeen shinglish". Simon sat down with a thump, and looked around the other players.

"*Don't understand Scottish eh? You won't know what a posh cunt is then Simon, eh?*"

Boyd said, under his breath, just loud enough to send Welsh into a coughing fit, a mouthful of beer shooting down his nostrils.

Ten minutes later, Simon was unable to hold cards in his hand, out of chips, and asking Gerry for a pen to write out IOUs, so that he could continue in the game.

"*OK Simon, time to get you home, I think, eh?*" Welsh said, standing and putting his hand on Simon's shoulder as Simon slumped over to one side again, in danger of going on the floor.

Simon looked up at Welsh, trying to focus, and smeared a combination of Lagavulin and saliva across his chin.

"*Nobody, but nobody, is putting any fucking wasabi nuts up my arse, Welsh*", he slurred.

Steph called a fellow taxi driver who was willing to take Simon home for the standard fee plus an extra tenner for drunks, and the promise of another twenty from Steph if Simon threw up, peed or shat in the taxi.

Then there were seven left at the table, with a bit more space and significantly more poker.

The game was dealer's choice, seven hands of the poker variation chosen by dealer, rotating around the table. As the deal moved, players were asked what the change of game was going to be, except for Boyd. He shuffled and dealt for his standard Omaha Bingo. He bet high and early, well above the number of chips that would give players the odds to call. He scooped the first two hands, taking everyone's blinds. In the next two hands only Welsh stayed in against Boyd's betting after the flop. They played between chatting.

"What you up to on Thursday this week Welsh – fancy a couple of pints at lunch time?" Boyd said as Welsh turned over the corner cards.

"Well actually, I'm thinking about taking an extended lunch with Alison, the receptionist on Thursday. I'm going to be eating at the 'Y'", Welsh replied, running his tongue around his mouth for extra emphasis.

"Aye, right, you'll be eating al desko, like every other bloody day of the week," said Boyd, dismissively, to some hoots at the table, *"just give me a shout if you're up for a drink."*

On the fifth hand of Omaha Bingo, Boyd pushed all his chips in pre-flop, for around thirty pounds. It was a typical Boyd bet; more of a joke, with only eighty pence in the pot. There was a familiar chorus of groans from the four players who had already put in big blinds. Boyd smiled, put his cards down and shrugged his shoulders. He put his hands out, over the chips, and held them there, theatrically, waiting for everyone to fold.

Players started chatting and Gerry and Barry tossed their cards into the muck pile of cards in the middle as the action moved to Christopher. He put his cards face down in front of him and stroked his chin.

"Come on Christopher, get them folded like everybody else," Boyd said, motioning Christopher to chuck his cards into the pile.

"You know what Boyd, I'm going to call you. You've been buying pots with your ludicrous bets all night, and I'm sick of it."

Christopher's voice was clear and his diction was more suited to Bridge than to poker, but there was a raw, nettled edge, none of the players had ever heard from him on a Wednesday night.

The side conversations around the table stopped.

He tapped an index finger on his two cards.

"You make these absolutely ridiculous over bets and it spoils the game for me, and I'm sure for others, even if they are too polite to say so."

Christopher voice was rising. He didn't look around the table for support.

"We come here to play poker, not to watch you make a mockery of the game."

The heads of the other players went down in embarrassment, at the display of too much authentic emotion at the poker table. Everyone looked away, apart from Welsh, who gaped at Christopher in slack-jawed shock. At home games Christopher was only ever known to play one way. It was simple, predictable and joyless. He would bet when he calculated that he had the best hand, bet big when he knew he had the best hand, scoop some chips and play tight for hours, eking out his winnings. He would cash out and leave at midnight precisely. He never got involved in any hands if the calculated odds were against him, and he was never tempted to build on his winnings by raising his bets.

Like other responsibilities in his life, he took the role of poker club treasurer very seriously. He kept the money right, to the penny, in the ledgers and enforced the rules of poker on club nights. It was very rare for a Wednesday to go by without Christopher intervening during a game, over some irregularity that he had spotted in play. Splashing the pot – betting by throwing chips into the pile of chips in the middle, rather than stacking them on the edge of the pile - was Christopher's bête noire. Other misdemeanours he could put down to players' ignorance or excitement, and he took satisfaction in demonstrating his knowledge of the regulations to correct these errors. But splashing the pot was more than a breach of regulations; it was inconsiderate, lazy and just plain rude. How could something as basic as putting chips forward properly when betting not been learned by everyone who played? He would correct it every time, throwing a hand over the pot to stop play, then methodically separating what had been thrown in haphazardly from what had been there already. He was polite and he was consistent, but it had happened so many times that even his patience was tested. It had become a battle of wills between him and Stevie and Russell, who, he knew, would splash the pot just for his reaction. It was the one regulation that he no longer derived any satisfaction in enforcing.

At poker tables players who threw in chips and failed to verbally declare a raise had the additional chips returned to them and informed that their bet was being treated as just a call. Players who failed to hear or notice a raise, because of lack of concentration or headphones or drink were asked to put in the additional chips to match the raise. Christopher would argue a point of order or a count of chips until anyone foolish enough to take him on gave up eventually out of exasperation or boredom. His swearing at the table was rare and clearly enunciated. His day job as a high school physics teacher gave him little in common with other players.

Even in home games he was a pedant for poker etiquette. It was around a kitchen table and there was more chat, less posturing and power plays but he let everyone understand that although it was just a friendly home game, with no league points at stake, the same set of poker rules applied - no drinks on the table, no use of mobile phones at the table, clearly declared bets, raises or calls at all times.

Christopher lived in the village as Gerry and had children at the same school. He had worked hard in his twenties to raise the capital for a mortgage, bought the house, then married and now had the two children. At home he was reliable, always, caring and loved. At poker, he was reliable, not popular, and apparently not bothered.

"Personally, I have had enough, and I think..."

"Aye, OK, OK, Christopher, we get the message. You've called my bet," Boyd said, cutting him off, looking again at his cards to remind himself what he'd decided was worth a thirty quid bet.

Everyone else had folded instantly on Boyd's bet and only Welsh was left to decide. He was one of the fastest poker odds calculator for any given hand at a table and also the person most likely to ignore the odds that he had calculated.

"*I'm probably behind right now*", he said slowly, looking at his cards and rubbing the bridge of his nose, "*but I've got a lot of possible outs, and that is a biiiig pot.*"

Welsh's loose play was well known and most players at the club avoided taking him on in cash games because, like Boyd, he would buy and rebuy up to three figure sums, just to win back what he had lost, and he usually did.

"*In fact, there's such a stack in that pot, that I'm all in too,*" Welsh said after another few seconds, pushing his chips stacks forward. He had just under thirty pounds in chips and the main pot and small side pot were quickly sorted out by Gerry.

The three players sat still, waiting to see who would show first, to gain some imagined advantage, until Welsh said, "*OK boys— let's turn them over and see what everybody has got so excited about.*"

Boyd turned over suited connectors, 6♥7♥ and a pair of black Queens, which was both a good made hand and a hand with good possibilities for Omaha.

He said, "*C'mon the Queens.*"

Welsh flipped over a J♥9♣ and then more slowly turned his K♥K♦, saying, "*'Mon the cowboys.*"

Christopher looked at both sets of cards, then stood up from the table as he turned over A♦K♠ and the pair of red Queens. This was a very strong starting hand, but now effectively just an Ace-King because of Boyd's Queens showing. There would be no more Queens to be turned over. There were a few gasps and one "*Ooya!*" from Barry, as Christopher's gamble on Boyd having bluffed started to look like a hot headed mistake.

The first card turned on the corner of the grid on the table was the K♣, followed by a 2♣ 3♠ 7♦ on the other corners, and Welsh let out a quiet, "*Yess!*" clenching one hand as his set of Kings hit the board. With three all-ins, there was no betting and the four other outside cards were turned. The 4♦ 6♦ 4♥ 8♣ low board helped nobody, and both Boyd and Christopher were fast enough to calculate was that they were drawing dead before the centre card, a 7♥, was turned. Welsh bit his lip to suppress any more obvious but less gracious expression of triumph.

His three Kings, ahead at the start, had become a full house with K♣ and the two 7s in a diagonal line across the board, Boyd had trip sevens and Christopher had just two pair, Kings and 7s.

Even as the 7♥ was turned in the centre of the grid on the table, Christopher was edging his way around his seat to the kitchen door, lips pressed tightly together, avoiding eye contact. He was down the hall and out the front door before players had looked up from the combinations of cards. Gerry looked over at Welsh and pulled a face; one eyebrow up, one side of his mouth down.

Welsh shrugged and used both hands to pull the enormous pile of chips towards him.

"*Well, what crawled up his arse tonight, Gerry?*" he said, starting to stack the chips into coloured towers.

"*He comes along here and usually plays about three hands in an hour, for buttons, then tonight all of a sudden he's Mr Wild and Dangerous, badmouthing me and chucking thirty quid into a two pound pot. What's that about then?*"

"*Ach, I think he's just had a hard week, Welsh, you know he's no usually like that,*" said Gerry, shaking his head, not wanting to criticise Christopher, but not knowing how to defend him either.

"*No, he's not usually like that - he's usually even more of an irritating prat than he was tonight, Gerry,*" Boyd chipped in.

"He loves picking people up for not playing the game that way that it's written in his book, and explaining to the world when anybody makes a mistake. If he cannae relax and play even in a home game without taking the huff like a big bairn for getting beat, he shouldnae play at all."

Gerry said nothing as he gathered in the cards and started to shuffle for the next hand.

Christopher sat outside in his car, in the dark, gripping the steering wheel, shaking. He knew that if he looked in the mirror he would see his four year old son's face in a temper tantrum looking back. It would be the same look of impotent anger when he didn't get his own way. He had allowed himself to react to Boyd, to show what he was feeling, and now he was feeling devastated over a fucking card game. He sat staring at the dashboard, powerless to move. After five minutes it was already too late to go back in and try to laugh it off. Others might have pulled it off, but for him it was too late to say, *"Sorry about that guys. I lost it a bit"*. He couldn't sit back down, and have them needle him about storming from the table in ten different ways for an hour and ignore them. It was too late as soon as he stood up and left, he knew, because he'd broken his own rules, by not playing his game, by rushing out with no handshake, no goodnight. Petty, petty, fucking petty.

All night he had been a mess, on tilt from the first hand that he lost, not wanting to be there, but not wanting to be at home either when he was like this. He thought he could make it through to his usual midnight curfew, just ride it out, betting on strong hands, being sensible with the chips, until he was too tired to think about it, go home, fall into bed and have the weekend to let it fade, at least until Monday. Boyd and his pointless, stupid betting – ten pounds, then twenty, then thirty - had got to him when he should have zoned it out. That's what made it worse; knowing even as he was doing it that it was wrong thing to do. He should have stuck to the game plan, avoided playing Boyd's childish toss-of-the-coin version of poker. He hated himself for not holding on, for being baited. Anger was the enemy, and going on tilt was anger.

In life and in poker, it was all about self-control, patience. Patience, experience and persistence; PEP. He had made it to Friday night, he told himself, almost held it together, so close to making it through another week, to finishing it, soul intact. He knew he was on tilt, angry at himself, at Boyd, and at the job. Thinking about those moronic kids who didn't want to be in his class, who told him, straight out, that they didn't want to be in his class, who *showed* him, very clearly, that they didn't want to be in his class, messing about with phones, drawing cocks on their books, shouting at each other like he wasn't there, looking everywhere except at the white board, turning their seats to face each other.

He hated it and he hated them. He didn't shout, didn't react, made it look like it washed over him, didn't touch him, but of course it did. It was costing him more and more, each week, each month, eating him from the inside, to keep the poker face in classes. He shouldn't let it eat him, he knew; focus on the teaching process, the Curriculum for Excellence, stick to the game plan and be professional, that was what he was good at. He played that role, being Mr Calm, controlling the level of chaos in the room, as much as it could be controlled for a group of fourteen year olds who were barely socialised, barely human. "*Lively students*", his head of department called them at staff meetings. Primitive pack animals is what Christopher saw when he looked up as they trooped in the door of his class. They were feral, living minute to minute, with no capacity for planning, no concept of cause and effect. Like animals, they had no idea of why they were held captive, incapable of learning new information or understanding why they should.

When he had asked Grahams to leave the class that day it was not for the first time. The relentless abuse from Grahams had found a gap in Christopher's armour.

"See, Mr Holmes, nobody cares about you and your physics, 'cause nobody is going to stop me in the street and ask me about your Laws of Physics or some shite about gravity that doesn't mean anything, and apart from that, you are just such a crap teacher."

More often now, as the months went by, he knew that only reminding himself of the consequences, of the rules of cause and effect, prevented him from reacting, from doing something in class that would make it very clear to all of them that he was the alpha male in this group of pack animals. He had imagined it and how good it would feel, but it would be wrong and it would be the end.

His first rule of poker, at the base of the any variations for conditions, was to play his game 100% of the time with no exceptions. His game did not include calling all-in bets with a pair of Queens in Omaha Bingo. His game did not include reacting as if Boyd was prodding him with a sharp stick. But he had reacted primitively, tried to show that he was a better poker player than Boyd and show the others that somebody had to take a stand on Boyd and his over betting. He had convinced himself that he could go heads up with Boyd before any cards had been turned, before any information on odds was available, and win the hand. Somebody had to curb Boyd's random and aggressive raises. It was excluding others from the game, ruining the challenge of playing poker, and he would take a stand. His judgement in the hand had been clouded by Grahams, and Hopkins, and McWilliams, and Quinn, and the rest of 3C, and he had lost focus. Sitting there, in the dark, in his car it was easy to analyse all that, to rationalise it, but it changed nothing. There was still the frustrated, powerless four year old in the mirror if he looked. He was sitting in a cold car replaying the same poker hand over and over in his head, trying desperately not to. Boyd was bluffing. He had to be, throwing thirty pounds into a one pound pot. He would take a stand, take him on, take the thirty pounds, make it last until midnight, cash out and go home. That was his game plan always; play very tight, win a few big hands.

He had ignored the lack of information about odds and how fast and how drastically they could change in Omaha Bingo. There was a clue in the title of the game. All in pre-flop? Calling the raise? That was just stupid. No logic or odds justified that move. In his rush of blood he hadn't even checked his table position, and he hadn't noticed that Welsh was still in the hand and likely to call on such a rich pot. He had jumped in, assuming that he would be heads-up with Boyd.

He should never have come tonight. They had enough players without him. He was a bad smell to them, like an embarrassing relative, the one always sitting on his own at family gatherings. At home games players would shuffle chairs together in a none-too-subtle attempt to prevent him sitting between them. Nobody spoke to him except Gerry, and that was only because it was easier than not talking to him. When he spoke players either ignored him completely or used him as a straight man for some crude come back, or to launch into some tirade that wasn't a reply to him at all, but just an excuse to run off at the mouth for the benefit of other players. He kept the books, banked the money, kept it legal, and signed everyone in when they arrived for club nights. But that was it; that was the totality of his value to the poker club. To other players he was as an administrative necessity. If they could find a machine that would do those things every week, they would buy it. He was an irrelevance in the cash games, just another body at the table, someone had to be invited because he lived locally and knew Gerry. When the poker league had started he had hopes of intelligent conversation each week, people with different interests who shared an interest in poker. In his head it would be a poker "league of friends", all feeling welcome in each other's company. There might be some status for himself as secretary. He would be the somebody that everybody in the club knew and respected, like a knowledgeable barman in their favourite pub. It was never that and it was never going to be that now.

Around and around it went in his head, impossible to resist: Boyd's all-in, his call, Welsh's call, Welsh's Kings, his Queens, feeling the despair again when Boyd turned over the other two Queens, Welsh controlling his celebration as he passed him, making for the door. He knew this would be a tape loop in his thoughts, intrusive and persistent, lasting until he played again, and that was three days away. The same hand would be played out again and again whenever he was not concentrating completely on something that left no space for anything else. When he was cooking, playing with Jeremy, chatting with Shirley at home, reading, driving or trying to focus on TV it would be there, as fresh and raw as it was now, and when the loop, the unwanted replay started to run in his head there was no stopping it.

It wasn't a bad beat. Welsh had hit it lucky, sucked out on him and won with some crappy hand. Boyd had overbet on his Queens, yes, but he was wrong to call such a massive over bet with the chip stack that he had. It was easy enough to do the simple analysis, file the hand under always-remember-to-revisit-your-blunders-to-see-what-you-can-learn-from-them or learned-another-poker-lesson-that-improved-my-game-today; that was the rational bit. Poker wisdom said that it was not the events at the table that caused you grief, it was how you interpreted them. It was an easy and glib way to rationalise the game, and clear away all that negative thinking, like wiping a memory. But right then and there, in his car, at eleven o'clock, knowing all that meant nothing. The only thing that would stop him thinking about it for the next three days was a time machine to take him back to 10.45 and play the hand differently.

CHAPTER 11

Double Draw Poker and Top Ups

There's always a second chance in poker games to do better, or at least it feels that way. In Double Draw poker there are two chances to improve the hand that you've been dealt. Players are dealt five cards, face down. There is then a round of betting. Players can then ask the dealer to replace any or all of their cards. There is another round of betting, then another opportunity to replace cards, before the final showdown round of betting. Weak hands can become strong hands and strong hands can become monster hands after the two draws.

Some games have top-ups. For freeze-out tournaments, players can be given the opportunity to buy more chips at the mid-point of the tournament. This can be a standard amount of chips, available to all players, or a re-buy when players decide how many more chips to buy, up to an agreed maximum. Players can be buy more chips as a top-up or as a re-buy even if they have been knocked out in the first half of the tournament.

The top-ups or re-buys give a player a second chance to succeed in the tournament. They will have fewer chips than most other players and will have to change how they play to avoid going up against players with the bigger stacks.

There were six left in Gerry's dining room, around the folding poker table, resting on two sheets of rubberised felt that protected the ash veneer that Gerry had patiently glued, ironed, sanded and varnished onto the old table surface

"*The bet's on you, Lee*", said Welsh.

"*Aye, right*", Lee mumbled, then took another swig from a bottle of dirt-dark beer, while the other players waited. There were some players who took dog's abuse for staring at their cards and keeping the table waiting. Working out all of the possible permutations of cards, or keeping other players waiting as a strategy for creating uncertainty were the two main reasons.

In online poker there was a button to bring up an onscreen "*Hurry Up!*" message when players took too long. At the club and at home games, there was, "*Just when you're ready*"(Gerry), or, "*OK, I'm going to have to put you on the clock here "*(Christopher), or *"Come to fuck, we've no got all night"* (Sleeve).

No-one told Lee to hurry up. He didn't speak much to other players except Welsh, and on club nights he would always turn up just in time to sign up for the game and leave as soon as he was out of the main tournament, avoiding chatter at the bar, the bad beat stories and the cash tables. He would shake hands with players he busted out of the tournament and those who took him out and he would nod to those who knew him, or knew his name at least. New players often mistook him for one of the group of eastern Europeans who came to play, because he spoke so little, and because the three day shadow on a well creased face gave him a look found in Scotland usually on golf caddies who had spent time in the sun and on the bottle. Lee could have been anywhere between 35 and 45.

It was rare to see Lee at a home game, but he had been to Gerry's house before. He had been invited because the numbers were low and he had taken a lift from Welsh. To those at the tables who asked, Welsh would say that Lee had moved through from Glasgow for work and didn't know many people in Perth. Away from the tables, Welsh would also say that Lee was a friend of his mother's, which just made the curious more curious, and brought predictable toy boy jokes. Welsh would clam up, or tell the curious that his favourite direction for them to fuck was off. For those who persisted, he'd tell them to go and ask Lee, if they really wanted to know, and nobody was that curious.

Lee was a brickie. That fact was the most advanced level of personal disclosure that Lee would go to. Starters from other players, like *"How's it goin'?"* and *"Awright Lee?"* were fine, and *"What is it you do, Lee?"* and *"Who do ye work with Lee?"*, would also get a reply, but anything beyond that got a shrug, a grunt, or was ignored. One drunken newbie at the club had sat down beside Lee one night, thrown an arm around this shoulders and launched in with, *"So, you look like a right hard bastard pal, what's your story?"*. Lee had got up and got himself another pint, despite having just started one.

At the few home games he'd been to Lee was a bit more relaxed, if you could call talking in sentences more unwound, but he was still the player who said least. He would chip into chat about the state of Scottish football. Despite being Glaswegian, he didn't have a team. He just liked to see a good game, hated divers and players who conned referees. He didn't talk much, but if you wanted to know about single skin versus retaining walls, or frogged or perforated brick, or using sharp versus soft sand, Lee was your man. He had done a homer for Gerry, after Gerry had negotiated through Welsh. The job was laying the foundations and nine-high brick base for Gerry's new greenhouse. Gerry got the bricks delivered and Lee turned up on the Saturday morning, as arranged, with tools and finished on Sunday night. Gerry agreed to labour for him to save a bit of money and to get the job done more quickly. By Sunday night, Gerry knew no more about Lee than he did on the Saturday morning, other than the fact that he laid bricks like a machine.

Gerry had to take the Monday off work, unable to stand up straight after the labouring. The brickwork was perfect, with the mortar lines so strait it looked like fake brickwork you would find stuck on the side of a mobile home. He had given Lee an envelope with a bit extra on top of the agreed price for the job, and he found the extra on his doormat in the same envelope, slipped through the letterbox as Lee was leaving. Gerry still raved to neighbours about the workmanship, and had put some other work Lee's way.

Welsh wished he didn't know that Lee had done time. He wished it more, and more often as the months went by. He didn't ask to be the only person who knew, apart from his mother. He carried the burden of this knowledge for his mother and he would not have carried it for anyone else. Just knowing turned him into someone he wasn't, every time Lee was playing poker, every time anybody spoke about Lee, and even at times when he thought Lee's name might come up. He went from easy going, slumped well back in the chair Welsh to some actor, pretending to be Welsh. It was like hiding a giant, exhausting poker tell, not letting anyone know what you had in your hand, pretending that you had nothing. In his head he switched between being the actor lying that he didn't know Lee's secret, and the liar pretending there was no secret.

Once, when he was out on a bender with Boyd, he'd almost let it slip. They slavered on about all kinds of gibberish when they were pissed. They'd been talking about how hard it would be to break into Perth Prison – not out, but in – and Welsh had said that he knew someone who would know, then had to invent some uncle, who was a security specialist in the Middle East, to cover his tracks when Boyd got interested. Luckily Boyd was so pissed that he didn't remember any of the conversation, or at least he never asked about it again.

But others wanted to know about Lee. *"Go and ask Lee yourself"*, Welsh would tell them, when somebody kept at it and at it and just couldn't leave it and Welsh ran out of energy for the lying. Every time he said it he regretted it instantly. It felt like giving up, letting Lee down, letting his mother down, and he wished he could take it back. But worse than that, it terrified him that just once somebody would go and ask Lee, and Lee would run out of energy for the lying too and get worn down with the same questions and all the evasion and he would just tell them.

He would tell them that he had been in prison, and then Welsh wouldn't have that secret to lug about any longer. But then Lee might decide, "Fuck it", might as well get it all out, and he would tell them why he had been sentenced to nine years. Just thinking about that had Welsh clenching the cheeks of his arse.

He was tired of putting on the lying act for so long. It was now giving him burning stomach cramps when he thought about it and when he lied. It could only end badly for him. He knew that finding out what he had been covering for, what Lee had done, was going to make all the lying pointless and whole sham house of cards was going to collapse not on Lee, but on him.

Who was going to believe that he didn't know, that he wasn't in on Lee's secret all this time? Absolutely nobody, that's who, not now, not after this long. He must have known, they would say. How could he know the guy for that long and not know? When it came out, Lee would be branded for whatever he had done and Welsh would be branded for the deceiving bastard that he had been, and for what Lee had done. He had brought Lee to the poker club, and into Gerry's home. His name would be shit stain among everybody who knew him.

"…and how's Lee getting on with everyone at that poker club William?" His mother asked the same question every Thursday when she phoned Welsh. It was never "the" poker club, or "the poker", it was always "that" poker club. His mother viewed playing poker on a par with other weaknesses in others that could be tolerated, like eating take-out food using fingers or watching reality TV. It wasn't a morally laudable game, like playing Bridge, but at least it wasn't in the category of vices you'd be ashamed to tell neighbours about, like gambling money on horses, and it wasn't in the category of degenerate activities such as drug taking or having sex in car parks.

Breeda Getty, mother of William and his younger sister Martha, wife to the late George Getty, was a woman who like to focus on one thing at a time in order to get the job done. House to be cleaned? Start with dusting all rooms, clearing all rubbish, wiping down all surfaces and then, and only then, vacuuming. Phone ringing while dusting? Leave it – they will call back. Dinner to be cooked? Clear the decks, oven on, wrap meat, prepare vegetables, everything cooking, wash up, clear the decks again. Orderliness was a virtue much under-rated in her view and many people could improve their life significantly by taking just a few minutes to organise what they wished to achieve and how.

When George died, she found that there was less to organise in the house but more time to do it. She surprised herself by taking on more work at the prison. Not paid work, of course; she realised long ago that the only place her current skills in office administration were seen was in TV dramas set in the 1980s. The offices that she had worked in were mostly managed by electronic calendars now, not by people. But she had other skills and she was confident that she had much to offer, helping others. She chose carefully, focussing on those that wanted help, of course.

The Justice Department warned of the "*dangers of visitors being drawn deeper into the lives of ex-prisoners*". The National Official Prison Visitors Association advised prison visitors not to keep in touch with a prisoner after release, and Breeda was of the generation that took official advice seriously. She saw nothing wrong however with Welsh keeping in touch.

She had become an Official Prison Visitor (OPV) two years after Welsh's father died of cancer of the spine. It killed him in ten weeks. Welsh was just finishing school when she signed up and he didn't pay much attention. His mother was still at home at the same times and his routine was not changed. She had been involved with setting up and running the visitors centre at the prison while his dad was alive. This was meeting and greeting wives and mothers and sisters and children who were visiting relatives in prison, and she was very good at being good. There was some charity and church connection involved in it all and Welsh had it filed under things-my-mother-does-that-get-her-out-the-house. He only noticed that she was doing something different at the prison when she stopped talking about it.

She could talk about the visitors centre with or without an audience, and even when Welsh or his dad were in another room.

"*Charlotte made a heap of fruit scones and brought them in for the visitors and they were gone in twenty minutes. She made at least enough for two each, so I think one woman took at least six of them and stuck them in her bag, but then you can't say anything can you? I mean, she probably needed the scones more than the others. We got more toys this week for the children visiting – something to play with while the mothers are having a blether. Most of these kids have never seen a real toy, don't know what to do with it, apart from throw it at somebody else. They learn that in those computer games, that's what I blame…."*

Welsh couldn't say exactly when she stopped talking about the visitors centre. His mother didn't talk as much in the house after his father died, and she only spoke when Welsh was in the room. After a break she did go back to some of her routine. First to her WRVS canteen work, on a morning a week at the hospital, then back to the prison. She would tell him snippets, just odd, funny bits that happened, but none of the previous blow-by-blow accounts like the fate of the home baking. Maybe she thought he didn't need to hear as much as his father did. That's how Welsh explained it to himself. He did remember coming to the house for his dinner one night, soon after he had moved out and she was talking about metal detectors and sniffer dogs and having a pat down at the prison and he remembered thinking it was strange that she would have to go through all of that to get into the visitors centre as it was outside the main prison blocks.

It still took him a while to twig that she was no longer serving scones. He found the leaflet one day when he stopped by for a quick lunch and she was out. *"The role of the Official Prison Visitor is to try to encourage the development of a constructive use of a prison sentence whereby inmates gain both a sense of belonging to the community and the realisation that they themselves have the ability to contribute to society's wellbeing."*

There was other stuff too, about how prison visitors could provide emotional support and *"intellectual enrichment that would normally be experienced through friends"*. He read that and he panicked.

His first thought was that his mother had become one of the weird women who befriend and then marry prisoners. She couldn't cope with his father dying and she was on some rescue fantasy, to save some sicko. These women, he knew from reading the tabloids, didn't befriend guys doing time for tax fraud or house breaking. On the front pages it was always the groom with the He-did-what! crimes that you saw, in a framed photo held up for the camera by a needy looking women in a wedding dress. Welsh remembered reading about a woman who had put her underage children up of adoption, just so her paedophile prison husband could come and live with her when he was released.

Welsh spoke to his mother. It was the first time he could remember ever having a serious talk with her when he wasn't on the receiving end of the difficult questions. He planned it, even wrote down what he wanted to ask her. As he tried to phrase the questions, a clear image of her as a jail bride kept intruding in his thoughts.

Welsh thought about three different ways of getting smoothly from, "*So Mum, how's the stuff up at the jail going?*" to "*Are you going to marry him?*" He didn't want to just blurt it out, getting straight to what he really wanted to know. He would feel stupid if he was way off base and he didn't want to embarrass his mother and himself.

As soon as they sat down after dinner and he didn't switch the TV on, his mother realised that it was something big. It went quickly from there, after she asked him if he was getting married and he made clear that he was not. He asked her straight questions and she answered them, managing to tell him both too much and too little at the same time. Too much about why she was doing it: she was seeing women she knew as children at the visitors centre ten years ago come back as wives to visit the next generation of prisoners and she wanted to do something that would make a bigger difference; she was spreading herself too thin, she said, trying to do wee bits here, there and everywhere and not doing much for anybody in the long term; she had more time since his dad had died. All this about why she was doing it, but she told him too little about Lee.

She wouldn't tell him what she spoke about with Lee. She wouldn't tell him why Lee was in jail and, most frustratingly, she wouldn't even say if she *knew* what Lee had done to get him nine years. She said it was all confidential, part of the contract that she signed as an Official Prison Visitor.

"Mum, it's me – just tell me. I can keep it quiet and I can promise you that I wouldn't say a word about it to anybody, but I just need to know! I'm worried about you and I want to be sure you know what you're taking on here with this guy," Welsh said.

"He's in jail for a reason, you know, and it's not a good reason. If you don't know what he's done, at least tell me that."

"All I can tell you William is that his name is Michael, although he prefers to be called Lee, and that's as much as you need to know. You let me do any worrying that's to be done." his mother said, in her best reassuring, motherly tone.

"He is just one of the prisoners serving his sentence and I have been allocated to him as his prison visitor. He is due to be released next year, having served eight years of his nine year sentence. What he has done in the past doesn't concern me, and it shouldn't concern you."

His mother would tell him no more. He tried again, a few weeks later, but got the same script. He was desperate to know, but there was no-one else to ask. He was left with the information on the leaflet and what he was able to find out about prison visitors online. *"Your experience may be rewarding, frustrating or heart-breaking depending on circumstances."* Yes, with no choice of which one, he thought.

Newspaper and court reports from eight years ago were a non-starter without a second name for "Michael" or "Lee" or whoever he was. Even with a name, Welsh would have no way of knowing it was him unless his photo was in newspaper archives, splashed across some tabloid and his mother would confirm it was the same guy.

He tried doing it in reverse; checking crimes that got that sentence in jail, see who had committed them and trying to find Lee. He gave that up fast. After 20 minutes online he had found you could get nine years for everything from being the "caustic soda rapist" to being some poacher who had dynamited the salmon in a stretch of river owned by the sheriff.

For a nine year stretch in prison, the story must be somewhere, he knew, but Welsh gave up searching. What he also knew was that whatever the story, it didn't have a happy ending.

CHAPTER 12

Chip and a Chair

Jack "Treetop" Straus (six foot six inches tall) died in 1988, aged 58, playing high stakes poker in Los Angeles. Six years earlier, he had played in the World Series of Poker Main Event in Las Vegas, which had 104 entries. During the second day of the tournament, Strauss had pushed all of his chips into the pot and lost the lot in one hand. As he got up to leave, he found a $500 chip under his napkin. As he had not said, "All in", when putting in his chips in the previous hand, he was allowed to continue in the game with his one chip. He played on, to win the 1982 event, taking $520,000. Strauss' performance is thought to be the origin of the poker expression "a chip and a chair", which means that as long as you have a single chip and a seat in a tournament, you can still come back from the dead.

You picked your games. Only sit down with players you knew and walk away when you had lost what you could afford and what you wouldn't miss. That was how Lee played it, inside and now out. He was never going to be climbing any poker ladder of winnings, heading for Vegas, but he made sure that he was never going to be the guy creeping about, watching his back by day and teeth grinding by night because he owed. Lee picked up the game by watching how others played, and got better by losing.

There were matches or wrapped sweeties on the table at the first place Lee was in, but nobody was really playing for those. When he was moved to the bigger jail he was gobsmacked to see sets of poker chips in the box with the rest of the board games. Gambling for cash was illegal in prison but playing games for recreation wasn't. It was keeping prisoners occupied, keeping prisoners off drugs, playing games that were popular in culture outside. But Her Majesty's Prison Service in Scotland ran hot and cold on poker. It only took one newspaper headline – *Poker School for prisoners at tax payers' expense!* and all of the chips, tables and cards disappeared for a couple of months until the publicity died down.

First timers were easy targets, especially younger, Pepsi generation guys, who didn't know the score. Invite them into a friendly game – meet the boys, just to be sociable – played for a few smokes. Play soft, let them win a few hands, up the smokes to cash on a secret tab, butter them up, offer to stake the fish in a bigger game, then wham, double bubble, they owed twice what they were staked and they were oxter deep in debt, with money and favours owing. Phones and skag smuggled in up wives' arses and fannies to pay off debts, then bigger favours needed because of growing interest on the debts.

Lee had seen the same routine with first timers, again and again. As easy as throwing out ground bait to get the fish feeding before they were on the hook, fighting for breath. He was seventeen when he went in and twenty five when he came out. He avoided the hook for all of those years, by watching, day and night, and by being terrified.

He was seventeen and it seemed like everybody he knew was seventeen. He found out that Shirley had been with Ben. Good old Ben, reliable and always ready to listen to anyone with a bad luck story. He was just someone who was around and available, like somebody else's enthusiastic dog that you could take for a walk and talk to when you felt like it.

Ben's parents had bought him a car, which was a big deal back then. Never the first one with ideas for the weekend or big plans for leaving town to see the world, Ben was just a follower who tagged along. He laughed at jokes and appeared in photos, but nobody missed him when he wasn't there. Years later, he had reinvented himself as a new, slimmer and wittier avatar when Facebook and Twitter took off. With the luxury of a long delay between thinking and opening his mouth and broadcasting unedited shite, Ben had tuned into how to become electronically popular. He recycled witty stuff from other pages and went from follower to being followed. But back then he was just someone you phoned if you were short of numbers for going out or staying in, or when you needed transport.

What was worse; that Shirley had been shagging somebody else or that she had been shagging reliable old Ben? Lee never worked that one out. He never managed to separate the two, even with all that time to sit and do nothing else but think about it. He could have just dumped her, phoned her or left her standing, walked away, then kicked some dents in Ben and his ratty car. But he had invested a lot in it and he needed to know why it had all gone to worms.

Janice, one of her best-mates-for-life had phoned him, coming over all conflicted loyalties and doing the right thing, but so obviously just loving it that she was first with the bad news. He decided he had to ask Shirley face to face. He told himself that he owed her at least that, after eight months together. He thought it through. Christ, he even remembered rehearsing what to say, trying it out to see how reasonable and mature or how raging nutty it sounded. He had to do it just right, make sure that he got it all across, check the facts before believing it, before judging her. She deserved that. He asked her to meet him at the Imperial. It was familiar, it was where they went before they went anywhere else. A barman who turned a blind eye to seventeen year olds, as long as they behaved like they were twenty. The Imperial had American diner booths where you could have a bit of privacy, on three sides of a horseshoe bar that was usually hooching with noisy regulars in the early evening; people on their way home or early drinkers on their way out.

Lee had thought how it would end. He'd pictured himself standing up and walking out when it was over, finishing it there, keeping a bit of self-respect at the end, no shouting and swearing, no calling her things he would regret. He was in the right and she was in the wrong. It was more than she deserved. He would do the self-righteous walk, up and out the door. It was much more than she deserved.

After Janice's phone call he had been gutted, totally devastated. Eight months was the longest he'd spent properly going out with anyone. Kidding at first that it was no big deal, but putting more and more into it as it lasted. It was the most he'd told anybody, ever, about what he was thinking. He knew it might end, but never like this.

She was late. He had two bottles of Becks and had convinced himself that her best-mate-for-life had phoned Shirley right after talking to him, when the barman in the Imperial shouted out this name, said there was a call. She said she was running late from work and why didn't he come and meet her on the green, go for a walk instead, since it was still sunny. They could go for a drink later, she said. So he'd left the bar. If he had stuck to the plan and said that he'd wait until she got there it would have been different, very different. She was found by a dog walker the next morning, early. She had disturbed the earth above her, punched a hole through the mud and leaves, but she was unconscious. If it had been a cold night she would have died. If it had rained she would have drowned. She was in intensive care for three days. The dog walker was in the same hospital, treated for shock. He asked for police when he phoned, rather than ambulance, because he thought he'd found a body. She twitched while he was waiting for the cops and he almost shat himself. Ben meant nothing to her, she had said. That's when he had lost it.

They had gone as far as the cycle path through the Burton Woods and he'd kept it light until then. How was work? Any difficult customers? Would she get time back for the overtime? He could feel it building though, when they reached the trees, beyond people lying about on the grass and parents kicking a ball and the paths starting, going left and right, offering different routes down to the river. None of the stuff he had rehearsed came out, none of the wronged man, dignified speech. *"Are you shagging Ben"*, was what he blurted out, saying it as fast as his mouth would move and making it sound like a reply rather than a question.

She kept walking, talking as calmly as he had hoped he would have been able to. She didn't deny it, said that it had just happened, that she didn't plan it. It was in Ben's car. In that ratty pile of junk, Lee thought, on the seats where he had sat.

She couldn't remember how many times, exactly; five or six, she thought when he pushed it. Ben meant nothing to her. That's when she had said it, turned and looked him in the eye for the first time since he had asked her straight out. Ben meant nothing to her. If Ben meant nothing, then he meant even less, Lee thought. She kept talking, saying what a bitch Janice had been for telling him, but he was no longer listening. His face felt hot and he could hear the blood pumping in his ears, with Shirley's voice in the background, like a radio with the volume turned down.

Lee had a thing about hands around his neck, even his own hands, since he was in Primary school. Even when his neck was tense from driving lessons, he would just roll his head about, rather than touch it. Just thinking about somebody touching his neck made him tense up. TV adverts for pain killers, with some guy pulling a face and massaging his neck was enough to set Lee off, the tendons on his neck standing out like a weight lifter's.
It went back to Tommy Jackson in Primary 4. Tommy was allowed to watch movies with his parents. He came in to school one day and started Kung Fu-ing kids in the playground. He was a wild man, walking through the crowd, with his head bowed, shouting "waayaa!" and "waaataw!" and karate chopping people in the arm, or rather on the sleeve of thick duffle coats and parkas. His circuits of the small playground got faster as he got worked up, chopping more than one of the enemy at the same time, shouting louder, more high pitched, standing on one leg and lunging forward. That's when he landed a chop on the side of Lee's neck. Tommy wasn't strong but he was chunky and Lee's neck was a smaller surface area then sleeves of coats. The force imparted when the blow landed on Lee's vagus nerve was enough to send his muscles into spasm and he collapsed on the ground, unconscious.

All he remembered before he blacked out was the fact that he couldn't open his mouth to call out when Tommy hit him. His teeth caught the tip of his tongue as they slammed together. Lockjaw, his mother called it and so did Lee until years later when he saw a documentary about First World War soldiers with tetanus and realised the difference. Lee had never put hands on anybody's throat, including his own, since.

She said it again, "*Ben meant nothing to me, Lee, he was just there.*"

It was like time was fast forwarded. His hands clamped around her throat before she had finished the sentence. He'd read later that it was very difficult to strangle someone with your hands successfully without re-adjusting your grip, because the muscles in the wrists and hands became tired quickly. That had not been a problem for Lee. He grabbed and squeezed in a single, flowing movement, squeezing until her eyes bulged and her face turned the same grey colour all over. He couldn't hold her weight and she fell to the ground in a heap. It was only then that he jumped back, looked at his hands, at the same time as tensing his own neck muscles.

Did he look around for anybody watching, or did he get on the ground and check her first? He couldn't remember. "*Fuck, fuck, fuck, fuck, fuck*". That was all he did remember, thinking it and saying it over and over. He might have shouted for help, but he had no memory of that, even when he tried to piece one together, to make himself feel better.

He put her in the recovery position first. That was the extent of his knowledge about First Aid and unconscious people, and his first reaction. She just lay there, completely limp, limbs flopping as he moved her. Then he rolled onto her back, fearing the worst, got his ear close to her mouth, tried to stop his own panicked panting to check if she was breathing. He couldn't hear anything except his blood, still pumping in his ears. Then five minutes of blowing in her mouth alternating with five thrusts on her sternum, getting frantic, going faster and faster with the mouth-to-mouth and the thrusts. He remembered hearing himself, making unintelligible noises, not words, sounding like a distressed chimp. Then he sat her up then, thumped her in the back, like she was a child that had swallowed a toy. He was getting more and more desperate for her to move, to make a sound, to show any muscle tone, anything. Finally, the Heimlich manoeuvre – that was how frenzied he got – trying abdominal thrusts like she was snow white with a bit of apple stuck in her throat.

He said her name, close to her ear, louder, trying to get a reaction. It was while he had her propped up, sitting with her head slumped on her shoulder, that he heard voices, further along the path, echoing off the overpass which crossed the river. With his hands still under her arms he dragged her off the path into the cover of some birch saplings and a screen of rhododendron bushes. She weighed next to nothing, he remembered, moving fast across the muddy ground, telling himself that was a good sign, convincing himself that the expression dead weight meant something. He waited until the two cyclists had passed, then started on her again with the mouth to mouth, blowing into her mouth first, holding her nose, then blowing up her nose, with his hand clamping her mouth, shaking her, even slapping her on the cheeks, seeing if she winced. Nothing.

The rest he remembered only because other people, the police mainly, and his lawyer, had told him. They were memories without any detail that he could add, like things he had done as a wee boy and only remembered because his mother had told him the holiday stories over and over and shown him the photographs.

If any real memories of what he had done next that night were still in his head, they were *"buried somewhere deep, away from the conscious mind"*, a prison psychologist had told him, which was a strange way to describe it, Lee thought, given what had happened.

There was a big spruce, pushed over by the wind a week before, ripping up its shallow roots on the way down. Lee had rolled Shirley into the pit left behind, climbed in, covered her up with the loose earth and leaves in the hole, then jumped out and kicked away at the loose banking until more moss and wet soil fell on top of her.

He had walked home, gone straight up the stairs and lay on his bed, staring at the ceiling until the police knocked on his door at six the next morning. He had been seen walking with Shirley and she'd been reported missing by her parents, but not found. The dog walker phoned in before Lee got to tell the police where she was, and that got him an extra three years on his sentence.

The muddy footprints on his stairs and Shirley's hair and saliva on this jacket were not needed at a trial. Lee pled guilty at the preliminary hearing, refusing to play the game with his appointed defence lawyer. The lawyer still tried to argue on his behalf, presenting background information to be considered in sentencing – first offence, moment of madness, excellent character references – but Lee's lack of cooperation didn't help his case. It looked bad. Lee had arranged the meeting with Shirley. He had walked her to a quiet spot in dense woods. He had strangled her, buried he body and gone home. Those were the facts.

A drunken fight with a cheating girlfriend would have got him six months maximum. Attempted murder with an attempt to defeat the ends of justice, concealing the body and attempting to flee from the scene got him nine years, even with the guilty plea. The sentence was read by the Judge at the High Court in Glasgow. Lee had few memories of the day. He did remember how shiny new the court looked, and words from the old testament wisdom of Solomon carved in limestone frieze, running around the walls. He had concentrated on these, avoided looking at faces. It was all very elaborate, with people in wigs standing up, sitting down, Lee's solicitor talking to him before he went in, the plea in mitigation and then the sentence.

Grabbing Shirley by the throat and burying her alive got Lee the nine year sentence, plus enough guilt and flashbacks to reduce him to a scooped out shell, even before he went to prison. For two weeks he was moving only when somebody told him it was time, or when he was about to pee or shit where he sat. The only time he could remember not being on auto-pilot in that time as a zombie was when his solicitor visited to discuss the possibility of appealing the sentence. Lee was across the table at him before he had finished suggesting it, ripping up the papers in his face and throwing them on the floor. There would be no appeal. Lee had done it, all of it, in the brutal detail that had been read out in court and splashed across the newspapers. Prison was there, with plenty of time every day, to make him remember that.

Shirley's mother, who had tolerated Lee as someone Shirley liked, had been encouraged by the prosecution lawyer to write a victim impact statement, but she didn't get to read out in court because Lee pled guilty. Instead, on the advice of the lawyer, she released the statement to the *Herald* and Lee had memorised every word it. Some of the language Shirley's mother would never use - "*Shirley now has a pathological fear of the dark and frequent night terrors*"- but there were enough words in the statement that were hers, enough words for Lee to hear them in her voice, in his head, over and over. In prison everything was relative. Murder and minimum 20 year sentences got you respect. Offenses against children got your food spat in, a blanket over your head and a regular kicking, if you weren't already in segregation. In between these, there were long termers with a reputation, serious robbers, and the rest.

Housebreakers, shoplifters and car thieves were the background in the prison. At one time these were guys all looking for short cuts to being richer, all with a different, hard luck story to tell, but now they were drug users, all with the same story, trying to get enough to pay off debts, or money to buy to sell drugs, or just enough for the next hit. Their crimes didn't qualify for a place on any pecking order and were committed so often that they were no longer interesting.

Looking down the pecking order made those higher up feel like their crimes weren't so bad, verging on respectable. Respect was everything. If you lost it, you had years ahead as a muppet, to be ignored, isolated and second to everything. Muppets could become fraggles, guys who started to lose it, on medication, slowly breaking down. When nothing much was happening in the prison, the fraggle became a good source of sick entertainment for other prisoners, seeing who could wind up the mental cases, get them to ding out and lose it completely.

Lee's crime, assault against a woman, could have put him in danger, down the pecking order, in with the wife beaters, but the one-off nature of his crime put him in a different category. The guy in the next cell had set two bull terriers on a 79 year old man because he complained about them running loose, and Lee's cell mate had come home drunk one night and panned his mother's head in when she fried his eggs to a crisp. Lee realised that he had to do his prison time without being a side-show attraction for others. Most of the prisoners were harmless fuck-ups, but there were a few who eyed him up as new boy entertainment.

Lee learned that keeping your head down in prison was a misnomer. What you had to do from the day you went in, to avoid becoming a muppet, was to keep your head up. To keep out of fights and not be quaking with fear every time another prisoner approached him, he had to create a new Michael, whom he called Lee. He shared as little information as possible with as few people as possible and never asked questions in case it showed how little he knew. Playing his cards close to his chest, very close. He watched everything that happened and he picked his way through the mess, carefully. Unless you were over 65 or in admin segregation, out of reach, you were fair game. He wanted to learn fast. The only information he got free was in his prison induction pack; laundry, showers, TV, prisoner conduct. But that wasn't going to tell him anything about keeping his head above water. In his first month inside he learned who to avoid. He identified and steered clear of the creepy loners and organised groups of guys who called the shots in the cash free society of tobacco or heroin or mobile phone top-ups and who owed what. He had a few scuffles with guys testing him but didn't get into pissing contests about who was hardest. He stood his ground when he needed to, but got the fuck out of it when he didn't.

"Security threat groups", in prison officer terms, and inside gangs to everyone else, were always looking for new recruits and a refusal, even a polite one, could offend, but Lee kept it civil. Friendly approaches were almost never what they seemed and he trusted nobody. Six weeks into his sentence, one of the main men in his block had come into his cell and stood toe-to-toe with Lee, to tell him that he could have him beaten in places that didn't show the bruises. Lee had said, "*I'm sure you could*," and left it at that, keeping the eye contact, and managing not to shake until the guy left.

He kept away from the stuff that was around, swallowed or cooked, to make your time go easier – bird killer, they called it, but it killed more than time in prison. He avoided anybody who carried a weapon, prison officers who took a dislike to him and prisoners who took a liking to him. He stopped smoking because it took him out of the game where it was easy to make a mistake by giving a cigarette or not giving a cigarette. Prisoners who didn't smoke, traded in tins of tuna, so he avoided tuna too. He watched the guys with newspapers, checked out which papers and targeted them for conversation when the desperation of talking to no-one got to him. That was how he met Tony.

Lee's mother wrote, by the third letter honest enough to say that she was too ashamed to visit. She'd moved to Newcastle, near her sister's family and as far she could afford to go from Shirley and her family. By the end of the first year Lee had enough information from his mother to write a dissertation on a comparison of the weather in the West of Scotland and the North of England. He liked the letters though, both getting them and reading them, and they were the only ones he got. His mother had taken up, or gone back to dressmaking, inspired by some reality TV show where competitors faced off under bright lights with sewing machines. She was making clothes for his Aunty Isobel's kids and it was saving a lot of money, apparently. She was also going to the bingo, just once a week mind, and she was getting a lot better with her felt tip marker, keeping pace with the bingo caller. His mother never asked questions about the prison or about "his trouble" as she called it, and Lee in turn kept it light, telling her about what he'd watched on TV and about his jobs in the kitchen and the library, even though he had neither.

The only people who visited him in that first year were paid to. His solicitor was still sniffing about for more legal aid work until he realised that the well had run dry. The chaplain, a punch bag of a man, did his rounds, multi-faith and smiling and, "*always available, Lee, even if it's just for a chat.*" Well what the fuck else was it going to be, Lee thought, other than a chat; some root canal treatment, or maybe a fitting for a new suit? Lee thought about her every day he was there, and that was his punishment. He didn't need someone to tell him that what he'd done was wrong, or to ask any Holy Joe preacher to forgive him.

There was Jenny, the prison social worker, doing family liaison work to keep the connections, and occasional bereavement counselling, using skills from her previous job. In a case load that was more firefighting than anything more planned, Lee was low priority for Jenny. He had no kids, no partner and therefore no pre-release support required.

In his first months in prison Lee had letters from gawkers – people who wanted to visit him because of what he'd done, just to have a look. He was surprised. Two were from guys he'd known at school, although all he recognised was the names. *"We were good mates and I'm interested to know what really happened"*, and one was from a woman –*"picture enclosed"*- who read about him in the Daily Record and *"felt compelled to write"*. Friends Reunited and women seeking men were different kinds of desperation, Lee thought.

It was almost three years before Lee did have somebody he was glad to see in the visitors' room. Tony (robbery of designer shirts and reset of same) had been finishing his sentence just as Lee was starting his. He was now working for another ex-prisoner, who had set up a home removals business, doing well, just on word-of-mouth recommendations. Tony was glad of the job and of the muscle mass that he'd put on during his sentence.

Lee knew Tony from the prison poker games and Lee suspected that Tony came to visit mainly for the buzz of walking into the jail and then walking out again. But that was OK. They'd have a crack about prisoners and prison officers and who had done what, then move onto getting outraged about prima donna footballers, getting paid the price of a house every week, to sit on a sub's bench. Tony would tell him about cleaning up, or about the bad beats that he'd had playing poker in the back of the furniture van during breaks. Tony could only get to Perth Prison about once every six weeks, so there was always plenty of catch up, never any spaces in the chat. It was nothing deep, and that suited Lee fine.

Two years in, Lee got onto vocational training and liked the bricklaying. At first because it was minimum talk, maximum labour, but then he found he was good at it, and he worked his way through the qualification levels with the guy who came in from the local college.

Lee couldn't remember if it was an opt-in or an opt-out request form, but he had ticked the wrong box, that was clear. The letter from the National Official Prison Visitors Association notified him that his assigned Official Prison Visitor would be Breeda Getty, the name inserted in capitals, and out of line with the rest of the text in the letter.

"The role of the Official Prison Visitor is to try to encourage the development of a constructive use of a prison sentence whereby inmates gain both a sense of belonging to the community and the realisation that they themselves have the ability to contribute to society's wellbeing."

Lee read it and wondered who would write this stuff, and who would believe it. Prisoners who have the ability to contribute to society's wellbeing? They must be keeping all of those guys in another prison, he thought, a very small prison.

"Prison visitors could provide emotional support and intellectual enrichment that would normally be experienced through friends."

That bit made him think back to his letters from the gawkers, and to personal ads for women seeking men. He knew that Breeda Getty was going to be a forty plus, plastered-with-make-up case, with a rescue fantasy, looking for a man who had been in jail for years and was even more emotionally fucked up than she was. She would be some hopeless, dried up saddo who was going window shopping at the jail, hoping for a bargain. As it turned out, he was wrong.

It was the only time in his eight years that he had requested a visit from the prison chaplain. It was a last resort. The National Official Prison Visitors Association had not replied to his letter, asking for no visits and explaining that he had made a mistake. Anything on forms in prison had a way of getting lost. The Prison Governor had told him that the Prison Visitors Association was an independent organisation over which he and his staff had no control. The visit from Breeda was two days away when he spoke to the chaplain, although Lee didn't get a chance to say much.

They met in the prison Chaplaincy Centre. After the first five minutes with the chaplain, Lee wondered if there was a Chaplain's Big Book of Tips on Speaking to People. The chaplain said his name at the end of every sentence, and slipped it in anywhere else he could. The amount of eye contact was like a staring contest.

"It's perfectly understandable Lee, and I've seen it with a lot of prisoners".

The chaplain's pose was legs crossed, hands clasped together on his lap, with thumbs free to tap together as he spoke.

"You're bound to be nervous, having second thoughts about meeting a stranger, and especially a stranger associated with your future and your prospects beyond prison, Lee. That can be a scary thought."

"But you don't get it, chaplain, I didn't ask for the visit, it was a mistake on the form," Lee repeated, for the third time.

The chaplain held up one hand.

"There's no need for formality Lee - it's OK to call me Roger. The business with the form is as may be, but perhaps it was meant to be? Your best course of action now is to embrace this opportunity, to welcome the chance to begin building a future with some self-respect and hope, taking those first small, important steps in communicating with others in society. Most men who leave this prison come back, Lee, but that doesn't need to be you....."

Lee had a few more attempts at explaining it as simply as he could, then gave up. The chaplain had a lot more to say and Lee realised that his own replies were just prolonging the sermon.

The day before the visit from Breeda Getty, Lee asked around about the consequences of refusing to leave his cell. At breakfast, his cell mate, jabbing his spoon on the table and spraying scrambled egg, told him to contact his lawyer and assert his entitlement under Human Rights legislation to stay in his cell for as long as he wanted. The prison guard on his block told him that he would be moved to the Segregation Unit with the kiddy fiddlers and other beasts if he was too frightened to come out of his cell. So he met with Breeda.

CHAPTER 13

Showing Your Hand

If a player wins a hand when all other players fold to his bet or raise, he is not required to show his hand. It is considered a weakness to show cards in this situation as it gives other players information about how that player plays certain cards. For example, it lets opponents know when a player was bluffing or was not bluffing and reduces the chances of that player successfully bluffing in subsequent hands. There are a few exceptions, when players will show cards, just to give false information and create an image. Showing Aces or Kings, for example, when everyone has folded, to create the impression that the player will only raise with strong hands.
Some players will exploit players who show cards, others will admire their honesty, whilst others will just be embarrassed by their naivety.

"*See, she thought she was an angel, and now she is, Gerry,*" said Arthur, "*I'm happier now that I've worked that one out.*"

They were stopped at road works on the way to the club. Gerry had noticed that when he picked up Arthur that night, for once he didn't start talking as soon as his arse hit the passenger seat. Gerry had felt obliged to fill the silence, moaning about the traffic, asking Arthur if he wanted the radio on.

Arthur didn't answer him directly.

"*Golf on the radio, Gerry, eh? Now who thought that one up? They could just pretend to have a stonking, exciting tournament and report on it on the radio, but not actually play it. It would save all the trouble and expense of those overpaid guys in pink tartan trews walking about for four hours for one game. And who would know the difference?*"

"*Aye, right enough,*" said Gerry, chuckling at the thought, "*maybe we could persuade somebody to broadcast poker on the radio – now that would be a challenge.*"

When the golf and radio chat ran its course they sat in silence for half a mile, until they hit the road works.

When Arthur started talking about Melissa again Gerry was listening, but he was distracted by Arthur's hands. He used them a lot when he talked, like a political correspondent on TV, adding emphasis to what he was saying, even when the pointing and waving and chopping bore no relationship to the words. But tonight Arthur's hands stayed in his lap.

He spoke without turning to Gerry and he spoke more slowly than his usual stream of consciousness rush. Gerry kept expecting the hands to burst into life any second, moving faster to make up for lost time, to catch up with the words, but they stayed folded one over the other, thumbs interlocked. Gerry wondered if they were restraining each other, silently wrestling, trying to break the hold.

"Sorry Arthur, I missed that last bit. What did you say?" Gerry said,

"I said that she thought she was an angel and now she is," Arthur repeated.

Gerry's participation was not normally required on these journeys, but the way Arthur paused made him feel that he was waiting for him to chip in something.

Gerry broke his rule of listening only.

"Aye it sounds like she was a good woman Arthur, and now she's at peace."

Gerry heard himself say it, and then wondered where in his head that phrase had been lying. It was the sort of meaningless mince that people said at funerals, stuff that was meant to comfort the bereaved but didn't. It was safe and meaningless but better than saying nothing, or trying to make up something new and getting it wrong.

The lights changed, but Arthur didn't reply until they passed the stationary traffic at the other end of the road works.

The hotel verified that the booking was for one night, one person, a double room overlooking the gardens. She'd signed in under her own name at 6.30pm and written the car number on the hotel registration. She'd taken dinner and breakfast at the same table, reading a book both times, paid for the room and checked out at 9.40am.

Arthur had phoned the police as soon as he came home and found the house empty and the car gone. On the recording he sounded frantic, demanding an All-Points Bulletin on the car and his wife, a helicopter and roadblocks.

The two officers who attended took his statement, one writing, one watching Arthur. His wife had been missing for between one and eight hours. She had not gone missing before. Her husband had so far phoned his wife's mother and sister and two close friends. The missing person had taken an overnight bag with her, but not her prescription medication, and this was one of the things that concerned her husband most. The officer watching also noted that Arthur stood by the window for the duration of the statement, looking up and down the road.

The car was found within thirty six hours. The hotel car park was for residents only and car registration numbers were checked against the register every night. The guest had checked out, but the car was still there next night and the hotel asked Kendal Rural West police to trace the owner. The check brought up the hit on the missing and stolen vehicles on the Police National Computer.

"You're right. I think she is at peace now, I do. I don't know if she ever was when she was here. She only married me because I kept asking her, and because she thought she might find more peace with me than on her own. Maybe she did, but it wasn't enough."

Arthur paused, just when Gerry thought he was ready to talk out the rest of the journey. His hands still hadn't joined in and Gerry had never seen him this calm, at least not without a book in his hands.

"When I first met her Gerry she was doing so many things I had to book a drink with her two weeks ahead," Arthur continued, smiling at the memory.

"She was in eight until six at the insurance office, then out nearly every night. I was a young guy, but I couldn't keep up. She did yoga on a Tuesday, spin class every other Wednesday and fencing at the week-end. Fencing, Gerry – I thought she meant putting in

posts and wire, but it was fighting people with swords, like Zorro!"

Arthur was still talking more slowly than usual, as relaxed as Gerry had ever heard him.

"I only met her because she was always on the bus I got home on a backshift from the plant. Pretty romantic, eh? Our eyes met across a slashed headrest, with "Jake wiz here", scrawled in felt marker pen…."

Gerry was focussed on what Arthur was saying, nodding.

"She always had her sports bag on the bus and her hair was always wet, tied back. Took me three weeks to fire myself up to speak to her, and that was only after another three weeks when we had started nodding to each other on the bus."

"I kept telling myself don't say, Been to the gym?, don't say Been to the gym?, say something smart and casual. I had even looked up lines on the internet, Gerry, and as soon as she looked up to nod that night, what did I say?"

They were moving faster now, as the front of the backlog through the traffic lights picked up speed.

"She had gone back to that hotel where we went on honeymoon. They found her car there, reported it. She was still looking, I guess, still trying to find whatever we had then, whatever she had then."

"We went walking nearly every day. It was weather like we had here today Gerry, but even hotter. The tar on the roads was actually melting and the news reports on the radio said that birds were falling out of the sky. Now that doesn't happen in Britain much does it?" Arthur laughed.

"It was a bit cooler up higher up, on the hills, but not much. There was a bit of a breeze to move the air around but it was still sweltering. We would pick a route over the morning champagne and the mushrooms, and then get out early doors, right after breakfast, and do a few miles, before it got too clammy and hot. I think that was the bluest sky I'd ever seen, anywhere."

"I know that it was only a walk Gerry, but it became like an adventure every morning. Melissa had done the research and she knew how long they would all take and

how steep it would be and how high we would be climbing above sea level. We would get
excited about choosing a better one each day, like trying to top what we had done the day
before. Some of them just skirted about the edges of Kendal and you could see the town all
the time you were walking, but as the week went on we were getting bolder and getting out
into the wilds in half an hour."

The search parties, co-ordinated by the police and the three mountain rescue teams, had used Arthur's map as a starting point. The pencil marks could still be seen, and each of the routes was labelled by day. There were a few Lake District scrambles but no high ridge or pike walking. Kendal Fell was as high as they had gone.

Arthur had gone through two ink cartridges, printing out individual posters, that he stapled-gunned to telegraph poles, trees and tourist information points in and around Kendal. There were plenty of volunteers, combining a walk on the hills with a worthy cause, looking for Melissa over two weekends and the days between.

They checked gullies and thick bush on the routes, pools and streams, and woodland in ravines. A red deer and two sheep killed by the winter were found in the same gully and an assortment of walkers' sodden hats and gloves were brought it for examination, but there was nothing belonging to Melissa. After interviewing Arthur, police used dogs to search the heart-shaped copse of trees near Tebay Gorge, the furthest distance Arthur and his wife had gone, travelling by bus from Kendal. According to local legend, the woods were the final resting place of two lovers forbidden to marry, who had taken their own lives rather than be kept apart. The trees in the woods were hemmed in by two walls, on a wedge-shaped piece of ground. Arthur and Melissa's initials were carved high on a tree, near the point of the heart, where Arthur had balanced on the dry stane dyke with his pen knife, but there was no other sign of Melissa having been there.

"When they stood down the mountain rescue teams I think I was actually relieved

Gerry," Arthur said, adding quickly, *"I know that might sound cold."*

It was like he was telling Gerry about something that happened at work; there was no distress in his voice, no painful searching for the next word.

"Her mother and her sister gave me such a hard time then, said we should be putting up more posters, getting Melissa's photo on the side of milk cartons, on Facebook."

Arthur paused again and looked down at his hands.

"But I knew Melissa. When we didn't find her in those first few weeks, I started to feel better. I thought that she had laid a trail for us, planned it the way she did, leaving the car at the hotel, then slipped away to start somewhere new. She was somewhere she could start searching again. I began thinking that she didn't want us to chase her. 'Course I was gutted that she was gone, catatonic, couldn't speak to anyone, but I thought at least she was somewhere that she might come back from, to visit me, or write or phone, in time, and that was much better than thinking about her lying injured on the hills, dying of pain and thirst. When all the king's men and all the king's horses couldn't find her, I convinced myself that she was OK. "

He smiled again and blew air out his nose, like he was remembering some detail.

"Melissa was clever, see, I mean really smart. She could do crosswords and Sudokus and Kakuros in the papers and then get angry with herself for wasting time doing them. I never saw her start anything and give it up because it was too hard. But disappearing? That was a really difficult one. I figured she'd decided to do it to challenge herself. To plan it, disappear and make a clean break. I was never half as smart as she was and I never saw it coming, her leaving me, I mean, and that was what wiped me out, I think. That was what damaged me, even more than not knowing where she had gone."

Arthur paused and Gerry looked again at his hands as they appeared and disappeared in the light between two underpasses.

"We were getting on all right, I thought. That was the first question that the police asked me. How was your relationship with your wife? But how do you judge that stuff Gerry, eh? Do you look at neighbours and think, well, at least we're not as bad as them,

or do you watch TV and think, well maybe there's something missing, something they have that we should have? I don't know, and we didn't talk about that stuff much, just sort of got on with it, let it happen. The going was good."

"Melissa was always searching for something when I met her, and she was still looking the whole time I knew her. You know that she's been in Glenalmond, in the unit, Gerry right? I mean, that's no big secret, I've mentioned that before, at least to you. She was just a bit knackered, burned out, doing too much with all that searching. Like one day I came home from the plant and she'd taken the day off work, rearranged all the furniture in the house, moved it all herself; couches, wardrobes, everything. Said she wanted to see how it would look. Next day the stuff was all back to where it had been. She'd get something in her head and worry it like a terrier, then just give it up as fast and move onto something else. She'd spend hours on her iTunes, organising songs into the perfect playlists, playing them once, then wiping them and starting again. Her doctor suggested some down time in Glenalmond, just to let her slow down a bit like."

They were ten minutes from the club. Without a word, Gerry flicked his indicator and took the exit for the Perth ring road, dropping his speed. He sensed that Arthur needed to talk and he couldn't go directly to the club tonight and not hear the rest, but he also knew that he wasn't strong enough to pull into a car park and let Arthur finish, without the distraction of driving. Arthur was on a roll. As long as they were driving it was OK, and he guessed that Arthur preferred that too. So they set off on the first of three circuits of inner road around the city centre.

A crime manager and a Missing Person Co-ordinator from Cumbria Constabulary gathered information about Melissa. An initial risk assessment and secondary risk assessment moved Melissa from the status of "absent" to "missing" quickly and established the grading of police response required. The fact that Melissa had previously been treated for mental ill health, even although it was two years previously, identified her as being a "misper" at medium risk, especially since her behaviour was considered out of character.

The bank reported no activity on Melissa's account, other than a cash withdrawal on the day of her disappearance, an amount that corresponded roughly with the hotel bill plus petrol. The room that she had slept in had already been cleaned on the day of her departure, but police checked it anyway and interviewed the hotel staff.

Bus drivers from the morning shift in and out of Kendal were traced and shown photographs, supplied by Arthur. Two drivers, one going north and one going south, thought they'd seen her, but couldn't be sure. The need for passengers to drop the correct money into the slot for fares made it more likely that drivers checked the coins, rather than looked at the passengers' faces.

There were three CCTV cameras in Kendal town centre, and a full set of multi-directional cameras at the railway station. Melissa didn't appear on any of these, or if she did she was under a hood or an umbrella like hundreds of others on a wet morning.

A Cumbria Community Messaging Police Alert had been issued.

Police are currently trying to identify the whereabouts of a missing female last seen in the Kendal area. The female is described as white, 5'7 in height, 35 years of age, short brown hair, cut in a "pixie" style. The missing female is believed to be wearing a waterproof grey jacket, black jeans and a light blue shirt or blouse. She is wearing hiking boots. Concerns for this person have developed since her car was found at a Kendal hotel a day after she checked out. Any information about this women or sightings should be reported immediately to the Police on telephone number 101.

One week after Melissa's disappearance, drivers whose regular route to work took them past the hotel were stopped. They were shown the same photographs of Melissa and asked if they have given her a lift, seen her, or seen anyone else give her a lift near the hotel.

In other parts of the country, the maxim for cases of missing persons where the circumstances were suspicious or unexplained was, "*If in doubt, think murder."* This maximised chances of preserving evidence. In the Lake District, the maxim was more like, "*If in doubt, look on the hills*", because that's where the majority of mispers were eventually found, alive mostly. The Patterdale Mountain Rescue Team had been trialling a search and rescue drone. The remotely operated craft with cameras could cover large and remote areas in a short time, weather and light permitting. They'd sent one up to fly a grid pattern over the least accessible, upper slopes.

The Missing Person Co-ordinator from Cumbria Constabulary was on the phone every day for the first week to Arthur, keeping him up to date on what was being done, and then to let him know when the mountain rescue teams were stood down.

"It took them eleven years to find a bit off that jetliner Gerry – do you remember it? It was a big chunk of metal in the middle of Manhattan, with all those people walking by, but nobody noticed it for eleven years. A six foot bit of landing gear from one of the planes that hit the twin towers, broken off on impact and wedged between the back of two buildings. It was just lying there with junk and piles of litter in this wee narrow alley. When they found it, it brought back all those hellish memories for people who had been in New York on the day and all the families who didn't have a body to bury."

They were on the second circuit of the ring road by then. Arthur was speaking more quietly and Gerry was having to lean toward him as he drove, to hear him.

'It took five weeks to find Melissa. I don't think she wanted to be found. She didn't want to be any bother, you see, just wanted to make a quiet exit. No fuss - that would have been what she was trying for, just to fade away in a bit of mystery and leave everybody with happy memories of how she was when she was well. To be an enigma. Is that the right word Gerry? That would have suited her."

There were more pauses now and Arthur sounded like he was running low on energy, struggling to finish.

'It was a guy working at the multi-storey in Kendal. Good eyesight he must have had.

He was on the top floor of the car park, looking for parking penalty notices people had torn off and chucked over the side. You're only allowed to park there during the day, see."
"Melissa had picked a good spot. The lane between the buildings was fenced off at both ends and it was dark most days. It didn't get much sun or light. All you could see at ground level was piles of rubble, left over from when they built the car park years ago."

Gerry realised this was it. He'd supposed he knew what was coming, and he'd heard Arthur talk around it plenty of times, without saying what had happened. Now he was going to finish the story.

"She was an angel and she thought she could fly, Gerry, that's the way I still like to think about it. I'm happy to remember her like that, because I know she was an angel, who would never harm anybody and never have wanted me to be hurt."

Gerry noticed Arthur's hands spring suddenly into life as he mentioned the car park for the first time. They turned palms up for a few seconds, then Arthur clasped them behind his neck, elbows pointing out the front windscreen.

"When they found her – well it wasn't really her, Gerry, it was just what was left to bury – I took it hard. That's when it was my turn to go to Glenalmond for the first time. Yep, that was my first trip to the big house with the locked doors. I don't mind people knowing about it. I think everybody does anyway. The guys at the poker know. I mean it's pretty obvious and Perth isn't such a big place that they wouldn't know. Nobody mentions it though, nobody takes the piss because I've been there and I appreciate that. Maybe they don't care. I don't remember much about going in, to be honest. I remember being off work, just moping about the house all day, on these horse tablets "for my nerves" as my sister called it. I'd slob about in the same clothes for days, minging, fall asleep in the middle of eating my dinner in watching some sad afternoon TV, and wake up with food all over me, drooling at the mouth. It was disgusting, Gerry, it really was, like a bloody comedy sketch."

Arthur laughed gently.

Gerry glanced at the dashboard clock and wondered if he should pull over and give Christopher a call, to let him know that he would be late. Christopher could set up the tables, but he would be major pissed off about having to do it by himself. When Gerry did it, the early arrivals – mostly guys who had to get buses – would help out, and the set up was done in 15 minutes. When Christopher had to set up, everybody who was there early would drift off to the bar and hang about there until all the tables were up and the chips were counted. Gerry kept driving, deciding that a phone call would be too distracting or disrespectful and would end Arthur's no-hands story.

"I came out of it and stayed at home for couple of weeks, then got back to work. Well what else was I gonnae do, eh? But I knew that I still wasn't right."

Arthur turned and looked out the passenger window and laughed quietly.

"You like this next bit Gerry, being a poker player. Funny enough, it was a gambling movie that finally put me in Glenalmond the second time – I remember that bit. A gambling movie and it wasn't even a poker movie either."

"I'd been lying on the couch on a day off work, eating Pringles – bloody addictive those crisps - flicking through the channels in the afternoon when I found The Hustler on one of those vintage movie channels. It was one of those channels with about half an hour of adverts in every hour, you know."

He stopped and turned to face Gerry.

"You remember it Gerry? Fast Eddie Felson and Minnesota Fats in the pool halls, Gerry? What a good movie that is! Eddie makes the mistake of scamming the wrong guys and gets his thumbs broken and all that, and then he comes back at the end, but it's all a bit empty by then. He's lost it. For me the Hustler's not a patch on the Cincinnati Kid, not in the same league. It is good, but the Cincinnati Kid's still my favourite gambling movie, apart from Rounders, but John Malkovich's Russian accent makes that a comedy for me. Anyway, I thought I'd drink some coffee and try to stay awake and watch The Hustler. It was better than all the hospital drama and game show dross that was on that afternoon."

"It had just started, about five minutes into the movie when I found it and Eddie and Fats are playing pool, on this amazing marathon game, with Eddie winning some but Fats always coming back, just wearing him down, grinding away, the seasoned campaigner. You remember it Gerry?"

"Yes, yes, I've seen it a few times Arthur. It is a classic," Gerry replied in the brief space Arthur had left.

"Anyway, Eddie's feeling good, starts off talking himself up, getting into it, trying to psyche out Fats."

Arthur's accent switched to mid-western Paul Newman.

"You know I got a hunch Fat Man, I got a hunch that it's me from here on in. I mean, that ever happen to you, when suddenly you feel that you just can't miss? I dreamed about this game...you know this is my table Fat Man – I own it."

Arthur's hands came from behind his neck, alive for a moment, chalking an imaginary pool cue as he played Fast Eddie Felson. He changed back to his own voice.

"That ever happen to you at poker Gerry, when you feel it's your night and every card hits? Usually lasts about ten minutes for me, then goes belly up when I play some donkey hand and lose half my chips."

Arthur laughed again and Gerry joined in, then took out a tissue and nervously blew his nose.

"So I was watching the movie and it got a bit further in and I wanted to know the name the actress who played Eddie's girlfriend. It was one of those things, you know, one of these things that doesn't matter, but you want to know it anyway, can't get on with the movie until you've got the answer. Talking about it with the psychiatrist later in Glenalmond, he said it might have been because the actress looked a bit like Melissa, and I could see what he meant, sort of. But I don't think that was it. I never thought about it at the time, but Piper Laurie, that's who it was, her hair was the same. Apart from that, I don't think she looked much like Melissa."

Arthur's speech has been speeding up again, almost reaching his usual, steady gallop pace.

"So I went onto Google on my phone for a cast list of the movie, and that was when I it went wrong. I just lost it," he said.

His hands came off his lap briefly, then slumped back down.

"I flooded the flat below mine. The woman that lived there came to my door first, then the landlord with a spare key, then the police, then the mental health squad."

Arthur's right hand rose from his lap and knocked on the door of his flat.

"It was just a tiny flat Gerry – I'd never had that many people in it!"

Now both of his hands moved to turn on taps.

"I had filled the bath to the rim and sat in it. The insurance covered it, but I still feel bad about that women's ceiling. She had to move out and have her flat gutted and re-decorated after all the water damage. They wouldn't even let me go back to get my stuff. Somebody put it in bin liners and brought it to Glenalmond."

They were on their final circuit of Perth. Gerry wanted to listen, but he knew that Christopher would be stomping about by then, stressed out, trying to collect the money, tick off the names, too proud or maybe just too realistic to ask anyone at the club to help him out.

"I had this thing about water, you see. Probably working at the plant too long, Melissa used to say. I know how this sounds. If you're near running water, Gerry, you get the benefit of the negative ions. It's a pure fact, as Rab at the club would say. But it is true, and the more running water, the more negative ions. So sitting in the bath with the taps on full bung, see, that made sense to me at the time, because there's a lot of ions belting out those taps!"

"When I went out walking with Melissa I always tried to go somewhere with moving water. The Tay was best, obviously, especially when it was in spate, moving fast, and I could feel myself getting high on the ions, like drinking good coffee, you know? Any of those streams cutting through the woods at the back of our flats were fine too. I could get a buzz on when I went walking up there. It's even better when the water was bouncing off rocks on the way down, because more ions get thrown off, into the air."

"When we went to the Lake District I felt like the whole damn place was head deep in ions, like we were walking through a cloud of them whenever we stepped out the door. Maybe that's why I picked it, I can't remember now, but I knew there would be a lot of water coming down the hills."

"Everywhere we went, I kept saying to Melissa, "Can you feel it here as well?". She just kept saying that she didn't know much about ions, but whatever it was, it made her feel finer than she had in years. I had never seen her like that. We went to this one place, Tebay Gorge. It was a wood shaped like a heart. There was a river there, raging it was, really hammering down the hill. I felt like I was going to overdose on the ions. We both got so high on it, I ended up climbing on a tree, carving our initials, like I was a fourteen year old!"

Arthur's hand leapt up again, to carve the initials in front of him. He paused and looked at his hand as it settled again in his lap.

"It was hard when we came back to Perth and the flat. We had some amazing photos of the Lakes and Melissa had these on her phone and all over her Facebook and kept telling everybody about the place, just raving about it. I wondered how long the ions would last. I got to thinking about it, about the science of it, you know. Was it like a suntan than still looked good for a while, or did the ions just leach out of you as soon as you moved away from the water? I still don't know the answer to that one."

Arthur paused, then spoke more slowly again.

"Anyway, it was at least a couple of weeks before the first time Melissa asked me to stop talking about the Lakes. She said it was like looking in the rear view mirror all the time, when we had to look at what was ahead instead, for me, for her, for us. She said a lot of stuff like that- profound like. I knew if meant shut up about the Lakes Arthur, and it did surprise me, because she's had such a good time."

Arthur's hands moved onto his shoulders, arms crossed over his chest.

"That winter, sitting in that flat, two jumpers on to keep warm, with nothing on the TV and only work to look forward to the next day, I guess we were both thinking that it would never be as good as it had been in the Lakes. Neither of us said it, but the Lakes

went from something we raved about, to something never to be mentioned."

"I started to get worried about her then, and it was about then that I got to thinking that a lot of the ions got lost in the pipes. We were on the fourth floor of that block and I worked out that most of the ions were falling off, just seeping away, or getting absorbed by the copper pipes as it got pumped up to that height. It made sense to me then. Water wasn't supposed to flow up the way, that wasn't natural. It's only good for you when you don't change it. When you boil it in a kettle or microwave it all the natural energy that's in it gets lost. It's like when you boil sprouts too much Gerry, you know, you start off with healthy green things that are good for you and you end up with a pile of limp seaweed. That's when I started to talk to Melissa about it. I told her we should move, find a place outside the town, somewhere with more space, but she didn't want to spend more time travelling to work."

"I wasnae welcome back to the flat when I got out of Glenalmond. The neighbours knew that I had been taken away to the big hoos, and all the kids in the block starting calling me psycho, asking me when I was going for a bath and writing stuff on my door. The social worker managed to get me another place. It was a farm cottage out towards Methvuen."

Arthur stopped talking. Gerry had turned on his indicator to come off the ring road, starting the left-right-left turns that would take them to the club in five minutes. He started thinking hard about what to say to bring the chat back to something light, something normal, before they arrived.

When Arthur started talking again Gerry almost missed it. He spoke so quietly that Gerry thought at first that he was talking to himself.

"It was the tag line in The Hustler that did it Gerry. A tag line? I'd never heard of them before then. I checked later and the line wasn't in the trailer for the movie and it wasn't even in the movie. The trailer just said something about Fast Eddie and Sarah and how they might be better off if they left each other alone. That got me thinking about me and Melissa again. But the tag line? It was there on my Google search Gerry, when I was looking up Piper Laurie's name on the cast of the movie. I read it when I was scanning

down the page. It was like somebody just pulled the plug of whatever machine was keeping me going, and that was when I lost it. "Only the angel who falls knows the depths of hell", it said. "Only the angel who falls knows the depths of hell". It was like somebody had written it just for me to read."

Arthur turned towards Gerry then and spoke again in his usual car voice.

"See, I can say it now, like that, without cracking up, because I've read it so many times since then and it's just words to me, but that one afternoon, when I read it for the first time it hit me so hard. What did Melissa go through before she got on that car park roof?"

Gerry became aware that Arthur was still looking at him and he became flustered as he realised that this one was a real question, not just another pause in the story. The space Arthur had left was for his answer.

He glanced quickly at Arthur, then looked back at the road, scurrying in his head for something to say. He feigned a cough as he realised that he couldn't drive and think up an answer for Arthur that meant anything. As they came around the bend he spotted a lay-by and pulled in behind a lorry, keeping the engine running.

Gerry looked across Arthur, rather than at him.

"Well ….I don't remember it, but I don't think that's what that line means Arthur", he said, buying himself some more time.

"It's about Fast Eddie in the movie, and how he's been up and then he's down and…"

Arthur's finger was pointing at the windscreen.

"Yeah, that's what they said in Glenalmond, Gerry, and I know that now, but it made me think about Melissa and how bad it must have been for her to do that. Not just to do it, but to plan it. To be in our flat and to be booking into that hotel, working out the dates, knowing that she wasn't coming back, deciding that her life would never be better. Only the angel who falls knows the depths of hell. She decided to do that and then we were still living together for what, a month, two months? I should have seen it in her, there must have been signs, must have been."

While Arthur spoke, Gerry listened, keeping his eyes on the back of the lorry. He was struggling, really struggling to find anything to say that he thought would help Arthur, and he knew that he was way out of his depth. This was counselling territory and Gerry struggled even to spell the word correctly.

Each time he thought he had the beginning of any answer, he would glance at the dashboard clock, and forget what he was going to say.   There was no way that there were going to make the start of the poker. When Arthur spoke again, Gerry held his phone down by the driver's door and used his right hand, sending a quick text to Barry, asking him to buy Gerry and Arthur into the game.

"When they interviewed me about how she had been before she disappeared, all I could tell them that she had been buzzing for the last two weeks, out with her mates, going to her evening classes, meeting up with me after work, cleaning the flat. She was saying goodbye, of course. I see that now, getting stuff in order before she went, but at the time I missed it completely."

Arthur stopped talking again, he and Gerry staring at the back of the lorry. *"Eddie Stobart. Trans. Store. Logistics"*, it said. It was dark with no wind and the only sound was the whoosh of cars passing the layby.   They sat for a full minute and Gerry was about to repeat his line about Melissa being at peace now, just to break the tension when his phoned beeped, confirming that Barry had paid them both into the game and the first hand was about to be dealt. With the sound of the phone, Arthur's hands suddenly sprung into life, both index fingers pointing at the lorry, like pistols.

"Fast Eddie Stobart. Occupation – hustler", he said in an American accent and smiled.

He leant forward in his seat and rubbed his face with both hands.

"Jeez, I'm sorry for rambling on like that Gerry. It doesnae take much to get me going, I know, but I don't know what got me started on that tonight."
He looked across at the clock on the dashboard.

"*And look at the time - I've made us miss the start of the game! Jeez, I'm really sorry Gerry.*"

"*No problem, Arthur, you're OK,*" Gerry said, shaking himself like a dog waking up and putting the car quickly into gear.

"*I got Barry to buy us in.*"

"*Thanks for that*", said Arthur.

He sat back in his seat and put his thumbs behind imaginary braces on his chest.

Reverting to his best Paul Newman he said, "*Fats, let's you and me go and shoot a game of straight pool.*"

Gerry laughed, "*Aye, well, I'm no so keen on the Fats bit Arthur, but let's get there and see what we can do tonight.*"

As he drove, he felt a tension in his neck and shoulders that usually only came when he'd played poker for too many hours.

CHAPTER 14

Final Table – Buried Pair

Before the 1980's and the rise of Texas Hold 'Em, the most widely played poker variation was Seven Card Stud. Unlike Hold 'Em, where on small blind and one big blind are put in by the two players on the left of the dealer, every player in Seven Card Stud has to put in a small number of chips at the start of the hand. This is called the ante.
Two cards are dealt face down and one face up to each player. There is one round of betting then, followed by betting after each of the other four cards are dealt face up to each player. The cards dealt face down to each player are called hole cards. When a player has a pair of hole cards, this is also known as a buried pair, as no-one can see them.

Rab was rehearsing.

It was a thing of beauty and it made him feel taller, just putting it on. He kept it on a wooden coat hanger in the wardrobe, protected by a bin liner. It was the only thing in his wardrobe that didn't smell like a charity shop on a hot day. Once a year he took it out and draped it over his shoulders. He liked that, the ceremonial draping. He'd lift over his head, hold it in the air for a few ceremonial seconds, then just let it drop the last few inches. It always settled perfectly first time around his neck and over his chest.

He had collected the silver plated emblems, and pinned them on over the years, the only collection of anything that he had ever owned. There was the All Seeing Eye, the Bible, the Crown and King William, and the purple badge spelling out LOL (Loyal Orange Order Lodge). The sash was four inches wide, bright orange, with purple stripes running along the edge, in silver bullion-wire fringe and braid. The squared off ends stopped just above Rab's waist.

The only thing missing from his otherwise perfect collection was a Lodge number, because Rab was "between Lodges" as he liked to tell anybody who noticed or asked. He had been asked to leave the local Lodge after twice writing to the Grand Master of the Orange Order in Scotland, querying why the Order had to spout all the Christian tolerance and liberty shite at every meeting, instead of focussing on the important business of the Faith, and fighting the enemies of William before it was too late. The Lodge gave him the option of withdrawing the letters and apologising, but Rab was no surrender through and through. If he backed off anything he knew it was the beginning of the end for him. The Order was a patriotic fraternity, all brothers for the cause, but sometimes he wondered if enough brothers were willing to give as much as he was and fight for the cause, to do what was necessary, now more than ever.

While he was between Lodges, Rab had tried to join up with the Vanguard Bears. They were the Rangers supporters who turned up to defend the Cause against *all* its enemies, come rain or shine, regardless of who or what they were, getting right in the face of the police, or catholic marches, or the national separatists, or whoever challenged. *Defend Our Traditions* is what it said on their banner and that was simple and attractive enough for Rab to pledge his allegiance.

The Vanguard Bears were well connected, with some of the boys going to Northern Ireland to fight the cause and some of the boys from there sending over boys from the Progressive Unionist Party to help out at big events against the big brother and other enemies in Scotland. They took no shite and kept one step ahead of the biggest gang in the world.

Nobody, not even some of the other blue nose defenders of the Faith liked the Vanguard Bears, and they didn't give a fuck. Hated but rated; that was just how Rab liked it. When they were challenged their motto was "deflect and deny" and they had a few boys who were clever enough with the words. These were the guys they could rely on to stand with a loud hailer on the back of a flatbed lorry in the pissing rain and fire up a gathering before a march, or come back at some smart arsed newspaper that questioned the motives of the Bears or the way of life of the faithful.

For weeks, Rab had tried to find a way into the Vanguard Bears, to meet, to offer his services, to serve. But the Vanguard Bears kept fobbing him off, saying they would get back to him when his application had been "*rigorously evaluated*", whatever the fuck that meant. He know that thousands of applications had been rejected and this just made him more determined to show that he was worthy of selection.

The 12th July was a supreme day for Rab, always had been, as long as he could remember. He felt the same excitement as he had when he was a young boy. Christmas and birthdays were just fucking painful reminders for him, but the Glorious 12th when King Billy shafted the papes and King James II at the Battle of the Boyne? Now that was truly special. It commemorated something real. You didn't have to buy people worthless trinkets to show that you cared about something, and cared deeply.

This was a Leap Year, otherwise the 12th would have fallen on a Wednesday and Rab would have missed the poker. But he went to the poker that Wednesday thinking about the march. He would tag in behind his old Lodge as they went by and work his way to the front of the march. All those pompous pretenders knew that he was barred from the Lodge, but none of them would have the balls to stop him marching, strong and proud.

At the start of the night, players were milling about in the club, shuttling between the bar and the poker tables. Gerry waited until most of the players were in the main room before reading out the usual list of messages from the Civvy Committee. He did his best to sound like it was him, rather than the Civvy blazers, who was asking everyone to please put their cigarette ends in the receptacles provided at the front door, to please avoid using the rear car park because of ongoing works, and to moderate their language in the main bar, but no one was listening enough, even to heckle him.

"*Rab of Orange wins again*," said Rab, scooping up his chips.

The game had been going for half an hour and he was feeling good. Stevie looked across the table at Rab, hurting at having his pocket Queens beaten by Rab's miracle King on the turn.

"*Maybe you can clear one thing up for me here Rab,*" he said. "*That King Billy of yours was a cowboy then, was he?*"

Rab looked up from the chips he was stacking, first at Stevie, then at Russell to see if this was one of their comedy double acts, trying to take the piss out of him.

"*'Cause in the picture of him that I saw he was on a big white horse,*" Stevie continued, "*and that's one of they pure facts that I don't think you've ever mentioned before.*"

Russell picked up the thread, "*Aye, puts all that stuff you've been telling us in a new light Rab, for me anyway,*" he nodded. "*Big Wullie, king of the wild frontier, riding about on his steed.*"

Russell mimicked holding a set of reins in one hand, while waving with the other.

"*On Dobbin*", he said, clicking his tongue.

"*Now this is the bit that I don't understand Rab*", said Stevie, warming to the theme and looking at others around the table now.

"*Does it mean that all those catholic punters you're always on about were originally Red Indians then, and you're carrying on King Billy's tradition, like a modern day Lone Ranger?*"

Rab had his head down, counting his chips into stacks and trying to stop his hands shaking as he put them into coloured piles. He spoke while staring down at the chips, enunciating each of his words clearly, his voice shaking.

"*The horse that he rode was called Sorrel, for your information, and it was black. The fact is that the white horse that you see in the photos is a symbol of King Billy's right to succeed to the monarchy.*"

"*Aye, Lone Ranger right enough,*" Russell came back, ignoring what Rab had said, "*'cause Rab's about the only fucking supporter Rangers have got left since that team went bust!*"

Russell and Stevie laughed and knocked knuckles across the table,

"*There was just one other thing I noticed in that photo, Rab,*" said Russell, trying to make his face deadpan again.

"*King Billy had a big wig on, a massive thing, down to his arse. Now that I think about it Rab, I think he had more hair than his fucking horse!*" he finished, wheezing out a laugh with Stevie and a few others at the table.

Rab was on his feet, catching his chair to stop it from clattering to the floor. Stevie twitched, getting half way out of his seat, then making it look like he was just moving to lean his elbows on the table when he realised that Rab wasn't coming across the table at him.

"*I'm goin' for a fag*", Rab muttered, pushing his chair against the table and sending his towers of chips splashing onto the green speedcloth.

He walked across the room like he was being filmed, taking stiff, self-conscious steps and keeping his clenched fists down at his sides. He took a crushed packet of 20 fake Embassy Regal out of his shirt pocket as he went through the swing doors into the corridor and crushed the packet some more.

"*Fuck-faced fucking faithless bastards,*" he muttered, trying to calm himself with the thought that he had taken half of Stevie's chip stack in the last hand. "*Just a pair o' snidy wee junkies, who know fuck all about burning the torch for the Protestant cause,*" he continued. He had a cigarette out of the packet as he walked, anticipating how the first draw on these fags tasted like rat shit, and probably was, considering how cheap they were. His thoughts of how he could do damage to Russell and laughing boy Stevie were side-tracked as he headed for the back fire exit. There were two, A-framed, "*Caution Wet Floor*" signs joined by a length of white string across the exit.

Without breaking his stride, Rab toe-ended one the yellow signs, thinking about Russell and Stevie's faces. Both signs slammed against the wall and slid back to the floor, flattened. Rab straight-armed the metal release bar on the fire exit, springing open both doors and stepped into the back car park. It was dark.

He cupped his hand around a match and lit up. As the left hand door swung back into place, Rab walked on at the same pace, lifting his head and blowing the rat shit smoke straight up. He knew that the taste got better by the third drag.

The light from the corridor fanned out in an arch to ten feet beyond the door. The back car park was empty and Rab slowed his pace, tucking his chin into his collar to inhale, then lifting his head back to blow into the cloudy night sky. He squinted as the smoke blew back into his face. His eyes had not adjusted to the dark and he was three feet from the edge of the hole before he saw it. He sensed, rather than saw the hole that workmen had dug in the car park for the water pipe repairs to the Gossip 'n' Envy's rusting cast iron system. The ground was suddenly darker in front of his foot. He did a jerky sidestep, his arms jutting out, putting his right foot behind his left and doing a full half turn quickly to go around the hole. He just kept his balance, and then was in the air as he fell backwards down the second, larger hole that had been dug for the main repairs. It was a bell hole; scooped out, steep sided with enough flat space under the pipe for two men and tools to work. Rab saw the right-hand fire door blowing shut as he went over the edge and his last thought when he hit the bottom, before everything went black, was a line from a banned song about being up to his knees in feinen blood. The back of his head struck a ring of bolts on the pipe junction and he was unconscious before the water in the hole had stopped moving. His limp body started to slide across the mud at the bottom of the hole.

At the cash table inside it was car crash poker, with players who had been knocked out of the main tournament going all-in every other hand, desperately gambling on their hand holding up and no Queen coming out. The card that was wild changed every time a Queen came on the board. Lee reminded himself, yet again, that he shouldn't bet or even play in these games with wild cards. He was usually out the door and on a bus as soon as he was out of the main tournament, but he stayed for a lift from Welsh because it was such a wet, wild night. Half his stack was already gone in just five hands of Barry's choice of Chase the Queen. His first three hands, a promising pocket pair, trips and a potential flush, had turned to mush after a Queen was turned, and after he had put sizeable bets in the pot to try to scare other players off.

Lee knew that the sensible, rational thing to do was to fold every hand in this stupid, no-skill game. That's what he told himself to do every time he thought about it in the post mortem. It was the simple logical thing to do, to avoid being sucked in to these wild card games and losing. It was only eight hands around the table, then the game changed with the next dealer, onto something else. All he had to do was fold every hand and lose one small and one big blind. It was that simple. But still he couldn't do it.

He'd look down at Ace King or a high pocket pair in his hand and think that this time, this time, maybe just this once, the random turn of cards would win him the pot if he stayed in, if he didn't lose his nerve and fold to some chancer's bluff. He'd convince himself that he had the pot odds, or that it was about time for his luck to turn, or that he could just sense that no Queen was coming out. All of which would go to worms and self-deluding crap the instant a Queen hit the board, again.

This time it was Jacks. He had the pair in his hand and the flop put another on the board and gave him the set. There were no Queens out, yet. He put in a pot size bet plus 20 percent, to get rid of the limpers, those players who needed a push to get rid of them and their no-hope cards. Only one folded. Right on cue, a Queen hit the board and instantly all the fives on the board and in players' hands became wild, giving a straight to one no-hoper and a flush to another. He knew he was beat even as he called the final bet.

"*Just deal me out*," he said, pushing back from the table.

He sat for a moment, looking on as the next hand was dealt, trying to calm himself, but it was no good. He was still following the deal, trying to work out which cards would have been his if he'd stayed in. It was too much what-if thinking. He decided to go for a pee, even though he didn't need to, just to take a break and let the crazy Chase the Queen move a bit further around the table. He'd come back when the game changed.

As he passed the other cash table, also full, he nodded at Welsh's mini-Manhattan of chip stacks and raised his eyebrows in admiration. Welsh gave a self-satisfied smile and nodded back. The cards on Welsh's table were laid out in three rows of three. It was Omaha Bingo, another game with more permutations of cards than Lee liked to try to calculate.

He turned the corner and felt the temperature drop. The cold draft stopped as one of the fire door swung shut with a muffled bang. He noticed that the wind had blown over the "*Caution Wet Floor*" signs, put there in the absence of anything more informative, to stop people going into the car park. Some Civvy official had come into the main hall at the start of the night and stood beside an embarrassed Gerry, as he tried to make an announcement, shouting above the loud chat at half empty tables. Last week it was about leaving fag ends scattered outside the main door and the week before it was parking in spaces reserved for Civvy members.

Lee went into the toilet and stood at the urinal, hoping that no-one else would come in to spoil his concentration as he tried to pee on an almost empty bladder. He leaned his head against the wall and closed his eyes, focussing. As he did so, he got a flash behind his eyes of the fire door closing again, the white door and corridor lights contrasting against the black outside. But there was something else in the afterimage, something else moving. It was beyond the door in the car park, a white ball, floating to the ground. He turned his head to one side against the wall and squeezed his eyes tighter, trying to see it as the image finally faded and disappeared.

The outer door of the toilet opened at the same time as his bladder as someone from the bar came in. He finished up and stood at the sink, dipping his hands in and out of the scalding water coughing out the tap, until he got them wet enough. He turned left out of the toilet, thinking about what game Kodiak would choose for the next round at the cash table. It always had to be something different for him.   He would go for a game that was played as a poker variation and make it a car crash by adding a wild card. "*Black eights are wild boys- this is a game I made up, called Crazy eights*"- or he would find some obscure three card river-boat-gambler game on the internet, but forget to read enough about how it was played, resulting in shouting and chaos when nobody, including Kodiak, could work out who had won a hand. It was still better than Chase the Queen, but for Lee, Snap! would have been better than Chase the Queen.

The fire doors rattled together as Lee walked back along the corridor and he looked back. He should close them, he thought, keep what little heat there was inside the building from leaching out. He had on three layers and he was still feeling cold. He turned and retraced his steps, past the toilet. Picking up one of the A-signs, Lee noticed a corner of yellow plastic from the sign had snapped off. He stood them both up as he approached the fire exit. He pushed both doors open, to get them in the right order to close, and looked out into the dark.

On the far left-hand wall he could just make out two white triangles that he knew were the *Anti-Climb Paint* signs. He had seen them when it was light. That must have been it, he thought, the white ball he'd seen. But the angle was wrong. He wouldn't have been able to see the white flashes from the corridor, because the signs were too high.

He stood with a hand on each door, ready to pull them shut, feeling the cold wind and knowing that he was about to miss the start of the Kodiak's choice of game at the table. He would take abuse for holding a seat at the table and not using it if he didn't get back soon. There were still players being knocked out the main tourney and some already standing about drinking, waiting for seats at the cash tables. But he stood and got colder and convinced himself that he had seen something falling into the cark park. Maybe it was just somebody's ball, punted over the car park wall, or a headlight from the road, bouncing off a window, but now that he had missed the start to of the round anyway, he decided that he had to know.

He stepped back inside, lifted the broken yellow sign and tried to wedge it in the hinge of one fire door to hold it open. It didn't work because it kept slipping out and it didn't make much difference to what he could see in the car park. Out on the rough tarmac, he stood to one side of the weak corridor of light from the door. There was only the sound of traffic on the main road at the front of the building. He thought he heard voices on the far side of the car park, but then realised they were coming from inside the building, bouncing off the wall.

He started to feel a bit stupid, standing in the dark, wondering how it would look if somebody saw the door wedged open, then found him out there. What would he say?   Stepping out for a fag?

It was probably just a ball kicked over the wall. But at half past nine at night when it was cold and dark, wet and windy, who's out kicking a ball about on that road with cars driving up and down?

"*Right*", he said out loud, which was what he usually did to get himself moving, out of bed or off the couch or up a ladder with a hod of bricks. It worked every time, like somebody pushing him in the back to get him started. He walked along one edge of the light until he was no longer throwing a shadow, then stood for half a minute, looking toward the *Anti-Climb Paint* and waiting for his eyes to adjust to the dark. It was then that he saw the first hole.

Standing in the dark, his imagination took off for a few seconds, as he pictured a white ball of light dropping into the car park from space, smashing its way through the black top, deep into the soil, still burning. His heart rate jumped as he took another step towards the hole. Not so much a step as a slow-march slide, feeling the edge of the hole with his toe where the dark of the tarmacadam surface turned black. Standing tense, with one foot forward and one well behind, he leaned forward to peer into the hole, keeping his head well back just in case something was about to jump out.

As his eyes started to adjust more to the dark, he made out the neat mound of stones and mud piled up at one side of the hole and he relaxed a bit, seeing that the pilot hole had been made by a digger with shovels, rather than blasted by a warp speed meteor, as he'd first thought. He looked back at the fire doors, thankful that nobody had seen him scared by a hole in the ground.

There was no ball of light. There was no light at all in fact when he stepped closer and looked in the hole. It was just a rough-edged black circle. Lee could then see the slope of a much larger mound of earth that rose into the dark beyond the hole. He took a step back and looked again toward the fire exit, where the wind had pushed the door halfway shut. The guys waiting for a seat at his table would be seriously pissed off by now, and he was out here, wasting his time, spooking himself looking for a ball of light. Kodiak's round of bedlam poker would be half over. He should go back in, buy a drink as his excuse, grunt an apology and get on with it. His hands were tucked up inside the sleeves of his sweatshirt now and rammed under his armpits, trying to find some warmth. He looked again at the fire doors as he felt the first splatters of rain. It was time to go back in. But like a poker game in which he had already committed a stack of chips to the pot, he figured he might as well see it through to the end and took another careful step around the smaller hole.

He thought he could just make out the lip on the far side of the hole, where the faint light there was from the fire door reflected weakly on the wet mud and stones. Around the edge where he stood the ground was being spotted by rain. Most of the hole looked like a giant, black puddle, filled just to the brim of the car park surface. He slid his foot closer, his toe touching the lip of the hole, and looked in. As his eyes adjusted he could see down one steep side, and at the bottom of it he could just make out a wide, mud covered pipe, running left to right. He followed the shape of the pipe to the centre of the hole, and that's when he saw Shirley.

Her face, the colour gone, was generating its own light in the darkness of the pit. He could just make that out her eyes were closed, and her mouth was open, a perfect circle where she had taken her last breath. She was lying on her back just as he had left her, at the bottom of the pit, covered in the mud and leaves he had kicked in to hide her body. The rich smell of wet earth and broken roots and moss from the base of the tree surged out of the hole and he could taste it on the back of his throat, like he'd eaten a mouthful.

His neck muscles went into spasm suddenly, first on the left, then the right, the tendons standing out, pulling his head forward and down. He was looking down at his hands, as they clenched and opened, the memory of crushing Shirley's thin neck sending his own neck into more severe spasms, being joined suddenly by the muscles in his stomach. The pain bent him over, making it difficult to breathe and he fell forward onto his knees, slamming them onto the hard tarmac, almost over balancing into the hole. His head moved forward toward his hands, now locked in the shape of hooks and held out over the lip of the hole. There were sounds coming from his nose, grunts and whimpering getting louder and more desperate, like a child asleep in a nightmare, until there would have been loud enough to wake any parent. His eyes bulged and a stream of snot ran over his top lip.

He willed himself to be quiet, digging his fingernails into the palms of his hands, listening for anyone coming along the path, or any dogs crashing through the undergrowth of the woods. Then he could hear the voices, faint shouts behind him, and he was terrified. Desperate not to be seen, but knowing that he would be, he tightened into a ball, his head over the edge of the hole, his eyes pressed shut. This was it. They had found him. She was in the pit and he was there, unable to escape or undo what he had done.

The voices grew louder, then faded. There was a star display going on behind his eyes, pulses of chequered diamond patterns, flashing black and white. The voices were replaced by a low hissing in his ears, rising and falling with the pulses behind his eyes. Both stopped suddenly, and he was in a blank nowhere, in total darkness unable to see or hear. His first frightened thought was not to move, to wait, not to make whatever it was worse. Like waking from unconsciousness, there were a disorientated and confused few seconds when he couldn't tell where he was, what time it was or what had happened. He flexed his eyes wider, trying to focus, but he could see nothing.

He realised that he wasn't breathing and the thought that he was dead came to him, the thought that it was over. He waited, tensing his muscles, staying perfectly still, accepting whatever was to come next.

The pain in his legs registered. He felt shooting stabs, running down his shins. The pain forced him to blow out the stale air he was still holding in his lungs and then he was gasping, taking rapid, ragged breaths. He reached forward to touch the knees of his jeans, reassuring himself that he still had a body. The jeans were wet from the puddle he was kneeling in, and his hands were clamped over where the tarmac stopped and the hole began. Then it came back to him in quick waves; the open fire doors, the ball of light falling in the car park, him searching, Shirley in the pit.

He raised his head and the *Anti-Climb Paint* signs came into sight again. He could feel the cold, the rainwater being absorbed, seeping into his jeans and his socks at the ankles. He kept his head up, forcing himself to stare at the signs, get them in focus, waiting until he had convinced himself that he was not in the woods, or dead, or in hell, but back at Gossip 'n' Envy. It took a full minute before he was ready to move.

It wasn't the first time that he had found himself back at the pit, looking in, seeing Shirley, but it was the first time it had happened when he was awake. Think about it, he told himself, digging his nails deeper into his hands, deliberately, blocking out the other thoughts pushing forward, still crowding to be heard.

How the fuck could Shirley be in a hole in the back car park of the Gossip 'n' Envy? That was impossible. The answer was that she couldn't. She was alive, married with two kids and living with a joiner in Newcastle, and he was kneeling in the dark in a wet cark park in Perth looking like the sad nutjob that he was. That was reality, he told himself. That was what had happened because he had stepped out the fire doors and looked in a hole. And what if somebody from the poker had come out the doors and seen him there, hunched up over a hole in the ground, shaking and sobbing in the rain like a bairn? How would he explain that? He wouldn't because he couldn't. There was too much to keep back, too much that he couldn't tell. One crack in the wall and the dam would be burst. He would need to walk away from the poker.

The Wednesday poker nights that he could do without talking. That's why he liked it. He could be there, every week, sitting down with that clamjamfry of souls, Perth's best and its worst, and all he needed to do was count chips and deal, all he needed to say was call, fold or raise. He had to put off the curious and the drunks, and paid the price of having nobody talk to him, but it was worth it, for now. Nobody knew what he'd done, not even Welsh. He admired and felt sorry for Welsh at the same time. Every time they spoke, he knew that Welsh wanted to ask, but didn't want to know. Lee had accepted that sitting there at the tables, week after week, listening to other lives was enough for now.

He slid his hands back from his knees to his thighs and held them there, straightening his elbows and squeezing his thigh muscles, steeling himself to look in the hole again. He focussed on the signs again, keeping his eyes wide until he could read them clearly, and then brought his head forward quickly in a nod, to look down.

It wasn't Shirley. The face was a death mask oval framed by the muddy water. The eyes were shut, the hair pulled back by the surrounding mud, creeping onto the forehead. Two days solid of torrential rain had pooled at the bottom, mixing with the dark earth from the sides of the pit and a slow leak from the pipe. The knees of the figure in the hold were sticking up, but the mud was deep enough to cover most of the upper body as it settled deeper. As Lee tried to focus, to see what was really in the hole, he saw the white face roll over, one of the eye sockets filling slowly with black liquid. He was up and slipping down the steep side of the bell hole, without thinking about it, feeling with his feet for holds and finding none before he started shouting. His throat was still constricted from sobbing and, *"Some help here!"* over and over again came out as a weak croak. He picked up speed as he went down the side and a displaced wave of slow moving, muddy water washed over what was left of the white face as he hit the bottom. Lee felt both feet sink into thick mud under the pipe and he fought for balance, his shins scraping against the rusty cast iron. He braced himself against the wall of the hole with an arm and got one foot free from the sucking mud, high enough to get it on the pipe. He looked down and grabbed a handful of T-shirt at the neck of the figure, yanking the face clear of the water. The head nodded, forward first with the force of being pulled from the water, and then lolling back, making a dull clunk against the pipe.

Shit! Lee swore as his left foot sank deeper in mud as he tried to get more purchase on the bottom. Changing his grip, he pulled on the T-shirt at both shoulders, the wet cotton stretching, then biting under the armpits as he dragged the body to a sitting position.

Lee knew it wasn't Shirley before he went into the hole, but he didn't know it was Rab until he got in close and caught a waft. Concentrated ear wax and acidic, underwear sweat, even after submersion. There was no mistaking that smell in the dark, confined space.

Lee came off the pipe and tried again to brace his feet against the sides of the hole, so that he could lift Rab clear of the water and sit him astride the pipe. His plan was to prop him with his back against the side of the hole with some more light and then check him as best he could. He didn't know how badly Rab was injured or even if he was breathing, but while they were both slithering about in the bottom of the hole, the recovery position and pounding Rab's chest to the beat of the Bee Gees *Staying Alive* were not going to be options.

But it was no good. His feet slid out from under him as soon he tried to lift Rab. Three times he tried. The only solid stance he could get in the hole was squatting with both of his feet braced on the pipe, but then he was too high above Rab to get any kind of grip that would lift his limp and slippery body out of the pool. He got back in the mud, setting himself with both feet deep in the mud and tried again to lift Rab onto the pipe, putting everything into it, but they both slid back into the water.

Changing tact after another five minutes, Lee got both feet in the deepest part of the hole. He arse shuffled in behind Rab, this time, his back against the muddy earth, where there were now a few extra streams as the rain got heavier and the wind picked up above. He slid his arms around Rab's chest with difficulty and locked one of his hands on the wrist of the other on Rab's chest, his grip centred on the image of Diamond Dan on Rab's t-shirt. He moved his weight from one foot to the other, trying to feel where the mud finished and the solid earth at the bottom of the hole, under the pipe, started. With his first pull, his angle was all wrong and his back slammed against the side of the hole, both of his feet and his legs sliding under Rab, leaving them looking like a two man bobsleigh team. There was a shock of cold as the mud soaked his jeans and a wave coming back off the side wall lapped over his waistband. He swore, then shouted out again, *"Some help here!"*, more in frustration than in the belief that he would be heard.

He shouted the same thing, louder, after each failed attempt to find a solid foothold to get the leverage to lift Rab. He realised now that most of the sound was going straight up into the dark sky, rather than anywhere near the fire door and corridor, where ears might hear it.

His next attempt at a lift from behind Rab was better. He stayed in a crouch and didn't try to stand up. It brought Rab's back out of the mud and he slumped-forward, chin on his chest, arms limp by his sides, like a puppet whose strings had been cut, propped against the pipe. This was an improvement, Lee thought, but he had to hold Rab's shoulders, to prevent him collapsing left or right.

They sat still in the mud for a moment, and Lee breathed hard from the effort of getting Rab's limp body into the sitting position. The rain was heavier now, with dozens of small waterfalls leaping off the cliff that was the hard edge of the hole and a larger stream cutting a stony groove through the earth on one side of the hole, where a dip in the car park above was channelling the water. Lee knew that he had done what was needed since he slid into the hole, acting fast, getting Rab's head clear of the water, with little time for thinking. He was soaked now, from above and from below. He shouted again, trying to direct it towards the building. Just then, Rab made a sound like a dog barking when it was dreaming and Lee pulled away from him with the fright, just catching him again as he started to slump to one side.

Being up close with Rab, the smell was strong, even in the heavy rain. Lee looked at the back of Rab's head for the first time and thought he could just see that the rain water flowing from his hair to the collar of his Diamond Dan T shirt was darker at the back. He couldn't see enough in the hole to make out if it was mud or blood but the steady flow of liquid across Rab's pale neck got him shouting again, and for the first time he could hear some panic in his own voice as his throat tightened.

He looked over at the encrusted, cast iron pipe in the hole and at the water settling around the protruding ring of bolts on a rusty six inch flange, next to where Rab's head had been. If Rab had cracked his head on that, from a straight dive into the hole there could be a lot of damage. Lee steadied Rab and starting feeling with his fingertips, starting at the base of Rab's neck and working up, through Rab's matted hair. He jerked his hand away instinctively as he felt two of his fingers slip under a wet flap of skin, just below the crown of Rab's head. He brought his hand close to his face, first trying to see, then smell for blood, but what he could see was in black and white and the smell of the earth in the hole and Rab's pungent body odour was all that he got. He put his hand back to Rab's head, patting around the wound, then gently touching again where the hair and skin were raised. He thought he felt some warmth in the tips of his fingers, and they were sticky when he rubbed them together.

Up until the point when he checked the back of Rab's head, Lee had been worried, but keeping it together, trying one strategy then another when that didn't work, going through the possibilities. As he sat behind Rab he'd been calm enough to think about how he would get cleaned up when they got out, and whether Welsh would have an old blanket in his car to protect the seats for taking him back to his flat.

He realised for the first time, his last beer rising suddenly in his throat with the thought, that Rab needed to be out of the hole fast, and that he was the person responsible for getting him out, or the person responsible if Rab died in that hole.

Images of Shirley's face, mixed with a flash of Rab's white death mask when he had first seen him came to him and he heard the hissing in his ears again as his blood pressure shot up. He blew out, hard, fighting the growing tension in his muscles. Then he started shivering, just a shudder across his shoulders, but then a spasm that went from this head to his fingertips. It was a combination of the adrenaline rush and the cold sludge now covering most of his feet and legs and soaking through his jeans and shirt. Think, he had to think.

Keep Calm and get the fuck out of this hole, he repeated in his head until he stopped shivering. He looked around the pit again, searching for anything he'd missed. He could see more of the walls now that his eyes had adjusted to the dark, but it was just the same wet hole with muddy sides, slowly filling up with rain. Apart from the rusty pipe, there was nothing to stand on, no footholds, and no miracle ladder or rope reaching down from the car park. He resorted to shouting again, in panic and desperation, making sounds that weren't words, just the loudest noises he could make.

He shut his eyes and pushed his head back against the small, sharp stones of the banking. They pushed through his hair, the pain distracting him for a moment from the creeping cold and his growing panic. Being stuck there took him back to his cell. Stuck in there, fighting to control the dread, like a belly full of something he regretted, constantly threatening to rise up his gullet and choke him. In the cell, it was the realisation that there was no way out, no matter what he said or shouted or did.

Those were long, terrible hours, the worst of that first year of his sentence, just trying to find distractions, anything that would stop the thoughts, push away the reality that he had no control, from rising up and suffocating him. Part of his recurring daytime nightmare, in colour and with sound, was an image of him cowering in the corner of his cell, hands on his head, gibbering and whimpering, finally overcome by the reality of being locked up, with days and weeks and years ahead, in that cell. If he ever went into the corner of his cell, that would be game over, he knew. The image came back, again and again, more often when he failed to find enough distractions.

In his waking hours his focus was on getting hold of anything to read, sniffing around like an addict for any words on paper. He would take anything. Newspapers were OK, but books were better, and lasted, even the prison library rejects. Books had to be really bad to be rejected by men locked up. The books donated were vetted for the prison library, but they were never rejected because the writing was just so crap you couldn't read more than half a page before giving up. Lee would spend hours just reading page after page of sentences, not knowing who was doing what or why or caring, going back to the beginning if no other books became available. Magazines were meaningless who-did-what-and-who-cares dross and the holy stuff, that the chaplain was only too happy to supply in volume, was so dense it was impossible to understand and gave him headaches.

Anything to count was second best. When it got to that he knew he was getting desperate, a couple stages away from cowering in the corner. The number of windows seen from his cell, the number of drainpipes, chimneys or pigeons per hour. Last chance saloon was song lyrics. Recalling a random line and trying to complete the song, he sometimes working on two at a time. On days and nights when he got down to songs, he knew that he was coming closest to losing it. He would up his game, concentrating hard, frantically pushing himself to fill his thoughts so that no room was left for the image of him cowering in the corner of the cell.

Rab jolted suddenly again, like he'd been shocked, sat straight up and then slumped forward. Lee lost his grip but shot a hand out, grabbing his T-shirt collar, just before Rab's face hit the water. He eased Rab back, holding him by the shoulders and looked up again at the edge of the hole. The rain that had fallen elsewhere in the car park had now found the lowest point and was pouring into the hole, creating a curtain of water around half the length of one edge. The water level in the bottom of the hole was now over Lee's outstretched legs, sloshing against the underside of the pipe.

He started to feel the same desperation of that first year in jail for the first time since he got out. He had no control over what was happening. He was willing himself to think harder, solve the problem, now tapping the back of his head against the sharp stones, trying to come up with any plan other than the obvious one.

He had to get out, leave Rab in the hole and go for help. But he would come back to find Rab face down in the mud, drowned. Rab would be dead and he would be fucked for years ahead, thinking about how he had almost killed one person, and gone on to kill another. Lee screamed out again, throwing his back against the cold mud wall in frustration and causing Rab's head to loll back and then forward again, chin on chest.

The Correctional Opportunities Programme - it came to him as he trawled through his thoughts of how he had survived his cell and how he could survive being in the hole. It was something to fill the hours, and it got him out of the cell, but it also gave him another trick or two, some distraction, to add to the reading, the counting and the song lyrics to fight off the suffocation.

Art classes he had started with, a prison project to design posters to decorate some rail station waiting rooms. His drawing and painting were like an eight year old's, but he was good on ideas for what other people who could draw might put on the posters. Then he signed up for eight weeks of the Emotional Management class, mostly because it guaranteed 16 hours out of the cell. He learned nothing, except that most guys in the class had problems that were an even bigger bag of snakes than his own.

There was a short programme in problem solving. It was short because only four prisoners turned up and one left on the first session, deciding that he wasn't that desperate to be out of his cell. Lee got the basics in week one. You define a problem clearly before tackling it, use some kind of structured approach, then celebrate success. It was an embarrassingly simple piece of piss, but it worked for him, getting him onto the brick laying by figuring out where he wanted to be when he got out -anywhere but where he had lived before - and what kind of skills he would need – some kind of trade that would allow him to move around.

"*Right*", he said out loud, straightening up and looking at the back of Rab's matted hair, "*problem solving*". He had defined the problem, again and again in the twenty minutes that he had now been in the hole. That bit was done. It was bad and getting worse. The water was still rising and Rab, with a gash in his head, would be shivering like him, if he wasn't unconscious and loosing blood.

After Lee decided that leaving Rab to go for help was a non-starter, the other possibilities became clearer. Worst case scenario was that somebody shut the fire doors and he and Rab were there until the morning when the pipe fixers turned up. Lee reckoned that he could stay alive until the morning in some state, by moving around, standing on the pipe, but Rab couldn't, either because he would die from the crack on his skull and the bleeding by then, or Lee would become too cold to hold him up and Rab would go face down in the mud. That meant they either had to get out together, or get help *into* the hole before the poker finished and everybody went home.

Lee started flexing his arms one at a time, thinking about one final attempt to lift Rab off the pipe while he still had some feeling in his legs. If he could somehow get his shoulders under Rab, he thought, he might be able to use a fireman's lift, stand on the pipe and slide him up the side of the hole, high enough to hoist him over the lip into the car park. His arms would be fully extended, to get Rab high enough, but it might work if he had enough strength left. He was stretching his back, trying to visualise it, trying to convince himself that he still had enough energy left to do it, when he heard snatches of laughter from above ground and he stopped moving instantly to listen.

"You were never winning that wi' two pair, ya fucking chancer…". It was definitely somebody in the corridor, the sounds of voices, breaking up on the strengthening wind as the sound came across the car park and down to him. He could only just hear them over the sound of the water flowing into the hole. If he could hear them, could they hear him? Did the sound only travel across the car park and down into the hole, like the rainwater?

He tried to think fast about what to shout, what they would notice, what they would hear, but in desperation he just started blasting out anything that might work, in a constant stream. *"Yo! Help!"*, then even louder, *"Need some help here! Hello! Help! Help! Help!"* He kept in going as loud as he could, until his voice was reduced to a rasp and he starting coughing. He stopped moving again and listened for any sounds from above. There was nothing.

He waited a few minutes, focussed, until he heard faint voices again and let loose, *"Help! Some help here. Hey, it's Lee! I'm in the car park!"*, repeating it over and over, the volume going down again as his throat got raw.

He was desperate, and the fancy problem solving strategy was looking less promising. The problem was that he was stuck in a hole with a man who might be dying and no matter how many ways you dressed that up, they were still in the hole. His thoughts bounced between keeping the shouting going and trying to lift Rab while he still had energy and was warm enough. He couldn't lift Rab and shout at the same time and he knew that if he had any chance of lifting Rab at all had to be soon.

When he tried moving his legs, to stretch, they were heavy and stiff, numb with the cold water, and aching at the joints. He had to use his hand to pull one of his knees into a bend. He was shivering again, and he knew his core temperature was dropping.

By listening, he worked that he could only hear people heading for the toilets if they were in pairs, and talking really loud, either because they were pissed, or because they wanted everybody in the corridor to hear them. He wouldn't hear the footsteps of anybody walking by themselves in the corridor, anybody who would be more likely to hear him because they weren't rabbiting on about some smartarse move they had made in the last hand, or how their chips had gone down in a bastard of a bad beat, or a donkey call.

He couldn't leave Rab, but he needed to do something and fast. The number of guys moving about in the club told him how long he had been in the hole. He couldn't see the time on his watch, but he worked out that they must be down to the last handful of players on the final table inside and that gave him about ten minutes before they started shutting up the building for the night, including the fire doors. Could he shout for those ten minutes and then put everything he had left into lifting Rab? He didn't know.

Bracing himself against the wet wall of the hole, facing the club, he stood up, sinking into the mud. The pain shot up his legs, his muscles like old elastic bands being stretched too far. He could feel the water running off his jeans, and the grit left behind on his skin. He moved slowly, stretching as he went, until he was standing with his face against the wall on the left side of Rab. He squatted down and lifted Rab's arm across his shoulders, tucking his own shoulder into Rab's armpit. Even with the cold, the shivering and the aching muscles in his legs, Lee still registered Rab's body odour when he got in close. It was like a toxic smelling salt.

Lee dug his feet in deep in the mud, adjusted his grip on Rab's wrist and around his body, said, "*Right, Rab*", took a breath and heaved, giving it all he had. Rab came out of the water about six inches, but by then Lee was already toppling forward, into the wall of the hole, his feet slipping from under him. He twisted and collapsed beside Rab, blowing hard. He struck fireman's lift off the problem solving list, without needing a second attempt.

He resisted sitting any longer against the pipe, because he knew that would be more thinking time, and not what was needed, with so little time left. He got to his feet again, looking up at the rim of the hole, judging the distance. He put both hands against the side of the hole and pushed, stretching his legs and his back, trying to keep his circulation going. He then moved his hand to hold Rab by the front of his hair, to keep him upright, positioning Rab's weight against his right leg, trying to hold Rab's shoulder against the wall with the back of his knee. His feet kept slipping in the watery mud as he tried to steady himself.

When he was satisfied that he had Rab's weight against his leg, he stretched and did a few more calf stretches as best he could and then he went for it.

By stretching full out, he got the fingertips of one hand on a stone that jutted out from the muddy wall. He then lifted his right foot out of the water, up past the pipe onto Rab's left shoulder. As Rab started to fall over on his side, Lee moved fast, shifting his weight, grabbing the stone with both hands and planting a foot on each of Rab's shoulders. With everything he had left, he pulled himself up, just high enough to see across the car park at ground level. Rab started to tip forward with the weight and Lee on his shoulders and he had just long enough to see that one fire door was closed before his arms could no longer hold him and he slid back to the bottom of the hole, grazing his face against the protruding sharp clinker near the surface as he did, and scratching at the mud on his way down, so that he went into the water and mud beside Rab, rather than onto the pipe. As Lee's hit the bottom the displaced water sloshed against the pipe, hit the side of the hole and came back in a wave, completely covering him and Rab, who had keeled over, his head between his knees.

He lifted Rab's face out of the water quickly and spat out the gritty water that had gone into his own mouth. Lee leaned Rab back against the wall. He steadied himself and stood up with his fingertips pushed into the mud, pressing his forehead against the rough surface. He spat out more mud from his mouth and shook his head to clear it from his ears. He was soaked and he could feel the coarse grit in a thin layer between his skin and shirt. His legs and his back ached from the effort trying to lift Rab and the strain of pulling himself to the edge of the hole. He could feel the raw grazes on his face, and the throbbing in his hands, where sharp slivers of stone had been driven under his fingernails as he tried to slow his fall. For all his effort he had gained a glance of the fire doors and the corridor. Big deal, he thought, big deal.

Looking around the hole again, the idea of sitting and resting beside Rab was suddenly attractive. Just sitting in the sludge for a few minutes, with his back against the pipe until the rain eased off, or until somebody came and looked in the hole and found them both. Lee reckoned that he couldn't get any wetter or colder or exhausted as he was then, and for all his fancy, problem solving strategies, and lifting and jumping he was still stuck in a muddy hole with Rab.

His best chance to get Rab out had been earlier, he thought now, before the rain started to fill up the hole and when there were more people in the corridor to hear him shouting, and before Rab had lost so much blood and before he had knackered himself. So maybe it was time to stop. Somebody inside was bound to notice that neither of them had come back to the tables and wonder why. Leave a pile of chips and just go home? That didn't happen. They might think that he and Rab had gone off drinking somewhere in the town, just abandoned the game for something better. Rab and him – drinking buddies? No, that wouldn't happen either. So somebody would come looking, sooner or later; he just had to wait.

Then, just as he stepped over Rab to find a space to sit beside him, it hit him. It was like a light going on in the dark hole. Something so obvious, but so cleverly done that he had almost missed it. It had been a long time coming and he almost smiled through his chattering teeth and numb lips at how it was being done. He was being punished, finally. The nine year sentence was the legal consequence, but this was the real judgement, the real price to be paid. It was God or fate or some higher justice's twisted sense of humour.

Crime: throwing Shirley in a hole and leaving her for dead. Punishment: being stuck in a hole and only able to get out by leaving somebody else to die. What a perfectly planned, cruel twist, like a poker hand played out by a master player over the flop, the turn and finally the river. Even although you were on the end of the shaft, you had to applaud it, you had to nod and shake your opponent's hand at the way it had been played, as other players tapped the table in universal admiration. You never saw it coming because you were distracted, weighing up the number of possible outs that *you* had, the number of cards that could hit the board to give *you* the winning hand and the chip stack in the middle. Whilst all the time you were being played, slowly sucked in, not seeing it, not suspecting. The play was exquisite.

It was only ever him that could have found Rab in the car park. It was always planned for him to be in the corridor, alone, to glance out the fire door just then, to see the flash of light on Rab's face as he fell in. Like the beauty of a great poker play, the timing had to be exact, no room for error. There could be no one else around and it needed enough time for him to be curious enough to go into the car park, to look in the hole, to be reminded first about Shirley, and then to have no time to go back for help, as he saw Rab's face slip under the water. He understood now that it was predetermined that it should end this way for him, from that first second when he grabbed Shirley's throat. He coughed out a short laugh, almost in appreciation at the play, and settled down beside Rab, putting his arm around his shoulders to hold him up.

The water covering his legs was cold, but not as cold as he thought it would be and the shivering and tension in his jaw eased off within a couple of minutes. He was wiped out, utterly drained of energy, and now of hope, and although he knew it would be impossible to sleep sitting in the mud, holding up Rab, the thought of shutting his eyes for just five minutes came to him. He let his neck and shoulders go slack, accepting that he'd done all he could, resigned to what had been planned for him, more relaxed, knowing that he no longer had the responsibility for what happened next. The rain seemed to be coming in steady pulses, a comforting rhythm, no longer headache cold. The two men sat, side by side, heads bowed, looking like happy drunks for a full five minutes.

Lee sank deeper into his reverie, his thoughts no longer racing. Rab had started to cough weakly, just a single spasm every minute or so and Lee was pulled back from his sleep each time. Rab gave three coughs together and then jerked violently without warning, pulling up his knees and doubling over. As Rab's wet shoulder slipped out of his hand, Lee grabbed and missed at his T-shirt as Rab went face down in the water again. Lee pulled him back up on one arm and held the back of his head, to prevent it flopping about. He eased him back against the pipe. Rab's skin felt like a piece of butcher meat, smooth and fatty, without any tone or warmth. Lee looked at Rab's outline in near dark and touched his neck, half-heartedly searching for a pulse but unable to feel anything through his own puckered, throbbing finger tips. He stopped, realising that whether or not Rab had a pulse was not going to make any difference to what Lee was going to do now or for the rest of the night. He was dispassionate about his actions now that there were fewer choices, less stress. No more leaping about, straining, exhausting and frustrating himself with all that false hope. What puzzled him was why it hadn't clicked earlier, why he hadn't realised in the first few minutes that he and Rab were supposed to be in the hole and were going to be staying there?

He put his arm around Rab's shoulders again and sat back against the pipe, the water lapping around his waist. He tried to will himself back to where he'd been, the calm where the cold was no longer hurting, the rain beating out a gentle pulse, his muscles relaxed, almost floating. But now there was something else gnawing at him, preventing him from settling back and floating off. It was a feeling that he'd missed something in working out all the details. His thoughts started racing again, going over the same ground about his past and how it had led up to this. He told himself it was the same hole, the same mud and the same justice he had coming. But something just didn't fit.

It was Rab, he realised. That was the bit that was wrong. Why did Rab have to stay in this hole and die as part of the master plan for what Lee had done? Lee looked up into the rain, trying to make sense of what had made perfect sense just ten minutes before. He tried hard to think of an ending where Rab came out of the hole alive and he didn't, some scenario where cruel justice was served. An outcome where Lee died a hero, saving the injured Rab. Nothing came, there was no series of events that finished that way.

But what if Rab made a spontaneous recovery in the middle of the night, woke up, found himself in the hole with a dying Lee, climbed out and walked away? Lee looked at Rab and saw light reflecting from the flat surface of his wet hair. He moved his hand from Rab's shoulder and felt the back of his head again. There was more swelling at the wound. The liquid was thick, and even through his shrivelled fingers Lee could feel some warmth in it. He didn't know if this was good news or bad. Did the fact that Rab was still bleeding mean that he still had blood pumping, or did it mean that he'd been bleeding for so long now that he had lost too much? Either way, he knew Rab wasn't waking up and climbing out of the hole.

He didn't know Rab and avoided talking to him, the same way he did with everyone else at the club. He did know that Rab was an obnoxious and offensive bastard at the tables, with no time for anybody. Lee could tune out most of the meaningless, rambling shouting across the tables, and focus down on the cards, but Rab's weekly rants were so rabid that they cut through it all. You couldn't not hear him. Rab spoke to no-one, but everyone at the table was forced to listen.

Was Rab as bad or even worse away from poker? Probably, Lee thought. But had he done something so terrible, so unforgivable that he had been condemned to this death hole with Lee, as part of some two-for-the-price-of-one economy justice killing?

Lee had learned over the months at the poker club how to calculate pot odds and inferred odds. He was good at it. It gave him an edge at the table when his hand was a thinker. If he was sitting with the sort of hand that looked good enough to call somebody's big raise, until you worked out the cold odds of how much you would be putting in, and what your odds of winning were. Those were the hands that you threw away and lived to fight another day.

It came to him then, clear through his exhaustion and numbness, that the odds were so remote to be absurd that both he and Rab would be in the hole at the same time, for this death-of-the-guilty-men set up that he had just invented. The odds that all the pieces of the puzzle that put them were planned by some higher authority now seemed ridiculous. His previous certainty, the comfort and acceptance about knowing how it had all been fated, unravelled in that instant and the frustration and anger came flooding back.

"*Ah, fuck Rab!*", he said, getting to his feet and slamming his fist into the hard soil wall, before going straight into another two minutes of shouting. This time what came out was, "*In the hole! In the hole!*", hearing himself sound like some demented American golf spectator. Lee turned his head in different directions, trying to convince himself that the sound would bounce off one of the walls, and somehow find its way out, but knowing that the direction of his desperate shouting wasn't making a difference. The combination of rain, the strengthening wind and the water flowing into the hole was now louder than any sound that he could make. His throat felt dry and raw and he now had to pause longer between hoarse shouts to make any noise at all. Like a battery going flat, his shouting would soon be gone, he knew, with nothing left.

He could hear a rush of noises from above now, just loud enough to reach the hole above the sound of the rain and wind. It was groups, guys talking, going for a pee before heading to cars and taxis. Lee knew that it was down to the wire. He looked at Rab and wondered again if there was some way he could wedge him upright in the bottom of the hole, tight against the pipe. The water would soon be up to his chest. Lee could climb out, run in, grab a couple of players from the toilet and get back; two minutes maximum he reckoned. If it worked, it would be a great move, a life saver. But wedged like that, Rab's face would be closer to the water, and if he slumped over and drowned in less than two minutes it would all be on Lee.

The voices were still faint, but he could hear a steady gabbling of sound now, no longer rising then fading away. He could hear whole conversations as people shouted to be heard over others. They must be queuing outside the toilet or just standing in the corridor. If he was getting out of the hole it had to be now.

With one hand, Lee pushed into the wet soil, two feet above the waterline, scraping slowly at first then at dog-digging speed to make a hole. His fingernails were still burning with pain from his attempt earlier, but the rest of his fingers were numb. The earth was packed solid behind the surface mud and through the cold he felt sharp stones bite into the tips of his fingers, splitting them as he scratched at the earth. He changed to his left hand as his right scraped less and less soil out of the hole.

When his fingertips felt the curve of a larger rock he realised that the hole would be no deeper. It had to be enough for the toe of his trainer. Steadying Rab by holding the top of his head, Lee got onto the pipe and lifted his left leg to test the height of the foothold.

Above, he could hear isolated shouts now, players heading off, saying their farewells. There were no more conversations coming from the fire door. Lee had one more howk at the small hole with his raw fingers, trying to make the bottom of it flat, angled down. Squatting down beside Rab, Lee positioned him with one shoulder against the pipe, and his back against the wall of the hole. He pulled Rab's legs forward, so that his shoulders were against the wall, making it less likely that his he would slump forward into the water. Lee cupped one hand, and scooped water from the muddy pool to his mouth, twice, quickly, trying to avoid anything floating on the surface. It tasted of rust and ashes. The grit in it made him gag, bringing some of the water down his nostrils. He repeated the move twice more, and forced more water down his dry, hoarse throat, hoping it would make a difference.

"*Right Rab, this is it*", he said, looking down. He felt for the foothold in the near dark, stuck the front of his left trainer in and pushed up. In the same movement, he jammed his right foot against Rab's shoulder, securing him against the muddy wall and made a grab for the lip of the hole. Immediately, the weight of his body brought on muscles spasms in his arms. The foothold he had made started to disintegrated as soon as he pushed with his toe.

His nose was at the level of the tarmac and he could see them. There were at least four of them at the door of the toilet. He had to shout something and they had to hear it. He swallowed once and what came out was a terrified scream, like the sound of a crime being committed, "*Man down over here, man down!*" It frightened Lee to hear it. There was loss of control in his voice. It was louder than before, cracking with the desperation. He didn't plan what he was going to shout, that was what came out. He concentrated on screaming it again as loud as he could, as the foothold crumbled and his fingers couldn't support him any longer. The weight of his right foot pushed down on Rab's back, pushing him against the pipe and then face down into the water again.

Barry reacted to his first shout. He broke off talking to Gerry and looked down the corridor, towards the main hall, confused, hearing panic in the shout, something out of place in the relaxed farewells as people left. His first thought was a fight, somebody drunk and pissed off. He looked at Gerry, then started to move towards the main entrance. Just then they both heard Lee's second shout, more desperate, and looked back towards the fire doors. Barry moved fast along the corridor, sensing the urgency and grabbing Gerry by the shoulder as he passed, getting him to follow.

It took five of them in the end, two going into the hole, to get Rab and Lee out. Gerry had to go back to the front car park to find three players who were driving, and might be sober enough to help. If Rab's neck or back had been damaged in the fall, the way that they dragged him out of the hole by his arms would have paralysed or killed him.

The staff in ER put the stench down to Rab having been pulled from the foul smelling sludge in the hole. He had a three inch gash in his scalp, blood loss, and what looked like a severe concussion. The priority was to clean and treat the wound, which was still bleeding, and to run a CT scan to check for any damage to the skull or internal bleeding. Rab gained consciousness briefly in the ambulance and had to be held on the stretcher as he rambled and struggled with paramedics muttering about being up to his knees in fenian blood.

Over the following 48 hours, Rab's pupil dilation, heart rate and pulse were checked regularly. The first CT scans came back clear. The behavioural and emotional reactions of Rab as he recovered in hospital caused the medical staff serious concerns however. They were put down to post concussive syndrome, and another scan was scheduled, until his full medical notes and NHS Advance Statement arrived and the consultant realised that what they were seeing was not, after all, a clinical indicator or a significant change in behaviour for Rab.

The workmen responsible for the hole had their collective arses kicked by the site manager, for having no barriers around the holes, and the contractor in turn had his arse financially kicked later, in the form of a fine, under Health & Safety Executive legislation, for being responsible for an accident to a non-worker (member of the public).

The site was sealed off for checking by Health & Safety on the Thursday and Friday following Rab's accident. The workmen were diverted to another job and only the foreman was allowed on site on the Friday afternoon to go over new safety procedures with the contractor.

When the workmen returned to the site after the weekend, they found that someone else had been in the hole. Someone who had either climbed into the car park over metal fencing blocking access, or had come over the shops and down the anti-climb drainpipe.

It was a simple brass rotary sprinkler head, bought in any garden centre, but fitting it to the cast iron pipe would have taken a lot of time. Centre punching the cast iron first, to ensure that it didn't crack, then carefully drilling a small hole, enlarging the hole by drilling at the same point with a larger drill bit, then again with the next size drill bit, until the hole was big enough. The sprinkler head had a thread that had been part screwed into the cast iron pipe, then sealed with a good quality waterproof compound.

The pressure in the pipe was low, but it was just enough to throw up a fine jet of water through the narrow sprinkler head, rising six foot clear of the hole. It was no Bellagio Hotel fountain, but as the diffused spray was caught by the wind and blown higher across the car park, the sunlight showed it as an intermittent rainbow, ending at the back door of Gossip 'n' Envy.

They were both back at the tables the next week. Lee had some rubber tips on his fingers and plasters on this hands, which got him out of dealing at least, and Rab, even darker eyed than usual, was in a Glasgow Ulster Rangers beanie hat, pulled over his bandages. Rab never did thank Lee for getting him out of the hole, but Lee never expected him to.

The games went on each week. If anybody did ask about what had happened, Lee ignored it and other players tried to outdo each other for the most cringe worthy jokes, until every reference was exhausted, which took a few weeks.

"Look Rab, let's not dig that up again,"

"Aye, being stuck in that hole must have been the pits for Rab"

"We shouldnae joke about it really— Rab's hole life passed before him",

"I think Rab wants to put the hole thing behind him now"

"Have you got a pair in the hole Rab, like last month, eh?" etc., etc.

Rab responded to all of them the same way.

"Shut the fuck up and deal," he said.

Shuffle up and deal.

Printed in Great Britain
by Amazon